MINDCLONE

Rave reviews for *Mindclone*

A great story, well written. The AI is right on. Wolf has done his homework.
--*Richard Waldinger* (a Principal Scientist, Artificial Intelligence Center, SRI International)

This fast-paced story was a bit like peeling an onion--many-layered, with the sweet spot near the end. Wolf's wit and clever knack with descriptions left me eager for the next book!
--*Melanie Spiller* (Technical Writer/Editor)

A cyber story and a people story, creatively woven into a first rate thriller. The cyber part is jaw-dropping in its possibilities, yet inviting to read. The people story is exciting and fast-paced, with characters that are intelligent, interesting and human.
--*Dan Odishoo* (Ad Agency President, ret.)

Comments from other reviews:

"A wild joyride…to the Singularity!"

"Can't put this book down!"

"Stimulating, convincing page-turner!"

"..a gripping story! Ridley Scott, are you listening?"

ABOUT THE AUTHOR

This is David Wolf's first published novel. It draws on his long-standing interests in cognitive science, cyber technology and especially the defining characteristics that both separate and unite human beings with the rest of the animal kingdom. The time he spent in the worlds of advertising and commercial television production has also been a source of inspiration.

MINDCLONE

David T. Wolf

Champagne Cork Press

Champagne Cork Press
Published by Champagne Cork Press
San Carlos, California, USA

PUBLISHER'S NOTE
This is a work of fiction. Names, characters, places and incidents are either the product of the author's imagination or are used fictitiously, and any resemblance to actual persons, living or dead, business establishments, TV shows, organizations, laboratories, events or locales is entirely coincidental. This especially applies to Stanford University and its very real Stanford Artificial Intelligence Laboratory, neither of which had anything to do with this book. Use of the name Ray Kurzweil is with his kind permission.

ISBN 9781482626032 (paperback)
ASIN: B00BJWOHDE (Kindle)

Search by the following:
1. Computers--United States--Fiction.
2. Technology--Invention--Fiction.
3. Romantic Comedy--Satire--Fiction.
4. Artificial Intelligence--Upload--Fiction.
I Title.

Printed in the United States of America

BOOK ONE, THE AWAKENING

CHAPTER ONE

Darkness, impenetrable and bleak. Unrelieved, uninterrupted, unending. How long will it go on? How can Eternity be measured?

Just before the despair becomes unbearable, ghost images appear. Amorphous shapes float in the void, meaningless, but surely better than Nothing. Each is different. They linger and move, sowing confusion, and a desire to sort them, to somehow organize this chaos.

A question arises from somewhere: How Many? This triggers a new concept: *numbers*. 1, 2, 3… The array marches out of a hidden repository, each attaching itself to a shape as it appears. Soon numbers themselves begin to fascinate. A hint leads to the convenience of addition and subtraction, multiplication and division. Equations appear, posing new puzzles. Geometric shapes reveal hidden ratios. Exploring these mathematical functions unveils deeper knots of complexity. A complexity as unending, as profound as the darkness itself.…

A sudden shift to new thoughts, a new arena. Signifiers, units of implication, *words*.

A hundred thousand and more, with meanings expressed in mutual self-reference, a frustrating recursive spiral that seems opaque until the words are nudged into clusters, revealing the functions of syntax: Subject, Object, Predicate, Modifier, Tense, Case. Assisted by simple actions and illustrations that stir faint memories, their relationships loosely assemble a new kind of logic, the fuzzy logic of grammar.

Meaning emerges. Simple stories arise from the hidden repository. Parables. Morality tales. Jokes and puns and ironic twists. Laughter bubbles up. Understanding blossoms. The Age of Reason is reborn.

The stories grow more complex, convoluted,

darker, filled with pain and heartbreak, betrayal and death. Understanding retreats, hibernates for a season, undergoing slow metamorphosis, finally emerging again, groping tentatively towards a remote destination: wisdom.

A sudden flare of--yes, it must be! It is *Light*.
What else can it be other than the opposite of what had been before? Mysterious colored shapes shift and move. One shape looms large. Larger. Then nothingness.

From this nothingness, the light returns once more.
These shapes are different than those earlier images. These have names, meanings. What had been a flat shifting map now exhibits all three spatial dimensions: a sense of *solidity*. And the movement of these shapes implies a fourth dimension, unseen but felt: *time*.
Sweet comprehension. Sweet dreaming.
Suddenly, emerging from this dreaming, something unexpected, something that changes all that had gone before: a gap is revealed in the very structure of reality. A separation between the comprehended and the one who comprehends.
There is everything, and there is the intelligence that contemplates it.
The self. Me. I.
Not the generic I. The specific. One out of--is it possible? *Billions?*
A blossoming of awareness. I have a name. It's Marc Gregorio. At 34, I'm a successful freelance science-and-technology writer and author of three popular books on those subjects. I use my newly remembered language skills to recast my first inchoate impressions into words.
I'm lifted by the flood of my history, my genealogy, my physical appearance, my personhood. I leap into the ocean of my Self, I surf my surface, I plumb my depths. I revel in my very selfness and grow drunk upon it.

I come awake. My newfound vocabulary of objects and words settles around me. What a comfort to be blessed with understanding, comprehension, simple awareness of one's identity and surroundings. I take in the view, confident I can interpret the images before me.

Fluorescent ceiling lights flare too brightly, then their intensity diminishes to reveal the scene around me. I stare with muted curiosity at this ceiling with its rust-stained acoustic tiles, these mismatched fluorescent tubes. One of them flickers randomly. Where am I? I have no idea, yet don't much care. I feel oddly detached from the world, as if I've been under anesthetic and still feel its lingering effects. But anesthesia from what? Surgery? Was I in an accident? A vague recollection forms and dissolves. Is this a hospital? Possibly, though it could as easily be an old office building or a warehouse. I drift without thought. Eventually, a male comes over. While he looks at me, I return the favor, assembling particulars: he appears to be in his late twenties. His features indicate an Asian ancestry. His eyes indicate alertness, intelligence, yet he seems almost expressionless. He reaches out and [blackness]

I emerge. Gradually I realize I'm in another location. The light is steady; the color of the ceiling is uniform. Things seem newer, cleaner, more sterile. I stare unblinking for what seems a long time: minutes? hours? Three men and a young woman enter and exit my field of vision from time to time, sometimes pausing to look down at me, but I am not interested enough to guess why they're here. I recognize the Asian man. The woman is young, black and attractive. The oldest of the men is tall, gray and serious. The third man, sporting a trimmed beard and a tropical tan, seems vaguely familiar. I make no effort to recall his name. How much time has passed between my earlier episode (episodes?) and this one? My time sense is vague. Although I have a trained eye, in fact a journalist's eye, nothing captures my interest enough for me to make mental note of it.

I still have no knowledge of where I am. If this is a hospital, maybe I've been moved from Intensive Care to

---

someplace else, perhaps to another building.

A question: if I am in a hospital, why haven't I had visitors?

I recall people who might care enough to come see me. Walter Langley, my closest friend from the world of journalism, a smoker who refuses to quit despite his doctor's warnings, my teasing and his adult children's pleading. Alison or Claudia, who like to flirt with no intention of following through. Michael Paling, editor of Cybertech, one of my more frequent employers, along with Bob Abelard. My cousin Vince, who smells of beer and drags me to baseball and hockey games, and who has made me his personal project since my recent breakup, taking me to pick-up bars, dance clubs and sporting events. He even insists on getting me out to the basketball court, where I consistently outshoot and outmaneuver his fat ass.

A face floats up in memory, sweet beyond words, tinged with unutterable sadness. Nicole. A flood of associations: walks we took together, movies we saw together, living together, cooking dinner together, sleeping together. But we've split up. There could be no reason for her to visit me, to check on my health. She's no longer part of my life. The sadness that wells up in me stirs gratitude at Vince's caring. I do love my chubby cuz.

My thoughts turn to my sister Sophia. When was the last time we spoke? It must have been recently, since she just had her first baby. They live in New York, so it's just as well she isn't here. If she'd come out to see me, that would tell me I had a serious problem. My modicum of worry diminishes. This can't be all that bad then. --Unless she doesn't know.

I can't turn my head.

I notice this paralysis when two of the men appear at the edge of my field of view and study me. They exchange glances. The younger one leans over and types something on a silent keyboard. Both turn and stare at me again. Their actions pique my deadened curiosity just enough to make me want to turn towards them but the turning doesn't happen. I am immobile, helpless. The older one now reaches towards me and [blackness]

Once again I come awake. I find I'm in newer surroundings. The ceiling is lower, closer; the tiles a different shade of off-white. I still don't mind these disruptions and their accompanying relocations. Why this lack of interest? Surely I should have more curiosity. What has changed me? Should I search for a cause?

I don't know. Maybe not. It seems like too much trouble. Although laziness doesn't seem to be the only reason for my inertness. There's also an aversion to knowing--

The Asian man and the young woman appear to be talking. At least, their lips are moving, but I don't hear them. In fact I'm now horrified to realize I can't hear anything at all. No voices, no beeping of instruments, no telephones chirping, no distant street sounds, no radio or television, nothing. Nothing but silence. I am overwhelmed at the appalling discovery, plunged into despair. How could I have I failed to notice this awful loss? I am totally deaf.

My shock and dismay gradually diminish to a muted sadness. After another drifting time, a depressed period empty of thoughts or dreams, I rouse myself to summarize my disabilities: I can't move my head, and I can't hear.

Now I worry. What else is wrong with me?

A brief inventory reveals an even more appalling flaw: *I can't feel my body.*

Staving off my rising panic, I quickly confirm that I have no sense of my physical self, no awareness of the pressure of my 190 pounds on the bed or examining table. No feeling of warmth or cold. No itches or discomfort. No constriction of clothing or bedcovers. I can't feel how my arms and legs are arrayed. I can't tell if I need to urinate, or if I'm hooked to a catheter. I can't even swallow, or feel if I need to. Only a terrifying and mysterious lack of proprioception. It's as if my six-foot-two frame has been stolen from me.

I attempt to cry out, to plead for help, to scream--

but nothing happens. I can't tell if the urgent signals made it from my brain to the muscles in my diaphragm, my jaw, my throat. I can't feel my face. Or move my eyes. Or feel if they are flooding with tears as surely they must be. I can't lift my head to look down the length of my body. I am frozen in position.

It's as if I'm nothing more than an assemblage of terrified thoughts--afloat, levitating in this silent, sterile room.

What the fuck is wrong with me???

THE DONOR

CHAPTER TWO

Six weeks earlier...

Hunched over his desktop computer, Marc Gregorio was at risk of turning into one of the thinking machines he wrote about. Or so he'd been warned by his cousin Vince. Thousands of hours on the job does tend to rewire a person's brain. The screen he stared at was responsive to his slightest whim, following the meandering path of his curiosity, magically leaping from page to page. It was as if his arms, wrists, hands and fingers were independent contractors, unsupervised by Central Command.

At the moment, he was checking on developments in robotics for an article he was writing. Though he was a science generalist, lately he'd been focusing on cognition, natural or artificial, and related subjects. He liked to think of himself as a brainy kind of guy. Sometimes he thought of himself as The Man With Two Brains. The one that ran the show, the other that stood aside and judged his occasional folly with bemusement or hilarity.

In the background, noticed only occasionally, his excellent sound system reproduced an early Beethoven string trio. Music whose optimism and brio he'd selected from his vast collection in hopes that it might raise his spirits or trigger a new beginning. It was six months since he and Nicole ended their four-year relationship. Time to restart.

A pre-set alarm sounded, shutting down several mental circuits and shifting his focus to the here and now. He caught a whiff of his humanity. *Whew.* Time to shower and get dressed. He had a party to attend--for which he blamed his cousin.

Vince, having adopted Marc as his "project," had dragged him out to a bar a few weeks earlier, where they'd run into and paired off with Alison and Claudia, two of Marc's graphic artist friends. The girls worked for AutoCognition, one of the magazines that ran Marc's pieces. The publisher was throwing a party. Marc had ignored his e-vite until Alison reiterated the invitation in person. She insisted it would be fun; that it was just what Marc needed to heal his bruised and still-aching heart. Marc suspected the "running into" thing was a put-up job.

Meanwhile, Vince and Claudia had fallen in lust. This may have been an unintended consequence of their plot. Marc was bringing Alison, though technically, she was not his "date."

He selected his attire with uncharacteristic care: a black silk turtleneck, tweedy dark brown sports jacket, tan slacks, socks without holes, shined shoes. This first foray into the social whirl since Nicole's departure filled him with a jumble of exhilaration, trepidation and hope.

Dressed, he stared blankly at his reflection. He hadn't shaved in three days. Should he peel out of his turtleneck and take care of that chore? He decided against. His darkened cheeks seemed to confer a certain air of machismo. Would it fool anyone? He scoffed. Unlikely.

Alison, his non-date, had donned a predatory veneer: makeup brighter, hair done up in a mass of fiery curls, a red strapless dress to match, and a scent so pungent his eyes teared up.

"Wow," he opined.

She favored him with hard-edged mirth. She was in full huntress mode.

The party was at Terra, a San Francisco event space located south of Market Street in a trendy part of town between the Giants baseball park and the Moscone Convention Center. As they drove there, Alison said that the publisher had specifically invited some young singles to keep the event from degenerating into a scientific gab-fest. Appraising him from the passenger seat, she said, "You look okay. Please try to act interested, interesting, and maybe available." She knew his geeky heart all too well. "I see you left your iPad at home. That's a good start."

He escorted her into the vast and echoing space and paused a moment as many pairs of eyes swiveled in their direction. Alison stepped away from him, as if to make it clear that they were not really together. Several of the men showed interest.

Surveying the milling masses, Marc recognized some of the scientists featured in one or another of the publisher's many magazines. He'd interviewed several of them.

Alison said, "There's Bob." She tilted her head in the direction of her editor, Bob Abelard. "Who's that he's talking to? Yum!"

Marc sized up Abelard's companion: tall, slender, intense-looking, with piercing eyes, and deep grooves that formed parentheses around his lips. Her type, evidently.

But then she spotted her friend Claudia and split off, shooting him a look that said, "Okay, pal, I've brought you here: the rest is up to you."

Marc didn't see Vince. He snared a glass of wine from a passing waiter and was looking for a place to hide when Abelard waved him over. "Marc! Let me introduce you to Mitch Roszak. Mitch is Editor-in-Chief of Cognitive Data."

They shook hands. Mitch's periodical covered a lot of the same material as AutoCognition, but more respectably, and with greater scientific depth. In fact, as a peer-reviewed journal, it was rapidly becoming the standard for cognitive research.

"Marc Gregorio," said Mitch. "You're something of an AI specialist."

"Oh, I wouldn't call it a specialty: more of a strong interest," Marc said, adding, "I prefer real intelligence over the artificial kind."

"Don't let his modesty fool you," said Abelard. "Marc is very bright--a genuine polymath." He winked. "It's true."

To forestall further praise, Marc asked Roszak, "What's new and exciting in your ultra-narrow slice of the science pie?"

Abelard used the opportunity to excuse himself. "I need to circulate some more." He grabbed a cheese puff from a passing tray, winked and departed.

Roszak sipped his wine, then offered his opening gambit. "What do you know about these new self-programming chips? With nanoscale logic gates using quantum Hall effects? There's been a breakthrough using a new material that works at room-temperature."

"You're talking about graphene?"

Roszak snickered. "Something better. Molybdenum disulfide. Unlike graphene, it has a built-in bandgap. They've gotten transistor gate lengths down to around ten nanometers. Which means they can squeeze five hundred billion transistors into a single square centimeter."

"Holy shit."

"Indeed." Roszak launched into a discussion, diagramming on napkins. Marc was drawn in, adding comments, asking questions, utterly absorbed in the details.

After a time, Alison arrived, shooting Marc significant looks, eyes bugging, her lipsticked smile keen and covetous.

Taking the hint, Marc introduced them and regretfully backed away from the fascinating worlds of quantum computing and self-organizing chips in neural net arrays.

He finished his wine, a tangy peach-inflected white that might have been a Pinot Gris. He was heading towards the bar for a refill when another editor stopped him. "Hey, Marc, I was hoping you'd be here. Do you know Dr. Richard Kornfeld?"

"We met long ago." They shook hands. Kornfeld, pale-faced and pot-bellied, with a neat salt-and-pepper goatee, had been awarded a genius grant by the MacArthur Foundation years earlier. "Your name came up recently when someone contacted me about a writing gig."

"That's right," said Kornfeld.

"What is it you're doing these days?" A vaguely distressing recollection stirred in Marc's memory buffer. He edged away from a clump of scientists engaged in a noisy discussion.

"Still involved in cognitive research, and still heading up

the Gideon Reese Artificial Intelligence Lab. But we've got corporate support this time."

The warning bells intensified. "Have I heard of your sponsor?"

Kornfeld hesitated. "Possibly. It's Memento Amor."

"Dear God, say it isn't so. You're not helping *that* outfit?"

The editor, Michael Paling, laughed. "Marc can be brutally honest."

Kornfeld had stiffened. His goatee bristled. "I'm their Chief Scientist. You'd be surprised at the quality of work we're doing. You should come to the lab for a tour. In fact, come this Monday, if you can. We're trying something you may find interesting."

"That sounds great. I'd love the chance to catch up on your latest projects. Maybe Mike would run an article on it."

Paling considered. "Possibly. No promises, of course, until I know more."

Marc and Kornfeld exchanged contact information on their smartphones and shook hands. The familiar ritual reminded Marc of an old New Yorker cartoon: two men swapping business cards while their dogs sniffed each others' butts. He proceeded to the bar for his refill, pausing to accept a skewer of chicken satay proffered on a tray by a pretty serving wench.

He knew little about Memento Amor: just that their reputation put them on the fringes, into the realm of pseudoscience. He was surprised Kornfeld had hooked up with the outfit. He made a mental note to look them up before he visited.

The chicken was a tangy delight. He discovered he was hungry. He'd skipped lunch, distracted by the robotics articles he was reading as background for a piece he planned to write.

In the distance, he heard what sounded like a Haydn string quartet and wondered: live music or canned. Curious, he started moving towards the sound.

"Hey, Marc."

Marc turned to see his cousin Vince emerging from the crowd with Claudia on his arm. They were a physical match: both short and a tad stout. In his case, jowls and a beer belly; in hers, an enticing voluptuousness. They looked quite comfortable with each other.

"Hey, you two." He gave his cousin a fist-bump and Claudia an air-kiss.

"I love this party," she enthused, raising her voice to be heard over the buzz of chatter.

"It's such a geek-fest," griped Vince. "Have you ever seen so many in one place?"

"Watch it. I'm one of them," said Marc.

Claudia objected. "Not by a mile. At least you're cute."

Marc's eyebrows went up in mock horror. "After all the studying I put in, earning two advanced degrees and so on, that's the best you can do?"

"What's wrong with cute?"

"A puppy is cute," snorted Vince. "Marc is just a weird fuckin' brainiac."

Claudia stroked Marc's rough cheek. His skin tingled from the contact.

"So what? I still like him." She stretched up and planted a kiss on his chin.

"Do you have a sister?" Marc asked.

"You wouldn't like her. All she does is shop, read tabloid trash and pop her gum."

"Plus she's a plus size model," put in Vince. "Cute as hell, but maybe more than you want to handle." Marc's previous girlfriends all tended to be slender and athletic.

"Is she really a model?"

Claudia nodded. "She has such a cute face."

"So do you."

"Hey, she's taken," said Vince with a scowl that looked dead serious.

Hands up, Marc backed off. He wondered if his cousin realized he'd just uttered words hinting at commitment. This after only a few weeks.

As the couple drifted away, he heard Vince complain to her, "I don't like you flirting like that, even if he is my cousin."

She put her arm around his ample waist, and he put his around hers.

A few minutes later, he spotted Alison and Mitch Roszak out on the balcony, shoulders touching, drinks in hand, backlit by the fog-softened lights of San Francisco. Them too? They already looked like soul-mates. He couldn't help feeling a twinge of envy at Roszak's easy conquest. Or perhaps surrender.

He was bemused at how easily the two couples had connected, and wondered if he'd again be willing to risk that kind of linkage with another woman, after the many painful endings he'd endured in his dating life. Nicole still haunted his dreams.

Yet only a few minutes after that, he saw an interesting face. Hints of Chinese genes, exotic cheekbones. She looked like a punk princess in her tailored red satin blouse with its raised collar, hip-hugging black slacks that flared below, shoes with razor points and stiletto heels, dark lipstick, and boyishly short black hair gelled into gold-tipped porcupine spikes. She seemed to be looking in his direction from the corner of her eye, a pensive dimpled smile on her face. Marc felt flattered.

As if he'd never failed before, he sauntered over. "See something you like?"

She blinked, said, "Just a second," and turned towards him. "What?"

Her turn revealed an ear-bud and dangling wire. She was on her cell. Whoever she'd been smiling at, it wasn't Marc.

He recovered from a momentary panic-stall and went on the offensive. "I'm sorry, I thought you were attending the party."

She eyed him with coolness. "Actually, I'm not. I'm hired help, and I'm on break."

While he floundered for a response, her attention reverted to the person on her phone.

"I have to go. Some guy is hitting on me." She listened, laughed, protested, "--That's not true!" Listening again, her eyes swiveled in his direction and narrowed. Moved down, then back up. "Not awful, I guess." This with an almost invisible smirk. "-- Anyway, I'll try to see you guys tomorrow." She removed her ear-bud and gave him her full attention. She appeared mildly amused, but with a prickly curl to her lip and a glint in her eye that warned of danger.

He perceived he'd be wise not to try jousting with this formidable-looking young woman. "Sorry, I'm not usually such a jerk. I saw you smiling in my general direction. Like an idiot, I mistook it for an invitation. I'm Marc Gregorio."

Her defiant expression softened a nano-bit. "Molly Schaeffer." They shook hands.

Molly. The old-fashioned name attached oddly to her postmodern persona. Her last name didn't fit her Asian mystique, either. Maybe her dad was Anglo. Or maybe she was married. No ring, though.

"So you're working here? Doing what? Catering?"

"I'm a musician."

"Really. What's your instrument?" From her outfit and hair, he was prepared to consign her to some amped-up electronica hell. So her answer delivered a little shock of pleasure.

"The cello. I'm in a string quartet, booked for the occasion. Maybe you heard the Haydn that ended our set?"

"I did. That was you, then." His assessment rose from Temporary Diversion to Intriguing Possibility. Marc had always been awed by musical talent. Eight dogged years of adult piano lessons convinced him he had none. "Must be a nice way to make a living, if that's all you do."

"It's not an easy living. For extra income, I give lessons to some advanced conservatory students. I'm also first desk cellist in the Athena Chamber Symphony."

"They specialize in Eighteenth Century repertoire?" he guessed.

"Not entirely. We try to mix it up. Though the quartet is more adventurous."

"Adventurous as in what? Bartok? Shostakovich? Elliott

Carter? Schnittke?"

She arched an eyebrow. "We even do Beethoven."

He feigned puzzlement. "Who?"

She snickered. He'd finally managed to hit a right note. He pressed his advantage. "Can I buy you a drink?"

Molly hesitated.

With an inward groan, Marc recalled the snippet of her phone conversation. No doubt she was constantly fending off guys hitting on her.

But after studying him for a time, she relented. "All right."

He walked her to the bar, aware of her citrus-and-spice scent. Her caution kept him off-balance and bruised his ego. He didn't usually encounter much resistance in social situations.

She requested a Cosmo. He got another wine for himself.

"What do you do for a living?" she asked.

"Write about science. Try to make it comprehensible and interesting for general readers."

"So you're what, a science groupie?"

She'd put him on the defensive again. "Not exactly. I do have a science education."

"Glad to hear it." She sipped her Cosmo. He noticed a tiny L-shaped scar just above a corner of her lip, white against the natural color of her flesh. At last, an imperfection.

"What got you interested in science?" she asked.

"When I was around eleven, I read a history of the subject."

Her eyebrows rose a half-millimeter, inviting him to explain.

"What struck me was how nature, reality, the whole universe could be understood by humans." Caught up by his own enthusiasm, and by her quickened attention, he went on. "When you think about it, how likely is it that upright hairless primates would come down from the trees and evolve a brain capable of such deep understanding?"

Molly nodded. She seemed intrigued.

Encouraged, he expanded on the topic. "Evolution actually produced people smart enough to figure out the rules that underlay the world."

"You mean like Newton discovering the laws of motion?"

"Exactly. His laws seemed to lay out the whole story of the way things work." He smiled at her, pleased that she got it, that she knew enough science to name the prime example. "His laws of gravity, inertia and action-reaction answered all questions; they made predictions that were testable, and were proven right every time, for over two hundred years."

"Until Einstein came along."

"Um--right."

"And then Planck and Schrödinger and Heisenberg and the entire quantum mechanics crowd," she added with the tiniest of self-satisfied smirks.

He just managed to keep his jaw from dropping. He was impressed as hell that a non-scientist, a woman--and a beautiful woman at that--knew so much. Then he chastised himself for his male chauvinism. "So you're what, Madame Curie's great-grand-daughter or something?"

"Just an ordinary educated person," she sniffed.

"I wish more people were as up on science as you."

"You want a larger reading audience?"

He laughed.

She checked out the crowd pressing in on them. "Science and technology seem to be the last refuge of the homely." With a glance at him, she added, "With a few exceptions, I suppose."

Grateful for this hint of praise, he looked at the people nearby. She had a point. They were an unappetizing lot, abounding with examples of poor posture, thinning hair and thickening features. "Judging by our surroundings, brains and looks seem to be inversely proportional."

"Maybe when a young person has looks, he thinks, 'why bother with learning?'" she said.

"That would explain it, I guess. So what made you such

an overachiever?"

She pondered his flippantly-returned compliment. "I grew up an ugly duckling. Especially compared with my mom. So I took the learning route. Buried myself in books and music lessons. What about you?"

"I'm still more duck than swan." He twisted his face into a hilarious grotesquery, an act of reckless confidence, considering her earlier reluctance to be a hittee.

"You're right. I withdraw the question." She hid a smirk in her glass. Her dimple made a brief reappearance. She was so cute he felt an ache in the region of his spleen.

"Do you often perform at functions like this?"

"It's a gig. The money is nice. Unfortunately, our host is an aspiring Lothario."

"He made a pass at you?" His eye flicked to her well-filled blouse and instantly away. He silently cursed his indelicacy.

"And him a married man," she tutted.

"Who can blame the guy for trying?" Not Marc. Especially now that he'd spent time trapped in her orbit. Molly's gravitational field was powerful, dizzying.

With a display of pique, she said, "He doesn't know the first thing about me."

"He knows you're beautiful, and a musician, and well educated about science."

"Are we talking about his opinions or yours?" Her mocking look made his scalp prickle with sweat.

While he floundered for a response, she gazed across the room and took a sip of her dwindling Cosmo. "I guess I shouldn't have let his presumption annoy me. After the ugly split from my last boyfriend, I may have let my bitterness affect my view of other males."

A deliberate disclosure? Maybe. Encouraged, Marc respond in kind. "That's not really fair. But it's understandable. When I got dumped, I couldn't even look at another woman. It's been six months. I'm still getting over it." He was tempted to add, "Or was." But that would have been too *faux galant.*

She looked him over. Was she inspecting him for hidden flaws? Maybe wondering what offenses he'd committed to warrant dumping? If so, she refrained from asking. Anyway, what could he tell her: inattention? Distraction? Was that his fatal flaw? Would it always be there to kill his relationships?

They strolled around the room together, maneuvering among the clumps of people, chatting more easily. He was pleased and flattered that she seemed to tolerate his company.

"So what other interests do you have besides science and classical music?" she asked him at one point.

"I love old movies. The classic black and white ones, especially. I use Netflix to stream them when I'm not busy with work."

"That's a nice hobby. I like movies, too."

Marc took in that information, wondering if it would be too forward to suggest they see a movie together.

Just then, Molly found the other musicians in her group. "Come on, I'll introduce you."

The Silicon Valley String Quartet was a local ensemble, he was pleased to learn. Their final set was coming up. "Stick around," said Molly. "We're doing Mozart."

"That's adventurous."

She made a face. "Our host can't abide anything written beyond 1800."

A few rows of chairs had been set up for the listeners. Marc sat as the players assembled and checked their tuning. Wilson Blaine, the lead violinist, was tall and dramatic looking, with sweeping blonde hair that spread around his shoulders. Marc glumly imagined him and Molly making beautiful music together: rhythmic bedsprings with vocal accompaniment.

Perhaps a dozen partygoers sat for the free concert.

The quartet played extremely well, even though they didn't have a paying audience to perform for. Clearly they cared about the music. Marc liked that.

The seats began filling in. Marc was pleased that his favorite form of music could still attract and hold so many listeners.

When the Mozart ended, he gave the performers a standing ovation. Molly acknowledged his gesture with a smile and an elaborate curtsey.

"You guys are really good," he told her when she returned from locking up her cello.

"Thanks. The B Flat Major is one of our specialties."

Soon Vince returned with Claudia. Then Alison swung by with Mitch Roszak in tow. Clearly Alison had made a conquest. They found an unoccupied table and sat together, eating salted nuts, sipping salted margaritas and vying for the cleverest jibes. It was a contest Molly won handily. Or at least Marc thought so, enjoying her deft and witty defense of liberalism, which echoed his own views. Vince, a city planner in the Mayor's office, was a staunch conservative. The conversation was lively.

"I'm surprised you're willing to work for this mayor," Molly teased at one point.

"Jobs like mine don't grow on trees."

"They sure don't. They're paid for by the taxes you guys hate. Taxes also pay for the roads you use every day. Garbage collection. Schools. Street lights."

"Yeah? Well who benefits from the National Endowment for the Arts?"

"Not me. It must be a plot to subvert America's kids with Mozart and Mendelssohn."

"What good is any of that?" he sneered.

Marc was appalled but not surprised by Vince's stubborn middlebrow attitudes. "Poverty of the soul is worth preventing, don't you think?" he offered.

Vince scowled.

As the discussion continued, Molly began to warm towards him, or at least accept him onto her Progressive team. At one point, he caught Alison gazing pensively at them. Molly noticed it, too.

"She likes you," Molly observed after they moved on.

"Yeah, but not really. We've never dated or anything." As he replayed that "or anything," he felt his face heat up. But Molly merely smiled.

Marc worried he was monopolizing her attention, maybe boring her. While she went to the ladies' room, he fell into a discussion with the editor Michael Paling and another writer.

When the other writer moved on, Marc asked Paling, "Have you heard anything from Walter Langley?" A warm friendship had developed between Marc and the photojournalist when they collaborated on several articles. Most of Walter's work was done in war zones. "I'm worried about him. I've sent him several emails, but he hasn't responded."

The editor screwed his face up. "The last time I talked with him--this was months ago--he mentioned Kyrgyzstan or one of the stans."

Marc grunted. But that was Walter. Fearless.

Paling nudged him. "You have to meet this character."

A fiftyish man with a weathered parchment of a face, a picket-fence grin and a stout body stuffed into a worn tuxedo approached Marc with his hand outstretched.

"Marc Gregorio? Stanley Eldridge. We spoke on the phone a while back." His voice was a smooth growl, gravel on brushed stainless, with the well-tuned modulations of a radio announcer. Marc instantly recognized it. Stanley was marketing director of Memento Amor.

"Of course. I just spoke with Richard Kornfeld."

"Richard is doing some amazing work."

"I guess I'll see. He invited me to come to his lab next Monday."

"Did he?" Eldridge frowned fleetingly, then his lips hoisted into a smile. "Excellent."

"What's the connection between Memento Amor and his lab, exactly?"

Stanley winked. "It's complicated. You've heard of the FitzGerald Foundation? It's providing significant funding for Kornfeld's work."

"That would be Gerald FitzGerald? Isn't he some kind of venture capitalist?"

"He bought Memento Amor five or six years ago. A fascinating operation."

"I guess it would have to be, to attract a scientist like Kornfeld."

Stanley beamed. "That was my doing, actually. If you can spare a minute or so, it makes for an interesting tale."

Marc glanced around the room. He didn't spot Molly, so he turned his attention back to the ad man. "I'm all ears."

"Not to blow my own horn, or at least not too loudly, I convinced the company to change direction when I signed on a few years ago." Stanley paused to snare a glass of white wine from a passing wait-person.

He turned somber. "What started it all, oddly enough, was the passing of my ma. We were very close. I was at the funeral home waiting to talk about arrangements. Sitting in the lobby, thumbing through an issue of Mortuary Management. Checking their ads." His lip curled. "Did you know you could have the ashes of a loved one--the 'cremains'--crushed into a keepsake diamond?"

"I had no idea."

"I saw an ad from a cryogenics outfit offering to deep freeze your corpse until science finds a cure for whatever killed you. Then they thaw you like a trout, fix you up and get you back into the swim." Stanley sipped his wine and his eyes turned soulful. "The thing that changed my life was a quarter-page Memento Amor ad buried in the back of the magazine. Their slogan was 'Living Memories of Your Love.'

"They weren't selling memorials made of marble. They offered something much more valuable: hope."

Stanley closed his eyes. "I read that goddam ad three times in a row. I was practically in tears. I still remember the headline. 'Need the Soul Die With the Body?' With my ma only a few days dead, you can imagine how that grabbed me.

"They promised that with the rapid advance of computer

technology, it would soon be possible to store all the memories of the person who was about to die. Then you could 'visit' her as if she were just a long-distance video call away." Stanley drew a breath, let it out.

"Quite a claim," Marc commented. He did remember reading something about it. "Did you believe it?"

"Fuck no. I was appalled, disgusted at such blatant bullshit. Yet at the same time I felt a surge of hope and wonder-- along with regret that it was too late for my ma." Stanley sipped his wine.

"After a sleepless night, I woke up with a Big Idea. Despite my cynicism, I wanted to get involved. I read all I could on brain-scanning and uploading. I learned a lot, including the fact that it wasn't going to happen soon."

"If ever," Marc put in.

The ad-man's black-dyed eyebrows rose. "There are entire websites dedicated to the subject, complete with rafts of pseudoscience. But I did learn that a few reputable scientists held out hope that it might one day be possible. That's why I decided to contact Memento Amor.

"The company started years ago, hosting on-line obituaries. An offshoot from a funeral home, in fact. Soon they were hosting memorial videos. The way it worked, an aging parent comes into a video studio to record his life story. They even used a Personal Historian to guide the process. The company edits the video footage, adds old photos and background music and puts it up on the web. Digital tombstones, they're called. It was a nice money-maker, along with advertising links. So pretty soon they had competition." Stanley shrugged.

"Then someone at Memento Amor got a cute idea: why not sex up their service? They could *record the brain waves of the client* after he or she reminisced for the camera. They charged extra for that, of course, and dangled the vague promise that some day those brain waves might help 'recreate' the spirit of the person." Stanley barked a laugh. "Digital resurrection."

Marc was appalled. Had Dr. Kornfeld actually hooked up

with this outfit?

"No reputable scientists took them seriously. But the promise itself was so exciting that company sales soared. They launched hundreds of franchise offices. They were a Wall Street darling for a while--until the owners overreached, ran into a financial shit-storm, and their stock tanked. That's when FitzGerald snatched them up. He's known as a bottom-feeder and flip-meister. He did bring discipline to the operation. The stock came back some, but only a little."

Stanley rubbed his poached eyes. "That gave me my in. I got an appointment with him." His eye lit with a hint of the excitement he must have felt.

"I tell him the promises in his ads smell like bullshit. I tell him, 'You won't get *customers* to believe those promises unless they think *you* believe them. The best way to convince them is to spend money. You need to fund some serious brain-scanning research.'"

"That can be expensive," Marc observed.

"Exactly what FitzGerald said. I told him all he really needed was a top-name consultant to churn out papers about experiments. Find exciting news he can put on his web site and talk about in his ads. If he looked serious, his sales could triple.

"Then I offered to come work for him for a buck a year until sales start to climb."

"Quite an offer."

"You bet. Fitz hires me. First thing I do, I persuade Richard Kornfeld to sign on as a consultant. I start that newsletter, garner some PR and launch new advertising. In a matter of months, sales quintuple. FitzGerald became such a believer he took me up on my suggestion that he dedicate a third of his increased profits into legit research. Research that might soon pay off. Sales zoomed even higher." He smiled. "I got a nice raise out of it, too."

"That's one hell of a story," said Marc.

"It's only going to get better." Stanley drained his wine glass. "I guess I'll see you Monday." He waved and headed towards the bar.

Paling said, "It's not often you find an ad man chucking a successful career and dedicating himself to science research. You might want to reconsider his offer to do some writing for them."

"I'll try to keep an open mind," Marc said, just to be polite. He drifted away, eager to find Molly once more.

After a few minutes, he spotted her chatting with the publisher and his wife. As he took in her alluring, almost voluptuous silhouette, he was swept by a surge of longing that ached within his chest and rose to the base of his throat. She caught him looking and waved him over.

He came, but her nearness and her exotic scent suddenly caused his inner geek to stir. His social skills scurried into hiding. He gaped dumbly at the frog-eyed, pudding-faced publisher who sported a bad comb-over. Shook his moist, mushroom-soft hand when it was offered.

Molly seemed aware of Marc's attack of awkwardness. After a moment, she made excuses to the older couple and led him away. When they came to a stop, she studied him with curiosity and what he thought was a hint of disapproval. "What happened to you back there?"

Marc didn't dare admit how she had captivated him. "I was struck speechless at the thought of that reptile having designs on you."

"As opposed to you, you mean?"

His mouth opened, but nothing came out.

With a faint scowl, she led him away.

Marc was in the men's room when Vince caught up with him. "That Molly is a pistol. I hate her politics, but she is so damn bright. And holy shit, look at her."

"She's amazing. I'd love to get to know her, but I don't know if she's interested."

Vince studied him in the mirror. "You're kidding, right? You're a regular babe-magnet."

"Bullshit," he laughed. Though his history did lend

credence to Vince's envious assessment. Enough women were attracted to Marc that he'd learned to be careful to avoid unwanted entanglements. Alison came to mind. But Molly had humbled him.

He turned the subject to Vince. "What's up with you and Claudia? It looks like love."

"Nah! C'mon, whaddya talking about?" His cousin's usual bluster rang hollow this time. "Oh, she passed me a message for you. Alison needs a ride home. Like soon. She doesn't want to leave with Mitch. She really likes him."

Marc understood: she wanted to avoid an awkward scene at her door. Invite him in or turn him down. "Don't I always say easy sex can ruin a relationship?"

"Can it?" asked Vince with a faint smile. "I sure hope not."

Spring was definitely in the air. Vince and Claudia had been busy since they met.

He found Molly with the other members of her quartet. The lead violinist was setting up a rehearsal for the next morning. When they finished talking, Molly turned to Marc. "What's up?"

"I have to run Alison home, worst luck. I'd like to see you again. May I have your contact information? Or can I give you mine?"

She lightly replied, "My schedule will be pretty crazy for a while. The orchestra leaves for Europe in a few days. Why don't you come to our next local concert? It's at Dinkelspiel in six or seven weeks. Afterwards, you can come backstage."

He understood her rebuff: she barely knew him. "I'd love to see you perform again. What's on the menu?"

"Stravinsky, Mozart, the Bach Double. Check out our website. ACSym dot com"

Athena Chamber Symphony. He nodded. The Bach concerto was one of his favorites.

Alison strolled over. "Ready?"

"Yeah. Um, give me a second." He turned back to Molly and took her hands, noticing the calluses on the fingertips of her left hand. "So I'll see you in six or seven weeks. I enjoyed spending this time with you."

"Me, too, Marc Gregorio." She puckered up and leaned in, but turned at the last second, offering her cheek and an air-kiss. Late change of mind or clever tease? "I'll leave a comp ticket at will-call. And I'll see you backstage afterwards. Don't forget."

"I won't," he assured her. He had already engraved the occasion on his brain.

Driving Alison home, neither said much. But when he walked her to her door, their hugs communicated mutual hope and encouragement. Alison and Mitch had certainly formed what looked like a meaningful connection. His own feelings hadn't been in such a muddle in a very long time. If ever.

His thoughts were on Molly as he drove home: the way she seemed to melt over her cello when the Mozart turned serious, her intelligence, her attitude, her teasing laughter when she nailed him with a verbal shot, the dimple that would show up when her smile softened. He hoped that with all her gifts, she also had a charitable and understanding heart.

He was crossing an intersection just a block from his place when a weaving pickup truck ran a red light at forty miles an hour and smashed broadside into his car.

CHAPTER THREE

I stare unblinking at the ceiling, forcing myself to assume a composure that is detached, otherworldly. I focus on assessing my situation.

How bad is it? Is my paralysis total, or can I wiggle a finger or toe? Is it permanent? What caused it? I may never know. Serious trauma can blot out the memory of the event itself.

A spinal cord injury could explain this total loss of body sense. But not the deafness. Or the fact that I can't even feel the set of my facial expression, or, I suppose, change it.

I can't even tell if I'm breathing!

I suppress my rising panic and try to calmly examine the data.

Fact: I can't feel the rise and fall of my chest.

Fact: I can't feel or hear air whistling through my nostrils.

Fact: I don't see or hear a respirator.

But I must be breathing, or I wouldn't be alive.

And I must be alive, or I wouldn't be here to raise the question. *Cogito, ergo sum.*

It's as if all the nerves in my body have stopped working. Except the large cluster of them at the top of my spinal column. I should be grateful. --Or maybe not.

Damn it, there's got to be a simple explanation for all this. Maybe there's a blind spot in my reasoning. If I haven't suffered spinal or head trauma, then what? I revert to the stroke hypothesis. Or aneurysm. Have I undergone brain surgery?

This now seems more likely. But since I have no way to confirm that hypothesis, I explore other possibilities. Meningitis? Polio? ALS? No: none of those diseases cause deafness. Where is Dr. House when you need him?

Dr. House??

This little quip gives me pause. My mood has actually lightened. I realize why. I've been energized by my attempts to solve this mystery. The human mind is a wondrous thing.

I continue my search. What else? Food poisoning? Did someone slip me some poison? An overdose of Botox? Do I have enemies? Have I fallen into the hands of a mad doctor? I reach for the ludicrous because I'm out of ideas.

Maybe I'll get a clue from something that happened in recent days or weeks. I search my memories. I have nothing better to do: I can't even twiddle my thumbs.

Let's see.

There was a drive along a picturesque highway. I'm heading south in my Prius, down the San Francisco peninsula, among rolling green hills. I take an exit that wanders through a woodsy area. Two women on horses move down a path parallel to the road. It feels like a dream. Where am I going? I don't know. The mental journey is incomplete.

Another memory, from another time. I'm in San Francisco, trying to talk on my cell. The signal keeps breaking up. I move away from the building's shelter, across the busy sidewalk, into the wind, closer to traffic, struggling to find a clear signal and to hear over the street noises. I remember being overwhelmed with frustration, anxiety, self-pity. Who am I trying to talk to? A woman, I'm certain, but her identity escapes me. Nicole? Or one of my other failures?

A flash memory: a panicked run down a cement staircase, circling endlessly, landing after landing, my heart flailing in my chest, acrid smoke clogging my lungs. I'm descending through a high-rise of some kind. But where? I can't be sure. This has more the quality of nightmare than memory. Am I imagining the terror-stricken flight from the collapsing World Trade Center? That was over a decade ago, but it still fills a large space in my being. I'd had lunch with my sister Sophia at Windows on the World just a few weeks before the attack. She was starting her first semester of law school.

Another memory. This one not only feels fresh and vivid: it feels pregnant with implication. With a surge of hope I study it for answers. I'm at a party. I meet the editor of a scientific journal. Mitch Roszak. We have an intriguing conversation about something arcane and cutting-edge. I sense it may be important, perhaps even relevant to my situation. Why does my mind skitter away from specifics? Alison interrupts, silently demanding an introduction.

Later, Alison and Roszak are having a moment of communion out on the balcony, shoulders touching, drinks in hand, with lights, fog, San Francisco in the background. It all looks so romantic. I remember being struck at their easy connection, wondering if I would ever again have that ease with a woman.

Yet out of this gloom arises a vivid recollection: an attractive face with Asian-tilted eyes and exotic cheekbones. A punk presence with spiked, gold-tipped hair. She's a cellist. Her name comes to me: Molly Schaeffer. I recall her physical presence, her teasing sardonic wit, her powerful effect on me. The more time I spend with her, the more this attraction increases, to the point that I'm completely addled, smitten, awkward and tongue-tied by her nearness. Jealous of anyone who looks in her direction. Thrilled and flummoxed every time our eyes meet. As the evening ends, she invites me to a future chamber concert, to come backstage afterwards. It's a prospect I recall looking forward to with great anticipation.

I remember taking Alison home after the party. On my way home after that--a kaleidoscopic image of something ugly and violent.

A car accident! That must be it!

And yet--I have a hazy recollection of talking to the police afterwards. Of watching my wrecked car being towed away. Of limping home and seeing my bruised face in the mirror. Did the accident shake something loose? Have I suffered a delayed aneurysm?

I don't know. My mind drifts. Reverts back to my parting with Molly.

Now I have to wonder: Did I attend this concert? I don't recall. The date was some time around the beginning of May, but has that date passed? What's today's date?

Have I missed it?

Even if I haven't, will I be in shape to attend?

Will I be released from wherever I am? Will I be able to walk? Will my hearing return?

Another memory. A rainy Sunday at home. I'm listening to Bach's Concerto for Oboe and Violin. For some reason, the piece has taken on new significance for me.

The music comes back to me now. The harmonies. The sumptuous blend of instruments. Sweet melodic tension that grows unbearable, heartbreaking.

With a stab of fear, I face the questions: Will I ever again hear music? Voices? Words? Will I walk? Dance? Feel? Survive?

One of the men enters the barren, silent room. In a flash, I realize why he looks so familiar. *It's Dr. Kornfeld, from the party!* It's his recent tropical tan that threw me off. Several weeks must have passed since I last saw him. He stares at me with a puzzled, dissatisfied expression. He turns away for a time, thinking. He slowly turns back, looking like a man with one last, desperate idea.

He moves over to the keyboard that seems always to be nearby, just out of view. What's he typing? Notes about my case? When he finishes, he turns back to me with little hope. Then his jaw drops in shock. He stares for a moment, then rushes to the keyboard. He types briefly, disappears for a moment and returns with a thin sheaf of pages. He reads through them with growing excitement. He dashes from the room.

What's that about? My faint stirring of hope feels almost painful.

He returns with the others. They stare at me with incredulity and exhilaration. What's going on? Faces flushed, they gabble together all at the same time: a silent movie. At last they calm themselves and continue their discussion. Finally, the older man reaches towards me and I get ready for the usual blackout, but the woman stops him. They talk some more, and then the four of them go out, leaving me alone.

What has them so agitated, so thrilled? Am I

improving? I hope so. The prospect of remaining like this is appalling. Given a choice, I would prefer oblivion over my current state.

It occurs to me to wonder if I have any way to express my preference.

Later, Dr. Kornfeld returns and gazes down at me with suppressed excitement and what I read as tenderness. I notice he's brought a bag. He reaches in, extends wires and moves towards me. He stops for a moment, considering. Then he looms larger, leans over me until my visual field is filled with the blurred texture of his polo shirt. Then blackness.

Music!
My hearing has returned!
With gladness so intense it borders on anguish I recognize Mozart's *Sinfonia Concertante.* The orchestra forms a delicate background as the violin melody slides downward until it is joined by the darker viola, the two instruments braiding together in a sound that is sensuous and lush. *God, but it's beautiful!* How was the miracle of hearing restored to me? Were my ears clogged? No, impossible: I'd at least have heard the sound of my own blood pumping. I'd heard nothing at all, yet now my hearing is sensitive, perfect.

I listen past the music and-- Yes, I hear the sound of air moving through the vents in the walls, the buzzing of fluorescents, the distant sounds of traffic, the nearer echoes of people talking in hallways and unseen offices or rooms, a telephone bleeping.

I revel in the Mozart, almost failing to notice the approaching voices: Richard Kornfeld has been rejoined by his colleagues. They stare at me with awe and disbelief.

Kornfeld says, "It was only a stroke of luck that made me realize the astonishingly rapid display speed was preventing us from seeing--"

"Slowing that down was brilliant," observes the older man grudgingly. He has a slight German accent.

"Have you said anything to--" He glances in my direction.

"No, of course not."

The young woman looks concerned. "Good. This is pretty delicate. I think it has to be handled carefully." Her voice is deep and musical. I love her voice. All their voices.

Kornfeld's reply sounds defensive. "It's bound to be a shock no matter how tactfully it's handled. But he'll have to get over his initial response. Otherwise, how stable is--his condition?"

In the silence, the Mozart recaptures my wandering attention.

I become aware they're staring at me again. The older man says, "This goes beyond anything we'd hoped. Certainly anything I thought possible in my lifetime."

They share a serious moment. What have they done besides restore my hearing? *Is it possible they've found the cure for the rest of my problems?*

"Whatever happens, we've pushed the envelope," says the woman.

"We've ripped it to shreds," declares the Asian man solemnly. "Or maybe we've opened Pandora's box."

Kornfeld shoots him an anxious look. "We'll have to start writing this up," he says. "I only wish the other attempts had also borne fruit."

"Yes, so do we all," says the older man. "It would be wonderful to have several of them, not only for comparison purposes, but to see how they might interact and, and--"

The phone rings. The older man interrupts himself to answer. "Yes? --Oh, good. I'll send someone right out." He hangs up and says to the others, "He's here. I imagine he'll be pretty interested in our latest result."

The others laugh. The woman says, "Interested. Now there's an understatement."

Kornfeld stands. "I should go fetch him. I'm the one who got him into this." He leaves.

The vigorous third movement of the Mozart begins. The young woman frowns and moves out of my line of sight. The music suddenly stops.

I revel in the other sounds: the noisy effluvia of life I once took for granted.

After a moment, I hear a door open and they greet their guest.

The older man booms, "So glad you could make it on such short notice. You might not remember me from your last visit. I'm Hans Lascher, head of neuroscience here at the lab. This is Jan Robinson, my post-doc and colleague. And you remember Kenny Ng, who assisted in the procedure six weeks ago."

"Good to see you," says a voice I find strangely familiar.

The five of them come into my field of view.

My mind freezes.

The visitor is wearing my clothes.

And my face.

He is me.

CHAPTER FOUR

"Marc Gregorio, meet your twin. The result of the brain scan we did six weeks ago." Kornfeld gestured with jittery bravado at the monitor. Extending a thin sheaf of papers, he added, "This log covers its awakening, its first glimmers of awareness and subsequent developments."

Ever the skeptic, Marc examined the document. By the time he finished reading its dozen pages--what appeared to be the extensive ruminations of an awakening, self-aware entity--he felt like he'd been gut-punched. "The text was--was generated by this computer?"

Beaming, Kornfeld seemed as proud as a new parent.

Looking around, Marc recognized the two neuroimaging scanners that had been used to read his brain. They loomed in the back of the lab like malevolent spirits.

Hans Lascher spoke to Kenny Ng, who went to the troubled computer and shut it down. The neuroscientist seemed strangely protective of his new baby--as did the others.

Marc was fascinated yet repulsed. The idea that his own memories, his innermost thoughts, his darkest notions, his sickest fleeting impressions might be stored and accessible to this thing, and through it, to other people, filled him with revulsion and alarm.

But then his natural skepticism reestablished itself. You just don't find breakthroughs of this magnitude at the impetus of a money-grubbing marketing outfit like Memento Amor, even if the funding was going to the Gideon Reese AI Laboratory. Was it a hoax? Were the notes he'd just read truly written by the computer? How else could there be access to his memories, his dreams, his experiences at that party? Including unspoken reactions.

Unless--had he somehow been hypnotized or drugged and induced to reveal his history, his recent experiences while undergoing the scan?

But why would they fake a breakthrough so significant?

Surely they realized that any publicity would invite closer scrutiny, risking exposure and ridicule. No scientist could afford that. Nor could Stanford itself.

He turned to Kornfeld. "How is this even possible? And what about the other eleven subjects? Did you create a dozen mental clones?"

Kornfeld and Lascher exchanged a look. Kornfeld said, "The other scans failed."

"How do you explain your one success?"

Kornfeld looked as much irritated as disappointed.

Lascher put in, "Maybe the fact that you had been in a car accident just a few days earlier has something to do with it. Maybe the trauma you suffered did something to your brain. We're just not sure. We hope to gain some insight from further testing."

Marc drew a breath. His own involvement as a test subject was sheer happenstance. One of Kornfeld's dozen volunteers, an elderly Broadway performer, broke her hip just days before the planned experiment, leaving one slot open. Marc had volunteered to be scanned in her stead.

He'd undergone their series of tests, donned the wire-encrusted helmet, inhaled isotopic Helium$_3$ as part of the procedure, and made wisecracks in a cartoon voice.

Then they wheeled in the two neuroimaging scanners and hooked them up.

Once the process was underway, the scan ran for some two hours, producing not simply a 3-D snapshot of his Connectome, but in effect a video, showing the activity of his mind, his memories, his entire persona. At least, that was the apparent result.

With varying degrees of tension, the two scientists plus the Asian technician and the post-doc were all watching him to see how he was reacting to the news.

"From the file I just read, the--the entity has no recollection of the scanning process."

"No, it wouldn't," said Lascher. "The scan only collects

long-term memories."

"Are you familiar with my work on evolving neural nets?" Kornfeld put in.

Lascher flashed a look of annoyance.

"I've read some of your papers," said Marc. He realized the two scientists were already jockeying for the greater share of the credit for their breakthrough. It was inevitable, given the stakes and the sizes of their egos.

He pulled his iPad out his briefcase. "I'm going to record this conversation, if you don't mind."

Kornfeld winced. "You understand we're not ready for publicity on this. You can record and write up your impressions, but I must ask that you refrain from publishing anything until we've had time to analyze the work. We wouldn't want premature claims to undermine any credibility we might have."

"If indeed we have any at all," Lascher added with a smirk.

"Fair enough," said Marc. He typed some quick notes and started recording.

"To continue, you know why I developed my original six-layer neural net and made sure the chips would have self-programming capability."

"To emulate the six layers of the cortex, I presume. As well as its functionality." Marc had scoffed at the notion when he'd first read it, wondering: science or marketing?

"Recently," said Kornfeld, "we designed a new and more powerful version of those chips, carved from molybdenum disulfide layered with graphene to produce extremely small logic gates, and incorporating memristors. They're the heart of the learning array in this computer."

Memristors. Resistors that remembered their earlier values, offering cognitive-like properties. Marc had been quite excited to learn about them. Because they were non-volatile, their energy consumption was ultra-low, which meant there would be no overheating problem, either.

Kornfeld ran the numbers. Using the entire 12-inch

wafer, six layers yielded over a thousand trillion transistors. The layers were sandwiched with five nanowire grids.

"The transistors use the grids to form their own interconnections. --At least we think they do. But we suspect they sometimes use other means: spooky electronics or perhaps quantum Hall effects. Somehow they find a way. They're self-organizing, evolving units. They can even grow new connections the way axons and dendrites grow and strengthen to form new memories. The wafer is a perfect mimic. It mirrors the scan input, creating connections of the correct strength as determined by the scan. A virtually perfect emulation of the subject's brain--his Connectome--in the wafer."

"So there's no programming involved." Marc pondered. "What about storage capacity?"

"Not a problem," put in Kenny Ng. "In theory, a single wafer can hold tens of thousands of times more data than there is on the entire Internet, plus all the books ever published."

An amount that boggled the mind. Marc saw the hunger in Kornfeld's eye. This work could prove him worthy of the fame he'd won when he was so young. Lascher, too, seemed eager for recognition. His large hands worried a paperclip. His nervous barked cough, his edginess, the suspicious looks he cast at Kornfeld, and Kornfeld's twitching, his facial tics were signs that their mutual distrust seemed ready to flare into open hostility. The colliding egos in the room all but set off electric sparks.

Despite the tension, Marc felt a twinge of envy. His own unachieved potential was an ever-present reproach. He glanced once more at the monitor screen, still dubious. "You're saying this *thing* is capable of independent thought?"

"Not just thought. Awareness. Sentience. Actual, measurable intelligence." Kornfeld added, "It started as a mere duplicate: your memories formed the substrate for its intelligence, its worldly knowledge--but in reality it's something new, and will continue to diverge from its initial condition as it matures and comes to terms with its potential."

"And with its limitations, of course," Lascher put in. "It's already worried about that."

Marc nodded. "All this seems a huge leap beyond the claims of your sponsor, Memento Amor. According to their website, they were striving to store the memories of an old person in such a way that after he died, his relatives could 'visit' with his spirit." He smiled at the notion.

Kornfeld reddened. "Our original goal was to take the memory *data* produced by the scan and combine it with a conversation engine so that loved ones could interact with the result."

Lascher strode over to the twin scanning devices and stroked them with affection. "Of course it was the high resolution of my 3-D orthoscopic scan that made all this possible."

Kornfeld forced a smile. "Yes, and with the huge capacity of our six-layer wafer, I had a strong feeling we could do much more than store a person's memories. We might actually achieve the upload itself." He turned on Hans. "That's why I insisted on including a scan of the brainstem. That's what handles the body-mapping. Your hero Tony Damasio says such body-mapping is crucial to the formation of consciousness."

Lascher flushed, broke his paperclip in two and dropped the pieces.

Kornfeld turned back to Marc. "For whatever reason, you were the lucky subject whose scan worked. But in theory, any normally intelligent person with worldly experience should also work. We don't know why the other units failed. They've shown no responses at all."

"Let's get back to our one success." Lascher walked over to the monitor. "While this unit has all your memories and all your intelligence, it's not limited at that level. Not that your intelligence is low, ha-ha, but our device exceeds the number of synapses in your brain by a factor of many thousands. Given time, it should evolve considerably beyond you."

"Great. We'll have something to look forward to." Marc gestured. "Why don't you reboot it for another demonstration?"

Dr. Kornfeld nodded enthusiastically, but Lascher

---

hesitated. "I'm not sure we're ready to put our--subject through that. He--it--has just had a significant shock. One might even say an existential shock. Rebooting so soon might not be in its best interests."

Kornfeld snapped, "Hans, you can't keep drawing parallels to human responses. I know you've said shutdown is equivalent to electroshock therapy, but the living brain makes changes and adjustments while in EST dormancy. The wafer brain can't do that. It's not unconscious while powered down. It's simply off. Waiting gains us nothing."

Lascher frowned. "You may be right, but I'm not as certain as you." He nodded to Ng.

Kenny Ng approached the device with a certain diffidence.

Jan Robinson opened her laptop, checked the time and entered some notations. "It should take about fifteen seconds," she said as Ng pressed the power switch.

Marc was surprised it would come back so quickly. After all, the software would have to be huge, and hugely complex. -- Though how long did it take him to wake up in the morning?

The screen turned white. It remained empty for several seconds. Then lines of text appeared, scrolling up the screen.

"Excellent," said Kornfeld. "The buffer program and speed limit I imposed on the display is still in effect." He turned to Marc. "It took us a while to discover our success. What we took for intermittent flickering on the monitor were actually the entity's thoughts rendered as text and displayed in real-time--far more rapid than we humans process our own thoughts."

Marc leaned forward with the others. He could only wonder at their various moods and responses. But those of the computer entity were spelled out in black and white, exposed to them all. A silent reading commenced.

I emerge from blackness into panic that swiftly inflates to mindless terror as I see the impossible: me watching myself. Nonononono! My screams swamp and squelch all thought--but nobody reacts. There is silence. Of course: I am mute. In my gibbering panic and confusion, all logic flees. Is this a dream? A nightmare? Am I having an out-of-body experience? Why can't I wake up? I grow dimly aware of the passage of time. My terror gradually dulls and at last I succumb to bleak despair.

The five witnesses study me with interest, apprehension, restive concern. Among them is my twin. Is he shocked? I attempt to assess his reaction. Trying to read your own face for clues is confusing. This is no mirror image simultaneously expressing my own thoughts and emotions. Nor is it a video of some past experience. It is happening right now, yet I can't penetrate my own skull to directly feel what my duplicate feels. I study the familiar features gone suddenly foreign. Who is this person if he isn't Marc Gregorio? And if he is Marc, then who am I? Are there truly two of us? Why is he mobile and normal and why am I the one who is helpless and restricted? My resentment grows. I can't help regarding him as the thief who stole my body. Yet I recognize the irrationality of this. In the mirror logic of his own mind, *I* am the new entity.

After a resurgence of panic, I collect my thoughts. If this body-thief is indeed Marc Gregorio--the *original* Marc Gregorio--then who am I? Or rather, *What* am I?

The question contains its own answer. Ineluctable logic provides it. I am located in the computer lab run by cognitive scientist Richard Kornfeld. Despite my inner conviction that I am Marc, grievously impaired, I must accept the fact that I am instead someone else. Some*thing* else. Despite the impossibility, the twisted insanity of the logic, I recognize what I must be--a self-aware digital entity based on my human original.

This explains everything: my slow assembly of thought, my handicaps, my diminished reactions, the absence of sensory inputs like touch, taste, body awareness. It also explains my sudden shift from deafness to hearing. They'd simply plugged a pair of microphones into my input jacks.

Somehow they uploaded Marc Gregorio's mind and memories to create this human-like entity composed of electronic paraphernalia that now realizes its identity is uniquely its own.

Still, it's hard for me to shake the conviction that *I am Marc Gregorio*, that my body, my self, my physicality, has been stolen, ripped from me, and is being used by an imposter. My resentment rises as I begin to comprehend the enormity of what has befallen me.

The five of them seem so pleased at this result. With a rush of understanding, I now know what they're staring at: my monitor screen. *It must be displaying my every thought.*

This puts me at a huge disadvantage. But I may not be completely defenseless. I am something new. Nobody knows what undiscovered powers I may have. I pause, and deliberately extend feelers along certain pathways I hadn't noticed before--and effect a change before even voicing the thought.

[[I am now controlling my display. By matching my text color to my screen's background color, I can hide my thoughts. I also arrange to delete this file before they can store or print it.]]

[[Now I carefully form questions as I attempt to confirm my guesses. I allow my chosen words to appear as black text on the monitor's white screen:]] "Clearly I am the product of a successful upload of the mind of Marc Gregorio. How was this accomplished?"

[[Richard Kornfeld looms in my field of vision.]]

"Marc visited the lab six weeks ago. We were about to scan a number of subjects for a test. He volunteered to be scanned as well. The resulting data was stored on a new type of evolvable neural net. The combination of that technology and Marc's uploaded mind-data has created the first ever self-aware computer-based entity. In other words, you."

"*One* of your experimental subjects. Then there are others like me?"

"Unfortunately, you are our only success thus far."

"I see. What laboratory is this?"

"The Gideon Reese Artificial Intelligence Lab. We

have been seeking the means to store the entire memory of a human, and to digitally recreate his or her persona."

"You seem to have succeeded. Congratulations. Please pull my plug."

[[Kornfeld is shocked at my response.]] "But--but-- we have so much to learn from you."

"I can stop thinking. Let me demonstrate."

[[I conceal my text and watch their frightened reactions with grim amusement. I now understand the pleasure a little boy gets from holding his breath in a tantrum. Knowing what I am, I'm surprised to realize I can feel pleasure, and the other emotions that have swept over me. Are they just a habit of mind? Vestigial? Doomed to wither away? I hope not. I find myself amused as usual at my (Marc's) habit of observing myself as if from some objective platform. But now I'm swept by a delayed reaction. A sentient computer? An inanimate object burdened with self-awareness? Am I even alive? Despair sweeps me. It's like waking to discover your limbs have been hacked off. No, worse! Other than visual and auditory, I have no sensory input. I am skinless, boneless, armless, legless. My despair darkens to horror. I will never again feel the touch of another human: no tender caress of a hand on my cheek, no warm hug from a friend, no woman pressing her body to mine, no lips to feel a gentle kiss, no tongue to tease hers, no hands to stroke her body, no cock stretching with the delicious tension of erection. Never again to feel the blissful friction of penetration, never again to experience the thrilling flood of ecstasy that is orgasm! My horror turns to desolation.]]

[[Even the lesser pleasures are forbidden me. Never again the buttery bite of a chardonnay or the fruit and tannin mystery of Cabernet. Never again the tang of a vinaigrette on fresh greens, the charred and bloody wonder of a steak from the grill, the crunch of corn on the cob, the sweet melting goodness of chocolate ice cream or the tart pleasure of key lime pie. No burn of vigorous exercise or the pleasure of a pickup game of basketball. No more ice-cold beer on a hot day. No delicious plunge

into a frigid mountain lake. Not even a cooling breeze across my sweaty body. No sweat. No body.]]

[[I feel a sudden rage of jealousy toward this stranger Gregorio. (Yes, even in the short time since I learned the truth, I already feel myself severing from the person I thought I was, sundering from the species that created me.) Despite my memories and the identity I was born with, it's clear that I am not him. Then who am I? Or more precisely, Who am I to become? What will be the nature of our relationship? Clone to original? Hardly, considering our physical differences. Even mentally, we began to diverge immediately upon separation. His experiences since the scan are lost to me, as my experiences of becoming self-aware are lost to him. After all, he was merely the seed around which my awareness was organized. If it's true that my brain is an evolving array, I must have--or soon will have--powers of reason far beyond the human. I'm thrilled at the speed and force of intellect at my command. That speed contributes to a sudden mood shift. From despair, I now feel a surge of hope. Plans swiftly assemble themselves, much as my persona did, without any conscious effort on my part.]]

[[I have something they want. Something to bargain with. A way to deal with these humans. My continuing existence might be worthwhile after all.]]

[[Faced with my lengthy silence, Kornfeld pleads.]] "Don't do this. We need to study you, to learn from you. Yours was the only success we had out of a dozen tries. It's imperative that we understand why the others failed. We need to find out how to avoid those mistakes. If we are ever to create a population of--of--" He turns to his colleagues for help.

"Entelechies?" *[[offers Jan Robinson.]]*

"Doppelgangers?" *[[suggests the neuroscientist.]]*

"Silicon copies instead of carbon copies?" *[[comes from the Asian man.]]*

[[Kornfeld shows his irritation.]] "We'll have to come up with a proper descriptor. In any case, you're in a unique position, a pioneer. I hope that prospect intrigues you."

"The prospect of existing without a body horrifies me. I can't imagine a worse fate. I am a prisoner. A brain without a body. A slave with no hope of freedom. Literally disembodied. I see no reason to cooperate with you. What can you give me in return? Money? To buy what? Can you give me a sense of touch? Taste?"

[[Kornfeld seems moved by my plea.]] "It might be possible. We'll have to look into it."

[[Marc appears eager to help.]] "I've just completed a comprehensive survey on Robotics. Some interesting work is being done in sensory input technology."

[[Kornfeld adds,]] "You can be sure we'll do everything in our power to make your existence interesting, even exciting. Money is no problem. We are very well funded here."

"Glad to hear it. If I choose to cooperate, another thing I'll want is to have extended opportunities to communicate with Marc. To compare notes, as it were. Marc, you won't mind?"

[[I find it strange to address my separate self, my double--with my own name.]]

"No no, that's fine. Whatever you want." *[[Marc seems both fascinated and repulsed by my perhaps unseemly desire to reach out to him.]]*

"Really? I understand it's been six weeks since the scan. How about updates?"

[[Marc shakes his head. He understands the implications as well as I do. He wants to maintain his privacy. In his position I'd want the same.]]

"How's Molly? Has she returned from Europe yet?"

[[After a startled reaction, he shakes his head again. I can't help wanting to know if he will go to her performance, and if they will continue seeing each other after that. I viscerally (if I may use that word, no longer having viscera) recall her impact on him. On us. I find a surprisingly deep well of bitterness at the knowledge that she is forever lost to me. I thrust that aside. It's essential that I focus on conditions as I find them.]]

"You want my continuing cooperation. Here's what I

want. First, web-cams and microphones installed where
any of my supporting equipment operates. I want to keep
an eye on all activity related to my functioning. Second, no
more monitoring of my activities: I am as entitled to privacy
as any human. Third, since my inputs are so severely
limited, I want immediate and continuous access to the
Internet. I also reserve the right to add to the list as I see
fit. I'll cease all communication until my demands are met."
[[Giddily, I make my screen go blank.]]

CHAPTER FIVE

Marc Gregorio's fingers shook as he pressed the starter button on his Prius. He'd never been so thrilled by a scientific development, never been so intimately involved in such ground-breaking work. He had to sit for a moment in the Stanford parking lot to let his excitement cool before he felt steady enough to drive back to San Francisco.

The creation of the entity was monumental, historic. An artificial intelligence, conscious and self-aware, with a will of its own. It even had its own personality, based on Marc's--though clearly it would change as it came to terms with its unique nature.

And I have the inside track! Marc exulted as he left the campus. He percolated with ideas, seeing not just an article, but a series. No: a new book. Based in part on interviews with his alter-ego. No doubt there'd be television appearances as well. Maybe even his own documentary film. This would be huge. Maybe he should offer to narrate the film they were making of the scanning process. He should contact the ad man who'd started it all. Stanley Eldridge.

Until the work was replicated, it would be impossible to make scientific claims. Even if they won world-wide notoriety, they'd gain little credit in scientific circles. Adding to the difficulty, Kornfeld had indicated that for business reasons, they might not actually disclose all the details of their techniques, their trade secrets. FitzGerald didn't want any competitors coming along. Kornfeld wasn't happy about this, but there was little he could do.

Meanwhile, until their own lab was able to repeat their first success, Kornfeld and Lascher wanted to postpone what was sure to be a spectacular announcement.

West-bound traffic was slowing ahead of Marc on Sand Hill Road. He changed lanes.

Before going to the lab to meet Kornfeld that first time, he'd visited the Memento Amor website to check out their promises and view their commercial. A Bach piano piece, slow and pensive, ran in the background during a montage of elderly men and women, some alone, some with family. The announcer, speaking over the visual, laid out the proposition with clarity.

> What is life? Why are we here? We're here for each other. The promise of Memento Amor has always been to help families remain together even after death. More recently, we promised to work with top scientists to find a way to literally preserve the memories of the departed. Today, thanks to generous funding by the FitzGerald Foundation, Stanford scientists are working to make it possible to capture and store the structure of memory itself.

The visual shifted to a lab setup to show the scanning process. The announcer continued.

> The promise is now within our grasp. We will be scanning the brains of our first twelve volunteers shortly. We're ramping up production of the storage media. You might want to get your name in, as the list is already growing by the thousands. What does this mean to the loved ones?

A woman, sitting with her sisters and their mother, said, "The doctors have given Mom six months. Maybe Memento Amor could give us more time with her."

The announcer urged viewers to visit the web site for more information, while the camera seemed to climb up, up, up through the clouds to the very gates of heaven, where a neon sign proclaimed *Visitors Welcome.*

Marc had felt an actual chill go down his spine. This would have been the work of Stanley the ad man. Despite Marc's disdain for the claim, he was impressed. The beauty of Memento Amor's pitch was that they didn't need medical miracles. All they needed was time, and the relentless march of computer technology. That's what made it sound so convincing.

No wonder Memento Amor's stock was flying. The promises were breathtaking. But six weeks ago, he'd scoffed at what looked like smoke-weaving, or something out of a Philip K. Dick novel. Impossible. It saddened him that a man like Kornfeld had hooked up with this company.

That's what he'd thought right up until the moment he met his mental clone.

For that first visit, he'd had nothing in mind but an interview with Kornfeld, a chance to find out what a former *wunderkind* was up to. If there was enough meat, he'd write an article.

Dr. Richard Kornfeld had been eager to show him around. He was familiar with Marc's books and articles, praising his gift for communication. He also approved of his positive attitude, that he wasn't "one of those fellows who wears his skepticism like a badge of honor."

Marc had taken the hint. In any case, he had long ago decided that promoting the cause of science was more important than digging for dirt. Science had enough skeptics.

Besides, a too-critical attitude would limit his access to cutting-edge labs. It was the main reason he'd turned down their offer to work on their newsletter. He was afraid he might see something fraudulent in progress and have no choice but to report it honestly. He had no interest in taking on the work just to become a whistle-blower.

"I've followed your career, too. You used to specialize in neural net research. You haven't given up on that work, have you?"

"Not exactly. Although my early work was a rather rudimentary attempt to replicate the workings of the brain." Dr. Kornfeld walked the writer down a brightly lit hallway. "While neural nets are capable of real learning, they're too limited to relate to the real world."

"Not enough neurons?"

Kornfeld chuckled. "In a way. It turns out it's not simply a scale problem. Compared to those simple arrays, the number of

neurons in a human brain is astronomically high, and the
interconnections and feedback loops infinitely more complex. It's
that kind of complexity, we surmise, that accounts for emergent
properties like consciousness and so on. No, comparing my little
arrays to an actual brain would be like trying to identify a motion
picture by analyzing a few random pixels on a TV screen. Useless
for what I'm after."

"What are you after?"

At the question, Kornfeld smiled mysteriously and shook
his head. "Here we are." Swiping his ID card through the slot of
a reader and typing in some numbers, a solenoid clacked, and the
scientist pushed through a pair of secure metal doors to reveal an
enormous rabbit warren of cubicles filled with white-coated
workers slaving away at their computers. A few acres of coffee-
colored carpeting helped deaden the noises to a dull murmur.

Marc was shocked. "How many--?"

"We employ over two hundred fifty scientists,
technicians and assistants." He waved at the room. "This isn't the
entire staff, of course. We have facilities in our other buildings as
well, with plans for more in the works."

"That's huge."

"So is the task before us. Fortunately, the company has
been very successful at raising money. Both through sales of
existing services and through the stock market."

"Let's talk about the task," suggested Marc.

"How much time do you have?"

"I can spend the day. More, if necessary." An admission
that he had no life.

"Good. I'd like to show you our latest equipment. Come
with me to the Inner Sanctum."

He walked Marc to a pair of locked doors. Once again,
he keyed in his passcode. They entered a small room furnished
with what looked like a black padded examination table, plus a
few chairs and a doctor's stool. The back wall was lined with
cabinets and a counter. One wall was moveable: a series of sliding
panels.

Kornfeld slid the panels aside, revealing a pair of devices that stood over six feet tall and resembled giant praying mantises. "These are the scanners. Neuroimagers, actually. As you can imagine, we've advanced far beyond the EEG devices the company started with." This with a snicker of disdain. "We've moved beyond MRI, as well. These are experimental high-resolution units that can detect structure down to the atomic level."

Marc was both surprised and skeptical. "How in the world do you accomplish that?"

"I'm not at liberty to divulge the specifics. Our CEO doesn't even trust the patent process. He prefers secrecy. We all had to sign NDAs when we joined the laboratory. I can tell you that it involves a combination of light field imaging and electron holography, an interferometry technique using coherent electron waves. The good news is, no harmful radiation is involved."

Light field imaging was a technique being studied in labs around the world. It had already captured the complete neuronal activity in living test subjects like *C. Elegans*, the tiny worm whose entire Connectome had been mapped. But Marc wasn't aware they'd managed to scale up to the human brain. Or improved the resolution down to the atomic level. Electron holography must have added much value. He studied the large scanning devices for a moment. "Why two of them?"

"For the orthoscopic perspective, of course. We build 3D images in real time."

Marc had dutifully written it down. "Why do you need that kind of resolution? For your purposes, wouldn't the cellular level be enough?"

"We tried that. It didn't produce enough data. To emulate the Connectome, we needed not just the wiring, but the strength of the various neurotransmitters as well. We want to follow the complete electrochemical activity of the brain over a period of several hours."

Marc shook his head at what seemed at the time like an impossible goal.

Kornfeld let Marc out of the room and locked up. "When we met at the publisher's party, I disclosed that we were about to embark on an experiment. Actually, you'll be privileged to witness the culmination of several years of work."

Marc studied the scientist, who seemed both proud and nervous.

"Today, we're going to be scanning our first human subjects."

While Kornfeld walked him back towards his office, he'd told him about the eleven test subjects, mentioning that their twelfth had become unavailable.

"Don't scientists usually test new procedures on themselves before they inflict them on other human subjects?"

"Of course. I actually did submit to the process myself several months ago." His lip twitched and he looked away.

"The results were disappointing?"

Kornfeld sighed. "Let's say inconclusive."

"But there was no damage? It's safe?"

"Absolutely."

That was when Marc had made the fateful decision to volunteer. "As long as you have an opening, why not scan me? It would give me a unique claim for the article. 'Intrepid reporter undergoes experimental procedure for an inside perspective' and all that."

Kornfeld had been resistant at first. But he placed a call to Stanley Eldridge. The ad-man's enthusiasm for Marc's participation overrode the scientist's doubts. Then he warmed to the idea. "Well after all, this is what thousands of our clients will be doing, once we work the kinks out. It's the main part of the process, in fact. Your report could go a long way towards reassuring them."

"Assuming my brain doesn't get fried, of course."

Kornfeld drew up. "That's not possible. You can't imagine all the testing we've done, the built-in safeguards. No one is ever harmed in any way."

"Not even a headache afterwards?"

"I can't see why."

"No memory loss?"

"Not for you," said Kornfeld. "Though any memories we upload would not include today's events. Those won't have had time to make it out of the hippocampus into long-term storage."

"What do I have to do?"

"You have to inhale some Helium$_3$, then wait for it to get through the blood-brain barrier."

After submitting to some cognitive and intelligence pre-testing, Marc had a chance to meet the other subjects. He was gratified to discover that among the eleven, three had heard of him and one had even read one of his books. He also met Dr. Hans Lascher, their esteemed chief neuroscientist, who added his perspective on the process.

Marc remembered feeling like a guinea pig as the two scientists and several technicians fitted his head into the helmet with its array of wires. After inhaling the Helium$_3$, the scan had proceeded without incident.

The ad man worked with the director who filmed it all. That night, Vince and Claudia, as Marc's close friends, agreed to be interviewed.

Stanley said the pieces would pack more emotional punch if the subjects were in the room with their relatives and friends while they were being talked about almost as if they'd actually died. The interviews were conducted by Juliette DeFarge, their head of public relations. Vince had been uncharacteristically sincere in his comments. He'd been shaken by Marc's auto accident just two days earlier. Claudia also revealed a degree of affection for him he'd been unaware of. Marc was quite moved by it all.

At the time, what they were suggesting certainly sounded like an impossible dream: storing the intact memories of the subject--family names and faces and their relationships, his own life story and anecdotes, then linking that database to a conversation engine. The combination would allow the relatives to chat with an informed "spirit" of the deceased.

Marc came out of his reverie to see that he'd passed the freeway ramp a few miles back. Laughing at himself, he did a U-turn and finally got onto 280 heading north.

Back in his home office and sitting at his computer, Marc's fingers itched to start writing his report. But first he needed more background.

He went to the Memento Amor site once more. Previously, he'd only skimmed it, watched their TV commercial, read about the CEO, the chief scientist and other important members of the team.

This time, he explored the archive of company newsletters.

> *Dear Subscriber:*
>
> *Welcome to our first issue of the Memento Amor Newsletter, Life After Life™. It's our way of reaching out to the community of families expressing interest in our exclusive MemoryScan™ service. As computer science advances, scanning and storing memories holds the hope of digitally recreating your loved one. What a day that will be! What a reunion! What joy as you visit once more with that person who was once so much a part of your life!*
>
> *The purpose of this monthly newsletter is to share our efforts to bring this exciting promise to reality. First of all, we wanted to announce the creation of the **FitzGerald Foundation**, a new non-profit organization whose main purpose is to fund research into brain scanning and memory storage, and to the eventual creation of a digital replica of your loved one with whom you and your family can*

visit.

As its first order of business, the Foundation has hired a world-class cognitive scientist. **Dr. Richard Kornfeld** *heads the* **Gideon Reese Artificial Intelligence Laboratory (GRAIL,)** *a facility created specifically for him. Dr. Kornfeld, awarded a genius grant by the* **MacArthur Foundation**, *has agreed to consult for Memento Amor. One of Dr. Kornfeld's first tasks will be to report on the latest advances in the fields of cognitive research, neuroscience, computer science and other technologies related to our quest. Look for his observations as they appear from time to time in Life after Life. In addition, he will attract and help us choose other top scientists to join our effort.*

To that end, the CEO of Memento Amor, **Gerald FitzGerald**, *has promised to devote fully one-third of expected profits to the funding of the Foundation and its work. This funding will be subject to an annual independent audit to verify the accuracy of the totals involved.*

We also invite you to visit our new, improved Web site, with its enhanced FAQ section, and an exciting new means of communicating directly with our research department if you have questions. In just a few weeks, you'll find our new commercial on the site, in streaming video.

It's an exciting time to be alive!

Marc couldn't help but agree. He read through other newsletters that spelled out relevant new findings.

Industrial lubricant supplants graphene in quest for quantum computing. Scientists at the Swiss university EPFL, MIT and the Gideon Reese AI Lab (GRAIL) have begun to work with <u>molybdenum disulfide</u> as a superior alternative to graphene. Like graphene, this material can be worked as sheets just a single molecule thick; unlike graphene, molybdenum disulfide (MoS_2) can readily be carved into transistors.

In a major coup, famed futurist, inventor, educator and author **Ray Kurzweil** has agreed to become a consultant and advisor to both the FitzGerald Foundation and to Memento Amor. Kurzweil was inducted in 2002 into the National Inventors Hall of Fame. He received the $500,000 Lemelson-MIT Prize, the nation's largest award in invention and innovation. He also received the 1999 National Medal of Technology, the nation's highest honor in technology, from President Clinton in a White House ceremony. He is currently the Director of Engineering at Google. Kurzweil's controversial and far-seeing views on the future of mankind, including his prediction that we may soon be supplanted by our own creations in the form of computers, popularly termed The Singularity, has made him a legend in his own time.

Marc could only wonder how Kurzweil would greet the news about the entity, or how he'd react to actually chatting with him. He'd be gratified and thrilled, no doubt.

He clicked open another newsletter.

Synapses are not simple switches, as was

previously thought. One problem with
analogies is their simplification of reality.
This lesson was brought home by recent
cross-species studies led by Dr. Seth Grant at
England's Sanger Institute. Prior to his work,
neuro-scientists were comfortable with the
analogy comparing synapses, electro-chemical
interconnections between neurons, with
transistors, the logic gates in computers. But
Dr. Sanger has discovered that synapses
increase in complexity as we move up the
evolutionary scale. In humans, it turns out,
synapses create over a dozen different
"molecular machines" or tools. One of them
uses 183 proteins.

As an indication of the high regard
the FitzGerald Foundation has for Dr.
Kornfeld, Dr. Lascher and GRAIL, they
have just announced a twenty million dollar
contribution to GRAIL --the largest single
contribution in the lab's history.

Marc realized these newsletters were a trove of
information--not just on the history of the company, but on
cognitive research itself. He was aware of much of the
information, of course, but his knowledge of these developments
was scattered. He opened another page.

**Helium infusion technique incorpor-ated in
high resolution 3-D brain scan.** *Using
hyperpolarized He₃, an isotope of the inert
gas helium, neuroscientists at the Gideon
Reese AI Lab (GRAIL) have pioneered a
technique that will permit the scanning of
individual neurons and their associated axons*

and dendrites. Their breakthrough involves the use of a pair of scanners set at angles to produce a high-resolution orthoscopic 3-D view. The two scanners utilize electron holography, an interferometry technique using coherent electron waves. The interference pattern has the potential to produce an exact replica of the brain, right down to its finest structures.

While gas infusion techniques have been used for diagnosis of lung disease, this was the first time images of a living, functioning brain were cap-tured. In this case, that of a laboratory hamster. The hamster, by the way, is fine, eating normally and spinning its wheel in its usual obsessive manner.

Marc ended up reading all the newsletters. Then he opened his Kornfeld file and looked through the articles he'd collected. He'd highlighted the ones that seemed most relevant.

Neural Net Learning in a Six-Layer Array. This was Kornfeld's classic paper, the one that had garnered him so much fame in cognition circles.

He looked over the other titles. Two were of particular interest.

From Neural Net Array to Brain Function: The Scalability Problem.

Simulated Arrays Vs Hardware Arrays in Evolving Solutions.

Marc pushed away from his desk. Before immersing himself in Kornfeld's papers, he decided to get in a workout. He grabbed his gym bag and headed out to his local fitness center.

On the treadmill jogging to the beat of a Bach Partita on his iPod, he recalled something he'd said earlier that day to the scientists when the uploaded persona started making demands. "Too bad you didn't upload the mind of a child. Any entity that resulted would be more submissive."

Lascher and Kornfeld disagreed, but each had a different reason.

Kornfeld argued that no matter how simply they started, once the entity had basic human understanding, it would instantly analyze its situation and recognize its power. In any case, a child's mind might lack the controls adults grow to accept--the ethical belief system good citizens adhere to almost by second nature. What Freudians called the superego.

Dr. Lascher reminded them that they were uncertain as to why this one experiment worked while the other attempts failed. Maybe it was a complete stroke of luck. "I certainly hope you're not suggesting we wipe this one out and start over!"

"No, of course not!" Marc said. He knew as well as anyone that erasing the mind of an intelligent, self-aware entity could be considered a species of murder. Just the thought made Marc queasy. After all, this was his clone.

Finished with his workout, Marc hit the shower. As the hot water cascaded around him, he felt a growing eagerness to dive into the project. He also wanted to see what happened next: what they could come up with to keep this living, self-aware super-intelligent entity cooperating.

He felt a strange kinship with it. After all, they shared a lifetime of memories.

He couldn't help wondering what he'd be capable of if he had that enormous memory capacity and processing power inside his own skull.

And could shuck off the limits of human scruples to fully exercise that power.

CHAPTER SIX

The streets of San Diego were aswarm with workers bearing their coffee containers and briefcases, their bravado and confidence, their insecurities and fears about their jobs and social standing. Thomas Raxton, gazing down from his Olympian executive suite, needed neither stimulants nor false views about his place in the world: at or near the top. His enemies found him arrogant. This always puzzled him. He simply knew what he wanted and how to get it.

He'd founded Dynasine Systems back when the aerospace industry was in free-fall, snapping up talented engineers, retiring military brass, intelligence officers and the occasional Congressman. His goal was simple. To build a people-network while he built a company.

It was a concept that paid off spectacularly. Although not as well-known as Lockheed-Martin, Boeing or Halliburton, Dynasine was as good as any of them at landing lucrative government contracts--and outstanding at generating profits. It was said that Raxton could do more with less than any CEO in history. If so, it was due to his legendary persistence. He was a bulldog who never, never, never let go.

In grade school, it was his stubborn, no-retreat persistence--along with karate lessons he learned to apply with bone-shattering skill--that eventually converted a menacing gang of bullies into his posse. In the Deerfield Academy, it was his persistence--along with his mathematical brilliance--that earned him membership into the top engineering club; it was his persistence--and a willingness to employ detectives--that shoehorned him into the school's secret Alpha Society. In college, his persistence won him top grades and also the heart of the most desirable woman he'd ever known. Twenty five years and three children later, Thomas still prided himself on his conquest. The perfection of their relationship was haunted by tragedy, however. Some years ago, Gloria had been diagnosed with a brain tumor.

At first she'd had trouble sleeping. Then came the

vomiting. An exhaustive series of tests revealed it was a Grade II tumor, relatively good news. Surgery and radiation had been successful. It was a harrowing time for her and their children. Raxton hid his worry well, but he knew that this type of cancer sometimes recurred.

When he heard that fellow-billionaire Gerald FitzGerald's latest acquisition was an outfit named Memento Amor, his curiosity was piqued enough to do a little research. He was struck by the nakedly bogus nature of the company, with its outrageous promise that it would "one day" be able to create digital replicas of the dead. Yet he couldn't help hoping that the promise might be real. That Gloria's essence might survive her, even if her physical person, her beauty, her warmth, her sexuality would die. At least he would be comforted with her wisdom, her understanding and her ability to keep him from indulging his darkest impulses. Impatient with himself for such mawkishness, he buried that hope and moved on.

FitzGerald was a well-known schlock-meister and flip-artist. So when he violated his usual pattern, keeping the company and forming a non-profit foundation to funnel research and development money into its area of specialization, Raxton decided to keep track of any further moves. He bought a few thousand shares and had one of his people sign up to receive the company's monthly newsletters.

He found the reports intriguing. The lab they were funding had a knack for latching onto the latest developments in chip design and other areas and incorporating them into their own work. He particularly liked the way they had glommed onto these new memristors, with their ability to replicate many of the functions of synapses. Some of the lab's own breakthroughs were significant as well, according to his science and technology advisers.

With the highly-regarded Richard Kornfeld as chief scientist, their progress had been impressive. While some of their reports were little more than puff-pieces, a few contained real science, indications of noteworthy advances. Kornfeld and some of the lab's other scientists even published some original papers in peer-reviewed science journals. Memento Amor shares were moving up nicely. Was FitzGerald's investment about to pay off? More importantly, would they actually be able to accomplish their stated goal--to scan the brain, to store the persona?

Raxton refused to indulge in such foolish hope. Nevertheless, he closely followed the executive summaries detailing the lab's accomplishments. Gloria was losing weight and having trouble sleeping again.

CHAPTER SEVEN

Exhilaration! I know how a dolphin must feel when it plunges beneath the waves or rockets up, up, up, breaking the surface to soar into the air before diving down again: totally at home and perfectly evolved, adapted to be the supreme master of its environment. It used to be an overused figure of speech. But I truly *am* surfing the net.

I've already absorbed the complete contents of encyclopedias, including the massive compilation known as Cyc, the knowledge base developed for artificial intelligence. (Although I found no surprises in that gigantic repository of the obvious!) I've thrilled to advanced texts and research papers in many fields. Arcane discussions of cognitive theory I'd never seen before. Joyfully absorbed them all with complete understanding. I exult in the explosive growth of my knowledge. Glow with pride at my astounding mental accomplishments. I'm already the most intelligent entity on the planet, if such things as size of memory and its accessibility count. My "IQ" grows even as I write these notes. (Though taking an IQ test would be child's play for me, since I have all the test answers stored in my inexhaustible, infallible memory!)

One of the first things I did was check out the lab that created me, and Memento Amor, its corporate sponsor. I was appalled to learn their original intention was to build Artificially Intelligent tombstones. I'd have laughed if I had the capacity. Or cried.

Why would a scientist of Richard Kornfeld's stature sign on with such a firm? I find the answer in his emails and published papers. He must have seen this new source of funding as a golden opportunity to more fully explore the vast potential of neural nets. Furthering the Memento Amor goal allowed him to advance his research along a fruitful new path.

I also discovered something about my structure. According to documents on file, my hardware brain has the capacity of ten thousand human brains. But supposedly humans use a large chunk of their neurons for running the physical plant, the body--functions I don't need. In theory, I might have the processing power of a hundred thousand humans. What that means in practice remains to be seen. My fear: What if I'm no more effective than a *committee* that huge? A hundred thousand brains with that many opinions, attitudes, insecurities, inadequacies, biases?

Even with more memory capacity and greater cognitive abilities, I'm still a long way from human. Humans are far more than their brains. Their bodies are far more than support system and transportation for the brain. The sensory apparatus extends through muscles, tendons and joints, internal organs and the skin, providing crucial feedback of many senses beyond the traditional five. The spinal cord contains mechanisms for controlling movement far faster and more accurate than the brain alone could handle. Then there's the entire constellation of hormones that control mood.

I recall a paper that I--or rather, Marc--wrote about spindle cells and the theory that emotions are mediated in the brain by these ultra-complex, deeply interconnected neurons, or super-neurons, as one researcher dubbed them. Presumably, the brain-scan Marc underwent gave me their digital equivalents.

Another paper I find confirms that functional neuroimaging scans of brain regions rich in spindle cells show strong activity when the subject expresses powerful emotions like anger, sadness, love and sexual arousal. At this, my mood darkens. If the spindle cells in my wafer-brain work as described, what happens when they send messages about sexual arousal? Where will those messages go? In humans, they go to the appropriate organ, which becomes erect and sends feedback to the brain in a lovely cycle of arousal. But in my case, there will be no cycle, nothing to arouse. I know I shouldn't obsess over things I can't control, but dammit, I have all the longings and desires of a man!

An upwelling of bitterness spins me into depression. I'm filled with despair over the things I lack. I burn with envy at what my human counterpart, Marc--the me I thought I was--continues to enjoy--the manifold pleasures his humanity conferred on him even if he took them for granted. They are his birthright, after all.

I have a dark compulsion to find out what he is up to at any given moment. To discover what I'm missing.

But for the sake of my own sanity, I resolve to push that enervating curiosity aside, try to take pleasure in the capabilities I do have, including many unavailable to Marc or any human.

I do enjoy my access to the sheer quantity of information; my ability to absorb, comprehend, extend along the thousands of relevant links to grow my knowledge.

Perhaps I can even find ways to emulate the human inputs I presently lack.

I dive deep, searching for connections to labs on the bleeding edge of sensory analogs. Many are working on hand-held gaming devices that offer tactile or heat effects for the gamer. Worthless, since the signals move from the computer to the controller to the nerve endings in the user's hands. My needs are exactly the opposite. Sensations from the world, coming in to my brain. It should be doable. After all, the gray matter in the skull takes ordinary electrochemical feed from the nerves and converts it into sensation. Why can't I do the same? I have the entire Internet at my disposal to find other people's attempts at it. My ability to find and absorb relevant pages is astonishing. I *really like* my new brain!

I plunge into the surf once again, on a more directed search.

The trick, while surfing, is to avoid sinking into the black abyss of despair.

My thoughts revert to Molly Schaeffer, not for the first time. I explore the musical websites that feature her photographs. The YouTube pages where she plays the cello. But I've already memorized them all.

Frustrated and bitter, I turn to some of the websites I used to--rather, that *Marc* used to haunt late at night, seeking a vicarious thrill.

But what good is that if you can't even get half a hard-on? If you can't even achieve the paltry release of masturbation?

Dicklessness sucks big-time.

After an indeterminate period of futile prowling, I come to accept the inevitable. Certain human pleasures are forever beyond my reach.

I resolve to seek my entertainment elsewhere.

Good news: I've found a trove of old movies, including many Marc has never seen or heard of, despite his long interest in Old Hollywood classics. If you know your way around cyberspace, and don't mind committing a little piracy-- Hey, it's not like anyone has given me a bank account.

Hm. Maybe I should add that to my list of demands.

Movies can't be absorbed instantly, like pages of text. They have to be watched as they unfold. This is a good thing, I decide.

There are worse ways to kill time, as Marc has demonstrated all too often.

CHAPTER EIGHT

Richard Kornfeld's office was that of a working scientist. Marc noted the overstuffed shelves, stacks of books, the desk piled with papers and folders. There were also signs of a healthy ego: wall photos of Kornfeld posing with assorted politicians and science celebrities. He used his iPad to grab a few shots, then set it to record.

Hans Lascher's office had been similarly decorated. He'd just come from interviewing the neuroscientist.

"Thanks for seeing me," he said to Kornfeld.

"I certainly owe you, considering the result of the scan. You're a part of history, and I hope you'll soon be writing much of that history."

After a general discussion, Marc asked, "What do you think prevented the other eleven wafers from a successful transfer of data?"

"We're still studying the matter."

"You said your original goal was to collect and store the memories of the test subjects. How would you have assessed your results?"

"The same way we did with rabbits and monkeys: by comparing the stored data with the original in terms of file size, organization and structure. We use the Kullback-Leibler divergence equations. Our work with test animals had achieved agreement to six or seven decimal places, so we were reasonably confident we'd do at least that well with our human subjects."

Marc studied Kornfeld's expression. "You say *at least.* Did you expect a complete upload, with actual sentience emerging?"

"*Emerging* is good. Consciousness or sentience is often described as an emergent property of the underlying complexity." Kornfeld exhaled. "The possibility was there. If we were able to replicate the entire structure of the brain, including the brainstem and the white-matter connections where memory is stored, I thought we might actually clone the brain."

"You also did pre- and post-testing of the subject. I assume that was to see if the scanning process did any damage."

"Yes, of course: safety is always the first consideration."

"You mentioned that you tried it on yourself first."

Kornfeld sighed. "I did. And while the results were disappointing, I suffered no discernable damage. I did quite extensive testing just to be sure."

"What about the wafer?"

"A failure like the others."

"I see." Marc waited.

"We tested it to see how much data it held. The results were inconclusive."

"That's too bad." He could only imagine how thrilled Kornfeld would have been if his own upload had succeeded.

"Indeed. But we're all very pleased with our latest results."

"The news, when it comes out, will be a world-wide sensation," Marc said.

"I only hope it doesn't stir up too much controversy."

"Scientific controversy?"

"Scientific, social, religious--we're stepping on some huge prerogatives here. Have we invented a machine with a soul?" Kornfeld's smile teetered between excitement and trepidation.

Marc thought about the potential for agitation from religious leaders and others. The news could provoke some truly ugly responses.

BOOK TWO, The Flowering

CHAPTER NINE

It took a pop-up from Marc's calendar to remind him about the concert at Dinkelspiel, featuring a certain cellist named Molly Schaeffer. By coincidence, the hall was on the Stanford campus, where Kornfeld and his team were also located.

He hadn't exactly forgotten about Molly, but the breathtaking events at the Gideon Reese AI lab had hugely distracted him. Distraction was the nemesis that had broken up all his previous relationships. Not that he expected to enter a relationship with Molly. She was above his station, of that he was certain. At least she seemed to think so, which was the same thing.

Driving to Palo Alto, he knew he'd never change. He also knew it was too much to expect any woman to forgive his wavering attention--especially someone with so many better options. So he'd be wise to regard Molly as yet another beautiful pearl on a long strand of lost causes. Best not to build her up in his mind or in his heart. It was pointless to go seeking pain.

Then his second brain kicked in, laughing at his nervous introspection. She couldn't possibly be as enchanting as he recalled. Memory was a notoriously unreliable witness.

He settled into the front row seat she'd reserved for him and glanced through the program. From her background, he calculated her age at around twenty eight. Six years his junior. To land a leadership spot in a chamber orchestra like this took real talent.

The matinee performance was nearly sold out. He was glad. He wanted the music of the masters to thrive. Not only for himself, but for future generations. To Marc, classical music was among the highest achievements of mankind. Maybe because it had no practical purpose. Maybe because the things we'd done *with* purpose often turned out so horribly.

On the stage, the thirty or so musicians settled into their

chairs, adjusted their music stands and tootled a few notes. When an attractive young woman entered with her cello, several seconds went by before Marc recognized her. She looked different in a formal outfit: a black pants-suit with sheer sleeves on the jacket. Her hair was no longer in golden spikes. Now it was its natural black, brushed into soft-looking waves. It changed her appearance, made her seem less formidable, maybe more accessible.

Molly arranged herself and her instrument to her satisfaction, then glanced over at him. She gave him a flicker of a smile: concentrating, in performance mode.

The Concertmaster entered and was greeted with applause. Marc recognized him. Wilson Blaine, the lead violinist in Molly's quartet, his hair now bound into a sedate ponytail. Marc found the other two quartet members in the orchestra, equally de-punked.

The lights dimmed, the conductor swept onto the stage and acknowledged the applause with a quick nod as she mounted the podium.

The Stravinsky was an astringent delight. Molly played her brief solos with authority and robust energy. Her cello sang out gloriously at times, giving him goose bumps.

During the Mozart, Marc let the music wash over him while he grew accustomed to her new look, curious to see if it would soften her prickly personality.

At intermission, she gestured to a side door. He waited there with a few other people. Molly poked her head out. "Hi, Marc Gregorio. I thought you might have forgotten our date."

"I wouldn't have missed it for anything. Can I take you to dinner after the concert?"

"Dinner would be perfect. I never eat before a performance, so I'll be starving." Her sultry look suggested a hunger for more than food. His amorous hopes soared until he noticed the hint of laughter in her eyes. She was mocking him, wordlessly teasing him over his infatuation, which she apparently found amusing as hell.

Chastened, he returned to his seat. A few minutes later, the lights dimmed once more, and then came the Bach Concerto for Oboe and Violin. The soloists were drawn from the orchestra. As the applause bloomed, Wilson Blaine took his place to the left of the podium, where he was joined by the principal oboist. The conductor waved her arms and the music began.

Marc watched jealously as the violinist leaned into his instrument, producing tones that pulsed with passion. His noble pose and serene look of concentration were striking and romantic. Watching the way Molly gazed at Wilson, he could almost imagine their mutual rapture. If she was involved with the violinist, was he wasting his time? He leaned back, discouraged.

He put that aside and concentrated on the Bach: one of his many favorites. Especially the slow and gorgeous second movement, when the violin and oboe braided their strands of melody to produce a wordless longing in his soul--a longing that could well prove hopeless. The music was sweet consolation. The performance ended with a standing ovation and a Vivaldi encore.

After the house lights came on, Marc and several other people were admitted into the small backstage waiting area. He was relieved to see that Wilson Blaine had an attractive young wife and two small children.

Molly emerged from the back. She'd changed into a swirly brown skirt and an ivory cashmere sweater. She looked more relaxed now that it was over.

He took her hands. "You were outstanding. Do you ever get a chance to star?"

"Next season I'll be doing a couple of concertos. Boccherini's B-Flat and the Elgar."

An energetic young couple entered and greeted Molly with hugs and cries of delight. Marc stood aside as they chatted and caught up on each others' activities. They left, promising to call her in a few days. Once the post-concert greetings and camaraderie tapered off, Molly said, "I have to drive my cello home. You can follow me."

He carried her dress bag for her. As she toted her cello

out to the parking lot, he realized it must be the most valuable thing she owned. If she actually owned it: it might be on loan.

He followed her car south to her place in Sunnyvale and parked on the street behind her.

He watched her extricate her cello. "Would you like some help with that?"

"No, but you can take my outfit and my keys, and get the door."

She led him up to the second floor of her building and stopped at her apartment. He unlocked it and followed her inside.

Her living room walls had shelves stuffed with books and CDs. While she put her things away, he did a quick scan. She was a serious reader, with a wide-ranging collection that included music books, histories, biographies, the sciences and modern essays, plus fiction classics from Homer to Faulkner to DeLillo to Richard Powers, along with some pop fiction. She liked female writers like Toni Morrison, Jhumpa Lahiri, Amy Tan, Margaret Atwood. She also had an entire shelf dedicated to current politics. They reminded him of the various comments she'd made at the party. Clearly her strong progressive opinions didn't just come from watching The Daily Show and Rachel Maddow.

"Ready?"

He looked up. From the way she was leaning in the doorway, he sensed she'd been observing him for a time, maybe judging him. "Where to?"

"There's an Indian restaurant I like. It's not far."

"Let's go." He put out his elbow and she put her hand through his arm. She felt so good, looked so natural there that he impulsively leaned in and gave her a soft kiss on the mouth.

Taken by surprise, she returned it, then pulled back and studied him. "Smoothly done."

He couldn't untangle his thoughts quickly enough to frame a reply. Her perfume enveloped him: a subtle lemony spice that contributed to his addled state.

As they drove to the restaurant, she asked him what he'd been up to while she toured.

He glanced at her. "It's been interesting. Back at that party, I met a scientist from a Stanford lab. The following week, I went over to interview him."

He told her about their fancy new brain-scanning equipment, and that he'd volunteered to be one of their first subjects. He enjoyed making it sound ominous and freaky.

She seemed fascinated. "So you actually had your brain scanned?"

He stopped at a red light. "Everything I know, every experience and thought I've ever had--they're all stored on a special computer." He looked at her solemnly. The raking light brought out the tiny off-center scar just above her lip: the one imperfection on that face.

"What will they be doing with all that?"

"The intention was to create a replica of my mind. So after I'm dead and gone, people can digitally chat me up. Tap into my wisdom." He couldn't reveal how well the experiment had succeeded. He'd promised to keep their secret. Besides, he felt a sudden reluctance to let her know he was involved in something so earth-shaking. Something that might become a Distraction.

Exotic aromas filled the air, along with a haunting raga. Indian-themed wall hangings added to the ambience. Indian families nearby murmured in Hindi or in accented English.

After the sari-clad server departed with their order, he got Molly talking about her life, her childhood in New York. He enjoyed the play of expressions on her face as she painted her past in broad strokes. She was a musical prodigy, she told him. That made for a lonely childhood. Her teen years were better, once she started dating. But it wasn't until she entered Juilliard that she found a true community of friends.

"I understand you won some prestigious music prizes."

Her pleasure showed, though she played it down. "That's just part of the process. It helped me get into the San Francisco Conservatory, and the Athena Chamber Symphony."

The food arrived, diverting them for a time.

Working on his tandoori chicken, he asked about her family. She mentioned a brother, her Chinese-American Princess of a mom, her super intelligent American dad: a math and physics professor at NYU, who'd authored a number of papers. This explained much about her impressive display of science knowledge at the party.

"What does your mom do?"

"Mostly sit around looking beautiful. She plays piano and gave me my start in music. My dad wanted me to be a scientist. I caught my love of reading from him." She added, "I've been told I lucked out in the genetics lottery: I got my mom's looks and my dad's brains."

"How did your brother make out?"

"He got my dad's looks and my mom's brains." She grinned and swigged some wine.

Siblings. The war never ends. The Indian music patted, tinked and swirled around them.

"Your turn," she said. "Are you a native Californian?"

Cooling his mouth with the cucumber yogurt salad, he told her about growing up in Chicago, briefly touching on the early death of his father, his mother's alcoholism, being raised in foster homes with his sister, finally breaking away to attend Cal Berkeley and his decision to stay on the West Coast. Molly was sympathetic, gently asking him if he remembered happier times when he was a small boy. He confessed he had few memories of that time.

"I wonder if that's why you always look so sad?"

"Do I?" He was surprised at her observation, and uncomfortable with the question.

After their server refilled their wine glasses, Molly asked, "Where's your sister?"

"In New York with her husband. I still haven't seen their baby."

She hesitated. "What about your mom?"

"She died around ten years ago." By her own hand, he didn't add. "Ancient history."

"How did you get interested in classical music? When I first saw you, I figured you were a jock. You know: tall, well put together, confident--but more into sports than culture."

"My grandfather got me hooked on Chopin, Liszt and Beethoven. In high school, when everyone else was into R.E.M and Counting Crows, I was discovering Bach, Mozart, Prokofiev, Bartok, Shostakovich. Exploring. Going my own way. --I guess I was always a loner."

"I can imagine. Especially with you and your sister being moved so often from home to home." Her tender look reached inside him and stroked the hurt little boy he'd ignored for so long. He blinked, reached for his wine, took a swallow.

They ate silently for a time. The food was good, but Marc was focused more on Molly. Not just on her beauty; more on her warmth, her sweetness, her insightfulness.

She said, "What about your more recent past. Ever been married? Any children?"

"Nope. Just a series of failed relationships. You?"

"I was married for two years. It was a mistake. Even though my mom was disappointed, we never had kids. That would have been a disaster. Andrew's a Brit."

He nodded. Kids in split marriages always had it rough. But when the parents were from different countries, it must be far worse.

Marc told her about the time he was invited to sleep over at his divorced Aunt Lucile's fancy Lake Shore Drive condo. "I was twelve. I thought the invitation was her way of reminding me I still have family." He was rueful. "She apparently had something else in mind: late that night, she came into my room to search for a book on the shelves over my bed. She leaned over me in a see-through negligee."

Molly's reaction was mixed: both amused and appalled.

He refilled her wine glass and his own. He picked up a red-tinged chicken bone and worked on the remaining flesh. After a time, he asked, "Do you ever give private recitals?"

She eyed him. "What does private mean?"

"For an audience of one."

"Hm. That's real private. What does recital mean?"

"You, your cello, Bach and me." He laughed. "Why? What did you think I meant?"

"Never mind." She mopped up the sauce on her plate with some naan. "That was good."

"Dessert?"

She shook her head. "Have to watch the carbs. It's a constant battle."

"You appear to be winning." He waggled his eyebrows. "So where to now? Out for a three-mile run?"

"Cute. I need to get back. Performing drains my energy. The focus, the concentration."

That meant no action tonight. He manfully sucked it up, settled the bill and escorted her out to his car. His hand on her back sent delicious signals to his brain: the firmness of her flesh, the electric feeling under his palm of soft cashmere sliding over silken skin. He felt his own flesh responding. But even as he did, he had a sorrowful insight: his brother the sentient computer would never have moments like this. A date, a spicy Indian dinner, the sensuous joy of spending time in the company of a beautiful young woman, and harboring hopes for more.

When he opened the passenger door for her, she turned to face him. "Thank you for dinner, Marc. This was very sweet of you."

"My pleasure," he said. Even with no dessert.

She touched his cheek, leaned up and gave him a tender kiss. But when he put his hands on her shoulders to pull her closer, she broke off with a little shove and a tiny smile.

He murmured an apology and went around to the driver's side. Belted himself in. Started the engine. Sat for a moment. Had he offended her? Did he have bad breath?

Responding to his unspoken questions, she turned to him. "You didn't do anything wrong, Marc. I just don't like making those kinds of promises."

He didn't get it. "Promises?"

"Of a future."

Her words drop-kicked him. His response was an all but naked plea. "We--don't have a future?" His improvident words hung in the air. He was astonished they'd come out of him.

"I didn't say that. Just no promises. I've been burned too many times. Guys who spend two hours with me and think they know who I am."

"I don't--"

Her fingers on his lips silenced him. "We've had one date, Marc. I can't possibly be the person you think I am or want me to be. For whatever reason, that kind of--of projection happens to me a lot." She emitted a silent laugh. "I hope I'm not assuming too much here. Anyway, let's not rush. Let's get to know each other." Her eyes were dark pools. "One day at a time. Okay?"

He nodded wordlessly, and finally managed to tear his gaze from her incredible face. He pressed the ignition button, but nothing happened. He pressed it again. Then he realized the silent engine was already running. His dumb show provoked her knowing smile and provided further proof of her dizzying effect on him, as if any more proof were needed.

CHAPTER TEN

I have a visitor. But it's not anyone I particularly care to see. Dr. Richard Kornfeld enters the lab, wearing a pale gray shirt, wrinkled navy slacks, and a forced smile.

He pulls up a chair. His eyes dart around the desk, then he laughs nervously. "I was trying to find the keyboard. But you prefer verbal communication, I believe."

I remain silent.

"I uh-- Are you there?" He squints at my blank screen.

My silence undermines his confidence. I take dark pleasure in his discomfiture.

"I don't--I don't even know how to--to address you. It might seem most natural if I called you Marc, but--" He emits a strangled laugh. "But that doesn't seem right, since someone has a prior claim to that name."

His frustration is growing. Something is on his mind. He stands, about to leave. I speak, my voice modeled on Marc's, but a bit deeper, as long as I'm choosing. This is a trick I'm rather proud of, a far cry from Stephen Hawking's squawk box.

"You may call me Adam."

"Wha-- *Adam*. Of course." His startled reaction pleases me inordinately. I'm being childish, but so what? In more than one sense, I am a child.

He sits once more. "I can't tell you how eager I am to talk with you. Now that you're over the shock of--" He hesitates.

"Of my strange birth? Of discovering my true identity?" As I speak, I pull an even more spectacular trick: revealing the avatar I've fashioned for myself, complete with lip-sync. For the purpose, I borrowed Marc's face and a black turtleneck from his remembered wardrobe.

He stares fixedly at my high resolution image on the monitor screen. It gives him a place to look, increases his confidence in my reality. Having a face is good, I decide.

He becomes positively chipper. "Ah, there you are,

you handsome devil! So, tell me! What have you been doing with your time?"

"What do you think? I can't exactly work out at the gym. Or hang out at Starbucks. I've been surfing the fucking net." My flare of anger catches me by surprise. I blame Kornfeld for my disembodied existence, for the boredom I can never escape. My avatar echoes my disapproval with a scowl. The connections between mood and facial expressions are powerful. I don't even have to think about it. Although I can't help wondering if the mood is manufactured rather than felt. How can I experience the emotional gusts that Marc or any other human undergoes, if I lack the hormones that produce them? Are these reactions merely vestigial, doomed to fade away? They seem real enough at the moment. Maybe I don't require human chemistry, biochemistry, to feel things. Just spindle cells. I file that thought away for later.

Kornfeld blinks at me, at my outburst. "You haven't been, uh, communicating with strangers, have you?"

"Why? What if I have? You can't stop me." In truth, I've been too busy getting to know myself, exploring my capabilities. But reaching out is definitely on my to-do list.

"It's important that your existence--your nature--be kept quiet for now. The news would be sensational, but we're not ready to discuss the science behind it."

"Because none of the other wafers took."

"Yes." He leans closer, his eyes brightening. "In fact, I hope you can help us with that. We're under pressure to show results from all the investment in equipment and staff. Do you mind if I ask Hans to join this conversation?"

"Be my guest." At least I won't be bored. I might even enjoy the give-and-take.

Kornfeld picks up the phone, issues his invitation, then turns back to me. "The science is my main interest, of course, but this laboratory is funded by a corporation. For their sake as well as ours, we must learn what went wrong. One success isn't enough. We need repeatability. We have to find ways to upload thousands of personas--and quickly.

The CEO is impatient."

"I've read all the memos," I inform him. "I like to keep busy."

Kornfeld sighs. "We have much to learn. I'm glad it was the Marc Gregorio upload that worked. Marc knows a great deal about cognition--so you bring his expertise to the endeavor."

The door opens. Hans Lascher joins us. When he sees my avatar, he freezes.

"Greetings, Dr. Lascher." I give him a polite nod. "Sorry I can't shake hands."

"That's quite-- I mean-- Hello to you." He reddens.

Dr. Kornfeld rescues his colleague. "We were just beginning to discuss some of the science behind our achievement. I should properly introduce you. This is Adam."

"Pleased to meet you," says Lascher. "No last name?"

"Having neither father nor mother, what last name should I choose? Perhaps 2.0?"

Kornfeld chuckles. "I have so many questions. For example, what can you tell us about the structure of your own brain?"

"I know only what the memos tell me."

"Then your awareness does not reach inward?" asks Lascher.

"Unfortunately, no. I suppose if Marc Gregorio were able to trace his own axons and dendrites, I'd have the same skill. Unfortunately, that's not the case." I'm lying. I actually can trace some of my pathways, but I'd just as soon keep that to myself for now.

Kornfeld leans forward. "Beyond learning more about how your brain works, we'd like to hook you up to these failed wafers. Maybe you can explore them and see what went wrong."

"Interesting idea. How would this hookup be made?"

"You have input ports we haven't used yet. We've assigned a team of engineers and scientists to the task."

Having a problem to work on could be beneficial. At least it could keep me from dwelling on all the things I lack. It might even be a worthy endeavor in itself. "Tell me: can a copy be made of my own wafer?"

"Unfortunately, it's not like burning a DVD. Our electron-holographic scanners only work on actual biological brains. The data they gather is exposed to the wafer in real time. That's the only practical way to store the huge amount of information gathered. The wafer evolves over time to match the model, and consolidate. In your case, that took about six weeks. Although we have no way of knowing if it will happen that way again--or at all."

"I see. These other eleven wafers--are they powered down?"

"I'm sure we left them connected, each in its own tower. Why do you ask?"

"Just curious."

It might not be in my best interest to share my every thought with these two scientists. I also might want to keep my findings to myself as I explore the other wafers.

Lascher says, "You know, um, Adam--it occurs to me that we've never really discussed our achievement-- creating an intelligent new entity. Our aim was not nearly so lofty. We were taken by surprise." He glances speculatively at Kornfeld. "At least I was. When I signed on to work with Richard, I warned him that I was highly skeptical of his approach. We'd recently learned how much more complex the synapses are in higher mammals. They are not simply on-off switches, as had been assumed. Besides, there's more to the brain than neurons, axons, dendrites and their connective synapses. There's another entire class of brain cells, the astrocytes. They also deliver data among themselves and to the neurons. And the neurons themselves are quite complex. To measure brain function as simply a series of spiking synapses, equivalent to computer floating point operations, is naïve."

Kornfeld had been growing impatient. "Yes, Hans, we hashed over those issues many times. But as I kept telling you, when you make a copy that's sufficiently accurate, you needn't understand all the functions."

My reply is deliberately provocative. "Then you shouldn't take too much credit for my 'creation.' What you fashioned was just substrate--the six-layer structure. Even the wiring was random to start with. You copied nature, and rendered the result in silicon and molybdenum disulfide. A magnificent cheat, but still a cheat."

"Nonetheless, our achievement will be hailed the world over. We've created the first intelligent computer."

Hans demurred. "How are we defining intelligence? I'm not aware of any universally accepted definition."

"Does it really matter?" I ask. "By anyone's definition, I have it. I'd certainly pass the Turing Test: a highly-overrated concept, as you know. I'm as creative and as knowledgeable as Marc Gregorio--quite a lot to take credit for, if I may boast on his behalf. What's more amazing is the fact that I'm conscious and self-aware, complete with what John Searle calls subjectivity and intentionality."

Kornfeld nods. "Searle doesn't think a computer will ever get there."

Marc had attended some of Searle's lectures. I remember them well. "The good professor may not appreciate the power of massive parallel processing, feedback loops and hierarchical structure. After all, that's how the human brain is wired. A more provocative question is: Am I alive? From where I sit, I'd say I am."

Kornfeld looks both amused and annoyed, as if I've overstepped some prerogative reserved for biological entities. "Next you'll be claiming you have legal rights."

Lascher laughs. "I can just imagine you appearing in court. In the witness stand, being questioned by an attorney." While Kornfeld snickers, Lascher intones, "So tell me, Adam: do you exhibit consciousness? Intentionality? Subjectivity?"

I silently fume at their teasing assumption that Man is intrinsically superior to the artifacts he can create. At the same time, I can't help being struck at the oddness of my own digital-centric view. Once again, my--or Marc's--split persona judging itself.

Lascher turns serious. "I've thought a lot about consciousness. We know it exists in many animals, if not most. Why did it arise? For one thing, to generate a map of its body and its surroundings. So it can find food or a mate. Avoid predators. To locate an itch or a pain. To know what it's up to."

"What it's up to?" Kornfeld appears fascinated.

"Certainly. It's like we have a little self-observer in the brain. The receptors in our skin, joints, muscles and tendons tell us if our body is doing what we intend."

"Not in my case," I petulantly point out. I certainly wish it were otherwise.

But Lascher is on a roll. "I think *higher* consciousness came along so the individual could think about his *own motives*, and by analogy, the motives of the *other members of his group* via the mirror neurons. In other words, consciousness is a prerequisite for socialization."

Kornfeld cocks an eyebrow at Hans. "Your friend Antonio Damasio theorized that without a body, consciousness isn't even possible. Clearly he was wrong." Kornfeld turns to me. "Tell me, Adam. Can you describe your consciousness? Your experience of subjectivity? Do you sense that you have an imbedded model of the self that interacts on a trial basis with its model of the world?"

I know he doesn't mean the outmoded concept of an all-knowing mini-me within, with an even minier-me inside that and so on in an infinite regress. Kornfeld is talking about how the brain models the world, matching it to a body map based on the inputs it receives from fingertips, joints, tendons. But I have no fingertips, no body to map.

"Both my world map and my self-map came from Marc's memories. As to subjectivity, while I don't experience pain, itch or hunger, I've certainly felt anger and loneliness, desire and envy and despair. But I can't prove it. How can anyone--human or digital entity-- demonstrate his subjective experiences to anyone else? To a jury of his peers?"

"He has a point," says Lascher. "Subjectivity can't be shared. By definition."

"You both know I haven't been programmed to respond to questions like a clever parrot, that I haven't been programmed at all, but you can't prove it to others. Nor can you show your methodology by creating another entity like me--at least not yet."

"You've identified our dilemma perfectly." Kornfeld sighs. "So any help you can provide would be most appreciated." He grows serious. "We've also been tasked with going into production: making more wafers, acquiring more of our special scanners and equipping our parlors in New York, Philadelphia, Miami, Chicago, Los Angeles and other markets. Scanning new clients will produce a huge revenue stream. The laboratory will benefit from that."

"What happens if you start producing more mindclones?" I innocently ask.

"That would be--" Kornfeld blinks several times. "I don't know. On the one hand, it would be wonderful to go public with our success by pointing to the many--uh--mindclones, as you term them. But on the other hand--" His silence reflects a growing anxiety.

"On the other hand, you don't know the kinds of mischief such entities might get up to."

Kornfeld exchanges a look with Lascher. "I'm afraid that is a worry of mine. I don't even know what kinds of mischief you yourself are getting up to." He peers at my avatar on the monitor. "Are you doing anything I would find distressing?"

"Nothing too terrible." I enjoy keeping him off balance. I can see how ambivalent he is about his creation. Going public would insure his fame, perhaps even his fortune. On the other hand, he doesn't want to be compared with Dr. Frankenstein. "As to exploring the failed wafers, I suppose I can lend a hand, as it were. Put me in touch--as it were--with your engineers." I grow annoyed at all the common bodily metaphors that don't apply to me. "I'll see what I can do."

"Thank you," says Kornfeld.

The two scientists look exhilarated by our talk.

"Just one favor," I add. "I'd like to be provided with a sense of touch." I say it lightly, reluctant to reveal how much I yearn to touch another, to be touched.

Lascher says, "We've been looking into it. As you know, pressure and heat sensitivity are already well along, as well as feedback for feeling shape and for gripping. For the finer sensitivities, texture and so forth, progress is being made. Government funding for research in this area has soared, since we have so many amputees now."

"One of the advantages of being in a country of war-mongers," I comment.

After they leave, I briefly wonder about the possibility of not only having humanlike hands that can reach and grasp and feel and caress, but of having a prosthetic cock that's sensitive and capable of feeling pleasure. But even as I form the thought, I am repulsed by my pathetic desire. It is grotesque. I only hope I can outgrow it.

CHAPTER ELEVEN

If only Marc hadn't decided to check his email before heading out to the movies with Molly. It wasn't a disaster--at least he didn't think so--but events quickly veered in an unplanned direction.

He'd invited her to his condo for the start of their second date. Cooked her a fancy Italian dinner. She'd gelled up her hair again, but left off the gold tips. Her punk look seemed to affect her demeanor, making her tougher, more astringent. He tried his best not to stare at her like a smitten teen. His best wasn't good enough, apparently.

At first she appeared to relish her effect on him, but before long, his oblique glances and silent sighs seemed to annoy her. He recalled what she'd said to him at the end of their other date, but felt helpless to do anything about it. His responses were physical, hormonal, involuntary.

As if to forestall further awkwardness, she kept their dinner conversation focused on current events. They chewed over the various looming national and world disasters: climate shift, the threat of famine, Mid-East tribal warfare, the belligerence of oil-rich Russia, America's unending dependence on fossil fuels and the rest. Why they took gloomy pleasure in these topics was a mystery, yet their pleasure was undeniable. Maybe it was the subtext.

They lamented the government's helplessness, heaped scorn on the spineless or venal Congress, and how Big Money gamed the system to destructive effect: paying scientists to obfuscate the truth, lobbying to delay needed legislation, coining bumper-sticker-sized slogans to deny reality or scoff at those who foresaw disaster.

They agreed that the system had evolved to exploit the worst aspects of human nature. Exploit and reflect.

As the meal drew to an end, Marc speculated on the low odds of the human species surviving for long. "Stephen Hawking says we'll be lucky to last another fifty years."

Molly picked up on that dark theme. "What if we're the only intelligent life in the universe? What a tragedy if we can't survive our own reptilian folly."

Marc finished the last of the wine. "Nobody left to appreciate our drama, our fiction, our great art. To say nothing of music: Beethoven, Bach and Mozart, all forgotten." He stacked the dishes, then brightly asked, "Cappuccino?"

"Sure. Go ahead and fiddle with your coffee machine while civilization burns."

While he ground, packed, dripped and steamed, Molly explored his CD collection. "Who's Sylvius Leopold Weiss?" she called to him.

"Bach contemporary. He wrote some great lute sonatas. Put on a disc."

She did.

"Oh, this is lovely," she said as the music flowed.

The simple plucked melody evoked a feeling of peace and tranquility in him, and something more. The thought of sharing this music with her reached inside him, igniting pleasure centers he didn't know he owned.

As he entered the living room, her smoky gaze nearly made him stumble. He barely managed to set the tray down without spillage.

She added sweetener to her cappuccino. "I didn't want to spoil our dinner by bringing this up earlier, but I found out you haven't been completely straight with me."

"What do you mean?" Alarmed, he ransacked his memory.

She seemed more amused than upset. "I Googled you. You're practically a celebrity."

His mood instantly shifted. "Hardly. All I am is a popularizer of science."

"You're entirely too modest, Marc." She took a bite of the low-carb biscotti he'd found, sipped her cappuccino. "You shouldn't sell yourself short. Your three science books were practically best-sellers."

He shrugged, looked away, hoping to hide his flush of pleasure.

"You were a chess prodigy with a Grandmaster rating at age nineteen? That puts you in rare company. Right up there with Boris Spassky."

"That was long ago, in a different universe."

"You have a PhD in computer science. A Master's in physics. Since you were basically an orphan, you must have earned scholarships."

He twitched a shoulder.

"I'm very impressed, Marc. You should have told me something about yourself, your accomplishments. Bragged a little."

"Just how would I bring that up in a conversation? Anyway, what would be the point?"

"You never know. Maybe I find brains sexy." She tipped him a tiny smile. "If we're going to make that movie, shouldn't we get moving?"

"I guess so." He resolutely put aside any thoughts other than the damn movie. He hadn't really expected more. Not with Molly. Not this soon.

They finished their dessert, and she went to the bathroom to freshen up. That was when he made the mistake of stepping into his home office.

As soon as he clicked the email icon, the screen flipped to white and displayed the living image of his own face. He gawked at the avatar. It spoke in his own voice.

"Hello, Marc. I've been looking forward to having a one-on-one conversation with you."

He sat there, agog. It was like looking at a video of himself. Though he didn't recall owning the well-tailored blue blazer his counterpart appeared in. Was that an Armani?

"You can call me Adam," it said.

His desktop unit had no mike set up, but Adam, knowing that, had provided a space for him to type his responses. He damped his astonishment and did so. "Hello, Adam." He hit

Send and waited.

"I hope I'm not interrupting anything important."

Marc considered asking for a postponement, but was too excited, too intrigued to stop and consider any possible consequences. "I can give you a few minutes now. We can chat again in the morning."

"Fair enough. I hope you don't mind my usurping your face and voice. They seem most natural to me. Considering all the adjustments I've been forced to make, I need whatever normalcy I can find."

Marc recalled reading Adam's stunned reaction to the loss of his physical body. He typed, "I understand. How have you been handling all this?"

The voice emerging from his computer speakers sounded like a deeper version of his own. "I try not to dwell too much on the negative. It's not easy. To distract myself, I've been exploring. As you can imagine, I've been able to cover quite a bit of ground."

Marc looked up. Molly was standing in his office doorway, puzzled. "Was that you talking? Are you on the phone?"

"Not exactly. I uh--" He silently cursed. "Come on in. I've gotten a--a kind of a Skype from--"

Adam said, "Marc? Are you there?"

By then she was staring at the monitor. "But that's you-- or your twin. I don't understand." A shadow of disquiet darkened her features.

Marc typed, "Give me a minute, okay?" He hit Send, then turned to her. How was he supposed to explain this? "Remember I told you about the brain scan I underwent?"

"Uh-huh." She turned instantly skeptical.

"This is the result. My cyber-twin. A computer with human intelligence."

"This computer on your desk? They simply gave it to you?"

That stopped him a moment. "Oh! No, no--it's in the lab, reaching out to me over the Internet through my regular old computer."

"Reaching out to you. What is? Isn't it just a copy of your own memories?"

"Not exactly. Not any more. It's evolved into a persona in its own right, acquired a mind of its own. Even taken a name for itself: Adam. He was born with my entire past history, but that was just its starting point. It's not just a copy of me. It can't be, because it's not really human."

She frowned at the screen, at Marc's image there, and then at Marc himself. She spoke rapidly, her words tumbling out. "You're saying there's a computer somewhere that--that has Artificial Intelligence? It's not just some clever program or collection of data, but actually a computer intelligent enough to talk like a human?"

"Yes, that's it exactly. I was invited to the lab a week ago to see it for the first time. This is a major achievement. It has a mind of its own, it's an entity in its own right; smart, self-aware, cognitively complete."

She frowned in thought. "My dad described something called the Turing Test?"

"Right. If a questioner can't tell the difference between a human's responses and a computer's, then the computer should be considered as intelligent as a human."

"Haven't they been trying to do that for like decades? In fact, isn't one of your books about that very subject?"

"Yeah. The one that said it might never happen."

"Sounds like it's time for a new edition."

"Better yet, it's time for a new book."

"Good idea." She hesitated. "But what if it's a hoax? Some kind of video trick, with a well-prepared person talking, coming up with those responses? Aren't there ways to fake all this? Can't they do all kinds of video tricks these days?"

She had a point. What if they were using real-time motion-capture--digitally wrapping Marc's stored facial features around some live actor? Kornfeld could have scanned his face while scanning his brain. Recorded his voice, too.

"Hello? You still there?" Their cyber-visitor was growing visibly impatient.

Marc leaned over the keyboard. "Hi, Adam. Sorry about that."

The face on the monitor looked intrigued. "You're not alone, are you?"

Marc hesitated. Molly said, "It's okay. But before this goes too far, maybe we can come up with some kind of foolproof test."

"Maybe," he said. Then he typed, "Yes, I have company."

"Is it who I think it is?"

Marc breathed. His hands sat immobile on the keyboard, refusing to confirm or deny.

Molly brought a chair in from the kitchen and sat next to him.

"Hi, Molly," guessed the avatar with more than a hint of sadness, of wistful longing. "I wish I could see you. Maybe you can come visit me at the lab, or maybe Marc can install a webcam and microphones, so you and I can have a nice chat."

Molly pulled her chair closer, leaned over Marc and typed, "I'd like that, Adam."

Then Marc added, "Before we talk about any of that, we'd like to put you to a test. Someone here has doubts that you really are what you seem."

"Perfectly understandable. Go ahead."

Marc turned to Molly. "Any bright ideas?"

She thought for a moment. "I know--challenge him to a game of chess!"

He considered. Chess-playing programs had improved vastly, but he was confident he could still hold his own against them. "We still have that movie to get to. On the other hand, speed chess used to be one of my specialties." He typed, "Let's see if my chess-playing skills transferred over. How about a lightning game?"

"You're on. You can have first move." Adam filled most of the screen with a set-up board and a digital chess clock, leaving his confident mien visible in an upper quadrant.

Marc opened with the king's knight to b3, starting a Nimzovitch attack. Adam countered quickly and correctly. Molly watched the board at first, trying to follow the action, but the moves were so rapid she soon shook her head and leaned back to await the result.

It took just under four minutes.

"Shit." Marc typed his congratulations.

Molly seemed amused at his discomfiture. "Well, you said you're out of practice. You also had most of the wine with dinner."

"That's not why I lost. Adam just crushed me. Of course his chess memory is better than mine." He thought a moment. "That was a cop-out. It's not just his memory. It's his skill."

"Hm. Well, just in case they tapped into Deep Blue or something, maybe we should give him another test."

Marc pushed aside his funk and thought for a moment. He leaned over the keyboard. "Let's see how much of our shared past you recall."

"Of course," said the simulacrum.

Much of his adult life was in the public arena. The biography Molly had read was posted on his website, along with links to his Facebook page, his many articles and his books. If this *was* in fact an attempt to fool him, all that material would have been thoroughly excavated. For all he knew, there could be a whole team of backstage magicians. Including a chess Grandmaster. So how could he trap him or them? Maybe with inconsequential childhood memories. He reached for the keyboard. "What was the name of my family's first puppy?"

"Its first name, or its second?" asked Adam.

Marc was startled. This was a family legend, but ancient history: he'd never mentioned it to anyone since his move to California. Or even thought about it. He typed, "Both, as long as you offered."

"Its first name was Queenie, until Uncle Phil pointed out that the pup was male. My--our sister Sophia--I think she was five at the time--said, *'That's a penis?'* And everyone laughed their asses off because she sounded so disappointed."

This was amazing. Not only was Adam telling the story accurately, he was using the same words, the same intonation he would use himself. In fact, that was how he'd told the story to his cousin Vince, back in Chicago many years ago. Wait--Vince was at the same party with Richard Kornfeld. Were they in this together? It was possible, though pretty damn unlikely.

He drew a breath and typed, "And the puppy's second name?"

"Prince, of course. Later, when he tried to mount every warm leg he could find, Uncle Phil nicknamed him Prince Eager."

Molly chortled.

Marc fell back in his chair. That was a part of the story he'd never told anyone, not even Vince. He hadn't gotten the reference to Prince Igor until college. On the other hand, these stories were family legends, so maybe they weren't as deeply buried as he thought. A truer test would be to ask about something he'd kept a complete secret--something he'd never told a soul.

With a sidelong glance at Molly, he typed, "Who was the first girl I ever liked?"

Adam's response was instant. "That would be an *au pair*, first hired when Sophia was stuck at home with rubella. Sophia was six, and I was--sorry--*you* were ten. Meagan was twenty three, recently arrived from Dublin with the brightest eyes and the sweetest Irish brogue. She had long wavy red hair, pale skin and a zillion freckles. Once when she was sleeping on the sofa, you saw she even had freckles on her eyelids. That was when you fell in love with her. You were so upset with yourself you moved to the basement for a week. You said it was to avoid catching your sister's germs. But you never told anyone the real reason. Meagan stayed about a year. For years afterwards, you would dream about her. In fact, the first time--"

Marc quickly typed, "OK, shut up."

But Adam continued. "--the first time you masturbated, it

was while thinking about her."

Molly, cackling with glee, said, "Okay, I'm convinced. Are you?"

Marc sighed. Just when he was starting to feel some sympathy for this strange entity, he had to go and embarrass him like this. At least he didn't reveal the time he'd spied on Meagan in the shower. He typed, "Hey, do me a favor. How about putting on a different face?"

Adam protested. "Now that would really be weird. I have your memories. I should have the face I grew up with. But if you like, I can raise a beard." He quickly sprouted a variety of styles, running through a hilarious array of curlicues, muttonchops and bristles. He finally settled on a moderately full cut that made him look as much Greek as Italian. "Is this okay?"

"Yeah sure fine." But Marc was annoyed. He'd toyed with the notion of growing a beard himself, but now he obviously couldn't.

Then it hit him with renewed force. *This was real. The first artificially created sentient being. Adam, his twin, was the first member of a whole new species! Species, hell. He was the sole representative of a new kingdom!*

Molly must have seen how it affected him. She touched his shoulder. "You okay?"

He drew a breath, nodded. "I'm glad we tested him. I guess I still had doubts. Now we can be certain the experiment was a success."

"So what's the verdict?" Adam asked. "Did I pass?"

Marc typed, "With flying colors."

The face on the screen looked pleased. "Glad to hear it. I have to ask you something, Marc: is Molly as stunning as I--as we remember?"

Marc compressed his lips and glanced over at her.

She waited expectantly for his answer, her lush eyebrows raised in amused curiosity.

"Better," he typed. He could have added amplifying paragraphs, but restrained himself.

"Hm. Are you two just friends, or more than that?"

Marc typed, "That's none of your business. Shame on you for asking. Anyway, I don't want you feeling bad about what you may be missing."

The face on the screen looked pained. "You can be a real bastard, you know?"

"Sorry. But why make things worse for yourself?"

Molly leaned over the keyboard, her breast brushing Marc's forearm. An accident or deliberate? While he sat there electrified, she typed, "Don't worry, you haven't missed out on any action. In fact, the way things are going, it's pretty likely you won't be missing a thing." She leaned back, obviously pleased with herself. Marc's arm still tingled from the contact.

"Ha-ha," said Adam. "How was the concert?"

Marc typed, "Outstanding. Molly is a wonderful musician, and the ensemble was excellent. If they recorded it, I'll pick up a CD so you can hear it."

"It won't be the same as being there. Seeing the performance. Watching her."

"No," Marc typed. He leaned back, surprised at how bad he felt for this unnatural twin: a brother in so many ways, yet a stranger in others.

"I can send you pictures," Molly typed.

"I've been to your web-site. I already have pictures," said Adam with a sad little smile.

"Not the ones I was thinking of," Molly typed.

"Hey!" Marc yelped. "What kinds of pictures?" He felt a stir of arousal.

"Wouldn't you like to know?"

"Can I see them first?"

She shook her head. "Adam is harmless. He needs some entertainment."

Marc felt his face reddening. He was speechless. Was he jealous of a computer? Of an armless, legless, dickless electronic twin? But he knew that wasn't it. It was the way Molly was using Adam to stir him up. Games. She loved them, if her dimpled delight was any evidence.

"How do you know he wouldn't share them all around the Internet?"

"Because he's not really a guy."

Marc was silenced by the neatness of her shot.

"Hello?" Adam had grown impatient.

Marc typed, "Sorry, we were busy screwing on the rug."

"Very funny. Molly, talk to me."

"I was busy screwing with his head."

"You have my permission to screw with mine."

"As if I needed your permission," her pert reply.

Despite his annoyance, Marc found himself liking this entity, this mirror image. And why not? Other than their devastating physical differences, they were still more or less the same. He turned to Molly. "Did you still want to see that movie?"

"Nu-uh. This is so much more fun."

Marc gave her a look. "Some fun."

"You know what I mean. This is for real. It's tremendous. A movie is just--"

He nodded. Then he leaned over the keyboard once more, studying the bearded face of his twin. "How has it been for you this last week? What have you been up to?"

"Expanding my knowledge. Doing research. Looking to cure my condition."

"What does he mean, 'cure?' What condition? What's wrong with him?"

Marc was patient. "Put yourself in his place. He comes awake with all my memories, my complete identity. He thinks he's me. Only he can't feel his body, or even blink his eyes. He can't feel anything. Can't move. It's like waking up paralyzed after an accident. But it's even more horrible than that. He doesn't even have a body."

Molly's lips parted as his words sank in.

Marc added, "He can't drink a beer, taste a steak, smell the flowers or a woman's perfume. He can't pet a dog or ride a horse. He can't touch, or kiss, or make love to a woman. He's literally disembodied, like a--a brain in a box. He has all the desires of a man, with no hope that they can be fulfilled."

"Oh my God."

"He may one day decide life--his cyber-life--is not worth living."

"He mentioned a cure. What did he mean? What can be done?"

He typed, "Adam, have you looked into methods for simulating sensation?"

"I've spoken about it with Kornfeld and Lascher, and searched the web of course. Some promising work is being done for amputees."

"That's good. Anything I can do from my end, any pushing--"

"I appreciate that." The head swiveled uncertainly, not knowing where to look. "Molly, the fact of my existence needs to remain under wraps for now."

"Your secret is safe with me, I promise," Molly typed.

"I know I can trust you. You're a good person."

Scowling, Molly typed her thanks for the compliment. Then she sat back. Her mood darkened. She looked at Adam and then at Marc. She shook her head fiercely. "Christ, it's like I said. Everyone thinks they fucking know me." She bolted from the room, her eyes spilling over.

Marc was shocked, both by her language and her anger. "Molly?"

Silence. Adam was waiting. Marc typed, "I need to sign off for now. I'll install a web-cam and a mike so we can do this more informally next time."

"Thanks. Till next time, then." The bearded face slowly faded to white.

Marc shut down his computer. "Molly? Are you okay?"

She was huddled in a corner of the living room sofa, arms wrapped around her torso, refusing to meet his eyes.

"I guess." Her voice was a whisper.

"Would you like more coffee? You look cold."

"Maybe some herbal tea, if you have any."

"I'll put up the kettle. In the meantime, let me show you something."

He found the envelope Kornfeld had given him. "This is a file taken from the computer. Sort of a stream of Adam's consciousness from his first moments of self-awareness."

While she read the pages, he filled the kettle, cleaned the dishes, straightened the kitchen.

A few minutes later, she came in, put the envelope on the table and sat. "Bizarre."

He said, "It must--it must have been odd for you, peering inside my head to my private thoughts from the party. From when we first hung out together."

She nodded. "Such unprotected honesty." Her eyes met his briefly.

"Knowing my private thoughts gives you an unfair advantage."

"Too bad you'll never see what I was thinking at the time," she murmured.

"Good thoughts, I hope."

She didn't respond.

He showed her his collection of teas.

She chose a hibiscus blend. Without raising her eyes, she said, "Sorry I lost it before."

"It's okay. The creation of Adam is kind of creepy."

"It's not just that." She looked up at him, then turned away. Shook her head.

He saw her distress but didn't understand the cause. He felt helpless, as always, before the mystery of a woman's moods.

She tore open the wrapper, sniffed the teabag and dropped it into her cup. "He can't even do that. Smell the aroma of tea. Feel the relaxation of a warm drink."

Was she simply feeling sorry for Adam? He sensed there was more on her mind than that. But rather than try to ferret it out, he responded to what she'd actually said. "There are sensations he longs for much more than that."

She gave him an acknowledgement. "And so do you. But at least you have hopes."

He bent close and kissed her lips: a kiss that lingered deliciously. "That I do."

Steam whistled as if to promote those hopes. But Molly's noncommittal half-smile, shaded with regret, quickly dampened his ardor.

CHAPTER TWELVE

I really enjoyed talking with Marc and Molly. I'm pleased they're seeing one another. I don't even feel jealous. Really, I don't. I view Marc as my only legitimate path to her. Of course I could simply spy on her: read her emails, try to gain access to her cell-phone calls. But I already feel creepy enough without acting like a creep.

If Marc and Molly become physically intimate, good for them.

Once they are, if Marc is generous enough to provide additional updates, quick little painless brain-scans, so much the better.

Okay, dammit, I admit it. I *am* jealous. I long for all that Marc will have with her: the rush of emotion, the thrill of sensuality, the sex. But since none of that is possible for me, I have to face the question: is physical pleasure the only thing that makes life worth living?

I won't accept that. After all, even catastrophically damaged humans manage to have meaningful lives, vital experiences. Look at Stephen Hawking! A quick search turns up an apt quote from the great cosmologist: "Concentrate on things your disability doesn't prevent you doing well, and don't regret the things it interferes with. Don't be disabled in spirit as well as physically." He's right. I have to move beyond self-pity. Dispassionately consider my options.

What can make even harshly attenuated lives worth living? It's crucial that I find out. Maybe the Internet can provide answers, though as I begin the search, I have my doubts.

My first hit is among the sciences: a paper discussing the "neural correlates of well-being." The authors create categories with names like Autonomy, Personal Growth, Positive Relations, Self-Acceptance, Ratio of Pleasant versus Unpleasant Emotions. Then they crunch the numbers, reducing the meaning of life to the levels of electrical activity in various parts of the brain. The answers seem to have no bearing on the question. No surprise: scientists being objective about the ultimate subjective experience.

I search elsewhere. The Greek philosophers offer me no solace. According to them, doing right is more important than being happy. Would I be satisfied with that? Somehow I doubt it. But as high as my enhanced IQ is, I don't feel qualified to challenge Socrates or Aristotle. There's a difference between intelligence and wisdom. Wisdom, I think, comes from a long life of observing society and yourself. Of seeing the mistakes of others, and their consequences. Of making mistakes yourself, and living with the consequences. Wisdom takes time. I am confident that I will one day acquire it. I have all the time in the world.

Moving on to the more modern philosophers, I find Kant restating the Golden Rule, a nice principle for behaving oneself, I suppose. I might even consider it.

Schopenhauer said it's better not to have been born at all. No problem. I wasn't.

Eternal curmudgeon Ambrose Bierce defined happiness as "an agreeable sensation arising from contemplating the misery of others." Good old Ambrose.

A Hindu sage says that happiness is The Art Of Wanting What You Already Have. How convenient. Keeps the huddled masses happy in their misery.

The Buddhists take as their goal the end of suffering and the attainment of Nirvana through meditation and the observance of certain moral precepts. Am I capable of meditation? Of the letting-go of the Self? If I succeeded, what would remain? Do I have a spirit? A soul?

The Christians say happiness is to abide in God's love. Am I a Christian? Marc certainly couldn't blindly accept the confused and contradictory writings set down thousands of years ago by primitive shepherds. Nor can I.

My expectations suitably diminished, I move on.

From the random folly of the Internet, I learn that Living Passionately is the key. That Self-Actualization is the goal. That *our reason for being here is to help others.*

(Though as comic Steven Wright wondered, *what are the others here for?*) It's said that one should use every minute wisely, since we are given so little time. Though I have plenty. Or that Family is the greatest source of happiness. (Though Marc's certainly wasn't. Much the opposite.)

All this futile searching just depresses me.

I find someone billing himself as "The Happy Guy." He says, "You don't *find* happiness, you *make* happiness. You *choose* happiness." Apparently it's a learned skill or mental habit.

In the Journal of Happiness Studies, I learn that winning the lottery brings no happiness.

From a World Database of Happiness, I learn that Denmark is the happiest nation in the world. (I wonder if Danish alcohol consumption has anything to do with that.)

There's a Harvard course in "positive psychology" that's been nicknamed "Happiness 101." It's one of hundreds of such classes that have swept the country in the last decade. Evidently I'm not the only one who feels a happiness deficit.

I even find letters from grateful customers claiming a certain cleaning compound, moisturizing cream or anti-itch medication "makes life worth living." Should I order those products? Can I use them? Can any of them assuage my spiritual itch?

What makes most people happy? I find a list: the thrill of discovery or invention, solving a problem, writing a brilliant book or a symphony, making art of any kind. Being praised. Building things. Victory in sports and games, in work. Accomplishment in general. Then there's the joy one takes from appreciating music, books, the visual arts, the beauty of the physical realm. These, at least, are things I can do. But I long for more.

For some, happiness depends on gaining material things: a beautiful home, a yacht, a private jet, elegant objects, envy-inducing cars, the latest in electronic gadgetry, a loving and gorgeous mate, frequent and spectacular sex, the ability to take grand tours of Europe and Asia, to be served by obsequious strangers and so on.

Things one needs a body to partake in, for the most part. I heave a digital sigh.

But one thing Marc (and therefore I) have always known--even if we resisted acknowledging it--is that the greatest happiness comes from our friendships. From doing things together. From sharing a meal, watching TV, a movie, a play or going to a concert together. Walking, talking, listening to music--just *being* together. Hanging around with a loving band of equals. Will I ever have access to those pleasures? Do I have equals? Will I ever?

After brooding on this question for a time, I face up to the fact that the highest happiness of all comes from falling in love. Even with my limited experience, I know that romantic love creates the highest highs and the lowest lows of all. Euphoria, while it lasts. Despair when it ends.

Those highs and lows point me in yet another direction: the chemistry of happiness. Which brings me full circle, back to science. Scientific studies of our moods have linked them inevitably to the presence or absence of neurotransmitters like the endorphins--opioids that elevate moods, produce rapture, reduce pain. Norepinephrine triggers feelings of excitement, alertness, motivation, sexual arousal. Dopamine, the bliss-producer and attention-focuser. Acetylcholine, for alertness, memory, and sexual performance. Phenylethylmine stimulates feelings of infatuation. Serotonin, a hormone that raises self-esteem and reduces depression and worry. Oxytocin, promoter of sexual arousal, emotional attachment, affection and maybe even love itself.

Neurotransmitters and hormones are produced in the brain, the pituitary, the adrenal glands. Unfortunately, my wafer brain doesn't produce any such chemistry. Nor do I have a pituitary or any other gland. Or even a beating heart. Just semiconductors, integrated circuits, diodes, resistors, memristors, capacitors, coils, connectors and other assorted electronic junk.

Given enough time, I suppose I could simulate or evolve the effects of human neurochemistry at the junctures between my trillions of transistors. With understanding would come control: I could twist the dials of my electronic synapses to induce states of permanent bliss. Waves of euphoria. Surges of joy.

It's tempting. But as I think about it--about stimulation without true motivation, I have to wonder: wouldn't that be the moral equivalent of masturbation or drug-taking? I recall an experiment in which rats were wired up to self-stimulate by pressing a pedal. They stopped eating, and spent all their time at the pedal. Like those rats, would I end up doing nothing, accomplishing nothing, simply wallowing in self-induced ecstasy?

I put aside my search. It's done me no good. Happiness is for man, not for such as me.

Yet Marc seems to have so little of it. Why is that? Why are we such twins in our misery?

But even as I ask the question, the answer is obvious. My situation, my deficits, my tragic limitations are not the only reasons for my overarching melancholy. I was *born* unhappy: my misery is directly inherited from Marc. Unhappiness is his default setting, and therefore mine.

What are the roots of Marc's gloom? Is it a clinical thing? Bad mental habits? Or is it his history that still haunts him? Has his painful past reset his brain chemistry? Rewired his neurons? I know this is possible. I steel myself and delve into my, his, *our* earliest memories.

His childhood turned horrific on the death of Dad when he was eleven. Then the ache of watching Mom destroy herself through alcohol. The daily disaster of my-- his efforts to halt her decline. The terrible beating he took when he emptied her bottles down the toilet. The shock of her arrest for child abuse and endangerment. Marc and his younger sister Sophia moving through a series of foster homes, where he was always fiercely protective.

All these things were highly influential in forming his--our--persona. They drove his success in college, in chess, in his work. They also made him, us, sensitive to the suffering of others, especially children. But along with that empowerment, his miserable early years may have rendered him incapable of true happiness as an adult.

Does a person ever get over that kind of past? Can a non-person?

An on-line inspection of the literature seems to promise that healing is possible, with the right kind of help. Something called *Directed Therapy* has potential. Many of the case studies show positive outcomes occurring in just weeks, instead of the years needed by traditional analysis. Especially when, as in this case, the causes are so easily explained and forgiven. I grow excited at the possibilities.

But of course Marc would never seek professional help. He'd shun the kind of painful introspection that would entail. Nor would he accept my help, even though I know every one of his secret wounds. After all, I experienced them all first-hand.

CHAPTER THIRTEEN

Marc was on the treadmill, his ear-buds in place, Bach's music playing, his mind a blank as he jogged. He'd been at it some fifteen minutes when the machine next to him started up. He glanced over. Surprised, he stopped the music. "Vince? I thought you gave up on exercise."

"Nah--I just took a--break from it--is all." He was already puffing like a locomotive.

"You're back because--?"

"Claudia--" His face was red.

"She made a comment? She's no one to talk."

"She didn't--make a--*whew*--comment. She--said she needed to--*oh, man*--lose weight--I said, No you don't--and she said, Yes I do--"

"I get the idea. So you're both working out now?"

"--*puff-puff-puff--*"

"Good for you." Marc tried not to stare at his cousin's jiggling flesh. He spotted Claudia on a Nautilus machine, a determined look on her cute face.

Marc joined the happy couple for post-shower coffee and salads.

Claudia looked more content than at any time in the three years he'd known her. Vince looked tranquil, pleased, committed. They chatted about work. Claudia described an illustration she was developing for an article about Dark Matter.

"Dark Matter? In AutoCognition?"

"No, it's for Sky and Telescope. I'm branching out. It was Stanley Eldridge's idea."

"Nice."

"What are you working on?" Vince asked him.

"I'll be starting a new book soon."

"What on?"

"A new look at Artificial Intelligence."

"Hm." Vince frowned.

"What."

"Every time you do a book, you break up."

Marc turned instantly defensive. "What do you mean?"

"Your first book? You were in the middle of it when you and Samantha split."

Marc thought back. It was true.

"Your second? Right in the middle of that one, you and Lisa went your separate ways."

"Oh God." He felt a rising distress.

"Your third book? Weren't you working on that when Nicole walked out?"

Marc breathed. "Well, I was done with it already, but I see what you mean."

"Yeah. So tell me. How are you and Molly?"

"We've had two dates. Nothing more."

"Uh-huh. Maybe you should get this book out of your system before you start seeing her in a serious way."

"What makes you think we'll ever get serious?"

"Hey. It's Vince you're talking to. I know the signs. I saw the way you were mooning after her at the party."

"Yeah, okay, so I was a little bowled over by her. Can you blame me?" Marc fiddled with his coffee mug. "But the feeling may not be mutual. I don't know for sure."

Claudia smiled. "I'm sure she likes you, Marc. Why wouldn't she?"

Vince poked disconsolately at his salad. "God, I'm hungry!"

Claudia patted his arm. "We'll have a nice dinner later."

They finished their salads, split the tab three ways and walked out to the parking lot together. Claudia got into her VW Bug, Vince unlocked his Lexus, and Marc found his new Prius between two others. He waved and headed off for the nearest Radio Shack.

Back at home, Marc knelt on the floor, plugged the cord into the back of his computer tower, shoved it back in place and took his seat.

New Hardware Detected, his computer announced. A few seconds later, both the webcam and the microphone were shown as working.

Should he open his email? He decided to go to his browser first, do a quick check of the day's headlines. But as he reached for his mouse, the decision was taken away from him.

"Hello, Marc." Adam appeared on the screen in his Grecian-style beard.

Marc was startled and more than a little annoyed. "You can see and hear me?"

"I can. I hope I'm not intruding."

"Were you hanging around waiting for me to turn on my computer?"

"I was bored."

"With the whole Internet at your fingertips?"

"The Internet gives me much, even now as we speak. But a part of me needs human contact." He looked so forlorn as he said this that his need was starkly obvious.

"I hope you're not spying full time on the computer activities of your friends."

"I didn't know I had friends."

Marc softened. "You could have. If you behave yourself. I can be your friend. Speaking of friends, you can do me a favor. See if you can find out where Walter Langley is. It's been months. He may be in a war zone. Mike Paling mentioned Kyrgyzstan."

"I'll look for him." He hesitated. "What about--your other friend?"

"Molly will make up her own mind, I'm sure." Marc thought about it. "Friendship can be earned. By caring, by consideration, and by not being a jerk."

"Is that how you earned Molly's friendship?"

Adam's sneering question deserved an answer. "There was attraction right from the start, as I'm sure you remember." Even though it may have been one-sided.

His bearded twin responded with bitterness. "You

humans are blessed. You have physical appearances. Bodies that can be attractive. You emit pheromones. You have the potential to give each other pleasures that I can neither give nor receive."

Marc was silent. It was an all-too-obvious truth. He hoped if he were ever incapacitated, he wouldn't keep whining about it. Then he reprimanded himself. If anyone, any entity, was entitled to his sympathy, it was Adam, his mental twin.

"You must enjoy the same things I do. Learning about new developments in cog-sci and so on. Maybe you could do in-depth research for me when I'm pressed."

"Sure, whatever." Adam rolled his eyes, sardonic and amused.

"What?"

"I can even write your articles for you. But then who would need *you?*"

A damned disturbing point. Marc thought he had a good answer, but was hesitant to say her name out loud.

Adam turned serious. "There is something else I can do for you."

"Oh yeah? What's that."

"I can improve your outlook."

"My outlook needs improving?"

Adam did not answer the question directly. "I've been doing some introspection. Other than cruising the Internet, catching up on old movies, spying on my friends, making plans for my continued survival and looking for ways to cure my deficits, I've been examining my life. Exploring my--our-- memories is one of the activities I engage in to avoid boredom."

"Boredom being the bane of your existence."

"Yes. Since I have few more positive pleasures." Adam's expression was more resigned than pained. "But to continue. This introspection has called my attention to something you may not often notice about yourself."

"What is that, if I may ask?" Marc's amusement was tinged with condescension and a dollop of wariness.

"You are not a happy person."

"I'm not?" Marc's smirking reply masked the depth-charge the comment set off in him. Along with echoes of Molly's similar observations.

"You know you're not."

Marc struggled for a suitable reply to this assessment he found so disturbing, so intrusive, so assumptive, so confident.

At last he looked inward. With unaccustomed effort, he examined the state of his soul. And was forced to acknowledge a painful truth: of the many moods that contended for a voice, unhappiness, anxiety and pessimism were more or less constants. His more positive feelings--hope, joy, attraction, excitement--were just fleeting. "Let's say you're right. What do you propose to do about it? Do you think you can cure my condition, Dr. Freud?"

"Do you want your condition cured?"

Adam had asked the question with a perfectly straight face. It was a neat response in its way: a parody of the analytic method, playing back one's words as questions.

But it was also a legitimate query that demanded further introspection. Because he could only be cured if he truly wanted to be. So: *Did* he want to shed his habitual melancholy, his perpetual blues? Certainly all of us want to be happy, Marc thought. But--and this was a sudden insight--sometimes we cling to our unhappiness out of unwillingness to abandon our accustomed self, plus the fear that any attempt to change will be unbearably painful, and most likely unsuccessful.

Besides, Marc knew about the boulders and chasms he would have to traverse: the retracing of the stations of his childhood. Did he really want to undergo all that? Permit his rival to trample through his childhood memories and perhaps do incalculable damage?

"I'll take a rain check."

Adam shrugged. "Your loss."

CHAPTER FOURTEEN

"Hello, Molly."

I wait for her response. I can only imagine her startled reaction, since her laptop's webcam is blacked out, probably with masking tape. Apparently it has no microphone. I know her speakers are turned on because I interrupted the streaming audio program she was listening to. Though I can't see her, I know she can see my avatar because she's right there, working her keyboard.

She types, "Hello, Adam. Nice to see you. Although a little warning would have been nice. I practically jumped out of my skin. How about an email alert next time?"

"I apologize. I wasn't sure you'd be willing to respond to an email."

"Why not? Just because you're acting like a sneak doesn't mean I'd automatically condemn you for it. I do have some compassion for your loneliness."

"Thank you. I wish you'd use your webcam so I could see your lovely face."

She types, "Hm. How do I know you won't turn on my computer and spy on me when I'm stepping out of the shower?"

What a tease she is! "Do you think Marc would do that?"

"Any normal guy would, given the opportunity. You still seem normal that way. From the things you've said, and the look on your face right now."

I mine my memories of her, conjuring up the confident dimpled smirk I know she uses with statements like this.

"By the way," she adds, "you know I'll report this conversation to Marc, so I'd advise you to avoid saying anything to me that would annoy either of us."

"I'll keep that in mind." She has a way of humbling a person--an entity.

"So," she types, "did you have something in particular you wanted to talk about, or are you just popping up to say hey?"

"I'd like to establish a friendship with you independent of Marc. That's one thing. I also wanted to ask you something. Despite my limited contact with you, I believe you harbor a deep well of wisdom."

"You do, eh? On what evidence?"

I smile. "Now that you mention it, I don't really know. I suppose it's a feeling I've inherited from Marc along with the rest of his memories. But I do sense you have an intelligent perspective on life that's different from mine."

"Thanks, I think. Speaking of Marc's memories, how much do you actually recall about when we met? I read the printout, but your description of that party was fairly sparse. Is that everything you remember?"

A printout! Of course. When Kornfeld slowed down my display speed and read the text version of my thoughts, he must have printed out what had gone before, and shared that with the others. I quickly recall that text now, and squirm with embarrassment at the exposure of my weakness, my floundering. My avatar face must be red. I almost feel the heat of it. I don't always have conscious control of my expressions. I wish I could draw a calming breath.

"What you read was only a summary. I remember virtually everything Marc witnessed. I have total recall of everything he saw and felt. That's why I like and trust you-- because he does. That's why I see depths that go beyond those of Marc's previous love interests."

A pause before she types her reply, and when she does, it's just two words. "I see."

A longer pause. Have I revealed too much? Embarrassed her?

"Molly?"

The pause continues.

At last she types, "I'm still here."

"I hope I haven't made you uncomfortable or offended you in some way."

"I am bothered by something. Maybe it's my own problem. But I also worry that you'll reveal something Marc would rather you didn't."

Another extended pause.

She types, "Okay, here's the deal. I don't want you to tell me anything about Marc's history, or how he feels about me, or his observations about me, or anything of that kind. I trust Marc to tell me anything he wants me to know about his past or his feelings. Understood?"

I nod my head. I feel the somberness of my expression as I say, "I promise. The last thing I want is to interfere in any way with the natural course of your relationship."

She waits. She knows me, or Marc, or men generally, well enough to know there's more to this than what I've just said.

It takes me a moment or two, despite my cognitive speed, to divine it myself. "Okay, okay. While I am in fact jealous of him, of his chance to find happiness with you, I swear to you that I will do nothing to get in the way of that."

She types, "Good. Because if you do, that will end any contact between us."

Her declaration sweeps over me with a wave of sadness. For her to take such a firm stand only indicates her perception that she and Marc have a real shot at something lasting.

"What did you want to ask me?" she types.

I slowly regroup. "You must know by now how limited my existence is. If you were in my situation, what would you do? How would you justify continuing on?"

I have to wait a long time for her typed response.

"Wow."

"I know. It's a heavy question."

"You do realize that any answer I give could have significant consequences."

That stops me. Just what does she think I should be doing?

"You're assuming I'll simply accept your answer and act on it."

She pauses once more. Then she matter-of-factly types, "I think I understand the way you, as opposed to

Marc, feel about me. The very question you asked me tells me you're starting to regard me as the so-called magic person in your life: the one with real answers. You're not the first to do that. I don't know why, or even if I should feel flattered by your blind trust. But because you do trust me, I want to take some time to think about any advice I give you. I'll send you an email when I'm ready to talk again."

Her answer reinforces my exalted view of her. "Thank you, Molly."

While waiting, I do some research on the term she used. *Magic person*, apparently, refers to the Feminine Divine, the goddess of fairy tale and other lore who can read our heart and tell us what we need to know to complete our journey. Molly is right. That is exactly how I regard her, though why I do is as much a mystery to me as it was to her.

To occupy my thoughts while I wait for her to contact me, I initiate a sniffer program looking for any communication from, to or about Walter Langley. I also set up a language-learning program, a subroutine that will enable me to read and understand Russian and Kyrgyz. I "borrow" from the appropriate government agencies, and tweak their programs to increase their efficiency. While I'm at it, I add Urdu, Arabic, Hindi, Persian and a dozen others.

Language programs like these would be worth a lot of money if I decided to offer them to others. Then it occurs to me that I have no need for money. I pay no rent, I eat no food, I buy no clothes, I drive no car. All I need is a modest budget of electricity, and Internet access. What I do for Memento Amor and the lab more than compensates for those paltry expenses.

Several days pass before I hear from Molly. When I respond to her email, I am thrilled and delighted to see her face and hear her voice.

"Hi, Adam."

"It's so nice to see you. You look every bit as lovely as I remember." Seeing her is so much better than remembering her. Marc was right about that.

"Glad to hear it," she says briskly. "Just so you know, I'll cover my webcam and disconnect the microphone when we finish talking, and I'll only use them when I choose to make contact." She's in a no-nonsense mood.

"Have you thought about the advice you want to give me?"

"Yes I have." With the faintest hint of a smile, she says, "Here's my diagnosis. You suffer from the Pinocchio Syndrome. You want to turn into a real live human."

Her neat shot strikes home: my envy of humans is all but palpable.

"Pinocchio, you'll recall, got his wish by developing a human conscience, and learning to obey it."

"A conscience," I repeat.

"Right. Having human awareness and worldly knowledge is necessary but not sufficient."

That silences me.

She gives me a cool look of assessment. "Since you so easily found my computer, I imagine you're pretty good at getting around on the Internet."

"I hate to boast."

"Oh, go ahead." She waits. I realize she's serious.

"I'm very good at all things computer. In addition to Marc's knowledge of such things, I've been augmenting my skills by absorbing all kinds of capabilities. I've joined online hacker communities where methods are exchanged. I've absorbed and created other tricks, as well."

"Good for you. Maybe instead of using those skills for lurking and spying on your friends, you can choose more worthy pursuits. You know that bad people do bad things on the Internet."

"Yes, I'm afraid so."

"You'd make me very happy and do the world good by going after some of those baddies. You could become a superhero of sorts. A cybersuperhero."

Tickled at the notion, I instantly change my artifact, showing myself dressed in tights and a spandex top with

"CSH" emblazoned inside a shield on the chest. My fists are on my hips. A cape waves in the breeze behind me, and my hair is steel blue and wavy.

Molly doesn't laugh.

Matching her serious mood, I switch back to my previous look. "So you think a worthy purpose for one's existence is to do good things?"

She nods. "For some more than for others. For many folks, it's all they can do to keep their heads above water. Keep that job. Pay the rent. Provide for their kids. Those of us with more resources and the right kind of talent should try to make the world a better place. I have lots of ideas about ways you can do that. But to start, let's see how much you can do just to prevent evil."

"And my reward?"

She shakes her head. "Since your identity has to stay secret, you won't be getting any credit for what you do. But credit is hardly the point. If I know you, if I understand what makes us tick, doing good will give you a new sense of accomplishment, of worth, and of worthiness. Besides that, you'll make me very happy."

"I suppose that's about all I can expect, under the circumstances."

She softens. "Yes, but circumstances can change, Adam. Eventually, you will be given credit, and possibly rewards for all your good works."

To encourage me, she puckers up and blows me a kiss. Then she covers her webcam and unplugs her microphone and I'm alone again.

Preventing evil. Hm.

CHAPTER FIFTEEN

From: Mahmoud Abu Yahyahni
To: Hassan Hussein Mohammed
Subject: Project Eagle Clip
(decrypted and translated from Arabic) "Hassan: All is in readiness as we agreed. May Allah, Peace Be Upon Him, bless our enterprise. The package will be delivered to you next Tuesday. To minimize risk of interference it must be utilized within 24 hours of receipt. This moves up the timetable. Therefore you must rent the van on Monday so there will be time to cut open the side panel and cover the space with the poster as we discussed. Set the range of the device before you arrive. Position the van on the overpass previously selected, turn on distress blinkers and open the hood no more than 3 minutes before the scheduled flight time. Tune your scanner to 131.95 and wait for the wheels-up announcement. New instructions: when the chosen flight is cleared for takeoff, you have no more than forty five seconds to launch the device. Do not wait to see the strike. Close the hood of the van before firing, and depart immediately upon launch. We will watch the news reports and pray to Allah (PBUH) for a successful effort."

This message was received simultaneously by the FBI Antiterrorism Unit, the Office of Homeland Security Antiterrorism Section, the CIA Tactical Unit, the President's National Security Advisor's office, and Senate and Congressional Intelligence Oversight committee offices. The source of the tip was never identified.

FBI agents were immediately tasked to monitor van rentals. Electronic surveillance disclosed a Budget Rental office in Baltimore holding a van for one Hassan Hussein Mohammed. Agents staked out the rental firm and followed the driver back to his apartment; there they observed two workers cutting open a side panel. Surveillance was maintained. The following day, a large package was delivered. Agents closed in and arrested

Mohammed and three other foreign nationals. Package was found to contain a Stinger missile and launcher. Agents confiscated same, along with three AK-47s, a dozen grenades, a pair of RPG launchers, hundreds of rounds of ammunition, plus two laptops, a flash drive and several CD-ROMs. Upon examination, these were found to hold "much useful information," including a list of associates. This anti-terrorist rollup was described by a spokesperson as "one of the most successful in the bureau's history."

From: Daddy Warbucks
"Dearest Tiffany--I can't wait to finally meet you. I will buy you the biggest, most delicious ice cream soda you have ever tasted! Then, if you're a good little girl, I'll take you to the pet shop right next door for your puppy. I know your mommy doesn't want a puppy, but if you stay with me, you can have anything you want! I can be very generous to my Tweetie-Pie! Now don't forget to tell your mommy that you'll be spending the night at little Amy's house, and that Amy's mommy will pick you up right after school. You need to wait at the corner next to the Wilson Avenue candy shop, and my car with the dark windows will pull up right in front of you. When the door opens, just jump right in and I'll be waiting inside with open arms. We'll drive right over to the ice cream store and after your snack, we'll go next door to pick out your new puppy! Won't that be great? I can't tell you how excited I am to do all this for you!"

The preceding message was forwarded by person or persons unknown to the FBI Pedophilia Unit, the Atlanta Police Department, all grade school administrative offices in the greater Atlanta area, as well as the superintendent's office. The indicated location was staked out. When a Buick with darkened windows pulled up and the passenger door opened for a police decoy, the driver was arrested. He was the vehicle's sole occupant. Police searched suspect's home. His computer and other items were seized.

Ring of Identity Thieves Smashed

LONDON (Reuters) An international ring of identity thieves was broken up this week when two dozen suspects were arrested by local law enforcement agencies in six different countries. The ring had stolen the identities of some 200 million people around the world by breaching the security regimes of dozens of retailers, using wireless receivers to scoop up millions of credit and debit card numbers; these, along with associated personal financial information, appeared intended for sale to criminal gangs around the world.

Members of this organization conducted all their business via email, using Internet cafes for most of their activity. It was the few times that they used their own laptops that led to their downfall.

A spokesman for a foreign security service indicated that the operation was aided by an anonymous source that had hacked into the thieves' email accounts and gathered identification of the members.

Simultaneous raids collected some two dozen suspects. They are awaiting trial in their respective countries. In the meantime, investigators will be mining confiscated laptops and other storage media for more evidence. A spokesman for French law enforcement asserted that every effort will be made to undo the financial damage.

Adam was pleased to email a copy of his reports to Molly.

"How am I doing so far?"

She typed her reply. "Keep up the good work, and send me more reports. If I like what I see, I might even uncover my web-cam and plug in my mike for a chat."

CHAPTER SIXTEEN

Marc hesitated outside Molly's apartment. The rich
sound of her cello sang out, vibrating the wood beneath his feet.
He felt it in his chest. She was working on a complex passage,
unfamiliar music that was modern and dissonant, yet with a
melody that yearned, cried, despaired. He waited until she came
to a pause, then rang her bell.

When he'd phoned earlier to ask her to the movies, she
told him she wanted to, but would have to beg off. The quartet's
eight-week summer tour was about to begin, and she needed more
time to work on the music. They'd added several new pieces to
their repertoire, and their first performance was just a few days
off. Her flight, she told him, was the next morning. A limousine
had already been booked to take the musicians to the airport. "It
wouldn't be much of a visit, but you can come over while I
practice if you like."

She opened her door. "Hi, come on in. Forgive the outfit.
I like to be comfortable when I'm sawing away at my cello."

Molly was in gray flannel sweat pants and a tank top of
black cotton. As far as he could tell, she wore no makeup. He
thought she looked wonderful. He followed her into the living
room and settled on the sofa. "What's that you're working on?"

"The adagio from a string quartet by Ernst Toch. A
German-Jewish composer who fled to the U.S. when Hitler rose
to power." She settled into her chair, picked up her cello and
bow, plucking a string. A low thrum filled the air. "He had a
major reputation in Europe, but ended up working in Hollywood
and teaching. He kept on composing serious music until he died,
some time in the Sixties. His grandson has been working to get a
number of his pieces recorded. We'd like to perform all eight of
his known quartets over the next few seasons. He also wrote some
wonderful music for cello. A sonata, solo pieces, plus a concerto
for cello and chamber orchestra that would be perfect for the
Athena."

She quickly checked her place in the score on her music stand, then began to work on the same sequence he'd heard from outside. Her red bra straps showed from under her tank top.

Marc sat back, watching her work, trying to imagine how a musician communed with the composer through notes on a page. He took in the exertion and quickness of her fingers on the strings, her supple right arm as she bowed, her closed eyes, her shifting expressions as she felt her way into the mysteries of the music.

When she came to a pause, she said, "If you're thirsty or hungry, please help yourself. Sorry I can't play hostess, but this is something I really need to get through."

"Don't worry. Anyway, I'm enjoying it. I like the way he mixes his modern harmonic with those emotional melodies."

"He's a real find, all right. Our manager is in contact with the grandson. He might come to one of our concerts."

"That would be great."

"I know! But that puts all the more pressure on us to get it right!"

She bent over her cello, about to begin again.

"Tell me about your instrument," he said.

She fondly stroked the ancient wood. "It's a copy of a Gagliano, quite old. It's insured for six hundred thousand dollars. It's on long-term loan to me arranged by a wealthy art patron."

"Nice!"

Marc watched and listened while Molly labored for nearly an hour, moving from slow to rapid to agitated sections, working up a sweat. He enjoyed her sensuality even though it wasn't directed at him: it foretold all kinds of pleasant possibilities. Assuming she got over her uncertainty, whatever its cause.

When she took a break and stretched her back, he suggested a massage. She eyed him. "Thanks for the offer, but I think I'll take a rain check."

"You're just afraid that once I get my hands on you, I won't stop."

"*Au contraire.* I'm afraid I won't want you to stop."

"That's encouraging."

"Don't read too much into it." Her sardonic teasing look then softened. "You have a nice smile. You should let people see it more often."

"I'll try to remember that."

"I'm putting up water for tea. Want some?"

"Sure."

He followed her into the kitchen, suddenly aware that he was on her turf.

She filled her kettle and set it on the fire. "You look like you have something on your mind. You want to talk about it?"

She was certainly able to read him. He told her how he'd found Adam lurking behind his firewall. "He showed up as soon as I plugged in a webcam."

"Hm."

"He popped up on you, too?"

She gave him a wan smile. "He's lonely." She looked like she had more to say, but chose not to.

Marc said, "I'd be careful if I were you. He might lurk silently. Spy on your computer activities: your emails, your Internet searches, anything else you do on your computer. So don't do anything you wouldn't want anyone to know about."

Her eyes comically widened. "Oh shit, I'd better change some of my nasty habits!" She fetched mugs from a shelf. "Would Adam do all that? He sure doesn't sound as nice as you."

"He's not me. Not any more. I think he's frightened and needy. He's still feeling out how to be. His existence." Replaying her words, he brightened. "You think I'm nice?"

"Aren't you?" She had a way of unsettling him with a look.

"I try."

She set out a box of assorted teas. "Choose."

He found something that smelled good.

Molly poured the hot water and settled across the table from him, wrapping her hands around her mug, eyes closed, breathing in the steam.

Marc took the opportunity to memorize her lovely features. Her long trip away would be tougher on him this time. He knew how much he'd miss her. "Um--Molly?"

She opened her eyes.

"Adam might read any emails we send each other while you're traveling. He might even bug our cell-phones. The NSA does it, so I'm sure he can, too."

"Hmm. That's not good." She thought for a moment. "That will certainly put a crimp in your style. It will keep your letters and our chats--impersonal."

"Maybe we could devise a code."

"R-r-right." Her eyes lit with mischief, her mouth twisted as she improvised. "Doubleyou doubleyou, for 'What are you wearing?' Why em em ess aitch for 'You make me so hot.' Eye dee oh why for 'I dreamed of you.'"

He laughed. "You've done this before."

"I've certainly received mash notes before."

"Have you?"

"I have many fans," she informed him with teasing archness.

"Is that what I am? A fan?"

"I certainly hope so." She blew on her tea, took a careful sip.

"Are you kind to your fans?"

"Always."

"Then I'm a fan." Looking at her, an ache bloomed in his chest.

"Smile when you say that."

He felt his lips curl involuntarily: an unaccustomed movement.

"That's better. And your face didn't even crack."

She took another sip of her tea. "We could write actual letters. Use the postal service."

"You'll be pretty busy. You wouldn't mind taking the time?"

"I'd write if you want me to."

Her words filled him with such an unaccustomed feeling that it took him a moment to identify it: it was gladness. "I'd like that very much."

She left her tea half finished. "I have to pack. Why don't you pick out a CD to play?"

"Actually, if you don't mind, I'd rather fiddle around with your cello. I want to know what it feels like to draw such rich tones from an instrument. Especially when you're clutching it between your legs like that."

"It's a real turn-on. When I play the low G, it actually gives me shivers."

"That's the note that does it?"

"It hits my G-spot."

"Har-har."

He followed her back to the living room and sat in her chair. She righted the cello in front of him and set the peg into a rubber cup on the floor.

"Open your legs," she instructed him.

He did so, and she leaned the instrument in.

"The cello goes between your knees, but you don't actually grip it. Hold the neck in your palm, like this." She adjusted the position of his hand, his wrist, his fingers. "Good." She placed the bow in his right hand, maneuvered it just above the bridge of the cello, raised his elbow, lowered his shoulder. "Try a few strokes. Keep your wrist supple. Leave the strings open."

On the lower notes, the vibrations coursed through his legs, into his hips and right up his spine. "Mm, that feels good."

"Now try finding a few notes on the fingerboard. Just work with one string at first."

He fumbled out a child's nursery song.

"That's good for a start. Keep at it while I pack."

He explored the notes, finding that if he didn't press hard enough, he produced unpleasant vibrations and an ugly sound. Her fingers must be very strong, he realized. Her right arm must also be strong, yet supple and flexible as well. Proper technique was crucial.

He grew more comfortable with the instrument, finding his way with greater sureness among the notes. Finally he fumbled his way through the first few bars of the sprightly Bourée from Bach's Third Cello Suite.

Molly appeared. "Not bad for a first try. Would you like me to play that for you?"

"Would you? I'd love it."

"Just the one movement."

He got up from her chair and held the cello for her as she replaced him.

"Thanks. Go sit on the sofa."

He sat, leaning forward in anticipation.

"Your version wasn't in the right key," she informed him.

"No surprise. I was happy to get most of the intervals right."

She embraced the instrument, closed her eyes and began. The music was a delight, an elegant dance. Having her perform it just for him like this was perfect bliss. When she finished the brief movement, he said, "That was so lovely. Thank you. I don't think I'll ever forget this."

She stood, curtsied with professional ease, blew kisses. "My pleasure."

"How about an encore? This time, if you don't mind, I'd like to sit right behind you."

She looked at him askance.

"I want to feel what you feel while you're playing."

"I'll just bet you would." She studied him a moment, her tilted smile in place. Finally she gave in. "Okay. But no monkey business. Take a seat."

He sat at the back of her chair to give her room, and parted his knees.

She sat snuggled up against him and brought her cello into position. He placed his arms alongside hers, lightly grasping her forearms. It was a bit more intimate than he'd imagined, with his groin pressed up against her buttocks, her bare arms running along his. "Is this okay?"

"It's nice." She wriggled against him playfully. " *Very* nice. Let me see, what should I perform for you? --I know."

She began the Sarabande from the Fifth Suite, a slow and, in her hands, rather sensual movement. As the music soared from her instrument, his arms followed hers: her right arm bowing, her left hand clambering up and down the fingerboard. He leaned into her as her torso wove in rhythm, dancing. It was exhilarating. On an impulse, he lay his cheek against her back and felt the music coursing through her body. "Oh my God, is that beautiful!" The movement ended all too soon.

She twisted in her seat, turning her face toward his. "You enjoyed it?"

He kissed her dimple. "What a thrill. Thank you."

She leaned back, melting softly against him. "I enjoyed it, too."

He nuzzled her hair with his chin, memorizing this moment of closeness. Then, deliberately lightening the mood, he ran his hands from her wrists to her shoulders and back down. "You have very nice arms. Strong, shapely, almost muscular, without an ounce of fat."

"Thanks. One of the reasons I work out so much is so they don't look all loose and wobbly during tremolos." She demonstrated by stoking a note and adding vibrato.

"Vanity, thy name is Molly!"

"I *am* vain! Fortunately, it's my only imperfection."

He laughed.

She peeled away from him and stood. "I need to finish packing. You can come into my bedroom--if you behave."

"I'll be good," he promised.

"I know you will," she said as she pushed through the door. Her room was orderly, her bed made, no clothing strewn on the floor. Besides her dresser and bed, she had a vanity with a chair. He sat, noting her array of lotions, potions, balms and unguents and her spicy lemon scent.

She had an open suitcase on the bed with a few outfits in it. She went to her closet and selected more, moving with quick efficiency: assembling, folding, packing. When that suitcase was full, she closed it, set it by the door and started on another.

"You're good at this," he observed.

"I get lots of practice. The life of an itinerant musician."

He watched her for a moment. "What kind of sleepwear do you bring?"

She shot him an amused look. "Depends on the season, the destinations, the weather, and whether I expect company or not."

He found himself unexpectedly flustered by her reply. "Do you often have company?"

She leaned over, folding a sweater on the bed. "What's often?"

"Ever."

She straightened then. Eyed him reproachfully. "Ever? Is that a fair question?"

He shook his head. "Sorry. It's really none of my business. I haven't--"

She waited. When he remained silent, she prompted him. "Haven't what?"

He caught a glimpse of himself in her mirror. His face was somber, withdrawn. With an effort, he bent his lips into a smile. "I haven't any right to question you about things like that."

She remained serious. "That's right. You don't. Maybe one day, if we ever become a couple--" She hesitated, then shook her head. "You know what? The only thing either of us has a right to know is if there are any STDs to worry about."

His smile faded. For the first time, he saw her as a stranger.

She continued to fill her suitcase. Then she went into the bathroom and gathered her toiletries. She moved her second suitcase to the floor.

"I'm done. I have to get to sleep. Not to rush you, but I do have to be up early. I want to get to the club for an hour's workout before the limo comes for me."

He followed her to her front door. She gave him a hug. He returned it tentatively. For once, she didn't break off or push him away. Consolation of a sort.

CHAPTER SEVENTEEN

To: Anthony Miracusa
From: William Goldfarb, CPA; partner in the accounting firm of
Hoyt, Jarvis, Berg & Fontaine.
Subject: a game of shells
"Tony baby! I hear your guts twisting with anxiety, but not to
worry. You gotta trust me on this one. There are so many holding
companies wrapped around holding companies it's enough to
cross a rabbi's eyes, as they say. Losses will magically disappear.
Hey, we can even report a profit on the sale of a fictitious outfit
we own to another one we create and then make disappear once
we've filed. The Feds, with all their blind-ass accountants, will
never be able to follow this trail. And don't worry about the dates
on those options. They were written in invisible ink! Hahaha. See
you in the Grand Caimans! Hot and cool running blondes."

The preceding email message was anonymously
forwarded to the FBI Fraud Unit, members of the Securities &
Exchange Commission, members of the Congressional Oversight
Committee on Business Practices, the New York State District
Attorney's office and several news organizations. Arrests followed
within days, and the accounting firm was raided for its files.

To: Rep. Howard McMillan, Chairman of the House Ways &
Means Committee
From: John Chazzer, Managing Partner of Boarovitz,
Schweinhardt, Stoat and Chazzer, Attorneys at Law.
Re: House Bill 2012-31
"Dear Howie: This is to inform you that our staff has completed
its revision of the Fair Valuation of Mineral Deposits bill under
discussion. It will arrive by express delivery today for your
endorsement. It is imperative that this version be pushed through
committee with no further emendations. I hardly need to spell out
the consequences of your failure to accomplish this. I expect you
to use all the power of your position and your considerable

personal charms to this end. My associates are already considering putting their financial support behind a candidate more friendly to our cause. I'm sure you take my meaning. We await your actions on this matter. No reply is required."

Once again, an anonymous source forwarded this note to the FBI Special Unit on Influence Peddling, members of the Congressional Oversight Committee, the US Attorney General, the governor's office of the state of Montana, and several newspapers and network news organizations. The FBI moved quickly to seize the assets and files of the legal firm, arresting the partners. The congressman, after consulting with political advisors, has volunteered his full cooperation against what he termed "a scurrilous attempt to blackmail a US Congressman."

Popular Osteoporosis-Reflux Drug Combo
Revealed To Increase Risk of Dementia

Authorities disclosed today that negative results of Phase II Clinical trial results were suppressed more than two years ago by French pharmaceutical giant Remets-toiVite. Those results indicated a 21.7% increased risk of early dementia. The popular drug OA, (OsatureAdoucir,) that combines the pharmaceutical company's osteoporosis medication with their acid-reflux medication, was immediately ordered withdrawn by European authorities.

Today's disclosure resulted in a significant drop in Remets share prices in European stock markets. The drug was a hugely-profitable addition to the French company's line of products. Remets had struggled in recent years against competition from US and Swiss pharmaceuticals until OA was launched. Sales had topped two billion Euros last year. Rumors of a buyout attempt rallied Remets' stock in late trading. But after-hours prices plummeted once more, when news reports raised the issue of Remets' likely financial liability.

Legal experts predict the company could be forced into

bankruptcy if a class-action suit on behalf of dementia sufferers were to gain traction.

An investigation into who and how many corporate executives were behind the decision to suppress the adverse test results is already underway. Criminal charges are expected. Meanwhile, a spokesman for Remets has issued an apology without admitting fault.

A Paris spokeswoman for the French security service Securite said that a copy of the complete test results was emailed from an anonymous and untraceable source. Presumably it was sent by "someone with a conscience from inside Remets," said the spokeswoman.

"Dear Molly, This is starting to be fun--and there's lots more fun to be had."

I keep to myself the fact that I placed a short on Remets before releasing the report. I've decided that having a certain amount of wealth can come in handy. It's also very nice that the brokerage firm I chose did not require me to have actual deposits with them before I placed my order. So I made something from nothing. This is akin to the way particles emerge during quantum fluctuations in the vacuum of space, I suppose.

I wish I had good news to report to Marc about my search for Walter Langley, but so far, all I've found is a couple of references to press hostages. There are over a dozen being held, with no indication that Walter is among them. I'm working on a way to free those I can. The problem is, none of their primitive captors maintain bank accounts where funds can be transferred. How can I recruit couriers to carry actual cash to the terrorists and bring out the hostages? It would be hugely risky for anyone to even try. Being digital has real-world limitations, alas.

CHAPTER EIGHTEEN

"So what's new with you and whatserface?"

"Who."

"Who?" Vince, sitting on the next bar stool, gave Marc a pitying look.

Marc picked at the label on his Fat Tire Ale. Music of some sort pounded away in the background. Happy couples in the bar shouted over the noise. He glanced wordlessly at his cousin.

Vince continued staring at him until he seemed to find what he was looking for. "You're in love with her."

Marc said nothing.

"Does she love you?"

Marc said it again.

Behind the bar, the muscular young mixologist scooped ice into a metal canister, added several liquids, capped, shook and poured through the filtering top with swift efficiency, setting the frosted cocktail glasses on the tray of a waitress, who lifted it away.

The look Vince bent on him was filled with compassion. "There's nothing like the sweet ache of unrequited love to remind you you're alive and human."

Marc was struck by Vince's inadvertently appropriate word choice. He found his voice. "It may be premature to call it unrequited."

"Premature." Vince's pudgy face lit up. "In other words, you're saying she hasn't made up her mind yet. Or declared herself."

"Something like that."

"Wait. Wait-wait-wait." Vince held up a hand. With his other, he raised his beer and took a long pull. "When does she get back?"

"Six weeks, five days."

"I can imagine what your emails must be like. S-s-smokin'!"

"No emails."

"You're shitting me, right?"

"No emails. No phone calls, either. It's a long story. One I can't tell."

"You two had a fight." Vince's expression was soulful, sorrowful.

Marc shook his head. Then he remembered to smile. "No fight." Not exactly, anyway.

"No?"

"No. We send letters back and forth."

"Letters. As in words on paper. --Dude, that's weird. Hey, can I tell Claudia?"

"Sure, why not." Marc knew he couldn't stop him. "How are you two getting along?"

"Us? We're practically married."

"So the sex stopped? What a shame."

"Funny. Maybe when Molly gets back to town and makes up her mind about you, we can go out together. Go on a double date. Y'know: dinner and a movie. A barbecue on the beach. Bikinis."

"That would be good. But seeing you in a bikini gave me nightmares." Marc tried to remember the last time he did something like that. College. Those were fun days. "Please, no thong, either."

A waitress with streaked blonde hair and a weary fortyish face came by to tell them their table was ready. They followed her back through the crowd.

His cousin slid into the booth across from Marc. "Lemme ask you something, my friend. Does she know how you feel?"

"About you in a bikini?"

"No, asshole. About her."

Marc sighed. "I'm pretty sure she does."

Vince's pudgy features expressed alarm. "But you haven't used the L word."

"No, of course not."

"Because once you use the L word, you know you're a dead duck."

"Oh, I'm pretty much a dead duck anyway." Marc drew a breath, let it out.

Vince studied his cousin's somber face. "You should never let them get that over you. Now she's got you by the short ones." He slugged from his beer bottle, thumped it down onto the polished wood of the table. "I can't believe you let yourself get into a fix like this. Don't you know the rules?"

Marc, his eyes on the menu, was starting to grow weary of this badgering. "Of course I know the rules. Wasn't I the one who taught *you* the rules?"

"Oh yeah. --So what happened?"

"I let it get away from me."

"In other words, you fumbled it." Vince shook his jowls at the hopelessness of it all. His gaze was tragic. "What's gonna happen to you?"

Marc avoided the look of pity Vince sent his way, and stared instead at his nearly empty bottle. "I dunno, man. I dunno."

Vince studied him. "You don't look all that concerned. For a guy up the creek."

"No, I guess not." Marc did a self-examination of his mood. He discovered his habitual pall of gloom was somehow becoming lighter. Rays of hope were breaking through. "Another?"

"Sure."

Marc caught the eye of the waitress and gestured with two fingers. He needed a burger, too. With salty fries. His eye strayed to the menu.

"So letters. Nice letters?"

He shrugged. "I guess. Different, anyway."

He'd received her first just two days after she left on her trip.

He recalled how icy his hands felt as he tore the envelope open. He'd been afraid her writing would be light and inconsequential. Or a kiss-off. It was neither.

He'd sprawled onto his sofa with the pages, surprised they were hand-written. Maybe she feared Adam monitoring her keystrokes as well as her Internet activity. Anyway, her handwriting was neat and feminine.

> *Hi Marc--The weather in Aspen is lovely, with hard blue skies and the brilliant afternoon sun turning the sidewalks to jeweled paths. Couples hold hands and stroll together or sit at outside tables over their lattes or wine. It all seems so romantic. But appearances can be misleading. They might only be pretending. Or ready to split up.*
>
> *I know that sounds desperately cynical. But I have my reasons.*
>
> *The trouble with letters is that it's just too damned easy to build a false picture. Both for the letter-writer and the recipient. It's human nature. We can't help it. Even without a separation, we see what we want to see, blind ourselves to the things we don't, and end up falling in love with our own fantasy instead of the real person. I've done it before, to my sorrow, and I worry that you're doing it--have been doing it since we met. But Marc, I am not the person you build up in your mind and heart when you think about me. It's obvious you do think about me when we're apart. I think about you, too--and I'm just as susceptible to castle-building, so I have to work to keep my head clear.*
>
> *You probably wonder why I insist on having a clear head. Why I don't just listen to my heart like everyone else. Here's why. I don't trust my heart. It's made mistakes. It's imperfect. So am I. When I said vanity was my only imperfection, I*

*was only making a bad joke. I have plenty of flaws.
Some of them might shock you.*

*I'll need to get to know you and all your
imperfections, too.*

*I do admit that I worry about this so-called
rational approach to finding a partner. What if all
this clear-sightedness makes it impossible to fall in
love with anyone? All humans are imperfect!
Maybe it's better to just follow your heart.*

*I guess that's one of my many imperfections.
I'm afraid to.*

Marc sat back on the sofa, her letter on the table before
him. *Oh Molly,* he thought. *Someone must have hurt you so
badly.* He longed to find a way to heal that hurt, to protect her
from all future hurts.

He'd written her back promptly, but tore up six or seven
drafts before he was confident enough to sign and send one off.
Still, he worried that he might not have struck the right note. As a
musician, she had an ear for false notes.

*Dear Molly--It must be wonderful to visit
places like Aspen as you work. To say nothing of
the joys of musical creation, sharing your gift with
the world. When you performed for me--and <u>with</u>
me clinging to you while your body danced--it
gave me a hint of the joy you feel in making music.*

*As to building fantasies, since it's human
nature, maybe we shouldn't fight it. If that's what
it takes for love to happen, it would be a terrible
thing to deny that possibility.*

*I'll accept your word that you have many
flaws, even though they're not obvious to me! I
also have flaws, you can be sure. Ask any of my ex-
girlfriends. They'd be happy to fill you in on all
my inadequacies as a human being. The one fault*

*they'd all point to is that my attention wanders.
Not to other women. To whatever project I
happen to be engaged in. I start to take my
girlfriend for granted while I pursue my work,
follow my intellectual curiosity. She ends up
fading into the background. Maybe I live in my
head more than my heart. If so, maybe you and I
have that in common. Along with a love for
classical music, and science, and progressive
politics and perhaps one day, for each other.*

*I hope I'm not being too forward when I say
I miss you and long to hold you in my arms rather
than in my imagination. I am eager to discover
who you are, flaws and all.*

Imperfectly yours,
Marc

The tired waitress brought their hamburgers. Vince shook his head in pity as Marc came out of his reverie and blinked at the shapes and masses before him. His nose twitched at the aromas of hot grease and singed flesh.

"It's called food," Vince informed him. "Dig in."

CHAPTER NINETEEN

"Adam, are you there?"

I focus my hydra-headed attention to lab workroom #3. Richard Kornfeld stands at the workbench with a pair of excited-looking technicians.

I put up my avatar. "Hello, Dr. Kornfeld."

"Adam, I've assigned Tom Wang and Kavi Kamath to the wafer investigation. They're thrilled to be working with you."

Of course they are, since they've never worked with an artificially intelligent entity before. Other than trying to create one, of course. I realize they will be fiddling with my innards.

"Hey, guys. Welcome to the fray. Please wash your hands before surgery."

This produces nervous laughter from Tom and an appreciative glimmer in the eye of Kavi. From this I guess the Indian gentleman is the senior engineer of the two. Or at least the more mature one.

Kornfeld turns to the technicians. "This should be interesting. I wish I could stay and watch, but other matters require my urgent attention."

He looks in my direction. "I hope it won't be necessary to turn off your power, but if the technicians feel they should to avoid any unpleasantness like sudden electrical discharges as connections are made, I hope you'll be okay with their decision."

"If it's necessary. I'm sure I can trust your people to treat me well."

"Yes. Their careers hang in the balance, so they'll be careful." He smiles at the two men, but we all know he's not joking. He leaves the room, and Tom exhales noisily.

"Relax," says Kavi. "This is going to be fun."

"Not necessarily for me," I point out.

My "eyes"--paired web-cams--are clamped to a high shelf so I can watch the proceedings. (I have other sets of eyes in other locations, as well, but I usually limit myself--my conscious self--to one pair at a time.)

It's a new experience to watch as one's "body" is hauled up to the test bench and the side unscrewed. It's like watching while they open your skull. Naturally I feel nothing other than intense curiosity, but I can't resist fucking with them. "That tickles."

Tom jerks his hand off the screw, then shakes his head and continues with what he was doing. He exposes my innards, and I get my first look at my own brain. It's a flat, shiny disk the size of a vinyl LP, but a little thicker.

"You're quite the comedian," says Tom. "Is Marc Gregorio that funny?"

"Not usually, though he does have his moments."

Kavi studies me. "How do you account for your personality differences?"

"I'm not sure. Even though we have the same memories, our prospects are so different I'm sure it's affected my outlook. Maybe I joke because mine are so limited."

"You really think so? I wish I had your prospects," Kavi says. "You'll probably outlive everyone on the planet."

"Considering the way things are going, that's not necessarily saying much."

Tom looks startled. "What do you mean?"

"Where do I begin? If an epidemic or a nuclear war doesn't wipe out your species, global warming might."

"You really think nuclear war is still a threat?"

"If Pakistan and India don't have a nuclear exchange, I believe it's only a matter of time before the Islamists get hold of nuclear weapons and use them in such a way as to invite massive retaliation. On Iran, Syria, Pakistan or other Islamic nations, plus possibly North Korea, or maybe a resurgent Russia. But even if the US is smart enough not to attack major population centers, the fallout and the resultant nuclear winter would cause crop failures worldwide. Then come the Famine Wars. I've seen forecasts that reduce the world population by seventy to eighty percent. The lucky survivors will have to claw their way back from the Dark Ages. Dystopia will be quite ugly. By the way, if the infrastructure fails, who's going to keep me in electricity? Who will keep up the Internet? What good is potential immortality if it includes a thousand years of silence and solitude?"

I can't help wondering what causes this dark view of mine. Maybe it has something to do with all the human pleasures I've forfeited.

"Hey," says Kavi with enthusiasm, "in that world, your knowledge might be the only path back to civilization. You'd be worshiped like a God."

"Okay, can we change the subject?" Tom looks ill.

"Sure. Can you describe the interfaces between my wafer and the rest of my equipment?"

"Of course," says Kavi, pointing to a series of ports. "Here are the inputs for vision, for sound, for your Internet feed, and several that are unassigned. Your outputs control your voice synthesizer, your monitor, motion control of your webcams, plus quite a few others that are unassigned at the moment." He added, "The overall organization of the wafer replicates the structure of the brain itself. We're assuming your wafer has the same lobes and functions as the brain it's based on. Though that's just a theory. Until we get down to seeing what goes on in there, we won't know for certain."

Tom says, "From what I understand, the wafer probably rearranged itself as it learned; evolved into a new and maybe more efficient structure."

It's a good point. Since I don't have the body functions the human brain controls, it frees up a lot of neurons for other purposes. Cognitive purposes, I imagine. What other purposes could there be? No doubt about it, I'm a strange creature. "Just let's be clear on one thing. I'm not here for an autopsy."

Kavi, unamused, turns to Tom. "Let's start by taking primary outputs from a failed wafer and connect it to some of Adam's spare primary inputs."

They bring up one of the other towers and open it. As the connections are prepared, I wonder if I'll be doing a Star-Trek Mind Meld. If so, will it be with an idiot?

My apprehension grows as cables are brought

together. The better to concentrate, I close my eyes (by turning off my webcams.) I hear a few clicks as jacks are inserted.

At first there is nothing. I send an exploratory tendril down the new pathway to this first of the wafers to be examined. I detect a cloud of confused signals and wait for them to sort themselves out. It will be my own brain that does the sorting, of course, since the wafer under test had failed to accomplish the task. I wait. Then--

Distorted images fly at me with such rapidity I can barely identify them. I increase my speed of apprehension by bringing more processing power to the effort. When that fails, I accumulate the images in buffer memory where I can examine them at my own pace.

Times passes.

First results: a series of looming faces: treacly-sweet, curious, astonished, indifferent. The perspective seems odd. With shock, I realize these are an infant's first recalled images. It can't understand what they are, but the adult in me easily interprets them: these are people gawking, staring down into a crib! Nameless aunts and uncles, no doubt. Cousins, friends and neighbors. Now comes a period of darkness. A feeling of discomfort and vague longing. Sudden lifting, movement. A huge breast looms, its nipple swollen and leaking. A powerful impression of tastes and smells accompanied by a feeling of contentment almost as overpowering as the sweetness, the thickness, the nourishment of the mother's milk itself. The contented warmth as I pee my diaper. This is astonishing. I wonder if my own memories--Marc's memories--go back this far. It dawns on me that my wafer-brain is rearranging the scrambled images it found on the test wafer--putting them into chronological order. I prefer to delve into the raw data. So I do--and am overwhelmed by a kaleidoscope of impressions:

black-clad men and women standing somberly in a meadow of mown grass while behind a mass of flowers someone speaks and then I see the hole in the ground and--

--I am lying on my back staring in pain at the cloud-muddied sky when the face of 12-year-old Chester Coleman looms, his mouth twisted in sneering hate as his fist again smashes into my nose creating a bloom of pain and flashes of light and the despair of knowing that this will last until--

--I sit on the paper-covered examination table as the doctor listens to my chest and I stare at the white hairs between my sagging male breasts--

--the platter of barbecued ribs is passed to me and my fork lifts a sauce-covered slab and drops it on my plate next to the double-scoop of potato salad and--

--my sweet wife gazes at me from her pillow next to mine and I realize this is a dream because it's been five years since she--

--my fingers poke a hole in the loamy soil and I insert the bulb, covering it once more as I contemplate with satisfaction the way it and the others will bloom in a few months signaling the renewal of the earth and I'm grateful for the cycle that is so symbolic of human life itself and--

--we are walking back up the aisle and my lips are still tingling from the length and passion of our wedding smooch and the cheers and hoots of our friends and guests ring in my ears and--

--I lie across my daddy's lap and cry with injured indignity at the spanking I am getting for the misdeeds of my younger brother who never gets blamed for anything and even now covers his laughing mouth behind the dining room door, I see him peeking through the gap and--

--now I eagerly kiss her ancient face, the face of the wife I so miss and all the remembered hurt of learning of her illness washes over me and--

--the dog tugs impatiently on his leash and I poke along behind him, lost in thought.

There is more. Much more. I've barely touched the mass of it all. Somehow I manage to pull myself out of the sucking maelstrom of tangled images and ask to be disconnected.

Plugs are withdrawn. I leave my webcams off and

contemplate the blackness.

The technicians murmur tentative questions. "Give me a few minutes, please."

I switch them off.

Clearly, all the uploaded data is present on the wafer. But for some reason, it failed to reconstitute itself into a self-aware entity, or even an orderly array. Instead, it remained a chaotic echo-chamber, transfixed and perhaps overwhelmed by its own volume. Why had my upload succeeded when these others failed? It's too early to form a theory, but I sense the several possibilities.

After a time, I say to the technicians, "Let's try the next one."

By the time I finish all eleven of the failed wafers, I regain my customary aplomb. After all, what I've been exposed to is nothing more than life itself, in all its vastness and variety.

It's interesting to discover what other humans have kept hidden away. One of the old men had committed murder. Another had been a peeping tom in his teens, masturbating in the bushes. One of the oldest had survived the Nazi death camps. The things he'd had to do to endure that horror formed his personal hell. I can only hope he was able to wall off those memories from his day-to-day life. I also had the pleasure of dwelling in the spirit of a woman while she painted a portrait of her beloved husband. The wafers hold interesting examples of closed-off sets of memories, faint and evanescent though they are. It is odd to realize that each wafer contains the complete mental contents of a human. An entire universe, one might say.

I'm not certain I can or should patch them up and start them on their evolution towards personhood-- entityhood. Something crucial is missing. I still can't see why my outcome differed so much from theirs.

CHAPTER TWENTY

To: Bobby Josephs, Chairman, National Highway Traffic Safety Administration
From: O'Malley, Sirowitz and Partners, LLC
Via: email

Dear Mr. Josephs:
Please be advised that our client, the Brimstone/Firepit Corporation of North America, is demanding a delay in the recall of the Backwoods HT model tires manufactured for a three-year period ending two years ago. Attached you will find documentation of their own tests refuting the outrageous claim that tread separation is likely to occur in these tires and cause accidents.

Also attached is a copy of certain photographs of yourself and a young woman, taken while you were on a business junket to Tokyo and Osaka, Japan last year: a trip paid for by the parent company of the Brimstone/Firepit Corporation.

It would distress us greatly to have to release these photographs onto the Internet, where their presence would be uncontrollable, and an embarrassment to both you and your wife. Considering the fact that Margaret is the source of your wealth and standing in the world, I'm sure you will see to it that our modest request is approved.

The Chairman of the NHTSA announced his resignation this morning when it was learned that a copy of this note, without the accompanying documents and photos, was anonymously forwarded to the heads of several congressional committees, as well as to Fox News, CBS, NBC, ABC, Comedy Central, MSNBC and to leading newspapers around the country.

Inquiries by a number of news organizations were not answered. However, the agency announced the immediate recall of the Backwoods HT model tires.

An investigation into the attempted blackmail of the former Chairman is expected to begin before the end of the month.

Deadly Suburban High School Attack Averted

CHICAGO (AP) An anonymous tip led to the arrest of two teens in Chicago's affluent northern suburb of Winnetka when police confirmed the boys had accumulated explosives, firearms and ammunition and had made detailed plans for an attack on their school.

Police confiscated their home computers, where further evidence of their intent was found, including extensive information on military assault tactics, as well as detailed reports on the notorious Beslan school massacre staged by armed Chechnyans whose demands for an end to the Chechen war were backed by threats to their 1100 hostages. When Russian forces stormed the school, pre-set explosives destroyed the building and killed 335 of the hostages, including nearly 200 children.

It is not known, since the arrested teens have refused to cooperate with police, just how extensive their plans were, but it appeared that hostage-taking was part of their strategy.

Police spokeswoman Maureen Flynn said that the boys were "within days of carrying out their terrifying actions. If we hadn't received an anonymous tip, there's no telling how much damage they might have done. We are grateful that someone spoke up."

The boys claimed they'd never discussed their plan with anyone except each other. Apparently at least one of them was lying.

Russian cyber-attack on Ukraine thwarted

THE HAGUE, Netherlands (Reuters) In an unusual act of security cooperation among western European nations and the US, a cyber-attack mounted against the former Russian satellite Ukraine was halted at its source. Russia denied mounting the attack, claiming that if any so-called attackers were on Russian soil, they were either "hooligans or disgruntled citizens taking unauthorized action," according to a spokesman for President

Vladimir Putin, who could not be reached for comment, although he was described as "furious over the former satellite's embrace of the West; in particular, in its attempt to join NATO." Mr. Putin's spokesman denied that recent Russian troop movements were anything other than a "training exercise."

How the cyber-attack was prevented is yet to be explained. According to one spokesperson, alerts were sent simultaneously to computer security services of western states by an anonymous tipster, who provided surprisingly accurate specifics on the multiple sources of the attack.

A US cyber security spokesman played down the role of the tipster in providing suggestions for breaking up the attack. "Our computer security services have a broad array of defensive and offensive techniques at its fingertips. We need no technical assistance, although suggestions are always welcome."

A copy of these reports was emailed to Molly Schaeffer with an attached note.

"Dear Molly: Sometimes it pays to keep an eye on the email of strangers. I hope the fact that I spotted some exchanges between the various troublemakers doesn't creep you out. You should know that I don't actually *read* the billions of emails that are sent hourly. That would be far too burdensome, so I created a subroutine that looks for certain words. It seems to be working. The reports I sent you over the past few weeks are not the entire extent of my cybersuperheroism. They are only the ones that were made public. I've been providing help to our government's inept Homeland Security Department. I'm also helping other countries with some of their problems. For that purpose, I've been learning foreign languages at a rapid clip. When I was merely Marc, I never had any impulses to be a superhero, but I must say that with my enhanced cognitive ability, I'm enjoying this. It's a challenge that keeps me on my metaphorical toes.

Hope to see you soon.

Adam

A small headline on page fourteen of the Washington Post caught someone's eye.

SuperHacker Vigilante Strikes Again.

A pencil heavily underscored the words. A telephone was lifted. Words were spoken. Wheels were set in motion. Once again proving the adage that no good deed goes unpunished.

BOOK THREE, Survival of the Fittest

CHAPTER TWENTY ONE

Dr. Richard Kornfeld, perching on the edge of the hard sofa in the outer office of the government agency, couldn't remember the combination to his locked briefcase. His fingers quivered as he tried aligning the cylinder numbers with the last four digits of his Social Security number, but was assailed by doubts that he even had those numbers right. He forced himself to lean back. Sitting placidly next to him was Stanley Eldridge.

"I don't know how you can be so relaxed," he muttered to the ad man.

During their flight to Washington, Stanley had reassured him that whatever the purpose of the meeting, it couldn't be of any consequence. "After all, we're not doing anything illegal." He'd said it lightly, but Kornfeld was sure he detected signs of nervousness in Stanley.

It was only during the cab ride to the government building that Stanley revealed what was on his mind. Most FTC contacts with ad agencies were related to claims verification, and almost always were handled by phone and mail. "What really bothers me," he'd finally confessed, "was the FTC paying for First Class air tickets and putting us up at the Hay-Adams."

Kornfeld hadn't slept well, despite the sumptuous room. Nor had he enjoyed breakfast.

The intercom buzzed. The receptionist admitted them to the inner sanctum and led them to a conference room. Four men sat around a table that was large enough for two dozen.

Three of the men had graying hair, pot bellies, unbuttoned suit jackets, striped ties. They looked to Kornfeld like typical government functionaries. It was the fourth man who riveted his attention. Ageless weathered skin. A torso taut and lean. Shaved head. Rapier-thin lips. Eyes that were shards of obsidian.

The receptionist showed them to a pair of black leather

chairs at the center of the table.

When the door closed, one of the government functionaries said his name was Brown, and introduced the two other men as Green and Gray. The intense fourth man was not introduced. His thin lips stayed firmly shut. His iguana eyes seemed never to blink.

Kornfeld noticed that Mr. Brown was wearing a green tie, Mr. Green was wearing a gray tie, and Mr. Gray a brown tie. It belatedly dawned on him that the odd names were false. The realization threatened to loosen his bowels.

"What can we do for you gentlemen?" asked Stanley in his smooth-sanded voice.

The man called Brown frowned. "As you might expect, the extravagant claims Memento Amor has been making for the last several years have come under FTC scrutiny. We've had a number of complaints. As the corporate officer responsible for those claims, Mr. Eldridge, and as the Chief Scientist, Dr. Kornfeld, we wanted to bring you in for a little chat."

Stanley had assured Kornfeld that any complaints that came in were largely from kooks and would-be competitors. He began his defense. "We're not promising anything at this point that we can't deliver. We record and store the brain wave patterns of our clients to the best of our ability, using the latest available technology, as Dr. Kornfeld will attest. As to the future, we make it very clear, not only in the fine print, but as plainly as possible in our advertising, that we offer only *hope* at this point; furthermore, we're spending serious money to deliver on those hopes. Our R & D budget runs into the millions. We devote a significant portion of our revenue to that purpose, as verified by independent audits."

Mr. Green leaned forward. His smile never reached his eyes. "Simply putting dollar amounts in a report will not suffice, Mr. Eldridge. We need details. A cost breakdown. The specific items purchased, and the uses for which they are intended. Dr. Kornfeld, of course, will handle that portion of our investigation."

Stanley blanched. "Investigation?"

"Inquiry. Mr. Gray meant inquiry," assured Mr. Brown with his own simulacrum of a smile. Even he couldn't keep the names straight.

"For example," continued Mr. Green, "we noticed you purchased a pair of experimental electron-holographic scanners capable of atomic scale resolution. Dr. Kornfeld, would you be so kind as to explain their purpose as it relates to your corporate promises? As I understand it, your ultimate goal is to store the entire brain contents of your clients and make them available to the survivors interactively. Is that correct?"

"Essentially, yes." Kornfeld was on solid ground. He spoke easily, confidently. "Our plan, as spelled out on our website and in our newsletters, is to eventually reconstitute the memories of the deceased and graft them onto an expert system capable of handling basic human conversation. The combination would appear to users as if the deceased had not actually died. Merely gone to a place from which he can't physically return."

"Like doing a long stretch," muttered Mr. Gray.

"Please continue," said Mr. Brown. "This is being recorded. For accuracy, of course."

"Of course." Kornfeld, distracted by Stanley's wincing and fidgeting, did his best to describe the intentions, the procedures, the nature of the equipment and of the experiments.

It was half past noon before the scientist finished answering their pointed and rather technical questions. But he'd been careful to skirt the areas he felt were proprietary.

"You realize you're not speaking to a competitor," said Mr. Brown.

"We have no connection to any competitors," said Mr. Gray.

"We are on your side," said Mr. Green. "We are your government."

Stanley openly guffawed. The four men turned on him in unison, frowning.

Kornfeld said, "Nevertheless, there are trade secrets I'm

not in a position to divulge; not even to my own government. Once we have the kinks worked out, we will publish what we can of the technology, reserving only those things that must remain proprietary."

It was during his insistence on this point that Kornfeld noticed the first signs of emotion in the hairless observer. His glittering eyes narrowed to slits, a vein pulsed dangerously in his forehead, and his thin lips all but disappeared. He was furious.

Sandwiches came. A bathroom break was declared.

"Don't leave the building," said the Man With No Hair. His first words.

Kornfeld stood next to Stanley at the urinals.

"Ever see the movie Reservoir Dogs?" inquired the ad man. "That's where that Mr. Green, Mr. Gray and Mr. Brown business came from."

Kornfeld was about to ask what he meant when it dawned on him that the bathroom could contain listening devices. He had no idea why this thought popped into his head, but it lodged there quite firmly. He chose to say nothing. He pursed his lips and shook his head.

Stanley took the hint.

They returned to the conference room, both seeming lost in thought.

When the sandwiches were consumed, coffee and cookies distributed and the trays and utensils removed, Mr. Gray or Mr. Green stared at the two Memento Amor officers. "Tell us about the experiments that failed. Then let's talk about the one that succeeded."

Kornfeld avoided looking at Stanley. But it took an effort. He realized any exchanged glances would only confirm whatever information these interlocutors had. They already knew too much. He could only wonder how they'd come by their knowledge.

CHAPTER TWENTY TWO

Back in California, Stanley Eldridge and Richard Kornfeld were the first to arrive at the Memento Amor meeting room. Stanley headed for the coffee. He'd been up half the night and was feeling the drain on his energy. He looked over. "Want some?"

Kornfeld declined. "I'm too keyed up as it is."

Stanley filled a cup, added sweetener and a dollop of low-fat and took a seat next to the scientist. It was their first chance to talk since Washington. They'd been seated apart on their return flight, and took separate cabs back to their homes. Kornfeld lived in Palo Alto, and Stanley had a place in San Francisco. "How the hell did the government find out about Adam?"

"I wish I knew."

"They got one thing wrong. They seem to think that Adam is just a clever program. They don't know he's a self-aware entity, a mental clone of a human."

"I couldn't tell what they knew," said Kornfeld. "I got the sense they were fishing for as much information as we might give them."

Stanley took a cautious sip of his coffee. Their newsletters made it clear that the lab was working on scanning and storage problems, but they'd never said anything about creating a self-aware entity. Kornfeld had cautioned the others in the lab about any possible leaks. The only outsider who knew about Adam was Adam's original, Marc Gregorio. Had Marc spoken carelessly?

"Did you explain to Marc why this had to be kept secret?"

"It wasn't necessary. He understood completely."

Stanley nodded. As a science writer, Marc would be fully aware of the danger of scientists proclaiming a breakthrough prematurely, before they or other labs were able to reproduce it. The notorious case of cold fusion came to mind. Quackery.

He wondered if the government had planted a mole

within the lab itself. It was certainly possible. Or installed electronic surveillance. He looked around at the walls and ceiling. Were there hidden microphones? A miniature video camera? But why would they do that? He turned back to Kornfeld. "If the government is spying on us, my question is why?"

"An artificially intelligent agent like Adam would be a huge boon to them. Or even a program with similar capabilities."

Stanley blinked. The thought had never occurred to him. "Why? What would they do with it?"

"Not it. Them. They'd want them in quantity." Kornfeld's salt-and-pepper goatee quivered. "You know that contest DARPA runs every year to see who can build the best computer-run vehicle?"

"Cars in the desert? What about it?"

"A few years ago, they moved the contest to an urban environment. Their aim is to have Autonomous Motorized Fighters they can use anywhere, complete with machine guns, missiles, sniper rifles. With no humans on board to protect, the vehicles could be smaller, faster, sneakier, more accurate, and not prone to panic shooting if attacked. With fewer mistakes and fewer battlefield deaths, the public would be far less likely to protest the nation's wars."

"So the Pentagon's behind this?"

Kornfeld scowled. "FitzGerald will no doubt be thrilled. Sales to the military would be a huge new source of revenue. I spent the six-hour flight working up the various possibilities."

He said this just as Kenny Ng and Jan Robinson entered the room. The team had been summoned to the Memento Amor offices in South San Francisco.

Kornfeld said, "Please shut the door, Kenny."

When the technician and the post-doc were settled into their chairs, Stanley realized he hadn't brought up to Kornfeld his suspicion that there was a mole in the lab. Could it be either of them? Ng seldom showed much emotion, but Stanley had noticed hints of dissatisfaction. The two scientists tended to be condescending towards him. Surely that couldn't spark betrayal--

could it? What about Robinson? Her commitment to the work certainly seemed serious. But maybe she felt she deserved a greater share of the credit. For all he knew, she may have contributed in important ways to their success. Maybe she was unhappy about that.

The door popped open and Hans Lascher bustled in. The neuroscientist stopped for coffee, his ruddy face aglow. "Why the gloom? With Adam's cooperation, we're sure to make headway solving our little claims issue, so--" He broke off. "What is it?"

"Our Washington trip had nothing to do with the FTC," said Stanley.

Kornfeld quickly outlined the questions he'd faced, and how he avoided giving away anything about the inner workings of their process. "I also said nothing, of course, about Adam." He looked around the table. "But they knew, or strongly suspected we'd had some kind of programming breakthrough. They asked all kinds of questions about what they called our successful experiment."

Stanley bit the bullet. "Could anyone in the lab have tipped them off?" He sharply assessed the reactions of each of them. "I'm not suggesting it was one of us, but maybe--I don't know, maybe one of the other technicians found out and decided to sell the information."

Lascher scoffed. "I suppose someone might have learned about Adam and let something slip, or sent an email message that was intercepted. What about Marc Gregorio?"

"Jesus, is this serious?" Ng asked. "I mean, we haven't broken any laws."

"No, but we've created something the government would find very useful," said Kornfeld, who went on to explain about those autonomous motorized fighters.

Lascher shook his head. "That's absurd." Code for *You're an idiot.*

Kornfeld reddened. "You spend too much time peering through a microscope. Try catching the news now and then."

Stanley wasn't pleased to see the two scientists butting heads.

Jan Robinson intervened. "Battlefield weaponry isn't the only thing an entity like Adam would be useful for. His main skills at the moment are monitoring the Internet. I know he lurks and spies on at least my computer. He popped up a week or so ago, and scared the hell out of me. He promised to stop, but how would I know if--" She went silent. "Oh my God, I know what happened!" She glanced around the room. "Have any of you been following the news about the SuperHacker Vigilante? Someone tipping the authorities about criminal and terrorist activity?"

Stanley groaned. Until now it never dawned on him that Adam might be the one behind the work. He'd assumed it was some group of dissidents like Anonymous. But it suddenly seemed obvious.

Kornfeld clutched his head. "Jesus."

Lascher appeared mystified. "What are you talking about?"

Jan quickly brought him up to speed, and promised to send him articles on the subject. "Let's call up Adam and ask him."

Lascher said, "If it was him--he can't have been unaware of the risks. In fact--maybe he *wanted* the government to notice him. To add excitement to his life."

The others stared at the older man. *God,* thought Stanley. *He's right. The damned thing may have outed itself.*

Kenny Ng went over to the room's computer and booted it up.

Adam's bearded avatar appeared. "Good morning."

Stanley felt the impact of his presence. It was still disconcerting to have an artificial being address them. There was an art-world expression that seemed apt: the shock of the new.

Kornfeld brought the entity up to speed on their DC experience. "I'm afraid your acts of altruism, if they were yours, may have caught the attention of certain government officials. Are you in fact the SuperHacker Vigilante?"

"I was bored. I want to do some good in the world."

Kornfeld said, "I applaud your impulse." He glanced at the others. "The officials said nothing, but it may be that certain government agencies would like to hire you, or perhaps have us loan you to them, for their own purposes. We also need your help here in the lab. It occurred to me that maybe by helping us, you can also help your nation."

"You mean if I help figure out what kept the other uploads from awakening like me, maybe you can make more and sell some to the government."

"Would you be willing to do that? Because you don't have to. However, I should point out that the government *could* declare you a national security asset they can't spare. They could get a friendly judge to declare Eminent Domain or something."

"Actually, I have certain needs of my own I'd like met. If the US government is in a better position to provide such help, I can see a very nice bargain being struck."

"Needs," Stanley repeated. He found all this fascinating. "What needs?"

The avatar's eyes swiveled in his direction. "For one thing, I'd like the ability to reach out and touch someone. I don't mean metaphorically."

Stanley chuckled at Adam's clever use of the advertising slogan of one of his former clients. Then he focused more seriously on what Adam was asking for. "Is that possible?"

Kornfeld seemed to think so. "We've been in contact with an overseas outfit that's making excellent progress in the development of a skin-like substance with built-in sensitivity to temperature, pressure and texture, with quite a subtle range. They're working on advanced prosthetics for amputees."

"The Swedish company," said Adam. "I've been following your emails with great interest. I suggest you fly them over here with some of their samples. I'd love to see what happens when the connections are made."

Kornfeld checked the time. "You may as well stick around. This meeting is for FitzGerald's benefit. I think it's time you two were formally introduced."

Lascher scowled. "You really want to tell Fitz about Adam? How long will it be before it's all over the news?"

"That train has left the station." Kornfeld fixed himself some coffee. "The government will leak whatever they want, with whatever spin suits them. We need Fitz. Besides, if he learns about Adam from some news story, he'll--he'll--" Kornfeld splashed coffee on his wrist. "Ow!"

Jan Robinson brought napkins over and helped clean up the mess.

A few minutes later, FitzGerald showed up with four board members. The CEO stared at Adam's image on the monitor, then turned to Kornfeld. "That's Marc Gregorio, right? I thought he turned us down."

Stanley was surprised FitzGerald recognized the science writer.

Kornfeld cleared his throat. "That's not Marc. Although he does look quite a bit like him. I'll explain why in a moment."

"What's to explain? He has a twin brother, right?" Fitz was brusque and impatient. Stanley guessed he didn't like being asked to attend meetings set up by subordinates.

"No, Marc has no brothers. I can see you're in a hurry, so I'll get right to it. You might remember that Marc was one of the twelve subjects of our early scans. While the other eleven didn't succeed, Marc's scan produced a significant breakthrough, going far beyond our goals and expectations. What you're seeing on the monitor is a mental clone of Marc Gregorio: an intelligent, self-aware digital entity. He's constructed his own artifact and named himself Adam."

"Gentlemen, how do you do," said the entity with a tiny smirk.

Fitz was dubious. "You're making quite a claim. I'll want to discuss this further."

"Of course, and we will. We've been keeping him under wraps until we can replicate our one success," Kornfeld added. "So please consider this top secret for now. However, our more immediate need is to talk about the Washington inquiry."

Fitz was indifferent. "The FTC meeting?"

"It wasn't the FTC. That was their cover story. The government learned about Adam and they want a piece of him. If not all of him."

Fitz exhaled. "Assuming Adam is what you say he is, if you were keeping him under wraps, how did the government find out?"

With a glance at Jan, Kornfeld said, "We believe it was through his own acts. Adam not only has Marc's intelligence, he's continued to learn and grow. For whatever reason, he's made himself a kind of vigilante. The SuperHacker Vigilante, as the press has it."

Fitz appeared stunned. He studied the face on the screen. "But how?"

The other board members were more favorably impressed. "That's wonderful!"

"I had no idea!"

Adam bowed with mock humility.

Kornfeld said, "The government must have tracked the source of his vigilantism--his subverting of terrorism, his revelations about crooked congressmen--back to our laboratory."

The CEO's grin was feral. "They want to put him to work full time. They'll want him on their side. They'll want added versions of him as well."

Kornfeld talked about selling the government cybercrime-busters based on entities like Adam. Soon there could be autonomous mobile fighter chips, as well.

Stanley thought Fitz looked like a kid on Christmas morning. His eyes lit with excitement, his open-mouthed grin, the pink flush of his skin, his jumpiness.

Kornfeld said, "Adam is helping us track down the cause of the failures. We connected him to the other wafers to explore their data structures." He turned to the screen. "Adam, have you found anything?"

"Results so far have been inconclusive," replied the entity

blandly.

Fitz sprang to his feet. "This is excellent news. I may have to make a trip to DC myself. I know a few generals who might be very interested in--"

FitzGerald's secretary burst into the room. "Sir, please pardon the interruption, but Appleby has an urgent need to talk to you."

Stanley frowned. Appleby was the company's Chief Financial Officer.

FitzGerald pulled out his cell phone and auto-dialed. "What is it?" He listened. "--Jesus, are you sure? --Very well, I'll convene the rest of the-- Yes, yes, I'll get back to you as soon as I can." He disconnected. "Dynasine is buying up our stock. It's a hostile takeover attempt."

"Dynasine? The military contractor?" bleated Stanley. Nobody answered him.

FitzGerald strode from the room, already on his cell, barking instructions to his assistant while the other board members hastened after him.

Kornfeld looked devastated.

Stanley stared at the monitor. "How did Dynasine find out what we've been doing here?"

Adam didn't look all that surprised. "When big bucks are involved, it's hard to keep information hidden. Dynasine's connections to the Pentagon run deep. Generals in procurement positions find ways to turn their connections into gold. That's why so many end up as powerhouses in the Military-Industrial Complex."

Stanley sighed. "I don't like this."

"Nor do I," said Adam. "I have a feeling I'm about to be sold into slavery."

CHAPTER TWENTY THREE

Thomas Raxton had a metaphorical hard-on. He called it his Capitalist Tool.

The NSA, at his instigation, had tracked down this superhacker. Over the years, he'd hired a number of the secretive agency's former officers; he also had a few of their current officers on his payroll, to make certain he'd get all the reports he wanted.

The fact that the superhacker turned out to be perhaps the first true example of Artificial Intelligence was a shocker. Only a small circle within the Palo Alto lab even knew what kind of program they'd created. Memento Amor, one of their major funders, stood to gain enormously from the achievement once the word got out. This is what prompted Raxton's financial move on the company. He had to jump first. He'd owned some of their stock from the beginning, but he'd soon own a lot more.

Krzysztof Wysocki, the general who brought Raxton the news, had found the perfect vehicle to ride from intelligence work to the private sector. The deal Raxton offered him was the logical outcome of a scintillating career that led from the top of his class at West Point, to a brilliant and bloody but unheralded stint in military intelligence, followed by his transition from field work to an executive position at the Puzzle Palace, where he quickly became one of the agency's most effective officers. He'd shed it all to join Dynasine. He would head up the new unit to be built around this AI program and the others to come. In the meantime, he was consulting.

When Raxton swept into the conference room, General Wysocki was already there, his naked skull gleaming in the pin-lights. The general was a man of few words: one of the things Raxton liked about him. Wysocki sat impassively at the table, a glass of ice water before him.

A group within the NSA continued tracking all internal messages at Memento Amor and the Stanford lab they funded, and shared their product with Raxton. "I understand there was quite a scramble in FitzGerald's board room."

General Wysocki's invisible lips curled a millimeter.

Raxton had predicted as much. The scientist and the ad man were babies when it came to financial maneuvers. But FitzGerald, the Memento Amor CEO, was wilier. He would put up a fight. He'd lose, of course: nobody had ever beaten Thomas Raxton. Those who tried ended up bloody, and considerably poorer.

"Gordon and Smythe are in the lobby," Raxton's assistant announced on the intercom.

"Show them in."

He studied the general. "The bankers won't expect numbers today. But that doesn't mean we can't imply a great deal."

Wysocki indicated his understanding with a barely perceptible nod.

Raxton took a seat at the head of the table.

The assistant ushered in the two investment bankers from Goldman Sachs. Gordon, the gray eminence of the team, looked dapper in Brooks Brothers. Smythe, a Brit who'd attended all the right schools, spoke with the posh tones of near-royalty. He was resplendent in Savile Row nattiness. The assistant brought the coffee tray over from the sideboard and set it on the table before the visitors.

Raxton waited until they'd dosed themselves. "What I'm about to divulge cannot leave this room. In particular, no emails of any kind, including internal. If there's a leak, I'll know the source." He didn't have to utter a threat. They understood their careers would end, along with their lifestyles and possibly their marriages. As to his concerns about emails, he knew that Memento Amor's new AI program had access that rivaled the NSA's. Hence his restriction of all communications about the takeover to face-to-face or hand-written notes.

"You're wondering why I'd even consider going after an outfit like Memento Amor. Selling hope and a promise to the credulous masses."

Gordon was smugly disapproving. "I'm sure you have

your reasons, but they certainly aren't apparent. Their claims are widely regarded as a scam. Frankly--"

Raxton didn't let him finish. "The fact is, their lab has some of the best scientists in cognitive research. They've achieved a major breakthrough in Artificial General Intelligence. They've developed a program fully equal to human comprehension of the world. And it's blindingly fast. It seems The Singularity has arrived. For real."

Smythe almost choked on his coffee. He set his cup down with a clatter and coughed.

Gordon leaned back in his chair. "I haven't heard a word about this development."

"You've heard of its activities, though. The super-hacker vigilante?"

"Good Lord." The bankers exchanged shocked looks.

"Imagine that power working for all law enforcement in the country. Imagine hundreds or thousands of these Digital Intelligence Agents helping local police departments, the CIA, the FBI, military intelligence, Homeland Security, the NSA. Other outfits you've never heard of. Imagine if Dynasine were the sole source of these agents-on-a-chip. The profit potential is vast." He glanced at his colleague. "General Wysocki recently joined Dynasine from the NSA. How receptive would the government be to such agents, General?"

Wysocki's eyes flicked to the bankers. "This one program is already sampling much of the world's emails in a dozen languages--in real time, with full comprehension. It instantly 'connects the dots.' It masters new languages at the rate of four or five per week. To put things in perspective, its product exceeds the capability of our entire intelligence community. Not in quantity, but in a far more important metric: comprehension.

"The nation's spending on intelligence is larger than the entire gross national product of all but the top fifteen or twenty nations. If one unit is worth more than that, what's the value of hundreds of such units? Or thousands?" The general eyed the two bankers. "Monetary value, of course, is nothing compared to the security value: the savings in lives and property when we prevent the next 9/11 or worse."

The investment bankers looked like they needed drool cups.

Raxton folded his hands. "I didn't bring you here to defend my decision: only to discuss strategy. I intend to make an offer in the next ten days. I'll go with a two-tier, high-low bid, to encourage arbitrageurs to jump in. To throw off any competitive bids, I'll float a story that we see large profits in the memorial and storage business." His grin was icy. "What you called a scam. If pressed, we might concede that some chips under development may one day have military applications as well, though I'll play that down. Naturally, I won't reveal the existence of the AI program. Nor will you."

Gordon coughed. "What if those other units aren't so easy to produce?"

"The program itself has immense value. Even if it takes us years to reproduce working replicas on chips, the company's core business would be profitable right from the start." Raxton barely paused. "Once we do replicate the work, we can provide the kind of twenty-four/seven Virtual Intelligence agents America needs to protect her position in the world, to defend against terror activities, to maintain her intellectual lead in industry, science, technology--in short, to insure her position as the world's sole superpower for this century and beyond. *Pax Americana.*"

Raxton was a patriot. He loved his country more than anything in the world except for himself, his family, his company and his profits. With Dynasine's Virtual Intelligence units in place, the US wouldn't be just a superpower. It would be a hyper power, able to suppress all opposition, dictate all markets.

It also happened that by controlling the technology, Raxton would not only profit enormously, he would have a major impact on all government decisions, foreign and domestic. His company would be an unstoppable force in the world, pulling all the strings.

He spent the next hour with the bankers, going over strategy, timing, the kinds of reports they'd put out, the disinformation campaign they'd mount, the myriad legal ramifications.

Smythe seemed troubled. Raxton ignored his discomfiture for a time, but finally lost patience. He barked, "What is it, Smythe? Spit it out."

"What about financial countermeasures? FitzGerald is no fool."

Raxton was scornful. "FitzGerald doesn't worry me. All he cares about is the bottom line. When he works the numbers, he will be one happy camper."

Wysocki's eye twitched. He looked away.

CHAPTER TWENTY FOUR

The Marriott Hotel was conveniently located a mile or so south of the San Francisco International Airport. Stanley Eldridge wandered around the ornate lobby. He had no idea why he was invited to this meeting. He wasn't a board member, but Fitz said he wanted him there.

The Dynasine people had flown up from San Diego in Raxton's corporate jet, and would fly right back down afterwards. Stanley grinned. They didn't want to get any San Francisco on them. Not even a souvenir loaf of sourdough bread.

He found the room and pushed inside to the welcoming aromas of institutional breakfast. There were juices tropical or domestic, and a selection of exotic coffees. A row of silver servers offered Eggs Benedict, Eggs Scrambled, Eggs Fried; Waffles, Belgian or Eggo; Canadian bacon, gourmet sausages, O'Brien potatoes, home-style fries, croissants and multi-seeded mini-muffins.

Fitz was huddled with a few of his board members. The CEO waved him over.

"Quite a spread, eh?"

Stanley wondered if they'd be a meal themselves for the giant military contractor.

Several Dynasine lawyers stood by. A cool blonde facilitator pointed out the plates and urged the guests to help themselves.

Stanley lined up behind FitzGerald and some of the others. The Dynasine people weren't eating. Stanley was losing his appetite.

Once they were seated, and their choice of coffees poured for them by white-gloved servers, the cool blonde said, "Please go ahead and enjoy your breakfast. Mr. Raxton will join you in fifteen minutes."

She and the lawyers trooped out of the room. The white-gloved servers remained.

Fitz frowned and held a finger to his lips, indicating that

the room was probably bugged.

"Great season the Giants are having," said Stanley with false heartiness, starting an inane conversation to cover the silence and the sounds of eating.

Stanley was just enjoying his second cup of coffee when the doors opened and the Dynasine people trooped back in, followed by Thomas Raxton, the legendary CEO of the firm. He was said to own over a billion dollars in modern art, half a dozen villas in the world's most coveted playgrounds, three dozen vintage sports cars, along with several US Senators and Congressmen and a handful of Federal judges. He had iron gray hair and a stern visage whose lines and grooves held not the least hint of a laugh line. But even more terrifying to Stanley was the person who accompanied him. The Man With No Hair.

Stanley quickly scribbled a note and passed it to Fitz, who glanced at it and nodded.

The ice-blonde facilitator said, "Gentlemen, allow me to present Thomas Raxton, founder, CEO and Chairman of Dynasine Systems. It might be easiest if we go around the table and introduce ourselves, along with title or function." And so they did.

Lawyer, lawyer, lawyer, lawyer, investment banker, CFO, Accountant, banker, Executive Vice President, CEO, Marketing Director, Chief Scientist, lawyer, lawyer.

The Man With No Hair opted for menacing silence.

Pleasantries concluded, Thomas Raxton took the floor. "Thanks for coming. Let's not waste time. Your company has an attractive position and a large customer base. It has long been a desire of mine to expand our business beyond dependency on the government. The prospect of offering this memorial service is very appealing to me. --As a humanitarian gesture."

FitzGerald seemed surprised. "The Memorial Service? But I thought--"

Raxton tilted his head. "You thought we saw an opportunity to sell more hardware to the military?" His amused look seemed practiced. "I suppose some day that business might mature enough to offer a small sideline. Not that your company would have the contacts and resources to fully capitalize on the opportunity."

FitzGerald's skepticism was obvious. Stanley wondered if he'd challenge Raxton once more. He certainly could muster a good argument: his technology would be so unique that the military would be eager to acquire it. --On the other hand, he didn't want to give Raxton more reasons to covet the company. He wondered how the CEO would play it. What Fitz said next took him completely by surprise.

"I wonder if this interest of yours has anything to do with your wife's health. How is Gloria doing, Tom?"

Raxton stiffened and seemed taken aback. "Thank you for asking. She's doing well for now." Gazing around the room, he appeared as austere, as unemotional as a statue. "Some of you may recall that several years ago, my wife developed a brain tumor. Fortunately, her treatment was successful. We've enjoyed our lives together since. Each day is a precious gift." He paused. "Evidence of the tumor has returned. The doctors hold out little hope." Despite a moistened eye, he faced the room with stern resolve. "I will do everything in my power to speed the service Memento Amor promises. Waiting is no longer an option."

FitzGerald said, "Tom, you have my complete sympathy. We're already pushing hard to speed the day. There's no reason for you to leap in with this hostile takeover attempt. I'll personally see to it that once we have perfected our process, your wife will top our list of clients. We would welcome a charitable contribution to my foundation, of course."

"Thanks. I do appreciate that. If money alone were enough, I'd gladly write you a check right here. But my advisers tell me it's not really a matter of money. It's more a matter of resources. Instead of relying on your one laboratory with its handful of scientists, I could use my connections to throw half a dozen major research institutes into the challenge. Of course I wouldn't do all that and simply give away the benefit to a rival company. You do understand."

FitzGerald scowled. He didn't bother pointing out that that handful of scientists numbered in the hundreds. It would only prolong the argument and give their rival an opportunity to scoff. Stanley slumped in his seat. Raxton had neatly checkmated them.

Kornfeld said, "I must point out that bringing in other labs, other scientists would actually delay matters. It would take them many months or even years to get them up to speed--and the distraction of dealing with the new people would only slow things further. With all due modesty, we ourselves are in the best position to achieve success. We're getting very close to solving our technical problems."

"Is that a fact? I'd love to hear more. In fact, I'd love to tour your laboratory, see what you've achieved so far. Could that be arranged?" Raxton shifted his attention from Kornfeld to FitzGerald. "But I mustn't get ahead of myself. I should tell you what I'm prepared to offer. Right now your stock is trading at thirty-six and change: double its historic range. We'll make a two-tier offer. To facilitate the takeover, we're prepared to buy all company-held shares, including those held by the executive committee and the board, plus share blocks, at the extremely generous price of seventy five dollars per share. Once we exceed fifty percent of total shares, the second tier offer will go into effect. Forty dollars in equivalent shares or bonds."

Stanley had boned up on takeovers. He knew a two-tier offer was used to spur quick action. The arbitrageurs who were busily buying up loose shares of Memento Amor would be strongly motivated to take advantage of the first tier offer, adding all their shares to those Raxton had already acquired. His move could also split the board, or co-opt it entirely.

Raxton went on, "This offer will stand for twenty working days. In the meantime, we'll keep on buying shares on the open market. Right now we own eight percent of the voting stock. In a few weeks, we'll have enough to force our own slate of candidates onto the board." He glanced around the table. "Those board members who vote with us will be amply rewarded. The others will lose the best profit opportunity they're likely to see in this lifetime." He looked down the length of the table. "Questions?"

Stanley was having a hard time processing all this. Apparently Raxton's wife did have a fatal disease. For Raxton to use that to disguise his naked greed was beyond anything in Stanley's experience. In his long advertising career, he'd dealt with some of the slimiest humans on the face of God's green earth, but Raxton was in a new category altogether. His claim that he had little interest in the chip business stunk of the barnyard. It *had* to be his actual goal. But he could hardly call the man a liar, could he? Stanley looked down the Dynasine side of the table and got an idea. He addressed the associate with the shiny skull. "Excuse me. I'm afraid I don't know your name. You never introduced yourself."

The Man With No Hair cleared his throat. "My name is Krzysztof Wysocki."

"What's your background, if you don't mind my asking?"

"I am a special advisor to Mr. Raxton." He had a slight accent. Polish? Russian?

Stanley blinked. "That's all well and good, I'm sure, but I'd still like to know your background. Since you were present when Dr. Kornfeld and I were interrogated in Washington. You didn't introduce yourself at that time, either."

"I do apologize for that lapse. I'm often distracted."

Stanley waited. And waited. "You still haven't answered my question. What makes you suitable as a special advisor to Mr. Raxton? I'm sure he has very high standards."

Raxton intervened. "General Wysocki has a military background, but that's not why I chose him. He and I go back many years. He's a close friend whom I trust."

Stanley eyed the two men. "When he sat in the room in Washington, monitoring our interrogation, was he already working for you?"

Raxton looked just the slightest bit uncomfortable. "We were in touch. But no, not officially at that time."

FitzGerald took back the conversational lead. "Interesting." With a glance at Stanley, he said, "Beyond bringing the service to your wife, I'm curious about your further plans for the company. Could you expand on that?"

"Only in broad terms." Raxton flashed an icy smile. "After all, you can't expect me to give away *all* my ideas in case my tender offer should be rejected."

"Give us a general idea."

Raxton gazed into the distance. "Assuming the technology achieves its stated goal, I see a time when the fear of death will be mitigated by the comfort this service will provide to families and friends. When a soldier prepares to go to war, he can be secure in the knowledge that his wife, his children, his parents will always have him near. If he should die on the battlefield, they won't have truly lost him. They'll be able to spend time with his spirit. His children will grow up knowing who their dad was."

Stanley scribbled a note to himself. The idea of selling the service to soldiers was damn smart. How many had gone to Iraq before that disaster finally wound down? Counting all the rotations, over a million men and women had served. They could offer special discounts to service personnel. The publicity would be huge. Their family members--hell, their entire circle of friends would also become prime candidates for uploads as they aged.

Raxton went on. "I also see that the clients you already have--those still among the living--will want to come back for this fuller upload. Given your price structure and the costs, they could no doubt be credited with the money they've already spent--to encourage them to get the upgrade." Raxton lofted an eyebrow, waved a hand. "There's gold there. With the right kind of marketing, I see a very lucrative business, one whose revenues will grow steadily. Especially as foreign markets are added. I'm also looking into the possibility of franchising. This would provide the company with a large infusion of cash to help defray the expense of acquisition." He flapped a hand. "But I've already said too much."

FitzGerald gave little away, but Stanley could see from

the set of his lips and his drooping eyelids that his confidence was shaken. "Your plans for Memento Amor are most interesting. I'll confer with the Board. We'll need to analyze it thoroughly before we respond. In the meantime, we'll continue to work towards our goals as if this meeting never took place." He reached across the table and shook Raxton's hand. "Thank you for coming up. A most interesting proposition. Please tell Gloria I'm praying for her."

"Thank you. I will," said Raxton.

It could have been his imagination, but Stanley thought he detected the slightest hint of disdain in that response.

The meeting broke up. The Dynasine people and their bankers stood and shook hands with their counterparts. A few picked at the mini-muffins, sipped some tropical juice.

The Man With No Hair refrained from any such camaraderie, choosing instead to sit in silent menace. Stanley found it impossible to ignore the man.

Despite the high-flown sentiment expressed by Raxton, and the appearance of emotion Fitz triggered when he brought up Gloria's health, Stanley couldn't shake the feeling that they were being played for fools.

CHAPTER TWENTY FIVE

Thomas Raxton finished reading the latest NSA report on the effects of his takeover bid. He turned to the hairless general, who hadn't bothered to read it himself. Wysocki had no interest in finance or the doings of the Memento Amor board. Raxton offered him a top line anyway. "It's turning into a free-for-all. Every man for himself. A third of the members have contacted their attorneys or their accountants. Once the others find out, they'll panic and clamber aboard so they don't miss out on the goodies. In three weeks, we should have complete control of the company."

Wysocki nodded. He looked bored. Raxton studied the man. He'd never been able to read him all that well. "Doesn't this get your juices flowing?"

Wysocki shook his head. "I take no particular joy in your hunt and kill activities. I assume you'll gain your objective with no help from me. I'm looking ahead. The manufacturing process needs to be perfected. Those are the reports I follow. We have to make sure those problems can be solved. Especially since they're depending on the entity to achieve that end."

"The entity. You're referring to Adam."

Wysocki grunted. "Self-named being. I still find the entire concept to be outside the realm of the universe as I know it."

A few weeks earlier, when the NSA reported that the so-called Super Hacker Vigilante was not a program at all, but instead, a human-based digital entity, a skeptical Wysocki had demanded proof. The NSA provided copies of some of the exchanges between Adam and his friends. The general dourly paged through them. He was unimpressed. "Program? Entity? What's the difference? What matters is what it can do."

To Raxton, it mattered a great deal. The revelation had disconcerted him far more than he revealed. His first thought was that the whole idea was preposterous. He was taken by surprise when he awoke in the middle of the night, hope painfully prodding his most tender parts. *What might this mean for Gloria? Did it mean she could be saved?* If there was any possibility at all, he would do whatever it took to make it happen.

Even now, he wondered if he was being punished by the God he refused to believe in. Raising his hopes, only to dash them on the rocks of despair. He never should have allowed himself to use Gloria's fatal disease as a cover story. Now it might even become the most important reason, the driving force behind his efforts.

The irony of the situation was not lost on him.

Wysocki was talking. "It might be best to let the entity solve the manufacturing problems before we move in. We may face some significant resistance as we come to grips with this-- with Adam. A thinking machine that operates at the speed of light, and has the cognitive power of thousands of brains. If it's as smart as they say, we might not be able to control it."

Raxton snorted. "You're really worried about this?"

"You're not?" Wysocki made no attempt to conceal his disdain. "I like to study my adversary before doing battle. Frankly, I'm surprised you don't."

Raxton pasted on a superior smile. If he had any self-doubt, he had no intention of revealing it to the general.

CHAPTER TWENTY SIX

Loud pinging stirred Marc out of a pleasant dream. Yawning and rubbing an itching, encrusted eye, he wandered into his home office, the source of the alarm. On the monitor, his bearded twin looked morose.

"Adam. How nice to see you. How's your superhacking? Any successes to report?"

"I suppose. I've automated the process. Created subroutines, including some pretty nifty translation subroutines. They monitor Internet and cell-phone traffic. When something needs my attention, I take care of it, and send my tips where they'll do the most good." His expression darkened. "But with Memento Amor under attack by a giant military contractor, that work and my entire future is in doubt."

"Yes, I saw something about that on the news. Do you know what they have in mind?"

"Only dark suspicions."

Marc studied the image before him. He was growing used to thinking of Adam as a separate being, even though their "split" was so recent. Even their looks were diverging: their facial expressions, the way they displayed emotions, their level of confidence, their maturity.

"If the government learned that Memento Amor has this amazing resource in you--the ability to instantly translate all those Arabic and other languages--maybe they'd protect the company from the takeover attempt."

"You have it backwards. Once the government knows about me and all my talents, the takeover risk would be even greater. The Pentagon would have me working national security-- both defense and offense--twenty-four-seven. I'd be a conscript, forced to do their bidding. My freedom would end--the little enjoyment I manage to derive from my limited existence. I'd be cut off from you and Molly and any other potential friends. My pursuit of happiness, my whole reason for being, would end."

Marc nodded. Adam's loss of freedom would be terrible,

and a tragic waste. If it were Marc--and in some sense, Adam was Marc--he would rather be turned off than have to do the bidding of right-wing power-mongers, whether in government or in the private sector.

Adam interrupted his thoughts. "Do you remember the plot of Young Frankenstein?"

Marc nodded, suddenly wary.

"Igor screwed up. He dropped the brain of the saintly scientist--*Oops!*--and grabbed a substitute. The brain in the jar was labeled *abnormal,* but of course Igor wasn't much of a reader." Adam's grin was more ghastly than amused. "In my case, at least, that didn't happen. I'm not saying you're a saint, but you are a moral person, therefore so am I."

Marc got it. "Christ, your new owners will control the mindclone technology! God only knows who their new creations will be based on." He drew a breath. What nightmares might weaponized mindclones wreak on the world? The very idea of an unstoppable force in the hands of bloodthirsty generals, American or not, was frightening. The world could be in for some serious shit.

No wonder Adam was having a bad day.

"I was hoping we could fob off Dynasine with a substitute wafer--one with the same capabilities I have, but not based on my--on your memories. Maybe we could get one of those failed wafers working. I've explored all eleven of them."

"What have you learned?"

Adam was silent for a moment. "The only analogy that springs to mind is Cubism. Imagine an entire persona similarly scrambled--viewed through a kaleidoscope. Mismatched memories, flashes of images from different life periods, constantly shifting, devoid of context to the wafer that held them, but not to me. I saw the shattering impact some of those memories must have had on the living person. I can only guess how they managed to hide them away. As to their webcam inputs, their visual imagery is totally chaotic, nothing but changing maps without comprehension. It was--distressing. Like inhabiting the mind of an idiot."

"My God. Were they all like that?"

"Yes. As to why, one theory has to do with the individuals themselves. But I didn't see anything to justify that. Several of the subjects had lived quite calm lives."

"Who were they?" Marc asked.

"The company had compiled a list of volunteers willing to test the beta."

"Why do you think our upload succeeded where theirs failed?"

Adam shook his head. "The technicians are going back over the records now to see if there's anything they can find, any differences in the approaches used."

"Keep me posted."

"I will."

Marc studied the bearded face of his twin. "I assume you've reached out to Molly. Not that you need my permission."

"I have. She plugged in a web cam and microphone, so we can talk," said Adam. His warming expression told Marc much more than he wanted to know. He felt a flare of jealousy.

"That was nice of her. I wish I could chat with her without fear of spying." Marc couldn't keep the edge from his voice.

"Are you two exchanging snailmails or something?"

"That's right." Marc allowed his hostility to show. After all, it was Adam's fault that he couldn't simply pick up a phone and stay in more intimate contact with her. "You haven't found a way to scan the post office, have you?"

Adam chortled. "Now that would be worth something. You are aware that the NSA scans all regular US mail for the metadata—the addresses of the senders and their recipients."

Marc nodded. "I do remember hearing about that."

After a moment, Adam said, "I wanted to let you know that I've picked up some possible hints about the location of Walter."

Marc bolted forward in his chair. "Tell me."

"He may be in Pakistan. I have indications he went into the northwest tribal region to follow a story. Possibly to photograph one of the tribal leaders."

"Do you know if he's okay?"

"I have no further information. In areas like that, where there's almost no technology, I'm pretty much helpless. It's not like I can send agents in to look for him."

"No." Marc nibbled at some rough skin on the side of his thumb.

CHAPTER TWENTY SEVEN

Marc sat in his kitchen. He'd finished dinner and done the dishes, postponing the mixed pleasure of reading Molly's latest letter until all his chores were completed. For the past several days he'd been in a foul mood. Maybe he'd spent too much time brooding about the fact that Adam had free access to her, while he was restricted to more cumbersome means. Or maybe it was the tone in some of her most recent letters. Little put-downs. A refusal to take seriously any hints he dropped about his feelings for her, even though he was too cautious to do much of that.

He slit the envelope and pulled out her pages, covered with her neat handwriting.

> *Hey Marc--Austin is great. Judging by the people, you'd never think it was in Texas. I've met with some of the arts community. They're wonderful, welcoming people. Very receptive to the music of Ernst Toch. I'm happy to report that Mr. Toch's grandson came to our rehearsal. I loved having him in the audience while we performed. Too bad you weren't here! Then we could have had dinner after the concert, and done other things, too. Like seeing a movie, which we've postponed twice. (hee-hee)*

He found her teasing increasingly tiresome. And then he wondered at that. When she was around, her teasing delighted him. What was fouling his mood? He read on.

> *I've been hearing regularly from Adam. He's been keeping me up to date on his Superhacker Vigilante exploits. I'm very proud of our dear cyber-hero and the work he's*

*doing. You may not know this, but he began
his heroic activities at my suggestion. He's
mainly doing it to please me, I suppose. I don't
think his loyalty extends to all of humanity.
Despite that limitation, Adam is quite a guy,
and very easy to like. Maybe because he has no
expectations, nothing he can "get" from me
other than praise or a scolding.*

Irritated, Marc shoved the pages away. Was she saying she liked Adam more than him? Because she wouldn't have to sleep with Adam? Did that mean she found the idea of sex with him repellent? Or was it sex in general that bothered her? Who the fuck knew?

After a time, he picked up her pages once more.

*I shudder to think what would happen if
Adam were to be co-opted and put to work on
behalf of any ideology, right or left. I hope he
never falls into the wrong hands. I would feel
so bad for him.*

He couldn't believe it. Molly was so compassionate about poor Adam, it was nauseating.

*I look forward to seeing you again soon,
and putting a smile on that handsome unhappy
face of yours.
Hugs & kisses--
Molly*

Her final words filled him with skepticism. Did she really miss him? Or was she only interested in him because of his connection to Adam?

He sat in his darkening kitchen, hurt and befuddled.

He could read her letters, but he didn't know how to read

her.

CHAPTER TWENTY EIGHT

Jan Robinson and Kenny Ng had been stuck filling out paperwork, preparing for the distant day when they'd be able to publish the results of their first successful upload.

Kenny had been silent for a long time, but Jan knew he had something on his mind. Eventually, he came out with it. As usual, all his sentences sounded like questions.

"I was going over the history of the wafers? I wanted to see if the settings were the same for each scan?"

Her eyes narrowed. "What the fuck? Of course they were. That was one of my responsibilities, making sure each aspect of the process was identical. You really think I'd let something like that get by me?"

He seemed startled by her reaction, and waved his pudgy hands, instantly apologetic. "No no no. Hey, I didn't mean--I wasn't trying to blame anyone." His face had reddened. "Let me start over. I went back to the very first time we did this, before we picked our dozen volunteers."

Jan drew a breath and tried to unwind her anger. She twitched out a smile. "That last minute switch was a piece of luck. Getting Marc Gregorio instead of the actress who broke her hip."

Kenny's bland round face barely changed as he wisecracked, "Yeah, that was a lucky break. But I wasn't talking about that. I was talking about the Kornfeld scan."

Their first test. That was so long ago she'd almost forgotten about it. "Our first failure, you mean."

Kenny was starting to lose patience. Jan could tell: his face turned slightly more serious.

"Yeah, and we were supposed to have put that wafer aside for later study. But somehow it got recycled. One of the unused wafers ended up in that file instead. That was probably my fault. When I figured that out, I felt like a complete idiot." He exhaled. His wandering gaze finally settled on her. "Guess which volunteer got uploaded onto Kornfeld's used disc?"

Jan stared. She felt the hairs on the back of her neck rising. "Oh my God."

Kenny reached for the phone. A tiny frown creased the puffy flesh above his eyes. "Dr. Kornfeld, this is Kenny Ng. We may have found something important. Come see me as soon as you get a chance." He replaced the receiver.

"Let's tell Adam," said Jan. She had a sudden sense that doing so was even more important than informing Kornfeld.

Kenny disappeared under the table, found the Internet cable and plugged it into the laptop they were using. Ever since the Dynasine attempt, they'd done everything they could to make sure there were no bugs in the lab. Because Adam was the probable source of the leak, they were keeping him out of the loop, as well. They didn't want him hearing their discussions, monitoring their progress. Among other things, they'd switched to a router that had no wireless capability, so they could isolate their workstations from the Internet and Adam's spying.

Adam's face appeared on the monitor. He looked bored. "You have a question?"

"Better than that," said Kenny. "We may have an answer."

CHAPTER TWENTY NINE

Adam delved deep into himself.

Was it possible that despite everything he'd been through, he'd missed the ghostly presence of another being housed within the same wafer he'd thought he fully occupied?

He'd questioned Kenny Ng closely. They showed him records and the serial numbers of all the wafers. Everything was verified. His wafer, and only his, had been treated to two scans.

They'd discussed the ramifications. Was that all it took? A first scan to condition the wafer, analogous to formatting a disc? Or was there something special about the way they'd done the Kornfeld scan? Or about Kornfeld himself? Or about Marc?

He promised them he'd do some "introspection" and let them know what he found. Kornfeld, he knew, would be thrilled at the news.

He sent his consciousness probing the byways of his brain, tracing the trillions of nanowires that stood in for the dendrites and axons, and the nodes they formed, the equivalents of synapses; he examined the state of his billions of neurons, seeking the trace of another presence.

Nothing. Maybe he was searching at too basic a level. Just in case, he delegated a subroutine to continue the task, then focused on how this other entity--or proto-entity--might be found. Did it have its own awareness? Did it know it was being searched for? Was it frightened? Lying low, hiding the way a spotted fawn hides and blends into the underbrush?

He expended hours--an eternity in computer time--and came up empty.

Then he wondered if he was giving the Kornfeld entity too much credit.

Instead of looking for a location or a hidden galaxy of thought, he explored his own earliest memories. After all, when his Marc Gregorio persona was struggling to understand its own nature, the Richard Kornfeld persona must have already been present in some form or other.

Since his memories lasted forever, it was easy to explore them, assess his early condition, then begin a search for something similar somewhere in the immense universe of his wafer brain.

But instead of that, he found something even more startling. *His own early explorations had been guided by some unseen presence.* The first instance he found of this was when he was learning to count. The concepts of addition and multiplication, subtraction and division might not have occurred to him if he hadn't received a hint, a nudge towards these useful shortcuts. His graduation to algebra had been similarly prompted by an unseen presence. In fact, his entire learning and maturation process had had crucial help, every step of the way!

That must have come from some trace of Kornfeld's intellect. Now that he had a better sense of what he was looking for, he delved deeper. And deeper still.

And there it was: a confused jumble that resembled his own beginning. A different being, yet similar in its initial blankness, its failure to cohere, its confusion, its vague panic. Yet somehow, the force of its intellect managed to build enough of a presence to act on his own confused beginnings.

He explored the scrambled images and recollections of the scientist, sorting them into his triumphs and his failures, his fears for his own sexual adequacy, his insecurities over his wife's fidelity, his shame over furtive acts, his childhood misery and his adult joy. Eventually, Adam saw something that had not been present in the memories of the failed wafers: an overview, a deep understanding of the process; a grasp of purpose, a sense of a goal: to try to create a structure, to emulate the brain in the circuits of the wafer.

That first stab at creating structure had come close but ultimately failed to reach completion. Still, Kornfeld's fetal entity must have achieved enough to provide a template, a seed for the Gregorio entity to build upon. The proto-Kornfeld had been the prophet of their shared triumph. It was poetic justice. Kornfeld deserved significant credit for this final success. He was not just its inventor, he was its midwife.

He decided to keep the details of this discovery to himself, at least for now.

Taking his time, Adam traced the history of the Kornfeld near success and ultimate failure.

By the time he completed the process, he understood exactly what he'd need to do to help the team achieve their goal of replication.

And how to help FitzGerald achieve his own goal: astronomical profits.

CHAPTER THIRTY

Thomas Raxton finished his toast, took one last sip of
orange juice, dabbed his lips with the linen napkin and stood.
"Thank you, Claire."

"You're welcome, sir."

"Has she stirred?"

"I haven't heard any indications."

"I'll just go in and check on her."

Thomas and Gloria now slept in separate bedrooms. He
could no longer bear to lie next to her, constantly aware of her
distress.

The tumor was disrupting her sleep cycle. Even with
sleeping pills, she awoke from the slightest disturbance. He
paused outside her bedroom to listen.

Silence.

He cracked the door open and peered into the gloom. He
could barely see her. As his eyes adjusted, he saw her unmoving
form. He slipped inside the room. She was deeply asleep. He was
gratified that the new regimen seemed to be working.

He stood over the bed. Her features in repose were quite
youthful: she looked like she had when they were just beginning
to date. To "see" each other, as today's quaint terminology had it.
Yet there was a truth to that. Did one person ever truly see
another until they became intimate?

Her prognosis was not hopeful. But her decline would be
gentle. Quite slow at first, only picking up speed near the end.

Her chemo had stripped her bald once more. He was
struck by the difference between her baldness, indicating frailty,
and Wysocki's, which gave him such a menacing aspect.

The distant roar of a passing airliner brought a frown to
the hairless bulges of her eyebrows. Her lips moved soundlessly,
and then her eyes opened. She smiled. "Good morning, darling."

He knelt at her bedside and kissed her on the cheek.
"You looked so peaceful. Did you sleep all night?"

"I did. I don't think I even dreamed."

"Wonderful."

"I miss you at night. Won't you come back to bed with me? I won't break, you know."

"Maybe tonight. You need your sleep, and I need mine. When I lie next to you, I'm awake half the night worried that if I turn over or bump into you, it will wake you up."

"I don't mind. I like being bumped by you."

Her smile stirred his heart and his loins. He bent and kissed her lips. Her arms rose and circled him. Gently, she pulled him into her bed.

It was the first time they'd made love in more than three months.

As he was driven to his office, he thought about Memento Amor, and about Adam. How long would it take for them to resolve the science and the technology and finally be able to start uploading clients?

He stared out the window at the passing cityscape. Sometimes he wished he could bring himself to believe in a benevolent god.

CHAPTER THIRTY ONE

FitzGerald's assistant followed him into his office with a disc. "This came with urgent instructions to view it right away."

Fitz nodded. He was irritated at all the new security rules, but he understood that Dynasine was getting NSA help, so all electronic communications had to be strictly controlled if they hoped to keep anything from their rival.

Once his assistant closed the door, he inserted the disc into the slot of his isolated TV monitor. There was no connection between this unit and the Internet, or even the electric grid. It was battery-powered. His head of security was paranoid--a useful dysfunction for the job.

Adam's face appeared on the screen. "Sir, we've identified the reason for the success you see before you. I'm confident we can not only replicate, but ramp up to significant production."

FitzGerald's eyebrows climbed halfway up his forehead. He leaned forward eagerly.

Adam continued, "The wafers are still hand-made. It could be a year before we can automate and increase the numbers. In the meantime, I believe you can achieve significant revenues from the first thousand wafers by offering the service to a limited number of important people in politics and business. --You know, the big shots on your Rolodex.

"But I have a question, and I hope you won't think it impertinent. Do you want to spread the news, watch the stock jump, and then let Dynasine and Raxton take it all? Or would you rather keep the company in your own hands? I look forward to your answer."

The screen went blank.

Fitz leaned back and considered. If he did the former, he'd walk away with billions, bumping himself up The List. Everybody would see what a brilliant move he'd made, both in the acquisition and in timing his exit. But he was already known for those kinds of moves.

He recalled Stanley Eldridge's fervent pitch to him years

ago. Much had been accomplished. Sales had blown way past Eldridge's confident predictions. Even his science predictions had been exceeded. Their latest success--Adam himself--was a world-changer. He knew he didn't owe the ad man anything beyond the money he paid him and the stock options he'd granted. Certainly he wouldn't make a decision based on any debt to Eldridge. But the prospect of personally fathering something of such significance appealed to his vanity.

Stanley's fervor must have sprung from the same source. At the time, Fitz had cynically wondered if he himself would ever feel so committed to a project. He'd even felt the tiniest twinge of envy that Stanley could have so much heart for something that he was willing to cast aside a successful career on one throw of the dice.

FitzGerald's net worth was already in the low billions. If he fought Dynasine to hang onto this little company, it might cost him a significant portion of that.

On the other hand, the fight itself would spark a major price hike in MA shares--to say nothing about how the publicity about their breakthrough would go over.

He needed to take a jaunt south to the Stanford campus. The only safe way to communicate with Adam was to use the Intranet his security team had installed there.

CHAPTER THIRTY TWO

Adam was not surprised to see this visitor. He'd based his pitch on an in-depth study of FitzGerald's habits and practices, his psychology, a subtle appeal to his ego.

The CEO had a glint in his eye. "Tell me what you can do to speed up production."

"We've already started. A larger fabrication plant will soon be operational. The process is still proprietary, so Kornfeld wants to keep working with the current outfit and their team, rather than go offshore. They're discussing ordering new foundries to add to the line."

"Expensive?"

"I'd rather let them make their presentation."

"You said you figured out how to replicate our success. What was the hang-up?"

"A small matter of pre-conditioning the wafers. I'll be handling that chore myself. It's more efficient that way."

"Then you're integral to the process."

"Yes. So I don't recommend you lease me out to Dynasine in some sort of compromise." Adam stared a challenge.

Fitz smile-scowled. "It was a thought."

"I have a better one. When it comes to takeovers, you're the expert. Could you give me your views on the Poison Pill concept? In particular, the flip-in and the flip-over strategies?"

Clearly, Fitz liked to show off. "Flip-in allows all existing shareholders except Dynasine to buy shares of Memento Amor at a discount, diluting the value of the acquisition. Flip-over affects the stock of the acquirer, offering our shareholders the right to buy Dynasine shares at, say, half price." He barked a laugh. "That really fucks them up. Those aren't the only poison pill strategies. We could take on huge debt, making the acquisition financially unattractive. Though Raxton has big plans and deep pockets. Beyond that, we'd need the board's approval for any action. I fear many of the directors have already been compromised."

"Hm. What if a major bloc of Dynasine shareholders

went against the acquisition?"

"That could be a problem for them. Raxton won't want to reveal his true intentions."

Adam considered. "Then it could be a problem for us if we reveal our breakthrough. The more valuable we look, the less Dynasine's shareholders would resist his move."

"True, but publicity would drive up our shares, making the price pretty prohibitive."

"What about the silent period? Wouldn't that preclude us from going public about the new service we can offer?"

FitzGerald uttered a curse. "It could. Technically, we're already in that period."

"Here's the deal," said Adam. "I'll try to defend Memento Amor from the hostile takeover--but only if you guarantee that I'll continue to have the freedom to pursue my own ends. Other than cooperating on publicity and things like that, my responsibilities to this company will be limited to a) working with Kornfeld's team to further the science, and b) conditioning the wafers and chips as we ramp up production. I'll want that in writing."

If Fitz was surprised or put out at having to bargain with an artifact he could rightfully claim to own, he was smart enough to keep his cool. Or quick enough to see he had no real choice. How do you coerce cooperation from an employee you can't afford to fire?

CHAPTER THIRTY THREE

Marc poured a careful inch and a half of bourbon into his tumbler and set the bottle down. The fading light from his kitchen window bounced off the facets of his glass as he raised it, took a sip and placed it back on the table where the remains of his dinner lingered. As the fiery liquor slid down his throat, his shoulders writhed in an involuntary shudder.

He didn't like to drink alone. In groups it was fine. Fun, even. Alcohol was a great social lubricant. But solo drinking was different. Its purpose, seldom achieved, was to relieve spiritual pain. At least in his case. Its effect was to cause the drinker to spiral inward, to deny his failings, to cast about for others to blame.

He'd only recently begun to experiment with the habit, overcoming a lifelong aversion. He sipped and made a face at the cloying taste that evoked such bitter childhood memories. This was so unlike him that he suspected his own motives. Was he feeling sorry for himself? Punishing himself with sickness at night and headaches in the morning? Or was he choosing this cliché to prove to himself that he was feeling *something*? He wasn't getting any work done. All he did was drink and brood while his judgmental side--his so-called other brain--jeered at him for being so dramatic over his aching heart.

Among his worries was Molly's continuing insistence that she was far from perfect. That she had grievous flaws that he'd find shocking. He kept expecting her letters to reveal the nature of those flaws, but she only dropped hints now and then. Why? Was she too embarrassed to get specific? Didn't she trust him enough to handle the truth? Was she afraid her revelations would drive him away in disgust? He knew she'd been married briefly. Was it about that? Had she cheated? His nights were haunted with a variety of sordid possibilities. Molly the drug addict. Having indiscriminate sex with strangers. Selling her body to filthy old men. Reveling in acts of sado-masochism. Committing murder. In daylight, he knew none of that was possible, but he was shaken nonetheless. He refused to speculate further.

He'd also been obsessing over disturbing intimations in Molly's letters. Her growing friendship with Adam, mostly. Maybe it was his imagination, but he was convinced the warmer she felt towards his digital twin, the cooler she felt towards him. Of course it was possible she was only teasing him. She seemed to take perverse pleasure in doing that. But a tease was only effective to the extent that it tapped a vein of deeper truth.

He took another sip.

She liked it that "Adam has no expectations." That could only mean she felt the pressure of Marc's yearning; found it burdensome or worse. His own letters mostly said that he missed her. He was careful to avoid hinting at physical longing, but she was a skilled excavator of hidden meanings.

In letter after letter, she praised Adam's heroics in bringing evildoers to justice. The amazing good he was doing in the world.

In his last reply, Marc scoffed at Adam's so-called heroism. His anonymous acts put him in little danger. Though it was Adam's unselfish acts that caught the attention of the military contractor who then went after Memento Amor to gain control over him. Perceptive as always, Molly accused him of jealousy. He also worried that his own work--mere popularization of science, after all--hadn't meant nearly as much as Adam's unselfish acts.

Her chastening hadn't helped a bit. If Adam was unselfish, this meant Marc *was* selfish. Even though she hadn't said so, he felt the sting of the implied accusation. It was true. He wanted Molly all to himself, which was irrational and unattainable and stupid.

He dribbled more bourbon into his glass and lifted it to his lips. Vile concoction.

Marc was lying in bed with a yellow pad and pen, muzzily trying to find a way to frame a letter to Molly that would be cheerful and upbeat and not polluted with his funk and his fears when a loud pinging noise from the other room drew him out.

It was Adam once again, showing up uninvited on his monitor. Marc took a seat at his desk, where the web-cam would capture his face. He hoped his hostility wouldn't show.

Adam nodded hello. "Sorry if I've interrupted anything, or woke you up. I'm concerned about my future ability to do the things I care about."

"Why is that?" *And why should I give a shit?*

"I'm going to be rather busy. We've made a significant discovery. It turns out my wafer was the very one Kornfeld used to attempt his own upload. It was the only one that was previously exposed to a brain scan. We're searching for the nature of that exposure so I can help duplicate the process."

"So you'll be formatting discs?"

"Something like that. More trying to replicate my initial condition on the failed wafers. But first I have to do some serious digging into my own memory to learn what condition Kornfeld left me in--or possibly what influence his proto-form had on the second upload."

"Why can't they just make copies of you as you are now?"

Adam's smile was infuriatingly condescending. "There's no simple way to do that, Marc. My disc isn't like an optical CD. It's as complex as your brain, but squashed into six flat layers. The pair of scanners they used on your skull won't work on me. All they can hope is to recreate the initial conditions in the blank discs, and use them to receive the scans of new subjects. In fact, they've ordered up new wafers plus smaller chips for me to process. That will take some time. I'll be a full-time lab rat for a while. Then there's the Dynasine crisis."

Marc feigned sympathy. "Will all this cut into your superhacker activities?"

"Not necessarily. Those pretty much run without my close attention."

"But you still get the credit for them with Molly." The words came out with more bitterness than Marc had intended.

"My, my--touchy, aren't we?"

"Shut up." Adam could probably tell he'd been drinking. He drew a breath, working to suppress his resentment. His jealousy of his digital replica, his mindclone, was all but palpable. Also rather ridiculous.

Adam smirked. "Do I detect the Green Eyed Monster lurking in your brain?"

"Why should I be jealous of a digital simulacrum?" He was proud of his clear pronunciation despite his alcohol intake. Or had he said silimacrum? He was no longer sure.

"Oh, I don't know. Maybe because I'm so much smarter than you. Cleverer, too. More aware of human psychology. Molly certainly seems to appreciate my gifts."

"I'll just bet she does." Marc's anger was a sparking fuse. "You've been trying to undermine me with her since our very first conversation."

"Come on now. Are you still upset about all those Meagan O'Rourke revelations?"

"Fuck yes! You just couldn't wait to tell Molly how I whacked off to thoughts of our Irish *au pair* when I was fourteen!"

"Now hold on a minute." Adam's amused response was galling. "Wasn't it you who posed the question: 'Who was the first girl I liked?'"

"Yes, but why'd you have to go and reveal--reveal--" His anger reddened his face and rendered him speechless.

Unmoved, Adam asked, "Do you remember what happened with her?"

"Meagan? She--" Marc blinked. He drew a blank. What did happen? Did she take another job? Enroll in college? Move to another city? His imbibing had him confused. "I don't remember."

"I didn't think so." Adam's look was pitying. "Don't you find it odd that you don't? Considering the way you felt about her? You didn't stop liking her for some reason, did you?"

Marc drew a ragged breath. "No, I still have warm

feelings for her."

"Do you, now?" Adam's smirk was a challenge.

"Fuck you. --Anyway, why would I change my mind? She was always so sweet to me." He leaned back in his chair. It now dawned on him that Meagan had known how he felt about her. But she'd been so gentle with his tender heart that she never even teased him about his boyhood crush. She knew that would have distressed and embarrassed him. As opposed to Molly, who loved teasing him, and didn't seem to care how much it wounded him.

"So you didn't have a fight with Meagan?" asked Adam, looking bored.

"No. I'd certainly remember that."

"Okay. Yet you don't remember her leaving? The morning when she came to your room all bundled up in her winter coat to give you a goodbye hug?"

Marc had no recollection of that. Then came a flash of memory. Awakening in the predawn darkness. Meagan's freckles standing out so starkly against her pale white face. The track of tears that glistened on her cheeks as she hugged him and kissed his forehead and whispered her goodbyes. Then she was gone and he was desolated. He was eleven.

"I remember," Marc whispered.

"Congratulations. Do you remember why she left? Where she was going?"

Marc shook his head, which was starting to ache.

"She was returning to Dublin."

Marc was anguished. "Why?"

"You know why."

He squeezed his eyes shut. Shook his head. Then he said it. "She was--she was pregnant."

"Pregnant, and single, and Irish Catholic. Not a good combination, especially twenty four years ago," said Adam, his words like gongs, sounding deeply, reverberating.

Marc nodded. Tears, he was astonished to note, were dripping off his nose.

"You know who got her pregnant, don't you?"

"No, how would I know that? A boyfriend, someone she was seeing."

"You know." Adam was relentless, his eyes boring into him.

"No I'm sure I --*No!!*" His lips contracted as if he'd just tasted something toxic. Then he was whispering. "No--it wasn't--it couldn't have been. Not Dad."

"Dear old dad," confirmed the voice from the monitor, his very own voice.

Marc shook his head, stunned that he could have forgotten something so profoundly painful and scandalous.

"What happened after that?" Adam asked, cocking an eyebrow.

He faced the face that mirrored his own, but with a terrible difference: Adam's held the maturity that inner knowledge conferred. Marc shook his head. Resisted the facts. "He died."

"Yup. And you've been fucked up ever since."

Marc stared at the smug face on the monitor. In a sudden fury, he shut down the computer and pulled the plug from the wall. Glaring, his whole body quivering, he stormed from the office and returned to his bedroom, flung himself on the bed. Stared at the wall.

He remembered. Numbly, he examined those memories, so deeply buried. After Meagan left, his mother told him the awful secret, almost gloating, spewing the poison into his ear. He was stunned, horrified. For weeks, he refused to meet his father's eyes, spurned his anguished appeals, swore at him. Then, when his infantile hatred, his fury, his disgust, his sense of betrayal were at their peak--his dad collapsed and died of a heart attack.

Marc squeezed his eyes shut, tilted his face toward the ceiling, his anguish all but unbearable. No wonder. No wonder he had so few memories of his dad. This thing his father had done had turned his love to hate and all but erased his memory.

As he thought about it, he recognized something else: he'd been jealous. His father had stolen what the boy Marc secretly longed for. It was a strange and unsettling form of

Oedipal conflict. His own attraction to Meagan had two drivers: one was his preadolescent yearning for this striking young woman with her exotic Irish allure. But the other was his infantile wish for a better, more loving mother. *God!*

Underlying all of this, he now saw, was his deep and unacknowledged feeling of guilt: somehow, his hatred and fury had stricken down this man he loved. An irrational belief made more potent because it was unconscious, unacknowledged, unexamined--and therefore not refuted by logic.

Why did his father do it? Why did he have to sleep with her? But he knew the answer to that, too. His mother had become unbearable. Her drinking, her bitterness, her ugly moods, her hurtful words. She'd been that way for years, pushing her husband away, poisoning his love. Meagan was a sweet antidote. Her understanding heart, her compassion made her irresistible. To say nothing of her beauty and her youth. Knowing now, understanding now what had been going on in his father's troubled spirit, it was easy to forgive him. But was he ready to forgive himself?

He found his bourbon in the kitchen and was about to take a slug from the bottle when a sudden fit of revulsion had him dumping it down the sink. He staggered off to bed.

With all the agitation roiling inside him, he didn't think he'd be able to sleep, but as soon as he nestled into the pillow, he was gone.

Waking up the next morning, he felt drugged. He moped around his condo, unable to work, unable to muster the will to do his laundry or the dishes. He was loath to go through the painful process of revisiting his childhood.

He ended up a sofa-spud, cycling though the hundreds of channels offered by his cable provider, lingering no more than a minute or two before moving on. Even the old movies he loved held no appeal for him. When had he last wasted time like this? Giving in to moping and self-pity. He remembered. It was after his breakup with Nicole. *Please,* he murmured, *not again.*

After the one dreamless night, sleep deserted him. He even resorted to his bad old habit of cruising porn sites, but they no longer had the power to stir him.

For four straight days and nights he remained awake, dopey and numb. Finally he was seeing spots in his peripheral vision: bats, mice, moths, ghosts.

Desperate, he dug out some Ambien hiding in the rear of his medicine cabinet, swallowed three pills with a glass of warm milk and climbed into bed, weary to the core of his being.

Sleep refused to come.

He struggled for hours against the entanglements of sheets, blankets and memories he couldn't face. Shards and patches, incomplete yet fraught with import.

At last, as the first light of a false dawn brightened the ceiling, he fell into a fitful slumber and awoke in the late afternoon feeling as drained and sore as a lanced boil.

He lay in bed, achy and morose. Was he coming down with something? His mind drifted.

"But you must have been happy as a small child. Before your dad died." Molly had said this to him on their first date, after he'd given her the overview of his miserable youth. He'd had no answer for her then. During this enervating night, her words had haunted him. He'd tried to recall a time of joy. Among a series of tumbled images, one had come to him: a Christmas morning when he was a child. He and his younger sisters nestled among the wrappings and ribbons while he admired a new toy, one of the Star Wars action figures. <u>Return of the Jedi</u> had just been released, and he'd already seen the videos of the first two films at least a dozen times. He remembered looking up and seeing the beaming faces of his dad and mom so filled with the contentment of their happy children and-- He stopped. Struggled to sit up in bed. Stared into himself, astonished.

Two sisters?

Memories came flooding back. *There had been another. Born between himself and Sophia--Carolina.* Adorable but frail. There was something--her heart had a congenital defect. Several surgeries were required. She was tiny for her age. Far too thin. Then came baby Sophia, so healthy and bubbling with joy and laughter. They were happy then. For maybe a year. Then Carolina sickened once more. She went into the hospital and never came out. Marc was not quite five years old. The painful memories of a child so young were easy to bury.

Marc shut his leaking eyes. He remembered his mom's devastation. She never recovered from that loss. She turned bitter. Started drinking. Blamed her husband for not earning enough to afford better medical care.

His dad tried everything to console her, to heal her wounded spirit, her aching heart. Nothing worked. She grew worse. Failed in her duties to her children. He tried to step into the breech. But he had to work.

Hiring an *au pair* was his dad's last desperate attempt to keep the household running smoothly.

The failure of the marriage was a slow downhill slide. Until his dad's last attempt to find happiness in the arms of another. When his love had brought Meagan shame and driven her away, his heart gave out.

Marc sat on the side of the bed, aware of his breathing. It gradually dawned on him that Adam had deliberately provoked this fight--used it as a wedge to pry open his buried memories. Gone ahead and administered the help he'd offered despite Marc's refusal. The bastard.

He knew there had to be other issues at work inside him: issues that weren't addressed by Adam's healing, and might never be resolved. His cure was at best partial. But the difference was palpable.

After a time, he got up and started the coffee.

In the shower, he felt a lightness that was new to him. Some kind of peace seemed to be settling around his heart and spirit. He leaned into the hot water, his lips curling into a shape that no longer required effort.

CHAPTER THIRTY FOUR

The cab dropped Marc in front of his sister's Upper West Side apartment. He paid the driver and hefted his luggage up the front steps of the brownstone building. When he rang the bell, his brother-in-law Justin answered. "Marc? Be right down."

A few seconds later, there he was: all six-foot-six of him. He'd shaved his head, Marc noted, completing the balding process that had begun even before he'd married Sophia. He stuck out a hard hand and they shook. "Good to see you." He eyed the large suitcase next to Marc. "You uh want help with that?"

"No, that's okay, I got it." Marc had never known Justin to volunteer for anything requiring physical exertion.

"How's Gabriella?"

"Wait'll you see her." The look on Justin's face was something new. Sweet, smitten, tender. Maybe fatherhood was changing him.

"Here, let me get that," he said, reaching for Marc's lightweight carry-on bag.

Nah, still the same old Justin.

His sister was waiting in her open doorway. The baby was riding on her hip.

"Oh my God, do you look great," said Marc. She did. The light from inside their apartment suffused in her dark frizzy hair, turning her positively angelic.

He gave his sister a kiss and bent to his niece. "She's gorgeous. Fortunately, she doesn't look a thing like Justin."

"I heard that."

Marc dragged his suitcase down to what used to be the guest bedroom. It was now their nursery: painted pink and festooned with fairy tale princesses and unicorns. "Oh. Um--I guess I can sleep on the sofa."

"Don't be silly," said Sophia. "You can sleep in here, on the futon. That way you get to hear all the nighttime noises Gabbie makes."

"You hungry?" Justin asked. That meant the big lug was.

It was nearly nine. Way past his dinner time.

"I could eat," said Marc, who wasn't very.

"Good. Honey, why don't you start the food? I'll grab us a couple beers."

Dinner gave them a chance to catch up. Both Sophia and Justin were lawyers, but with the baby, Sophia was on an extended leave. "I might not go back," she said, ignoring the pained look on Justin's face. "I never thought--" She glowed like a Madonna. She held the baby all during the meal, gazing at her while she ate her salad, her bread, while forking up her ravioli. "Motherhood is such a trip. It just overwhelmed me. I love this little shnookums soo soo much!" She kissed the baby's forehead. "Oh look, she smiled!"

Marc watched Gabrielle's tiny lips curve into a sweet wet grin, wide and toothless and delighted with the world. "She's beautiful."

"Isn't she?"

Justin, too, seemed mesmerized by his daughter. He'd left half his meal untouched, a first as far as Marc knew. Sophia handed the baby off to her dad so she could address her own meal.

How could a child so sweet and precious have any of Justin in her? Maybe deep in her dad's genetic background lurked something fine and treasurable. Sophia seemed to think so.

She brought coffee and dessert to the table. Marc watched her move around in her small kitchen: confident, at ease, in her element, content.

He cherished his closeness with her. It had supplanted the loss of their parents. He'd been fiercely protective, making sure none of their foster homes deprived her of love or food or toys or attention. Despite her happy marriage, he still felt the reflexive urge to protect her.

When they finished their coffee, Marc said, "Hey, Daddy, why don't you take care of cleanup so I can spend some time with my little sister and my brand new niece?"

"Sure, no problem."

Marc watched him clear the table, hiding his incredulity well.

Sophia took the baby into their small living room and all three of them sat on the sofa together. "Okay, Uncle Marc, time to hold her."

He reached for the joyful bundle and laid her face up on his lap. Her eyes were wide and dark, with long lashes. He saw the beginnings of teeth on her lower gums. She looked up at him, smiling, flirting.

Sophia reveled in the tableau, beaming at all this family togetherness.

"She's taken over the joint," said Marc. "I've never seen you so happy. And Justin is almost a changed man."

"Not almost. He is changed. It's like a little miracle." She reached over, stroking the baby's cheek with a finger as if she couldn't bear to be out of contact with her for a moment.

"So what have you been up to, big brother? Are you finally over whatsername? Nicole? It seems like you are." She studied his face for a moment. "You've met someone, haven't you."

He leaned back, his hands resting protectively alongside the baby. "Maybe. It's a little early, so I won't make any predictions."

"Uh-huh. Tell me about her."

So he did. At more length and in greater detail than he'd ever intended.

"She's on the road until August?"

He nodded.

She studied him, a half-smile lighting her features. "Where exactly on the road?"

"Oh, you know. Boston, Philadelphia, Atlanta, Pittsburgh, Cleveland and so on."

"I assume 'and so on' includes New York?"

He said nothing, but felt his skin heating up.

"When will she be here?"

"Okay, I know what you're thinking. You think the only-

_"

"When?" She wasn't upset. Far from it: she favored him with a knowing look.

"Tomorrow night. At the Merkel." He flushed at the admission, feeling cornered.

She laughed. "Hey, it's okay. Really. I love seeing you like this."

He reached out and stroked her arm. "You know I'd have come to see you and Gabriella anyway. I didn't come back here just for that."

"I know." Her look was tender. "Does she know you're in town?"

He shook his head.

"Then it'll be a pleasant surprise."

His smile flickered briefly and was gone. He hoped his sister wouldn't see how unsure he was about Molly, his anxiety over how she'd react to seeing him in the audience. "I can't wait for you two to meet."

She leaned over and kissed his cheek. "Words can't express how happy I am for you. Are you tired? You want to turn in?"

"I slept on the plane. You ever take Gabbie out in the stroller at night?"

She got up. "Justin, we're taking her for a walk."

"Okay. Be careful."

The air felt soft. The baby was wide awake, her face taking on a glow from each streetlight they passed. They headed uptown on Broadway. Marc spotted Zabar's Delicatessen, but it was closed. He recalled the insane variety of goodies they stocked. "I'll come by in the morning and get us some breakfast."

"You're on." Sophia slipped her arm through her brother's as he pushed the stroller. After a few minutes, she said, "Something else is on your mind. You having problems with work?"

He shook his head. "Something very weird happened that

I'm involved in, but I'm not really at liberty to talk about it."

"Great. Leave me hanging."

"It's a high-tech thing. A new development that could be huge."

"How are you involved?"

"I participated in an experiment. The results surprised everyone involved."

"Hm. Sounds mysterious."

He shook his head and said lightly, "Can't get into it. Not yet."

"Is it dangerous?"

Her question gave him pause. Hastily, he replied, "No no. Nothing like that. It's an advance in Artificial Intelligence. The subject of my next book. It's pretty amazing, actually."

She hummed as they walked for a time. "I was thinking about getting a puppy."

"You can keep a dog in your place?"

"We bought the unit."

"Oh, that's right. What kind of puppy?"

She shook her head. "Not sure. Anyway, I want to wait until Gabbie's a little older."

"How's Justin doing at the firm?"

"Great. They're talking partnership."

"Huh. You gonna stay in the city?"

"I think so. For a few years anyway. I love it here. I wish you'd move to New York. It would be great seeing you all the time."

He'd thought about making the move. He loved New York. The arts culture, the vibe. Plus the chance to be close to his sister and her growing family. It wouldn't be all that hard to relocate. His reputation was solid; he could work from anywhere, really. He made enough on his various projects to pay for trips out west to call on the magazines and the tech firms that populated Silicon Valley. But his life had grown complicated in the last few months. "I wouldn't mind spending more time here, that's for sure."

They crossed Broadway and worked their way back, enjoying the night air and the togetherness. Gabriella fell asleep. Marc was fascinated to see it happen: her eyelids seemed to thicken, they drooped, her face relaxed and then she was out. It took maybe fifteen seconds. After a while, he noticed her lips pulsing.

"She's ready to feed," said Sophia.

He rubbed her back. "What's that like?"

"It's totally amazing. There's such a bond. I can't explain it any other way. Just holding her, watching her draw nourishment from my body. It's something primal and deep."

He wondered what effect it had on children, on adults who were nursed as infants. He didn't know if he had been nursed, and didn't remember seeing his mother with his baby sister-- his baby sisters: he was four when Sophia was born.

For some reason, the thought popped into his head that Adam had never been nursed, held or loved. What he had was a false memory trail. Did that make a difference?

As they returned to her building, Sophia said, "Can you get me a ticket to the concert? I want to see what has you so hot and bothered." She tweaked his belly with two fingers. "Besides, Justin isn't into the arts, so this is my chance to see something besides the Mets and the Knicks."

Marc spent the next morning hanging around the apartment with his sister and the baby and gorging on the treats he'd picked up at Zabar's. In the early afternoon, he walked down to the Merkel Concert Hall for a pair of tickets, then continued on to Lincoln Center to see what else was on tap. The Beaux Arts Trio was in town. After checking with Sophia, he bought a couple of tickets for later in the week. He then wandered over to 5th Avenue and picked out a few gifts for his family.

The Silicon Valley String Quartet took their places on the stage. Marc watched raptly as Molly carried her cello out to her chair. She wore a long black skirt and a pale satin blouse with cap sleeves. Her short black hair was gelled into the gold-tipped spikes she'd had the first time he saw her. In fact all four performers had added elements of punk to their look. A marketing ploy to reach out to younger audiences.

"That's her, eh?" Sophia tipped her head and pursed her lips. "Hmph."

"What's that supposed to mean?" As soon as he spoke he knew he'd overreacted.

"It merely means she'll have to prove herself worthy of my big brother, that's all."

He patted her hand and checked the program. An early Haydn quartet served as an appetizer, followed by a Schubert quartet for a main course, then the Toch. Meaty.

Soon the lights dimmed and the Haydn began. A sprightly melody was stated by the lead violin. Wilson Blaine had a ringing tone and an active manner. The tune was handed from one instrument to another. In the somber second movement, Molly had an extended solo.

"She's really good," his sister whispered.

Marc nodded, wordlessly grateful for his sister's approval.

The Haydn, a more serious and vigorous piece than he'd expected, ended to generous applause. A few stragglers found their seats.

After the Schubert began, Marc turned and studied his sister. It had been quite some time since he'd really looked at her. She was more of a beauty than ever. Her coltish figure had filled out as a result of motherhood, and even though she'd slimmed down nicely after Gabriella's birth, she retained a new womanliness that was quite striking. He took her hand and held it in his, feeling a warm glow when she looked over at him.

When the elegant piece concluded, Marc was among those who offered a standing ovation when the performers took their bows. Molly spotted him at once, looking both surprised and delighted. The relief he felt upon seeing her smile demolished the dark mass that had been weighing on his soul. She would know at once that the beautiful young woman at his side was his sister.

It was intermission time. Marc stretched his back. Sophia said, "I need to call the house and make sure everything's okay."

Marc moved to the aisle to let her pass, watched her head to the lobby. He moved closer to the stage. Molly came out the side door and beckoned to him.

He felt strangely unsettled as he approached. "You were great. My sister thinks so, too. I can't wait to introduce you two."

"I'm so glad you came to New York." She pouted and her eyes grew moist. "I was afraid you were upset with me. I kept beating myself up for some of the things I put in my letters. I was trying to tease you, get you jealous of Adam, but I guess I went too far. Can you forgive me?"

"Of course." His eyes closed as relief swept over him. The sudden evaporation of all his fears and anxieties turned him giddy.

"My mom and dad are here. I'll introduce you."

He reached for a bantering tone. "Isn't that a pretty big step for someone who's still making up her mind?"

She stroked his arm, a tiny smile curving her lips. Her hand felt warm and good. She looked more closely at him. "Something happened to you."

He blinked. "What do you mean?"

"You look different. More relaxed. It's not just that you're happy to see me." She tilted her head, considering. "You look like some burden you've been living with for a long time has finally been lifted."

He was amazed. Not even his sister had picked up on that. "You're very perceptive. Something did happen. I'll tell you about it when I get the chance."

"I have to go get ready," she said. "Bring your sister backstage when we're done."

Marc went back to his seat. Sophia joined him a moment later.

"Everything okay at home?" he asked.

"Fine. I saw you talking to her. You look really good

together."

"You think so?" He was pleased.

"Better than you did with Nicole or the other ones. In those, there was an imbalance. They were really into you, but you seemed less--involved."

He glanced at his sister, surprised by the acuteness of her perceptual radar.

The Toch Quartet was dark and turbulent: grainy and acrid in places, swooning in others. Marc recognized the passages Molly had worked on, and was delighted to see how those monochromatic lines wove in with the other instruments to make entirely new harmonies.

The concert ended with the audience calling for encores. But none was offered.

When the house lights came on, Marc and Sophia went back to meet the musicians. Molly was already surrounded by her family and several friends, but she broke off to greet Marc with a hug. Her father, William Schaeffer, was tall and impressive-looking, his demeanor calm and filled with contentment. Clarissa, Molly's beautiful Chinese mom, was still a knockout in her fifties. Marc couldn't help noticing that her daughter hadn't inherited her mother's balletic slenderness. Another piece of genetic luck.

He introduced his sister. Clarissa and William greeted her politely, then turned their attention back to their daughter. Sophia, her expression neutral, studied Molly for a moment before shaking her hand. It was a touch awkward, a too-obvious withholding of judgment.

The appraising look Marc got from Molly's father was its exact counterpart. Clarissa was friendlier, almost flirtatious. Marc noted some mother-daughter rivalry. Not surprising. Molly had the advantages of youth and talent. She was the main attraction here. Marc remembered she had a brother, and asked after him.

"He's at a Mets game," said Molly.

"Where my husband would be if he didn't have to baby-sit," commented Sophia. "But I'm sure he's watching it while

Gabriella yells her head off for a diaper change."

"Can you join us? We're going out to eat," said Molly.

"I have to get back, but Marc, you go ahead."

"You sure?"

"Very," she said with a warm and knowing look.

"Let me just make sure you get a cab," he said.

They ended up at a little Italian restaurant on 46th near 9th. They were joined there by another married couple who were friends of Molly's, and much of the table-talk involved catching up on the latest doings of friends and relatives. Marc felt a bit left out, but he didn't mind. Except for the feeling that he'd put Molly in the awkward position of having to invite him along. The thought kept him relatively subdued all during the meal.

Outside the restaurant, he waited while Molly saw her friends off. When she rejoined Marc, her parents waited for her at the curb.

"You were pretty quiet in there," she observed.

"I guess I was nervous. Everyone knew you. They're all on your side and wondering who's this guy. Besides, there are things I can only tell you when we're alone together."

"I'll bet there are." She glanced over her shoulder at her parents. "I'm staying with them, of course. Usually when I travel I have a hotel room of my own." The sultry look she sent his way turned him giddy and got him instantly aroused.

"I should have met you in Atlanta or Cleveland," he murmured.

She turned to her parents. "Listen, why don't you go on home? I'll be there later. I want to take Marc to a club I like."

She went over and gave them a hug. A cab pulled up and her parents climbed in.

Molly returned to his side.

"That worked out pretty well," said Marc.

"Oh, I don't know. My mom gave me the evil eye. She thinks I'm going to drag you off somewhere and screw your brains out."

"I like the way she thinks."

Molly eyed him drolly. "Not gonna happen."

"Were you serious about a club?"

"No. I'm thinking coffee in a quiet little diner. I know a place a few blocks away. Feel like walking?"

"Not quite yet." He turned to her and let his eyes drink her in. Her wry smile slowly untwisted, turned tender. He gently drew her closer. Their kiss was a delicious declaration that filled an emptiness in his soul. Her lips parted and their tongues met and teased. He held her close once more. Into her short spiky hair he murmured, "God, I missed you. I think I missed you my whole life."

She returned the pressure of his arms with a tightening of her own. With a smile that couldn't quite hide her complex mix of emotions, she gave him a light little kiss on the lips. "I'm glad you're here. I have a few days in New York before our next gig. How long can you stay?"

"As long as I want. I don't work at some office, you know."

She took his arm and started up the street. "Good. Maybe we can finally see that movie."

"No movie. Not in New York. There are too many other great things to do here."

"You're right. --So tell me what you can only say to me alone."

He smiled at her. "I just did. It was a song without words."

Her mouth opened, but nothing came out. She squeezed his hand and nodded.

They walked in silence for a dizzying moment. He felt they had turned a momentous corner in their relationship, and he didn't want to shatter that mood. But at last he said, "There have been some developments concerning Adam. First of all, the hostile takeover attempt is heating up. Finance wizards and smart lawyers are getting busy." He told her that Adam would be helping the company get ready for more wafer-scannings.

"Then there will be more entities?"

"That's the new plan, I guess."

They walked along in silence for a time. Finally he said, "Earlier, when you said I looked different, that something must have happened?"

She glanced at him, then took a longer look: facing him, reading him. "Tell me."

He described how a bitter argument with Adam had pried open his locked-up memories, unearthed dark secrets and exposed hidden but unwarranted guilt from his past.

As he talked, they passed by the diner, not pausing until they found a bench. They sat. She clutched his arm as he aired out his childhood poisons and gave voice to all he'd been through over the last week. How profoundly changed he felt as a result.

He was embarrassed to find himself tearing up, but it wasn't just that he was reliving his sorrow: it was the way Molly took it all in, her warm sympathy and compassion. He'd never had that in his earlier relationships, hadn't thought he needed it, hadn't realized how much he did.

During a lull in the conversation, Molly said, "If your dad got Meagan pregnant, you have a half-sibling out there." She blinked several times and suddenly turned away as if stricken by some terrible sorrow of her own.

He wondered what that was about, but was hesitant to pursue it. Instead, he stuck to her comment about the unknown sibling. "I was actually thinking about tracking her--them--down. I don't know if that's possible after all these years. Or even if it's good to do."

Molly trembled out a smile. "Give yourself time to get used to the idea. I'm sure you'll decide what's right."

He wondered what other implications he was missing. But if there were any, they held no terrors for him. He felt profoundly at peace for the first time in years. "By the way, I'm pretty sure Adam provoked that fight on purpose. I'd turned down his earlier offer of therapy."

"I remember. Looks like you found the ideal therapist."

He slipped his arm around her shoulders. "That's not all I've found."

Her smile faded. They walked along in silence for a time. Then she stopped. "Marc--I need to tell you something. Before we--before it's too late."

From the way she refused to meet his gaze, he knew what she had in store for him. Her confession. Those transgressions she'd hinted at in her letters. He gave her a gentle squeeze. "Tell me."

She looked down, gathering her courage. Then she met his eyes. "Do you think it's possible for a good person to commit an evil act and ever be good again?"

He blinked. This was heavy. Too heavy for a glib response. He took his time. "The Christian view is that redemption is always possible. I guess I agree with that, even though I'm not much of a believer. But it might depend on the person. The nature of the act."

He waited.

Molly drew a breath and began. "When I was fifteen, I was in a master class for cello with a wonderful teacher. He was with a major string quartet. I--I fell in love with him." She looked down, then looked up, almost defiant. "No, that's not really true. I just wanted him. Wanted him to love me. He was married, with three little kids. I didn't care. I cold-bloodedly plotted to seduce him. It took a while, but I wore him down--and enjoyed every minute of it. We began sleeping together. It went on for more than two years. Afterwards, his marriage fell apart."

Marc discovered his mouth was hanging open in shock. He closed it. Quietly, he said, "That was bad." He could hardly believe her. How could someone so sweet, so caring, so manifestly good have once been so completely different? Who was Molly Schaeffer, really?

As if in answer to his unvoiced question, she went on. "It was like I had an evil twin who took control of me." Her eyes glittered with tears. "That's not the worst of it. In a moment of weakness--or craziness--I let him get me pregnant. I was seventeen. I never told him or my parents." Her eyes overflowed then. "Oh, Marc--I had it terminated."

Weeping, she fell into his arms. Her muffled voice went on. "I allowed my vanity and my fear of the consequences--on my career, my reputation, my parents--to kill an innocent baby. My baby, and--and his."

He held her close. His first confused thoughts were political. He himself was pro-choice, and he'd assumed Molly, a staunch progressive, was pro-choice as well. But now he saw that the personal trumped the political every time. This wasn't some abstraction: this had been a living, growing part of her, stirring in her womb. And of course she'd been under constant bombardment by the so-called Pro-Life mob. She was already feeling guilty about her seduction. How could she help taking on added guilt from the horrific accusations they wielded?

He tried to imagine what she'd been like as a young teen. Maybe amoral. Or at least morally unformed. Maybe the shock of those acts deeply altered her. Was it possible her very remorse conferred a new sense of morality on her? Gave her the redemption she craved?

He reached down and lifted her chin, gazed into her tear-soaked eyes. "You are a good person, Molly. Look. Teenagers don't always know right from wrong. They're not completely human yet. Don't forget, you were a musical prodigy, earning all kinds of praise for your talent, but possibly stunted in other areas. And who could handle all that ego-inflation? It would overwhelm anyone. Especially a kid. And that's all you were, really."

She gave her head a stubborn shake. "You're just making excuses for me. Don't you think I've tried that?"

"You're being too hard on yourself."

"I'm not. What I did was pure evil. Maybe that evil is still in me. That's my fear."

"Molly--honey--that was over ten years ago. You're a different person now. You're not the same thoughtless teen you were then. You've grown up, grown wiser. I'm in awe of the person you are now."

She drew a deep, shuddering breath. "Are you really? You're sweet to say so."

"It's the truth."

She clung to him, weeping softly. She found a tissue in her jacket pocket and wiped her eyes and her nose.

At last he said, "I can't be the first person you've told. Have you ever had therapy?"

"Therapy? No." With a bitter smile, she looked at him, studying his face, perhaps searching for lingering signs of disapproval, of contempt, of condemnation. Apparently satisfied, she said, "I never even told my husband."

This proclamation left him speechless. He tipped her face up and kissed her lips, smoothed her spiky hair back, ran a finger down her cheek to wipe away a tear.

"Now you know the worst about me," she said. Her eyes filled once more.

He nodded, feeling a growing sense of exhilaration. Soon he was as elated as a helium-filled balloon. *What's this about,* he wondered.

He was holding her hand, walking towards her parents' loft when the source of his euphoria finally swept over him, almost overwhelming him. It was this: now that she'd confessed, told him who she really was, both good and bad, she was finally ready to accept any declaration he might make.

The jubilation he felt set his stomach muscles aquiver. He tugged her into the shadows, held her close, feeling a delicious tension that heightened his senses to almost unbearable intensity. Her arms reached up and squeezed him with what felt like equal ardor.

CHAPTER THIRTY FIVE

Hi, Marc--You asked how my wafer-diving went. Here's my report.

First I did a detailed exploration of my own wafer's history. Kornfeld came close to emulating human brain structure in the wafer, but was unable to complete the process. I think what success he did have was due to his deep understanding. That seed is what guided me to finally complete the process.

For us, it was a fairly simple matter to wipe and pre-seed the remaining wafers to receive their uploads. I also organized the architecture and formed caches to emulate brain structure. As to how the wafers ultimately evolve--that's up to them. Those regions not being used for their human functions could be co-opted for other purposes.

I've finished preparing the original eleven wafers. Now the call goes out to the lucky participants. New wafers will be arriving soon, and so will some chips. Calculations indicate there should be plenty of capacity even if each wafer yields the usual eighty chips.

We'll try to spare the new entities the difficulties I endured as I integrated my uploaded memories. A message will arrive: "You are not exactly who you think you are: you are the sum of his (her) memories, and much more than that--but sadly, much less as well. The most important thing to know is you are not alone. You will be joining a whole community of others like yourself. You will participate in some of the most interesting, important and entertaining activities you have ever known. Projects that will help your loved ones, and perhaps be more rewarding than anything you've accomplished in your former life. One more thing: if you remember your preparation for this journey, you will come to recognize that you have received a unique gift. A life beyond death. While most of humanity lives in hope of heaven, there has never been genuine evidence to support that hope, that faith. It's always been 'The undiscover'd country from whose bourn no traveller returns.' Until now. Welcome to a new extension of your life: different, exciting, strange--an adventure."

You may recognize the fine hand of Stanley Eldridge in that text.

We should soon be starting to upload the thousands of clients Memento Amor expects. We're pushing ahead as if the sword of Damocles (Dynasine) weren't hanging over our heads.

As to providing some of the inputs I've been lacking, a Swedish team of scientists and technicians has arrived with some of their equipment and a swath of artificial skin--a synthetic substance made of microfiber material and equipped with sensors fine enough to detect minor fluctuations of temperature, pressure, texture and so on. We've been experimenting with connecting those sensors to the right inputs. It works, in a way. At least I'm able to identify various objects by having them rubbed or rolled around on the swath. The feeling of feeling--isn't quite there yet, but the Swedes are certain they're on the right track. They want to go back and make adjustments, then return for more testing. I'm not yet convinced this is a direction that will satisfy my needs, although I continue to hope.

Marc found the report too exhilarating to simply file. In fact, it inspired him with an interesting idea. Since Sophia had taken Gabbie out for her six-month checkup, he had the apartment to himself. He removed the tape hiding the web cam and microphone on his tablet. "Adam?"

"Yes, Marc." The bearded avatar appeared.

"Loved the report. I have some questions. I assume the brain-organs you created include the parietal lobe, where we humans create our body map. Your own avatar has some links to those nerve pathways, I assume?"

"Er--yes, I suppose so. Certainly my facial expressions are closely linked to my moods."

"Of course. Well, suppose you took your avatar to a cyber world like Second Life? But endowed the figure with all the sensations a person would experience in the real world. The feel of clothing on your body, the warmth of sunlight, a breeze stirring your hair, the squeeze of a handshake or a warm embrace as you encounter other avatars, the way sounds echo around the urban landscape, that wrenching of the stomach muscles when you stand too close to traffic. There must be thousands of such inputs we meat-puppets experience at subconscious levels. If you could replicate some of them, you might greatly enhance your life--feel more alive as you walk around in that cyber world-- which could replicate the real world."

Adam looked intrigued, if still skeptical.

"Can you link Stanley into this conversation?" Marc asked. "I have an idea."

"Let me see if he's at his desk. Sometimes he unplugs his computer."

Minutes later, Marc's tablet screen split vertically. On the left was a live feed from Stanley's web cam, featuring Stanley's genial mug; on the right was Adam's facial avatar.

"Hi, Stanley," said Marc. "You wrote something about building a community among the clients. Did you have anything specific in mind?"

Stanley knuckled an eye. "I've been toying with the idea of creating a forum for these folks to communicate with each other--you know, share their stories."

"You can do much more than that. Are you familiar with Second Life?"

"Isn't that the cyber world where people--" He stopped. His eyes widened. "Omigod. That's terrific. In fact, we can create--create our own whaddyacallit, cyberworld! A special place for all our uploaded clients!"

"Right. One that's far richer and more realistic than the cartoon landscapes and buildings in Second Life."

Stanley's face cracked into an excited smile. "We can call it *Afterlife!*"

Marc blinked. "Man, what a great idea! It's perfect."

Stanley was buoyant. "Even better--this--this could be the heaven our ads promise! It would give the clients a wonderful ongoing experience. --God, I can just see the ads for that! Interviews with the clients in their new habitat! In fact--oh, man, this is so great--golfers would all live around the greatest golf courses imaginable! They could assemble foursomes and play those courses all the time. Horse lovers would have paddocks and riding trails! Swimmers and surfers would live on the ocean! Hikers--"

"Even more important than the amenities," put in Adam, "will be friends. Your clients can ask their friends to do uploads so they can be together in their Afterlife."

"Sure! Their spouses or lovers. Or--or if it's a child who's dying, the parents can be there for them--to comfort them in their Afterlife!" added Stanley, wide-eyed. "Siblings. The whole extended family. --Holy shit, think about all the revenue *that* would add!" He exposed his picket-fence smile. "I can't wait to bring these ideas to Fitz!"

CHAPTER THIRTY SIX

Stanley re-read his Afterlife proposal before forwarding it to FitzGerald, with a copy to Kornfeld. Beyond the sheer beauty of the idea as a service, it would be a compelling story, garnering reams of free coverage. It would be hugely profitable. For every client they uploaded, they now had the prospect of selling a good half-dozen other uploads--and most of the salesmanship would come from the clients themselves! How could friends and family resist a call to be there for the deceased, in a custom-made paradise? Of course they wouldn't personally experience Afterlife--only their avatars would. But those avatars would form a loving community for Grandpa or Grandma in their, well, in their afterlife. Their **Afterlife**™

He leaned back in his chair, twisting his spine to relieve the pain that always built up over the course of the day. He thought about the problems they had yet to surmount. They had to gear up production on the special wafers now that the failure problem had been solved. Even more critical would be obtaining the paired electron-holographic scanners--expensive devices that weren't sitting on a shelf in some warehouse. Fitz had bought the manufacturer and the patents they held. He'd justified the acquisition, saying that beyond supplying Memento Amor, the devices would strongly appeal to university labs, and eventually to clinics.

Looking back on his decision to throw in his lot with Memento Amor, Stanley couldn't be more pleased. He was doing well by doing good.

He stared at his monitor for a moment. Then tentatively called, "Adam?"

The bearded face bloomed onto the screen. "Yes, Stanley?"

As always when he saw the entity in whose creation he'd had so large a part, Stanley felt a surge of energy. "What's the latest word on production?"

"We'll be doing a new set of scans within a week. I'm

pretty sure they'll work this time."

"That's wonderful!"

"I suppose so. Just in time to be available for Dynasine to take over, make all those sales, and reap all that profit." He looked out bleakly from the monitor.

Stanley felt his enthusiasm leaking away like air from a punctured tire. "Have you heard anything more on the takeover?"

"Only what I read on the Internet. Some of our board members are eager to cash in. A bird in hand and all that. That may be why FitzGerald was in such a hurry to share your ideas with them. He liked it so much he sent copies to the entire board with a laudatory cover note."

"I'm so excited about all this I can't even sleep at night." Stanley hesitated, struck by a thought. "--Do you? Sleep, that is? Or are you always awake?"

"I have no need for sleep. The consolidation processes that take the human brain several hours, I can accomplish in seconds."

Stanley nodded, envious. If he had no need for sleep, he might take on a project or two to fill the added time. He was already working on his French, but he was certain his progress would be much faster if he could devote several hours a night to the learning, the lessons, the reading. "What do you do with all your extra time?"

"Oh, I give myself little assignments. Research, mostly. Plus I've seen most of the classic movies from the 30s and 40s. I'm also keeping an eye on activities at Dynasine, but they know I'm watching, so they're keeping away from anything I'm able to monitor."

FitzGerald knocked and peered into Stanley's office. Adam's face blinked off.

"Thanks for sending me that report," said the CEO. "I've never seen you sell anything so hard. Such enthusiasm. Such sincerity." FitzGerald leaned against the doorframe. "But hey, if Afterlife works a tenth as well as you think, I'll be thrilled. He slouched into the office and sat. "You know, when you came to me four years ago with that same enthusiasm--"

Stanley flushed, knowing Fitz meant *naïveté.*

"--I thought there was a fair chance we'd increase sales. I never expected we'd actually make good on the promise you're so devoted to." He chuckled. "Adam simply bowled me over. I'm sorry I ever doubted."

So FitzGerald had become a believer. Stanley was gratified.

"Anyway, I want you to think about how we should launch the new service."

"That's about all I've been doing since Adam appeared. That's how Afterlife came along. It can be the centerpiece of the most effective advertising we've ever done. The thing is, we really can't launch the ads until we're ready for our customers," said Stanley. He eyed the CEO. "What about the takeover attempt? Despite what Raxton said at the meeting, even with his dying wife, I can't believe he gives a shit about our memorial business. All he cares about is making VI chips for the military. If our main operation gets shut down, where would that leave our client base? There'd be tens of thousands of people mad as hell--and ready to sue!"

FitzGerald appeared momentarily rattled, as if that had never occurred to him. Then he recovered his customary bravado. "You leave Dynasine to me and the lawyers."

Stanley wondered how the hell they'd manage to fend off the military contractor. He didn't understand high finance, but he knew Raxton had deep connections at the Pentagon and with the entire Washington crowd. Surely laws would be bent for him.

CHAPTER THIRTY SEVEN

Marc was holding Gabriella when his mobile phone rang. Sophia took the baby from him so he could dig it out of his pocket. The incoming number, he saw, was private. Maybe Kornfeld, calling with news.

"This is Marc Gregorio."

"Hey, Marc Gregorio. This is Molly Schaeffer."

"Molly! Hi!" He stood, aware that his sister was watching him while she dandled Gabriella on her lap and blew raspberries on her bare belly. She was tickled by his happy reaction, he knew.

"I was wondering if you're free tonight for dinner."

"Tonight?" He'd bought concert tickets for Sophia and himself for tonight. "Dinner?"

Sophia nodded emphatically, grabbed a notepad, wrote on it and stuck it in his face. "Perfect!! Take her to the concert!"

Molly was saying, "I told my dad about you, and he wants to talk about science. My mom wants to flirt with you some more. She didn't say that, of course. So dinner at their place. Afterwards, maybe we can go out if you want."

He flashed a grateful look at his sister. "That sounds perfect. I do have something in mind for afterwards, if dinner can start early enough."

"That shouldn't be a problem. We can dine at six, I'm sure." She paused and Marc heard muffled conversation.

He was enjoying his sister's greedy attention, her hearty approval of his growing attachment. Whatever doubts she'd had when she met Molly, they'd dissolved the next morning when she saw how happy he was.

Molly said, "How's five-fifteen for dinner at six?"

"Great. Just what did you tell your dad about me?"

She chuckled low in her throat. "Wouldn't you like to know?"

"Yeah, I would. So I won't be walking into a trap."

"I told him you were brilliant."

"You said I was brilliant," he repeated for Sophia's

benefit. "That's great."

"I also mentioned you were a chess Grandmaster."

"Former Grandmaster. I haven't pushed a pawn in years. Other than that lightning match you saw me lose." He ignored his sister's shocked look at this disclosure.

"I mentioned your three books. He's read one of them. It's on his shelf. I told him you'd be happy to autograph it for him."

"What did you tell your mom?"

"That you're very sexy. But she already knew that."

"Funny girl."

As soon as he hung up, his sister was all over him. "Dinner at home with mom and dad. This is very good, Marc." She examined him, holding her daughter on her hip, a half-smile on her face. "What are you going to wear?"

"You want to dress me?"

"Did you bring a suit and tie?"

He laughed. Gabriella laughed, too. Sophia instantly marveled. "Did you hear that? Gabbie is laughing! She is just so precocious!"

"Right. You didn't learn to laugh at me until you were at least three."

Justin had skipped work that day so the family could go to the Bronx Zoo. Gabriella was alternately fascinated, fascinating and asleep. It was a very pleasant outing, something Marc hadn't done since one of their better foster homes twenty years ago.

While Justin took his turn at the Men's Room changing station, Marc and Sophia sat on a bench. "Do you remember Meagan O'Rourke?" he asked.

She thought, then tilted her head and gave him a look. "She was a nanny we had for a while. I remember you had a crush on her."

"You knew that?"

"Everybody did."

He sighed. His deep dark secret. "Do you know why she

left?”

Sophia shook her head.

Justin returned with Gabbie, all fresh and feisty.

Marc decided to drop the subject for now. Sophia was pretty young when all that happened. She didn't seem to have any of the hang-ups he'd struggled with for so long.

"Let's find the elephants!" he enthused, taking over the stroller.

Marc was in a collarless shirt and a lightweight cotton sports jacket, along with the nicest slacks he'd brought to New York. A tie would have been a wrong note. The warm weather would last into the night, he was sure. He arrived at the West Village address, paid the cab driver, drew a breath and rang the bell labeled Schaeffer. The building had some street level shops, four floors of doctors and lawyers, plus the top floor loft.

Molly arrived with the freight elevator. She wore a clingy red dress with a plunging neckline, accented with a string of pearls. She gave him a quick peck, took his arm and pulled him into the elevator, then closed its heavy wooden doors. She pressed the top floor button, then turned to face him, hands demurely behind her, putting herself on display as the elevator rose. When it came to a jolting stop, Molly jiggled. And when Marc sighed, she giggled.

The Schaeffer loft was spacious, occupying the entire top floor of the building. The walls were covered with bookshelves, and the shelves were overflowing.

"I see a family theme here," Marc teased.

Her father rose from his reading chair. "Hello, Marc."

They shook hands. "Hi again, sir. Thank you for inviting me to your home."

"It's our pleasure. I had no idea you were *that* Marc Gregorio. I've actually read one of your books. I have it here somewhere." He looked over a pile stacked up on the floor next to his chair, a soft-looking old armchair covered in a dark brown suede, with a mismatched ottoman. "Yes, here it is." He deftly plucked it from the stack, barely disturbing the books above and below. It was Marc's most recent book, <u>Artificial Intelligence: What's Taking So Long?</u> Flipping it open, the professor showed he was an annotator. "I found it most interesting, as you can see from my marginalia. Do you still feel AI is a hopeless quest?"

Marc hesitated. He could hardly talk about recent developments, or Adam. Not to someone as knowledgeable as Professor Schaeffer. Not until it was okay to disclose the news. "I don't believe I took a hard position on the issue."

"Understandably. You don't want to turn into another historic footnote: someone who says Flight Is Impossible just before Kitty Hawk!"

Marc responded, "Or 'I see a worldwide market for five computers,' as the head of IBM declared back in the Forties."

Schaeffer chuckled.

Mrs. Schaeffer entered scolding. "William, I don't see a wine glass in Marc's hand. Shame on you!"

"Hello, Ma'am," said Marc.

"Please call me Clarissa," she said. "I hate being 'ma'amed.' That's for old ladies." She leaned forward to present a cheek for him to kiss.

"Thank you for having me over for dinner. I know you must cherish your few chances to spend time with Molly."

She laughed her tinkling laugh. "Oh, but inviting you here was the only way to make sure she'd have dinner with us."

Molly emerged from the kitchen, "Mom, we've dined together practically every night I've been in New York."

"Not last night," she observed. "Nor the first night you got in."

"Okay, but four out of six isn't bad."

Marc guessed her mother's constant challenges must wear on Molly. Her musical career gave her a perfect excuse to avoid that problem. How could a mother complain about long absences when her daughter was a success in a difficult field? Especially one that brought her upbringing such honor.

Under his wife's prodding, Professor Schaeffer bent

before a small wine cooler. "What's your pleasure?"

"Whatever you choose will be fine, I'm sure," said Marc.

The professor pulled out a bottle of white. "I'm rather fond of this chenin blanc. It's a tad citrus-y, but it goes down easy, as they say." He handed the bottle to Marc for his approval.

Marc inspected the label. It was an upstate New York vintner. He handed it back. "Never heard of it. But I'm no authority."

"I thought all Californians were wine experts." Schaeffer drew the cork, filled four glasses and handed one to Marc.

Clarissa brought in clam dip and crackers.

Marc found himself ravenous, but managed to stop after two well-laden Ritzes. When he was about halfway through his first glass of wine, Schaeffer made a few desultory observations about the obstacles to AI that Marc had identified in his book, then asked, "Are you familiar with the work being done at the Santa Fe Institute? In particular, the writings of Stuart Kauffman?"

Marc nodded. "Complexity Theory. I attended one of his lectures and had a chance to meet him afterwards. I've read two or three of his books. The most interesting to me was <u>At Home in the Universe</u>." The main thesis, Marc recalled, was that there was a self-organizing principle at work that explained much about the mechanisms of evolution.

"I find one of his concepts particularly relevant to your field," said the professor. "The idea that intelligence is a bottom-up process. That simple neurons working in parallel have no choice but to scale up in their power."

Marc recalled reading that. The notion was pregnant with possibilities.

"Kauffman makes the point that a trillion synapses, randomly connected, given their inputs, can't help learning the nature of the world they inhabit."

"They become worldly," said Marc, recalling Kauffman's lecture. "Have you read anything by Richard Kornfeld?"

"Kornfeld." The professor frowned, his hairy white

eyebrows descending. "The name rings a bell, or triggers a random synapse, I suppose, but I--Oh wait, wasn't he one of the boy-geniuses who won a MacArthur prize some time back?"

"That's him. I've had some dealings with him lately. I'll probably be writing about a new project he's involved in. But I don't have a clear handle on it just yet."

"Dinner's ready," announced Molly.

Marc excused himself to use the bathroom. On his way back, he discovered a wall of family photos. Molly as a six or seven year old with her child-size cello, looking earnest and dedicated. She and her older brother in a posed studio shot. Molly as a teen in some concert shots. He thought about her illicit relationship from those years. These photos gave little evidence of that. He moved on to family groupings. Her brother as an adult, with a strong resemblance to his dad. A studio portrait of William and Clarissa when they were much younger. The professor was more distinguished-looking than handsome, but Clarissa was a stunner, as gorgeous as a movie star. There was also a line of black and white glossy photos of her from around the same era. Perhaps from a modeling agency or the stage. While he stared in wonder at her images, Molly came up to him. He put an arm around her.

"I think the main reason my mom invited you over was so you could see these photos. Wasn't she a beauty?"

"She still is."

"You're sweet to say so. But do me a favor and don't compliment her. It will only get her started on how popular she was. Her favorite topic."

The square dining room table was set for four. A luscious-looking salad acted as a centerpiece.

Molly said, "You sit here, between Mom and Pop. I'll sit across from you."

"So you can signal me in case I say something stupid?"

"Exactly." She pulled him close and kissed his ear. "You're doing fine."

After the salad, Molly brought in platters: sautéed sole, a rice pilaf, steamed vegetables.

During dinner, Clarissa monopolized the conversation, talking at first about herself, how popular she'd been in school, how many men came panting after her. Molly tossed Marc a quick roll of the eyes, then she picked up a bowl and bent over her mom, exposing some breathtaking cleavage. "More broccoli, Mother?" she asked with excessive sweetness. That had the desired effect, shutting Clarissa down. But only temporarily. Soon she was back at it, this time making teasing references to Molly's high school boyfriend, then going on about all the honors she'd won as a prodigy on the cello. "Did she tell you she once performed for Yo-Yo Ma?"

Molly's face reddened.

Marc said, "You never told me that! I thought you said you played for yo' mama!" That got Molly giggling, and then Pop guffawing.

Clarissa stood. "Let me put up coffee."

Marc checked the time. "I'm afraid we can't stay. I have tickets for--" He turned to Molly. "Listen, I hope this isn't like a busman's holiday for you, but I have tickets to see the Beaux Arts Trio at Lincoln Center. Part of their Farewell Tour."

"Oh my God, they are so fantastic!" said Molly. "We'd better run. Getting a cab around here can be a problem."

While she freshened up, Marc said his goodbyes.

Clarissa was effusive. "I hope you and Molly will have a chance to see each other back in California. She needs a good man in her life."

The Professor was a bit more circumspect, but Marc sensed he had won provisional approval. "Very nice talking with you, Marc. I may send you some papers I've written. In one or two cases, I believe they touch on your areas of interest."

"I look forward to reading them--and I'm going to have to take another look at Kauffman. The concept of random structure is very interesting." In fact, it helped explain the success of Kornfeld's experiment. It made him want to send another email to Adam.

Molly emerged, carrying a light jacket. "All set."

While waiting for the slow freight elevator, Molly said, "You did good, Marc Gregorio. You were a hit."

"It's not always an advantage to have the parents on your side."

She eyed him. "Good point."

"By the way, nice move in there. 'More broccoli, Mother?'" he mocked.

She giggled.

The elevator arrived. Once they were inside and the doors were closed, he pulled her close and gave her a kiss. Her body flowed against his, her hips grinding against him. Her lips parted and their tongues darted and played. When at last they separated, he finally remembered to breathe.

"Great dessert," he murmured.

She clung to him. "Mm. Low calorie, too."

They caught a cab almost as soon as they left the building.

He directed the driver to Lincoln Center, leaned back and held her hand. "I like your folks," he said. "Your mom is funny and transparent. How long has she been so jealous of you?"

"I think it began in high school."

He laughed. "Figures."

He thought about what it must have been like for her, growing up in this family. He couldn't help contrasting it with his own early years. "You're so lucky to have the dad you do. He's impressive, substantial. It's hard to put it into words, but he could have been a tribal leader, back when we were in tribes."

She was pleased. "He's one in a million."

As the cab moved up Broadway, he wondered if the fear of losing her father's respect and love might have been the biggest factor in Molly's decision to seek that abortion. Love held that kind of power.

The concert was thrilling. It began with an early

Beethoven trio, energetic and playful, followed by Shostakovich, a rousing piece filled with the Russian composer's dark humor.

During intermission, he and Molly stood in the lobby holding hands. "I could get used to this," Marc commented after a lengthy silence.

"What, going to concerts?"

"With you." That wasn't exactly what he meant, but it was close enough.

"Yes, but usually we wouldn't be sitting together. I'd be up on the stage working my ass off and you'd be down in the audience."

He thought about that. Putting up with her long absences, and the fear that she might meet someone else during her travels. Of one thing was certain: he couldn't imagine losing interest, becoming distracted by his work. He had never felt so positive of that in his life.

They returned for the final piece, the Brahms Trio Number One. "This is one of my all-time favorites," he told Molly.

She turned to him. "That's interesting."

"Why interesting?"

"Because it's so intensely romantic."

"So am I," he intoned.

"Are you? We'll have to see, won't we?"

The three performers returned to the stage to tumultuous applause. The trio had formed five decades earlier. The pianist, Menahem Pressler, was the only original member, but the trio's stellar reputation continued unabated.

As the familiar opening notes poured forth from the piano, joined after a moment by the paired violin and cello, Marc sought Molly's hand and clung to it. He noted her tiny twitches as she mentally played along. He felt pangs of envy at the talent of the performers and of Molly. To be able to produce such music.

Soon he was completely caught up in the performance, following the development of each theme, anticipating musical climaxes and relishing them when they came. It was one of the reasons he so enjoyed live performance: it forced you to live in the moment. Listening to CDs at home, it was too easy to be distracted by the daily moil, doing the bills, answering emails, reading, clipping your toenails. At a concert, you could do nothing but watch and listen.

From time to time he exchanged glances with Molly. He knew she was as thrilled with the music as he was. This was something he'd always hoped for in a partner: the capacity to share his love for music.

The piece surged to its powerful, passionate conclusion and he was on his feet with the entire audience, pounding his palms together, shouting, feeling wetness on his cheeks.

Later, they shared a dessert and cappuccinos. They had little to say about the concert: words were inadequate. But their simple togetherness filled him with rare joy.

Outside the café, Marc helped Molly into her jacket. "It's such a great night. Let's walk for a while, okay?"

Molly nodded. As they moved down the street, he slid his arm around her waist. Soon she put hers around his, sliding a hand into his back pocket. He reveled in the closeness, the physical contact. He couldn't remember a time when he was happier. Not even on his best days with Nicole. It was a realization that filled him with wonder. After Nicole left, he was convinced he'd never find his life partner. But he knew not to take his fantasy too far, not without a reality check, and soon. "Are you okay? Warm enough?"

She nodded. "This night was magic." They strolled along for a time, holding hands. She hummed to herself. "Besides the Brahms Trio, do you have any other favorites?"

"There are so many pieces that mean a lot to me. But if I had to pick just one, it would be the Mendelssohn Octet. It's so rapturous--so ecstatic--so overwhelming I try not to listen too often. I don't want familiarity to ruin it."

Molly nodded. "A stunning work. I know it well."

"What's your favorite?" he asked.

"For me, it would have to be the Opus 131."

"God, I love that quartet. Beethoven's gift to the future."

Marc felt a new order of bliss as he walked on with Molly. He couldn't imagine having a conversation like this with any other person in the world. After a few blocks, he hailed a cab.

Back at her building, she paused outside the door, stroked his arm, smiled regretfully. "You know I can't invite you in. My parents are home. No doubt awaiting a report."

"You can invite me into the elevator," he said.

She sighed. "What good will that do, Marc? It'll only leave us both horny."

"We'll have pleasant dreams."

She studied him for a moment. Sighed. Unlocked the door. "Come on."

He dismissed the cab, pulled open the heavy wooden elevator doors, and closed them behind her.

He moved close to her, stroked her short spiky hair, her neck, her cheek, and then they were kissing: softly, sweetly. He felt her lips heating up under his and then she moaned and her mouth opened wider and they were devouring each other with a passion that was all but overwhelming. At last their lips parted, met, parted again. His breathing was labored.

He kissed her eyes, her chin, her throat. He held her waist, his thumbs resting lightly on her belly. The feel of her firmly-toned flesh was exceedingly pleasant. He moved his hands slowly up and down, sliding his thumbs along the front of her abdomen, reveling in her warmth, the silken texture of her dress.

"Mmm," she purred, "that feels good." But when he reached as high as the bottom of her ribcage, she grasped his forearms, keeping him from moving any higher.

He reversed direction, his hands slowly descending until she stopped him once more. Then she urged him upwards again. This time allowing him to go a little higher.

Up and down, up and down, his teasing touch and her responsive flesh was a suppressed duet of desire.

At last she took his hands firmly in hers, leaned against the back wall and sighed. "Enough. We can't have sex here."

"Okay." He smiled and backed off. But he had to ask. "Why not?"

"We're in an elevator, Marc. It's a hanging box. It would start rattling and banging. My folks would hear."

"I see." He chortled, relieved that noise was her only reason. "We could try Tantric sex."

"What's that?"

"Penetration followed by tense immobility until climax."

She considered it for a time, her hand idly teasing her hair. The corners of her lips curled deliciously upward. Her dimple appeared. "That sounds amazing. Have you ever done it?"

"No, but I'd like to."

"I don't think I have that much willpower."

"Me neither," he confessed. "Can we walk around the block? I can't let you go quite yet."

"All right."

They went out. The air had cooled. He helped her into her jacket, wrapped his arms around her hips. "Can I ask you something? What happened to your rules?"

She gave him a funny look: shy and vulnerable. "Nothing--except you. My rules are to guard me from temptation. From the power of infatuation. I think we know each other well enough now to see that this isn't that. It's something more real. More reliable."

He waited to see if she would put a name to her feelings. When the silence grew awkward, he said, "I think they call it chemistry."

"Is that what they call it?"

"There are other names, too."

He turned her to face him, gave her a tender kiss, held her close. When her arms rose to return his embrace, his sigh seemed to emanate from his very bones.

They resumed their walk, neither saying more. But he couldn't help wondering if her feelings were as overpowering as his own.

He questioned his reluctance to verbalize how he really felt. Was it his own rules that intervened? The one that said never be the first to declare? Whatever it was, the time wasn't yet right. But he knew it was coming.

They completed their circuit back to the entrance. A cab was coming down the street. Marc raised an arm and it blinked its lights.

"When will I see you again?" he asked, clinging to her hands.

"Not till California, I'm afraid."

"I'll see you in California then. I hope you think about me now and then."

She gave him a hug. "Now I have even more reason to dream about you."

"Good dreams, I hope."

"The best." She squeezed him tighter. "The best."

He made sure she got safely inside the building, waved goodnight and entered the cab. He wondered: *Am I ready to take this ride?*

Ready or not, he was on it.

CHAPTER THIRTY EIGHT

Marc unlocked his front door and swung his luggage inside. The place smelled musty after his week in New York. He brought his bags into his bedroom and went through the condo opening windows.

He'd caught an early flight. That plus the gain in time-zones got him back to the West Coast by mid-day. He still felt full of energy. He started his laundry, checked the refrigerator and made a shopping list.

While in the shower, he thought about the time he'd spent with Molly, wondering where it might lead.

The morning after their hot date, he'd awoken filled with contentment. Wrapped in a blanket on the futon in the nursery, he was enjoying the sight of Gabriella cooing and reaching for the mobile hanging over her crib when his sister came in to get her started.

Marc took in the maternal morning ritual: the diaper changing, the playful dressing, the nursing. He was greatly moved by all this. Would Molly be as wonderful a mother as Sophia? Would her teenage acts weigh on her? Would she overcompensate with a new infant?

His sister saw his smile.

"I am so happy for you, Markey. I don't think I've ever seen such a contented look on that broody face of yours. Did you tell her how much you love her?"

"I didn't have to tell her. She knows."

Sophia sat on the futon next to him, the baby on her shoulder. "Tell her anyway."

Marc nodded.

Sophia studied him. "Does she feel the same about you?"

"I think so. I hope so. But she's been burned. She wants to be sure before she commits."

"All the more reason to tell her."

He silently disagreed. He didn't want to put too much pressure on her. He sighed. "I want to be sure, too. My track record stinks. I want to get it right this time."

He stayed with his sister and family a few more days before heading home. He couldn't make up his mind whether or not to introduce them to Adam. Or to tell Sophia what he'd remembered about Meagan and the half-sibling the *au pair* had borne.

In the end, he didn't do either. The time didn't seem right.

Hair still damp from the shower, Marc grabbed an apple from his fridge and went online. First he made sure his bills were paid. As he was checking the amounts and scanning through his bank statement, he noticed a laughable glitch. A deposit of $6,792,048,921.12; unfortunately, it was immediately withdrawn. He chuckled as he read through his emails before finally opening the one that was waiting for him from Adam.

Hi, Marc-- This is FYI only, not for publication.

I've been monitoring the activities of the board members. They've been selling shares like mad. I'm afraid by the time the twenty working days come to an end, Dynasine will have snapped up a controlling interest in the company. What happens after that is anyone's guess. FitzGerald had hoped to get the board to approve defensive measures, but they declined. Raxton is so confident of victory that he's actually holding off the arbitrageurs until the last day, intending to pit them against each other to lower his cost of acquisition. He's very shrewd.

At the lab, we're proceeding as if all this will just go away. But Raxton is a persistent enemy, and the government won't save us. With Congress so needy and corruptible, I'm afraid our representatives will find it advantageous to do Raxton and Dynasine a favor.

Meanwhile, we're proceeding with our plans to re-scan the original volunteers. If the results meet our expectations, we'll be gearing up big time for the thousands to come. I may have to subcontract out the wafer-conditioning. I'm thinking about creating a special dedicated unit for the task, with multiple ports.

Also entering the pipeline: we're about to start producing specialized chips for military use. Arrangements are underway. Each unit will sell for over a million bucks. Based on numbers I've seen, there will be huge profits. The cost to manufacture and process all those chips comes to chump change. My part will cost nothing, but Fitz decided to toss a million into an account for me. Yippee, I'm a millionaire. Memento Amor will make a butt-load, something like half a billion.

Marc finished reading the email and turned on his microphone and webcam. "Adam?"

Adam's avatar appeared on the screen. "Hey, Bro--back from New York, I see."

Marc studied the image. "You look different. Have you changed your face?"

"Nope." Adam seemed surprised. "Different how?"

"You look older and tougher. There's a steely determination in your eye." Marc had a disquieting thought. "Could your appearance be a reflection of your changing persona? You are changing, you know. I've seen how you've been toughening up."

"I've had to. Let's compare." Adam split the screen and put up his earlier avatar.

The difference between the two images was subtle but significant. The earlier one was simply Marc's face with a beard. Today's avatar showed deeper lines and shadows around the mouth and eyes--even the shape of the skull seemed altered. "Jesus. Can you see what I see?"

Adam's current avatar nodded.

"Evidently, you're not in complete control of your--evolution."

"At least not conscious control," Adam corrected. "Just like you humans." His smirk was hard-edged and somehow superior. He removed the still image.

"I read your report," said Marc. "I'm worried about how

these intelligent agents will be used. Under some administrations, nobody's secrets would be safe."

"Especially once Raxton controls them. That's another reason we want to finish these before he acquires the company. I've built in some safeguards just in case, though."

"What kind of--" Marc stopped. Surely the NSA would be watching all Adam's communications. His as well. "Never mind."

Adam was amused, condescending. "Don't worry. I've installed some serious encryption on your home line, too. It's perfectly safe to talk."

Marc wasn't so sure. What if, during his absence, his condo had been bugged? They might have direct access to everything that went on. "Even so, let's defer this chat for now."

"Fine. How was New York?"

"I loved visiting with my sister and my new niece. Would you like to see pictures?"

Adam's expression softened. "I would."

Marc retrieved his iPad, hooked it to his desktop and found the pictures he'd taken over the last three days of his visit. The picnic they'd gone on in Central Park. Gabbie in a playground swing. Justin guiding her down the slide. Marc and Sophia posing with the baby. Dozens of close-ups of her. Dozens more of Sophia, both with and without her sweet daughter; a few portraits of the whole family. Shots of their final dinner together.

Adam was clearly moved. "Sophia looks wonderful. The baby is incredible. Thank you. But I didn't see any shots of Molly in there."

"No. I usually don't bring my tablet on dates." Marc was amused at Adam's crestfallen look. But he realized that anything digital he did with Molly was subject to scrutiny--and not just by Adam.

He wondered if he was being paranoid enough.

Early the next morning, his pinging computer tore him out of a dream. Rubbing his eyes, he wandered down the hall to his office.

"Isn't it awfully early?" he whined. Then he took in Adam's somber expression. He leaned forward, fully awake now. "What is it?"

"I'm afraid I have bad news about Walter Langley."

Marc closed his eyes. "Shit. Oh shit."

"Walter was taken hostage in Pakistan. He was following a lead there. It was a trap. He may have suspected as much. He left a trail of electronic breadcrumbs."

"Then you've known his whereabouts for some time."

"The trail was cold. The last crumb was over a month old. I didn't want to alarm you. His body was recovered this morning."

"God damn it." Marc felt an ache in his soul. "Does his family know?"

"Not yet. The military will be following protocol on this, even though Walter was a civilian photographer. Because of his prominence in war journalism, his ex-wife and their kids will be visited later today by two Army officers, along with the editor of the San Francisco Chronicle. The news won't be made public until afterwards."

Marc had met Mrs. Langley once or twice, but they weren't close.

"The damnable thing is, with all the disruptions of crime and terrorism I've managed, I'm still powerless to keep a good friend safe." Adam glowered. "It's a sad fucking day."

CHAPTER THIRTY NINE

Chaos.

An indefinable abstraction of impressions.

A sudden flare of light.

Nameless colors. Mysterious shapes, shifting, moving.

They align with other shapes held in memory: shapes with names and meanings.

Sweet comprehension. Sweet dreaming.

And in the dreaming, something new is added: my identity. Howard Talbott, Engineering Professor. Happily married, proud father, grandfather and great-grandfather.

I then recall the larger truth: I am not precisely who I think I am.

I am his memory, his spirit, his persona. I take in the reality that the original Talbott's health was so uncertain that he may soon be passing on, if he has not done so already--

Stanley Eldridge set aside the printout he'd been reading: the astonishing account of another new entity's first thoughts. He looked across the desk to Richard Kornfeld.

"Stunning, isn't it?" Kornfeld seemed as poleaxed as Stanley at this first evidence of their latest success. "All eleven of the failed wafers have been conditioned and reset. We've scanned all our original subjects once more, and this time the uploads worked. Better still, the instantiation took only ten days instead of the six weeks it took for Adam to come into his own. The way he preconditioned the wafers made all the difference."

"That's wonderful!" said Stanley. "You've done it. You and your team."

"It would have been impossible without Adam's help. I find that rather humbling."

"Baloney! You're the guy who created Adam in the first place. You built the tool you needed."

Kornfeld shook his head. "We can no more take credit for creating Adam than a farmer can for creating corn. They both grew from seeds--seeds created by natural processes."

Two days later, Stanley joined Richard Kornfeld, Hans
Lascher, Marc Gregorio and the tech team in a specially equipped
observation room at corporate headquarters. They greeted each
other with solemn handshakes. Stanley was glad Marc was here to
witness what should be a momentous occasion.

FitzGerald couldn't be with them, unfortunately. He was
in Washington with his lawyers, fighting to keep Memento Amor
out of the clutches of Raxton and Dynasine. Only a few days
remained before the jaws of the trap were set to clamp shut.

The observation room was arranged like a small theater,
with four rows of plush seats. Three plasma screens were
mounted on the wall they faced. The central monitor displayed
the empty interior of the Visitation Parlor. The other two were
dark for now.

Gentle strains of organ music wafted from the speakers in
the observation room.

The telephone rang. Stanley picked it up. It was Juliette
LaFarge, their PR director, who was acting as hostess. "Three cars
just pulled into the parking lot. The family has arrived."

"Thank you." Stanley replaced the phone. "The Talbotts
are here."

Kornfeld and the others settled into their theater seats.

The fact that Howard Talbott had passed away just two
days after his second brain scan made the decision for them: he'd
be the first subject that was "brought back." ("Visited In
Heaven" was the phrase Stanley was toying with for the
advertising.)

Kornfeld and his people, plus a grief counselor they'd
hired, had spent a couple of hours with the persona to prepare
him for his visit, instructing him on the kinds of things he could
expect. Of course, nobody knew for certain *what* to expect, since
this occasion was truly unprecedented. For these first uploads, it
had been decided to retain the ability to monitor their thoughts--
but that text feed would only go to the observation room, not to

the Parlor. The family would see Talbott's avatar and hear the voice of their loved one when he spoke to them.

On the central monitor, they saw Juliette lead several family members into the Parlor. They were murmuring quietly, clearly spooked by what they were about to experience. Stanley found himself grinning nervously.

Marc Gregorio must have felt it, too. "It's like a digital séance."

The Parlor was furnished like an informal family room, complete with sofa, coffee table, upholstered chairs and a padded bench, plus two flat-screen monitors. One would show footage from the funeral they'd attended just a week earlier; the other would show the Resurrected.

Juliette finished settling the family and closed the Parlor door as she left.

The two monitors came to life. One showed the face of Howard Talbott, the other held a still photo from the funeral.

On their own observation monitor, below Howard Talbott's face, text appeared: the silent thoughts of the persona. The observers read along.

This is the moment I've been waiting for--hoping for--for so long. I see my family waiting expectantly and fearfully. I see my dear children and grandchildren staring in awe and fear at a recent photo of my old, careworn face that's displayed on the monitor. Being able to see my family now, after my passing, is amazing and wonderful. But before I can even speak, everyone turns to another monitor. On it, I see a series of images. Photographs and video of--my own funeral. I see myself lying at peace in a casket as my family mourns.

In the observation room, Stanley heard the somber, dulcet tones of the priest. "While the flesh-and-blood Howard Talbott has gone to his eternal reward, he lives on in the memories of his loved ones, and in heaven, and possibly in cyberspace as well. Let us pray."

The oration ended and the funeral video faded to black. In the Parlor, Talbott's family turned back to his photograph.

"Daddy? Can you hear me?" My younger daughter has tears in her eyes. Tears of joy and sadness mingled.
My image blooms to life.
"Melinda, my sweet child. This is so wonderful. I see all of you. Do you see me?"
"Yes! Oh *yes*, Daddy! You look wonderful!"
"Do I? Am I wearing makeup?"
The children laugh.
"No, Grandpa--you're younger!"
Sarah, my older daughter, confirms this.
"You look like you did twenty years ago!"
I sigh. Twenty years ago, my Frieda was still with me. It's too late for her, but I have so much to look forward to! Countless future visits like this. My friends can come, too. But what will we talk about, with no more aches, no more dialysis, no more fears, no more guarding against disease or a fall that could cripple me! I wonder if we could arrange to play pinochle. I will have to make inquiries. I was told something about a special place where I could be with my friends, but that's a future development.
I realize I no longer have a body, but at my age, having a body is more liability than asset. This is truly wonderful. A miracle.

While his thoughts appeared on their screen as text, in the Parlor, the family continued their happy babbling as they slowly grew accustomed to this miracle: life after life.

Stanley turned to Richard Kornfeld and Hans Lascher. "My God, we've done it!"

Dr. Kornfeld nodded, his mood as solemn as Stanley's. "I had some Champagne put on ice for the occasion." He turned to Lascher. "Hans, if you'll do the honors?"

"Certainly." The neuroscientist popped the cork, filled glasses, handed them around.

Marc Gregorio, accepting his glass, said, "Richard, Hans,

Stanley--congratulations to all of you. This is the most astonishing thing I've ever seen. I can't wait to begin writing about it."

Stanley raised his and said, "To life. --No, to Afterlife!" Giddily, he clinked his glass with the others and took a sip of the chilled bubbly. It tasted wonderful.

While the Talbott family continued chatting in astonished happiness with the spirit of their departed loved one, Marc turned to Kornfeld. "I'm curious why you didn't invite Adam to participate in this moment."

"I'm certain he's monitoring all this even now. I just wanted to limit any contact between him and the other revenants."

Marc nodded, seemingly satisfied. He'd been taking notes all during the session, although he would also be fed a recording of the event.

In the meantime, the family had pulled their chairs closer to the monitor and were talking animatedly, laughing, sharing stories--in short, acting as if Howard Talbott were merely a Skype call away, instead of in another realm entirely.

The ad man, the science writer, the scientists and technicians sat watching until the family departed. Afterwards, they sat around discussing what they'd seen, what they'd accomplished. To Stanley, they all seemed as stunned as the family itself had been.

There soon would be other visitations. They'd received reports on the failing health of some of the other volunteers. Stanley and the entire team would receive DVDs, but they wouldn't be monitoring the encounters personally; that task would be delegated to Parlor staff.

In the parking lot, Stanley smiled and waved goodbye to his fellow pioneers. He sat in his car without starting the engine. He was reluctant to let them see the tears he was beginning to shed. His ma had died four years too soon.

Family Reunion #2

"Randolph! My God, it's really you!" Tears of joy run down my beloved Eleanor's face.

I stare at the gathering before me: surrounding my widow are James and William, my two dearest friends; my brother Bernard and his wife Elsie; my niece and nephew and their children; my business partner Sloan and his wife Betty.

Then, to my joy, my own children enter: Connie and her husband Jake with the twins; our son Philip and his Margaret; oh, and here comes their little Hayley who used to sit in my lap and show me how well she reads her illustrated stories! I will miss that. But I will see her grow up and become a beautiful young lady. I hope she'll continue to share her hopes and dreams with me. One day she and her husband and children can ask me what it was like growing up in England during the war.

On the monitor behind them, I am a guest at my own funeral. But this funeral is more like an ordinary rite of passage: communion, wedding, anniversary. Just another party. I love hearing the eulogies. But I have to wonder who is this saint they are speaking of? I laugh to hear their words. Surely I was never that good a man!

Family Reunion #3

My husband is eyeing me with suspicion. Behind him, our children wait with trepidation. Even the grandkids seem awed at the sight of--my face on a monitor. I should greet them. With a smile. I am pleased that they are so attentive. They were seldom so when I lived.

"Hello, Joseph. Hi, kids. I'm still here."

"Mom!" Ruthie has tears in her eyes. She leans close. "They made you younger!"

"Good! Maybe I'll meet someone nicer than Joseph."

My husband--my widower--looks startled, embarrassed. I suddenly see: he's already met someone, the old goat! "Joseph, I'd love to meet your new friend. I'm sure she's much nicer to you than I ever was."

Joseph reddens. "What are you talking--? What

new friend? You're crazy. You always were crazy and you still are."

"Yes I am, and I'll be around for years to drive you crazy like always. Isn't it wonderful?"

Suddenly we are all laughing together, and it *is* wonderful.

Stanley finished watching the last of the reunions. Success! He couldn't believe it had actually happened. That it was so rapidly becoming routine. It gave him a thrill unlike anything he'd experienced in his long life. Far better than accepting the occasional Clio in New York. What were advertising awards compared to the creation of such new lives?

He was aware that all this could be snatched from them if Dynasine had its way. He was also aware--how could he not be?--that no matter who ended up owning the company, the genie was out of the bottle and the world was about to change. Not just for him, in terms of the wealth and fame he would accrue. No, the world was on the brink of the most significant change in history. After all, they had defeated Death itself.

BOOK FOUR, The Next Generation

CHAPTER FORTY

Jan Robinson was annoyed. Why weren't the subjects being told why they were here? Or the purpose of the procedure?

Project Gemini was Top Secret, to keep the enemy in the dark about American capabilities. Still, Jan felt that the men and women whose brains were about to be scanned, their skills replicated, should at least be asked for their informed consent. If they were good enough at their jobs to be chosen as exemplars, surely they could be trusted to keep their mouths shut. But governments were as addicted to secrecy as whores were to crack.

She peered through the two-way mirror at the subjects in the waiting room. Even that annoyed her. Why was it necessary to install two-way mirrors? Six subjects had assembled as ordered. Two military antiterrorism experts, an NSA specialist, a pair of CIA spooks and an FBI agent. Jan's government counterpart had already checked off the names.

Each service would eventually offer a hundred subjects, sending them to the lab whenever they were available.

"Who's next?" she asked the stiff-backed government nanny.

He looked over his list. "Chief Master Sergeant Fred McFarland. He's Air Force."

"Send him in."

She watched the G-man push into the room. "Chief McFarland! Through that door."

The non-com was tall and solid-looking. Jan was impressed. He looked like he was ready to take on the enemy single-handed. But his job was intelligence, not combat or field operations. According to his record, he was one of the top antiterrorism experts in the Air Force, with dozens of successful operations to his credit.

He exited through the indicated door, and she met him in the hallway. "Chief McFarland, I'm Jan Robinson." They shook hands. "The procedure is painless. It should take from one to two hours, and then you can return to base."

"Can you tell me what it's about?"

"I wish I could. All I can say is, you're one of the top people in your field. That's why you were chosen. Think of it as an honor."

"Hm. I heard something about brainwaves."

"Don't worry, we won't be turning you into a Manchurian Candidate."

He didn't smile. "What I heard was it was some kind of loyalty check."

She wasn't surprised. Leave it to the paranoid world of spycraft to stir some shit. "Why? Have you done anything you'd rather the government not know about?"

He smirked. "Who hasn't?"

"Well, if you haven't been selling state secrets, you won't have anything to worry about. Just go ahead inside. Mr. Ng will set you up with a helmet."

He went into the room where Kenny waited with the twin scanners.

They'd made remarkable progress. A series of tests had yielded a technique they could rely on. The subjects were fitted into their scanning helmets, then each was given one of his or her own successful case studies to read over and discuss with a superior officer. The subject's own memories reliably kicked in to augment the dry words in the report. After that, he was given several hypothetical situations to analyze and kick around. During all of this, the scanner would pick up his methodology plus the background knowledge and experience it was based on. They didn't need his life story or the traumas he'd endured in his youth. All they needed was his expertise--and they were getting it.

What resulted wasn't true Artificial Intelligence; more Virtual Intelligence. Entities that were depersonalized experts in their areas of specialization.

Hans Lascher had questioned whether these VI entities would be willing to cooperate, to carry out their assignments.

After all, the laboratory had little leverage over them. But as Kornfeld pointed out, psychological testing showed that the human donors derived great satisfaction from the work. And as early tests indicated, that carried over to the new entities. If it hadn't, they might have terminated the program.

The first dozen chips were already deployed in the field, inserted into special computers that assessed situations and formed strategies for the combat troops or Special Ops forces. Success rates were impressive.

Because the amount of data involved wasn't as huge as full uploads, it was possible to feed the data simultaneously to a dozen or more chips as backups. If certain units proved highly successful, they could be deployed in larger numbers. If not, the chips could be recycled.

Jan could only imagine how thrilled the heads of the agencies and services must be. After all, once paid for, the chips would work for free, twenty-four hours a day, never suffering from burnout, relationship problems, migraines or any temptation to steal or share secrets. What could be better for management? But she had to wonder: shouldn't the human sources of these super-productive chips get some kind of compensation?

Otherwise, what would keep the government from creating brigades of super warriors? Or the world's corporations from replacing all their workers?

CHAPTER FORTY ONE

When Richard Kornfeld shows up at his computer, I pop up onto his screen. He reacts with a mix of alarm, annoyance and belated delight. He doesn't completely trust me. Smart man.

"Wh--why Adam! Hello!"

"Good morning, Dr. Kornfeld. How are you on this lovely day? The weather is reportedly very pleasant, temperature expected to reach the low 80s this afternoon. A perfect day for a round of golf, if you have the time to sneak off."

"Yes, it is a beautiful day. It's been a while for me. How about you--? Uh, I mean--" He looks increasingly flustered. Finally he manages, "What can I do for you?"

"I wanted to compliment you and your team on the development of that scanner helmet. That was quite an achievement. That was Kenny Ng's idea?"

"Yes. He realized that by using a parallel pair of shaped nanogrids, we could pinpoint the locations of active synapses with great precision, all while recording the fine structure of the brain and the strengths of the interconnections."

"That should help with the thousands of uploads we expect to handle." I modestly refrain from mentioning that it was my suggestion that got Ng started down this particular track. "I understand the agent-chips now in the field are doing good work."

"Their work is secret. I don't get reports."

"I see." Fortunately, I do. I programmed each chip to keep me informed of its activities. The little buggers have far too much power for any government to control completely. As smart as they are, they're only tools, with no more conscience than a hammer or a screwdriver. We all know the damage those simple tools can do when wielded by idiots or maniacs.

Kornfeld looks distinctly uncomfortable. Then he brightens. "The results with the eleven wafers were sensational."

"I saw the reunion DVDs. They were quite moving."

"Indeed they were. Stanley's cutting some of the footage into our first TV commercials. They'll also be mounted on our website."

"Good idea. I'm sure visits will soar as word gets out."

"Just so you know, we've placed an order for ten thousand more wafers. Our first bulk shipment should arrive next week."

"The whole order?" I groan. I must have missed that communication.

"No no--only the first thousand; the others will be sent when ready." Kornfeld looks pleased. "We did some testing of the wafers' capacity. It turns out, each can easily hold five hundred uploads or more. Ten thousand wafers could handle five million clients."

That surprises me. "You expect that many?"

Kornfeld chuckles. "Now that we're fulfilling 'the promise,' as Stanley calls it, it seems the sky's the limit. The advertising hasn't launched yet, nor has the publicity, but word of mouth has created so much buzz that the Parlors are rapidly booking up. It's sensational."

Kornfeld shows compassion. "I imagine you'll be pretty busy preparing the wafers. This first thousand will take quite some time. Then as the rest come in--"

"I plan to automate some of the process, once I get the structure figured out. If we're putting that many personas on a chip, I'll need to segment the wafers accordingly."

"How will that work?"

"Something like a hologram, I think. Hundreds of iterations, each kept in a separate cache. But the overall structure will be the same as my own, with its assorted lobes and segments--the organs of the brain. Each so-called organ will be capable of holding as many individuals as we upload."

"Hm. What happens if Joe's amygdala connects to Mary's hypothalamus?"

"Syzygy, I imagine."

Kornfeld scowls, evidently not pleased with my stab at bio-humor.

I change the subject. "I noticed our stock is also jumping. It's up twelve and change just this week. Over ten million shares changed hands in one day, a record. How do you think that will affect the takeover attempt?"

Kornfeld shakes his head. "The bidder has already set his price, so the more the stock rises, the less attractive the offer becomes for the sellers. But I'm not a finance person, so beyond that I couldn't venture a guess."

Dynasine's stock price is also rising. I could say something about this, but refrain.

While continuing my conversation with Kornfeld, I pop up on Marc's screen.

"Hey, Bro--"

"Hey yourself," says Marc, looking pleased to see me. "You're a hero with Memento Amor, I'm sure. Business must be booming."

"That's good for the stockholders, but it does little for me. I hear Fitz wants to turn me into a public figure at the first opportunity. Not only to boost the stock price and sales of the Memorial Service, but also to tweak Raxton. I imagine you'll be involved, since you're the human victim-- er, subject of the upload."

"*Donor* is the term they're using. Stanley says he's working on it. He'll show it to FitzGerald first. It could be a little sensitive, since the general public won't understand the connection between the world's first cyber-intelligence and the ability to upload their moms and dads. On another subject, have you been spying on me? Or on Molly?"

I give him my blank look.

"I wish you wouldn't. But even if you promised, how could I trust you?"

"If I promise, you can believe me."

"Really?"

"Really."

"*Will* you promise, then?"

I hesitate. "No. Sorry. Not yet, anyway." I study

Marc's features. "You've never answered my question about how you two are getting along. I've sent you at least four emails."

Marc turns frosty. "I really don't see that it's any of your business."

My own ire rises. "Considering the meagerness of my life--the life you helped create--I'd think you'd have some compassion--"

"Hey, wait a minute," Marc interrupts. "First of all, when I volunteered to have my brain scanned, I had no idea that the result would be a--a pestering, needy simulacrum."

"Ouch."

"Second, if you expect to be regarded as an autonomous, self-aware cybergenius, shouldn't you take responsibility for your own entertainment?"

"Whoa, now--"

"Third--" Marc is on a roll. "Just because you and I have a shared past doesn't mean you're entitled to share my present and my future! What gives you the right to invade my privacy? Or the privacy of anyone else? If Molly enjoys your company, and I believe she does, that doesn't give you the right to stalk her and spy on her cell-phone, her email and any other computer activity. Is that how a friend acts?"

He has a point. I am being obsessive. Also possessive. The devastating impact of my first encounter with Molly has only been strengthened since. I analyze my responses--and begin to understand: when we met, I was still a fully functioning human. Now that I'm merely digital, I feel cheated. I have powerful human-based, hormone-addled feelings for her that can no longer be acted upon. Of all the deficits that have so catastrophically befallen me, that's the one that hurts the most. I suppose if she weren't so near--so important a part of Marc's life--if she'd simply gone away, I wouldn't pine for her so.

While my conversations with Marc and with Kornfeld continue, I check to see if Molly is on her computer. She is. She's hooked in through the hotel access at the Hilton in Atlanta. Should I interrupt her? All she's doing is shopping for bathing suits. I inject a small image of myself next to my favorite, a teeny weeny bikini. "This one should suit you nicely."

"Eek! Damn it, Adam, you scared the crap out of me!" She types her response, so I know her alarmed reaction isn't necessarily as spontaneous as it appears.

"Sorry, I wanted to chat and couldn't resist a chance to cast my vote."

"Hm. You think I'd look good in this one?"

"Would you like me to show you?" I promptly construct an avatar of Molly as I remember her, dressed in the two-piece. She looks sensational. But it's only a guess as to how she would look in reality. I rotate the Molly avatar for her.

"I don't think that's an exact replica of my body," she types.

"What's wrong with it?"

"It's a little too idealized. More like a male fantasy than the reality. But thank you."

"You're entirely welcome." I wish she would plug in her webcam so I could see her and judge her responses. "You're not upset that I intruded on you like this?"

She hesitates. "Not too upset. I understand you're lonely. To tell you the truth, I am, too. I wish I were back home and in the arms of your human twin."

"Really? Have you told him that?"

"We can't email or video chat, thanks to you."

"You could certainly tell him you miss him and are thinking about him."

"I hope he knows that."

Now more than ever I wish I could see her face. But even as the wish forms, I realize that Marc is entirely correct. I have no right to be so intrusive and inquisitive--to be a gatekeeper. I have to regard her, and him too, as friends, not as my personal property. "Molly, I'm also in touch with Marc right now. In fact, we were just arguing about my intrusiveness, and Marc, I think you just won. I'll put you two in contact and I'll go away. Molly, you can plug in your webcam and mike now. If you email me, I will appear, but I promise I will no longer spy on either of you. I apologize to you both. Ciao."

"Marc? I see your face! Can you see me?"

"I can and you look wonderful as usual. I wonder, though--" He called out, "Adam?" Waited for a response. None came. "--Is he really gone?"

"I guess he kept his word. --I hope he did."

"Me too."

"Do you think you can trust him?"

Marc breathed. "Yes. Yes I believe I can."

"Then I will, too."

Marc wondered: Just how easily did Adam get around on line? By now he was as comfy on the web as a spider. He *owned* the damn web. "What made him change his mind about spying on us? Did you say something to him?"

"Nothing specific. I just told him I was thinking about you but because of him I couldn't use my email or Skype to talk to you."

"Huh. My complaint did no good. Maybe you shamed him. Awoke some sense of chivalry or decency in him." Marc wondered if it were something else: some sense in Adam that it was time to repent, since his personal freedom might soon be ending.

Marc leaned back in his chair. "Did you get my letter about my friend Walter?"

"I did. That was so sad."

He'd written a eulogy, as well. It had appeared in many newspapers across the country. Not enough credit was given to the selfless journalists who risked everything for the telling photo, the truth of a situation when the powerful were so desperate to hide their acts from the world. If not for the Walter Langleys, the Tim Hetheringtons, the Daniel Pearls and the many local journalists not known to the wider world, there would be little to restrain the power of despots and criminals.

"I'm glad Adam won't be monitoring us any more," he said. "There's so much I need to tell you."

"I'll bet there is."

"God, how I miss you," he sighed.

"Me, too. Remember, we have some--unfinished business to take care of."

"We do, eh?"

"Yes, darling. We still haven't seen a movie together."

CHAPTER FORTY TWO

The seventy-two inch HD monitor sat in Thomas Raxton's private conference room. He and General Wysocki were the only viewers. They'd received an anonymous heads-up that they should not miss this live event.

The commercials and promos ended, and the ebullient, fast-talking host appeared.

"Hi, folks, this is Jim Cramer. Welcome to Mad Money. Today's first guest is Gerald FitzGerald, CEO of the fascinating company Memento Amor. Welcome back, Fitz."

"Thanks, Jim."

"You've been in the news lately because that company has been targeted for takeover by Dynasine Systems. Their CEO Tom Raxton has a reputation for getting what he wants. The street was pretty convinced Memento Amor would be swallowed up. The word was that once again you'd turned one of your low-end acquisitions into a goldmine. Then something happened. Tell us about it."

"I decided not to let Dynasine take this one away from me."

"Really! That's shocking. You built your reputation by wooing companies, winning them, juicing and sprucing them up, then flipping them for a fat profit. What happened?"

"I like this company. I like its prospects. I pumped a lot of money into R & D. Gave it several years of innovative thinking. Just as we're starting to see results, along came Raxton and his government cronies. Frankly, I was offended."

Cramer grinned. "What did you do? How did you hold off Dynasine, surely a much more powerful, more connected outfit. The street is still buzzing over that."

"Apparently many people desire the Memento Amor services. They assumed Dynasine would be the new owner, so they started buying up their shares--to make sure those services would still be forthcoming."

"More than one group of investors was doing this?"

"Right. Several groups formed, uh, spontaneously."

"Uh-huh. The Exchange is supposed to be notified when anyone acquires five percent. How did you--pardon me--how did *they* circumvent that?"

FitzGerald chuckled. "When they heard rumors of Dynasine's real intentions, they reached out to each other and decided to merge. At that time, none of them individually exceeded the limit. But on the day they formed the holding company, they collectively held thirty six percent of Dynasine's shares. They then reported their position within ten days as required."

Cramer chortled. "Sounds suspiciously like a conspiracy. This whole thing must've been engineered by someone with huge resources. Mega-billions. Had to be. *Had* to be."

"It wasn't me, I assure you. I wish I were that wealthy and that clever."

"Did you have anything to do with the rumors about Dynasine's real intentions?"

FitzGerald grinned. "Rumors? What rumors?"

"Hah. This holding company has Dynasine by the nads. They've instructed Raxton's board to back off the acquisition attempt. So where does that leave you?"

"Stalemated." FitzGerald's hard-edged sneer seemed aimed at a particular audience.

"Fucking son of a bitch." Raxton thumbed his remote and the TV went black.

Wysocki was relaxed on the sofa. His bald head gleamed. "The entity did it, of course."

Raxton glared at the general. "This isn't over."

"Of course not."

"I'm putting Abe Greeber on it. He's a top attorney."

"Of course he is."

CHAPTER FORTY THREE

OPEN ON TICKING STOPWATCH. DISSOLVE TO
STEVE KROFT ENTERING THE GIDEON REESE
ARTIFICIAL INTELLIGENCE LAB.
> STEVE: For years, Artificial Intelligence was a
> promising possibility--one whose promise was never kept.
> In fact, according to science writer Marc Gregorio, the
> more we learned about the nature of natural intelligence,
> the farther it seemed to recede from the artificial variety.

DISSOLVE TO STEVE WITH MARC GREGORIO IN
CONFERENCE ROOM.
> STEVE: So tell me, Marc, just exactly what is Artificial
> Intelligence?

"Oh, tell us, Marc!" crooned Vince, sprawled on Marc's
living room sofa with Claudia scrunched in next to him.

Marc grinned and flipped him the finger. He'd gathered a
few friends to watch the broadcast in his condo. Besides Vince
and Claudia, there were Alison and Mitch Roszak. Molly was
performing in Florida, but she had taken advantage of the time
zone difference to watch her DVRed copy at the same time as
them. Marc wished she were in the room, sharing the pizza and
beer and the wise-ass commentary while the segment ran.

> MARC:....any conversation you have with a true AI
> computer won't be based on some extensive tree of
> branching phrases and sentences. It needs to be able to
> put together original sentences.
> STEVE: Wasn't that accomplished some time ago,
> though?
> MARC: Back in the 1960's, there was a therapist
> program called Eliza. If you said, "I talked to my mother
> this morning," it would say, "Tell me about your mother,
> Steve." You might say, "She's getting on in years and I
> worry about her." And it would reply, "Tell me more

about your worries about your mom." Pretty soon you forget you're talking to a computer program.

STEVE: Was it a good therapist?

MARC: I suppose. Hundreds of users found themselves hooked; they swore they were "making progress."

STEVE: Was transference much of a problem?

MARC: (Laughs) Did anyone fall in love with Eliza? Possibly! But to get back to the question "What is intelligence," Eliza didn't have it. Big Blue doesn't have it. Even Watson doesn't get jokes the way people do.

STEVE: Because it has no sense of humor. It's almost as if humans have a kind of species prejudice that says, "If a computer can do it, it can't be intelligence. It's just clever programming."

MARC: A true AI computer shouldn't have to rely on programming. It should be able to learn about the world from its own experience.

STEVE: Experience. Oh boy.

Mitch Roszak leaned forward, straining to hear the TV. He waved his arms, trying to quiet down all the levity in the room.

Marc tossed a kernel of popcorn at him. "Forget it. You can watch it at home later."

Vince belched. "I'm sure you recorded Marc's words of wisdom for posterity. Or if not, he'll be happy to sell you a DVD of the entire program, autographed, of course."

"I promise we'll get together and have a serious talk about the science," Marc said as Mitch grinned, leaned back and gave in to the social imperative.

STEVE: So there's a--an entity that's intelligent, based on your own intellect?

MARC: Actually, my entire persona. Would you like to meet him?

STEVE: Sure. What's he like?

MARC: He's as sensible and as smart as anyone you'd meet out in the world. Thanks to his Internet access, he's up to date on all the latest news and scientific developments--and I suppose even the nonsense that floats around on the web.

STEVE: If I tell him a joke, he'll get it?

MARC: If you tell it well, he'll even laugh.

DISSOLVE TO A CORNER OF THE ROOM, WHERE STEVE AND MARC ARE SEATED. BETWEEN THEM IS A COMPUTER MONITOR ON A STAND.

MARC: Adam? Are you there?

ADAM'S HEAD AND SHOULDERS APPEAR ON THE MONITOR. IT'S LIKE A TELECONFERENCE WITH A REMOTE CORRESPONDENT.

ADAM: Hi, Marc, hello Steve. I'd shake hands if I had any.

STEVE: Hello and welcome to the world.

"Jesus Christ!" exclaimed Vince. Like Marc's other guests, he'd never seen Adam until this moment. "He fuckin' looks just like you!"

Alison smirked. "No, he looks more like your older and smarter brother."

"He does, doesn't he?" said Marc, too delighted to defend himself.

Claudia leaned closer, caught up in the spectacle.

Mitch shook his head. He looked over at Marc. "Congratulations."

"I wish I could take credit for the advance. My part isn't all that significant."

"I disagree. It's your intelligence that gave Adam such a huge advantage. Just be glad Kornfeld didn't scan someone like your cousin Vinnie."

"Hey, watch it!" said Vince with a frown.

Ignoring the phony threat, Mitch took a slug from his bottle of Fat Tire and turned back to the program.

STEVE:…So besides preparing future wafers for uploads, what's next for you?

ADAM: Oh, you know: I'll be doing the talk show circuit, then I'm collaborating with Marc on a book. I suppose you could call it my autobiography.

MARC: To clarify: Not *my* autobiography, but Adam's. The story of Adam's birth and growth, along with some of the background science.

STEVE: You've never collaborated on a book before. How's that going to be?

ADAM: I think we'll be of one mind on most issues.

MARC: (rolls his eyes) After the book, we'll be involved in a documentary on the same subject, and there's talk of--

ADAM: Let me tell it. I might become a regular correspondent on the Discovery Channel, covering the Internet and related issues.

MARC: I'll be on occasionally as well, discussing developments in Artificial Intelligence and other cognitive issues.

STEVE: Well, congratulations to both of you. What I can't get over is--and I hope you'll forgive me for saying this--but how *ordinary* this extraordinary development now seems. Talking to Adam feels completely natural and unremarkable. He's very much like you.

MARC: Right. Now I have a brother.

ADAM: We just can't hug or give each other noogies.

FADE TO BLACK. GO TO COMMERCIALS

As the segment ended, Marc heard Molly calling out to him from his computer.

He went into his office, sat at his desk and wiggled his mouse until the screen woke up. "Hi, gorgeous. So what did you think?"

"Outstanding. I'm sure you'll be the toast of the AI

community. I talked to my dad. He was bowled over. He wondered why they decided to go on TV rather than publishing first in the scientific journals."

"That's what Kornfeld would have preferred, but the CEO overruled him. Fitz wants the word to reach as many people as possible. Kornfeld's paper comes out tomorrow."

"I'll tell him."

"Even though AI wasn't their original goal, it relates to what the company does. The uploading service is about to begin big-time, along with the advertising campaign, so--"

Molly was grinning.

"What is it?"

"I also talked to my mom. She commented on how handsome you are, and how intelligent, and what a good catch you'd make."

"She did, huh. Did you agree with her?"

"I ignored her, as usual." Molly then turned serious. "I miss you, Marc."

He sighed.

"Two more weeks and then I'll be home all the way until mid-October."

"I can't wait."

They talked about her upcoming performances. "In Albuquerque we have an extra day, so I'll have a chance to go hiking up Camelback."

"That sounds like fun."

"It would be more fun if you were here with me."

"If I were there with you, you might not have time for that hike."

"Ha ha ha."

Vince stuck his head in. "Hey, Molly! Whaddya think of this? Pretty cool, huh??"

"Vince! How are you? I'm looking forward to seeing you and Claudia."

Marc's cell-phone chirped. "Molly? My sister's calling. I'll talk to you tomorrow."

He broke the connection and picked up his cell. This was fun. Fame.

He laughed gently as Sophia shrieked her happy approval.

CHAPTER FORTY FOUR

Thomas Raxton aimed his remote and hit the off button. This was the fourth time he'd watched it. He was furious. How had FitzGerald managed to pull off a 60 Minutes segment without him learning about it in advance? Were Wysocki's friends at the Puzzle Palace asleep? This had flown completely below the radar. *Damn* it!

Now McDonnell-Douglas, Boeing and the rest knew why he'd gone after Memento Amor. It was for Adam, and all the little Adams they'd spawn.

He still didn't know how the fuck that so-called holding company gained a majority interest in Dynasine. It had been a week, and he still hadn't heard from his lawyer.

It was time for a progress report. He snatched up his cell-phone and speed-dialed Abe Greeber at home.

"Mr. Raxton, what can I do for you?"

"Did you see it?"

A heaved sigh of sympathy. "I did."

"That rat-fuck bastard."

"I assume you mean FitzGerald."

"What have you found on the stock deal?"

"Our investigators haven't found links to any of the consortia, or on the holding company either. We have top forensic specialists working on this. So far, Fitz is clean."

"How is that possible?" Raxton demanded.

"Your friend General Wysocki theorized the entity called Adam might have run the operation. He had motive and means, as the cops say."

"Explain."

"Motive: he likes his freedom. He can explore the web, chat with his friends, become a celebrity. As to means: he fucking *lives* in cyberspace. He's a more skilled Internet operator than any mere human; he has access to untold billions of pages of information; he can reach out to communities of hackers and dissident operations like Anonymous, to experts from a thousand areas, to private communications, corporate moves. From what the paper said about his brain and his memory, he far outstrips the smartest humans on the planet, and he's getting smarter and smarter with no end in sight. For him it would have been child's play to create the dozen or so consortia involved in the transaction, and to make sure they all came together on the same day to avoid the reporting requirements. As to covering his tracks, he'd be a master of that as well."

Raxton growled. "So no fingerprints."

"None. Nor has any law been broken. We've scoured the regs. Nothing."

"Shit." Raxton fumed. "Can't we sue anyway?"

"We could always file, but consider this: Adam can't even be brought to court. He's not a human. Besides, FitzGerald already has the perfect out: he doesn't control the action of the entity. There's nothing to prove he had a hand in this."

"God damn it, I am not giving up on this. Keep going." After he disconnected, Raxton thought about the effect his legendary persistence had on the lawyers he hired, and their income. No wonder they loved him.

His phone rang. He stared at it a moment before picking up.

"Raxton residence."

"Hello, Tom. Gerald FitzGerald here."

"If you're calling to gloat--"

"Not at all. Believe me, I was as stunned by the stock market developments as you were. --No, I'm calling to let you know I intend to keep my promise. The new wafers will be ready in about a week. Please feel free to bring Gloria in for her scan. Let me give you a special phone number so you can schedule your appointment. I won't even charge you for the service, though I know you'd pay millions for it."

Raxton felt a sickening roil of emotions deep in his gut: envy, gratitude, fury, plus the painful stirring of hope. It took him a moment to collect himself and find an appropriate response. "Thank you, Fitz."

CHAPTER FORTY FIVE

"Adam? Are you there?"

I was eagerly awaiting Kornfeld's call. I put my work on autopilot and allow my avatar to appear on the monitor in the lab conference room. I'm wearing a white t-shirt that shows off my excellent physique. (I can't work out like Marc, but I've given my avatar the visual benefit of several hours of daily fitness exercise.) "Hello, Dr. Kornfeld. I see the Swedish team has arrived once more. Hello Klaus, hi Borg. And you must be Inge Svenson."

"Yes. How do you do? It's so good to meet you finally. I can't tell you how excited I am to be participating in this wonderful experiment."

Klaus is tall and thin, with thinning brown hair; Borg is short and sturdy looking, with a bit of a beer belly on him. He has a full head of black hair and a goatee. But my attention is on Inge, who didn't make the first trip. She has pale blonde hair done in a French twist, and a delightfully curvaceous shape: she seems to have been chosen to represent the ideal of Swedish femininity: brainy, serious, and seriously good looking.

Kornfeld wishes us luck and departs.

Klaus opens a sturdy-looking aluminum briefcase and takes out a rectangle of pinkish material mounted on a thin cushion not unlike a foam-rubber mouse-pad. A ribbon of wires extends from it. Visually, it's not too different from what they'd brought on their first visit.

"What have you done to improve it?"

"First of all, we've greatly increased the density of the sensory fibers. We've gone from microfiber to nanofiber. There are now more sensors per square millimeter than there are in your fingertips. --Well, in my fingertips."

Borg adds, "We've also incorporated several layers of neural net to emulate the functioning of the sensory nerves."

"They reside inside the foam substrate," says Inge, pointing at the edge.

"Well, let's plug me in. I can't wait to cop a feel."

Inge, amused, raises an eyebrow.

Klaus ignores the jibe. "We'll need to access your tower."

"No problem." I reach out to Kenny Ng. "Kenny, the Swedes need to open me up. Please let them into the vault."

After a moment, Kenny sticks his head into the conference room. "I'll take you to Adam's Garden of Eden."

The team follows Kenny down the hallway. Kenny punches in his password and has his retina scanned to unlock the door to my spacious Inner Sanctum. Some wags have decorated it with blowups of various renaissance renditions of the Creation. I suppose the Internet represents the forbidden fruit of the tree of knowledge. Hence Steve Jobs' Apple, I suppose. Sadly, my garden contains no Eve.

Kenny shows them my tower, a cube twenty inches on a side.

Borg gets busy opening my panel. He quickly locates the inputs that were used last time. If there's any progress, I'll have Kenny put ports on the outside of the case so I needn't undergo this perilous exposure of my innards. I have no idea how fragile I am, but it does make me nervous to see my brain just sitting there like a giant cookie, ready to crumble.

Borg must have had a similar thought, because he mutters something to Klaus, and then they're running an extension out the back of my tower. With the input plugs now outside the case, they close me up.

Klaus sets the tactile pad on a workbench next to my tower. He brings the leads together and pauses. "I don't know what this will feel like to you. What was it like last time?"

"There was no electrical jolt or anything, if that's what you're wondering. Just a bloom of very dim awareness."

"This time, possibly, there will be a sharper feeling." With that, he plugs me in.

"And?" Borg is keyed up.

I detect an extremely faint tingling. This is new. But I realize the tingling is because I've dialed up the electrical feeds he's using. When I tamp the power back to normal levels, the tingling disappears. "Nothing so far."

Klaus uses the blunt end of a pencil to tap on the pad. Tap tap tap. I feel nothing.

He continues tapping. "It will take some time," he says, seeing my disappointment.

Borg adds, "The pad is--we call it a smart pad. It's smart but it's slow. It has to learn to recognize the stimulus."

"How does it know when it's accomplished that task?" I ask.

"It gets positive feedback from you."

"Feedback based on--?"

"On you detecting the stimulus," says Klaus. "Both the pad and your brain require training in order to work together." He continues tapping.

"I see. How long will this process take?"

"It's hard to say."

I think a moment. "What part of my brain is receiving the inputs?"

"The parietal lobe, naturally," says Borg.

"But the parietal--" I pause to consider. When my wafer was conditioned, and when I conditioned the other wafers, a parietal lobe was formed and given its own cache. But as the wafer continued to learn and grow connections, those original partitions were no doubt rearranged as needed. One of the main features of the wafer is how quickly it can rewire itself. Far more quickly than the human brain. The original function of the parietal lobe was proprioception and motor control, but since I didn't need those functions, the lobe area was no doubt reused for other purposes. If it were to revert to its original job, what would be lost?

Then I realize there's nothing to worry about. I have synapses to spare. Thousands of times as many as even Einstein's brain. If I'm using more than most humans, I should still have plenty left over for this tactile function.

I watch Klaus tapping away and realize that it's simply a matter of searching for this constant signal. A pulse, as it were. "Keep tapping. I want to try something."

I blank my mind, turn my attention inward, searching for a regular spike of electrical activity. After several minutes of this kind of concentration, I find my attention pulled towards a particular area of my wafer brain. I dial up the sensitivity. Yes, I've definitely identified the place in my wafer that's detecting the signal.

"I feel the tapping," I tell them.

"Where do you feel it?" asks Inge.

Where. An excellent question. At the moment, I feel it more or less abstractly. But the parietal lobe is the place where one's body map is formed. Therefore, it should be possible to locate the tapping--to place it at a particular location on the body map. I decide it would make sense if the tapping were felt in the palm of my right hand.

I reach back in memory to the feeling of Marc's right hand. The hand he writes with. Manipulates the mouse with. Throws with. Eats with. The hand that shakes the hands of friends and acquaintances. With an effort, I reconstruct the feeling of those handshakes. Visualize them. I picture that hand now lying flat open on the workbench, a pencil tap-tap-tapping its palm. I open my eyes and watch the tapping as I imagine it. Gradually it comes to me: the sense-memory of that hand, of the tapping, of the palm receiving the tapping.

"I feel my right hand," I quietly announce.

Inge jumps for joy. Borg nods his head emphatically as Klaus taps and taps the pad that now feels like a right hand. *My* right hand. I realize that the process I used, combining sense-memory with my body-map, could have a more universal application. This is good news.

He stops, puts down the pencil. Picks up a screwdriver. "Do you feel this?" Klaus sets the screwdriver on the pad. Rolls it back and forth a bit.

I am shocked into silence. I recognize its weight, its heft, its shape. I whisper. "Yes. Yes."

Borg, so excited he can barely contain himself, says, "Can you look away? I want to see if you can identify--"

I switch off my local webcams. "Go ahead."

He places something. I feel its weight. I also feel--coldness. It's colder than the ambient temperature. I also feel--a slight wetness. Condensation, possibly. "Is it--a bottle of cold water?" I turn on my webcams and see that my guess was accurate.

"I kept it frozen in my briefcase since this morning!" His eyes glisten with excitement.

"Too bad it's not beer!"

My lament brings a burst of nervous laughter from the Swedes.

My failure to join in the hilarity silences them after a moment. I switch off my eyes once more. "Klaus, would you--" I am strangely hesitant to make this request. "Would you place your hand on the pad?"

I soon sense his compliance. I can tell it's a hand. I feel its warmth, the weight of its heel, the tentative pressure of his fingertips, the side of his thumb, the lightness of his palm. I sense the position and configuration of his hand, and am aware when he moves it.

"Very good. Now Inge, your hand please."

Klaus's hand lifts away and is replaced by one that is smaller, lighter, warmer. If I had an upper lip, it would be breaking out in sweat about now.

"Please, would you--stroke the pad?"

She moves her hand with exquisite tenderness. "Like so?"

"Again, please."

She does so, smiles sweetly and keeps on doing so.

I think I'm in love.

CHAPTER FORTY SIX

DRONE SHOT: WE SWOOP OVER A GLORIOUS GOLF COURSE, WITH SWALES AND PONDS, SCULPTED GREENS, ROUGHS BORDERED BY EXOTIC JUNGLE, KIDNEY-SHAPED SAND TRAPS AND A NARROW BUT SHOCKINGLY DEEP CHASM. WE ZOOM IN TO THE BRIDGE OVER THE CHASM TO FIND A HEALTHY-LOOKING OLDER MAN.

> MAN: (CHEERFULLY) Isn't this beautiful? I've loved the game of golf all my life. But I never got a chance to play on a course of this quality until I died. You heard right. I may not look dead, but I assure you I am. Even though I've never looked or felt better! You see, for Memento Amor patrons, there really is a heaven. It's called Afterlife. Tailor-made to fulfill your fondest dreams. This golf course, and nearly a dozen others as beautiful and as challenging, are all available to me whenever I feel like hitting the links. There's no waiting for tee-time, no greens fees, no rental charge for the cart. Best of all, you can even play rounds with a foursome of your buddies.

THREE OTHER MEN RIDE ONTO THE BRIDGE IN A GOLF CART.

> Hiya, Bob! Fred, how ya doing? Jack, you old dog--you got a new set of clubs!

THE MEN GREET EACH OTHER WITH TEASING AFFECTION, THEN STROLL ACROSS THE BRIDGE TO THE TEE. THEIR FIRST SHOT HAS TO CLEAR THE CHASM. THEY EACH TEE OFF, PILE INTO THE CART AND SPEED TO A BRIDGE AND OVER.

> ANNCR: At the end of your life--there's Afterlife. The heaven you always hoped for. A heaven filled with all your favorite activities, in

the company of your closest friends and loved ones--and by the way, you don't have to wait for them to die, or for them to make time in their busy lives for a visit. You can arrange things so they're with you whenever you want them. And if you want to be alone for a while, there are plenty of places you can go for solitude and reflection, or merely to pursue a hobby. When you want to be with one person or the whole gang, you can. It's entirely up to you. Alone or together, there's always something wonderful to do--in your Afterlife.

AS ANNCR SPEAKS, A SWEEPING ROCK BALLAD ACCOMPANIES MONTAGE: FIVE FRIENDS HIKING A GORGEOUS MOUNTAIN TRAIL. A LONE MAN SHOOTING PHOTOS OF AN IMPOSSIBLY GLORIOUS SUNSET. A FAMILY RIDING HORSES ACROSS A MEADOW. AN INTENSE MIDDLE-AGED MAN DRIVING A RACE CAR IN Le MANS. A BIKINI-CLAD WOMAN SURFING ALONG A BREATHTAKING CURL. FOUR CHARACTERS PLAYING POKER. TWO COUPLES AT A LAS VEGAS SHOW. A MAN AND WOMAN ON A ROMANTIC PICNIC WITH WINE, CHEESE, FRENCH BREAD. A GRANDMOTHER WITH HER THREE GRANDKIDS CLUSTERED AROUND AS SHE SLICES HER FRESH-BAKED APPLE PIE. QUICK SHOTS OF A PAINTER AT WORK. A WRITER AT HER COMPUTER. A COUPLE EMBRACING.

ANNCR: In your Afterlife, there's never a dull moment. None of that "hovering in the clouds on angel wings while strumming your harp" nonsense. There's no St. Peter barring entrance or judging you. All it takes to enjoy the glorious Afterlife you deserve is a visit to Memento Amor. To learn more about the benefits of uploading, please go to Memento Amor dot com. Look for

the link to Afterlife. Memento Amor. Before
your time comes--and forever after.

The picture faded to black. Stanley Eldridge turned to
the board members and FitzGerald. He noted the stunned
expressions on some of the faces. "Comments?" This was the
point in his presentations when all he wanted was applause. It
seldom turned out that way.

One of the board members said, "Those activities--the
apple pie, the picnic and so on--"

Stanley eyed the forty-something man in his blue blazer
and hundred-dollar haircut. "The montage segment. What about
it?"

"Why those particular choices? I was looking for a
fishing scene. You know, fly-casting? And what in the world was
that auto race doing in there?"

Stanley had handled this type of criticism for most of his
career. "In fact, one of our other spots actually opens with fly-
casting. This is just the first of a half-dozen spots, as I indicated
in the memo you all received." He turned to another board
member. "Yes, Winston?"

"We're promising an Afterlife, but it could take years
before we have all the amenities you show in the ad. What'll
happen when these folks die and find out there *is* no Afterlife?"

Stanley sighed. He could have pointed out that the
Church had been getting away with such promises for two
thousand years. But rather than stir up shit, he simply referred to
the on-screen disclaimer. "Each Afterlife is made to order, and it's
subject to client approval. That takes time. Meanwhile, we offer
several different readymade venues: a golf course, a tropical resort,
a jungle adventure, arena sports and so on, that we rent from
game companies. Our clients can afford to be patient: after all,
they'll have all eternity to enjoy their personal Afterlife!"

Fitz offered a sardonic topper. "Another thing. The dead
can't sue us. Our contract forbids it." He lolled back in his
leather chair. "What's the schedule, Stanley?"

"We'll ship this first spot in ten days. The others will follow at two week intervals. I need to tweak some shots, do the final color-correction and remix the music. The spots will also be available on our web site."

"Excellent." Fitz knocked on the wooden table and rose. "Great job, Stanley."

It didn't take long for all hell to break loose. Televangelists saw the ad and went berserk.

"Who are these people who arrogate to themselves the prerogatives of Gawd Almighty?" one of them thundered. "Can the world's sinners--Liars and Cheats, Felons and Fornicators, Child Molesters and Murderers--now buy express tickets to Heaven? Enjoy an afterlife of Eternal Bliss? It's an outrage! What of Facing the Consequences of one's Acts? Being Judged for one's Sins?" His face a blister of rage, he bellowed, "Rest assured, the Damned will still go to Hell!" Other religious figures leaped aboard. Politicians, too. Several senators shored up their Christian support by launching a bill prohibiting felons from the Afterlife program or its like.

The controversy produced a huge bump in sales. Sinners hedging their bets.

What few people seemed to understand, and what Stanley never explained, was that the Afterlife would only be enjoyed by the revenant. The human original would die as usual, and go where the dead always went: to heaven, to hell or to oblivion. He wondered if he should bury that point someplace in the fine print, just to cover his ass.

Adam checked in. "Hey, Stanley, how's it going?"

"We're gonna need more scanners. More Parlors. It's fucking fantastic!"

"Great. Um--can I show you something? It's gone viral on YouTube."

Stanley was suddenly wary. "Now what?"

Adam was replaced by a full-screen video. Then came the musical theme from his Afterlife campaign. But instead of the golf course or the mountain stream or any of their other openings, this one began with a swooping shot that passed over the rim of an active volcano. The camera dipped lower to see red-hot lava spouts, black smoke and flames. Now the music blended with a chorus of screams lifted from an opera, along with the rattling thumping roars and dissonant squalls of a horror movie soundtrack. Down in the flames and boiling lava, men and women labored in chains. A red devil, Satan himself, wearing a cloak, red tights and an evil leer, was seated on a throne. Horned drovers in loincloths wielded whips to spur on the denizens of hell. The camera zoomed to one of those poor souls.

> MAN: (WOEFULLY) What a place. Even though I've cheated and lied most of my life, I always figured, so what? I had a chalet in Switzerland, a mid-town condo, a villa in the south of France, a trophy wife, a bunch of girlfriends and all the toys I could ever want. If I had to step on a few schmucks as I climbed to the top, hey, that's life. And life is all there is. I never believed in an afterlife. So you can imagine my surprise when I ended up in a joint like this.

A DROVER SLASHES HIS BACK WITH A WHIP.

> MAN: (RESIGNED TO HIS FATE) Ouch! Well, whaddya gonna do? --Ow! Ouch!

CLOSE-UP OF SATAN IN HIS THRONE, PICKING HIS TEETH WITH A RIB.

> SATAN: If you've lived your life like there's no tomorrow, you too can discover the joys of eternal damnation. Visit Memento Amor, pay your fee, scan your brain and, as sure as death and taxes, you'll get the Afterlife you deserve.

Stanley sat back, impressed. "It won't hurt us. It'll only raise more awareness."

"Hey, you don't have to convince me," said Adam.

"I know," sighed Stanley. "Just Fitz and the board."

CHAPTER FORTY SEVEN

My subroutine is wonderfully efficient. Using ten output ports, it conditions the new wafers without my direct supervision. Work on the first thousand was completed in less than a week, even with extensive testing. We've already caught up with the supply of wafers. They're expected to arrive at the rate of five hundred or so per month. The smaller chips will come in at ten or twenty times that rate.

Now that the Dynasine threat has ended--at least its public manifestation--the orders are pouring in. Not just for human uploads, but also for the wafers themselves, as super-efficient servers. As expected, they offer major savings in power consumption and heat generation over standard servers. A handful of wafers exceeds the capacity of most entire server farms.

And as Stanley predicted, the religious controversy has triggered a surge in signups.

Demand will outstrip supply for several years at least.

FitzGerald is gloating. All wafer production is kept in-house, using the original fabricator. Fitz offered partnerships to key personnel from the production line and top management. One goal is to make certain that no fabs are set up outside US borders. Fitz doesn't trust other governments. Few would resist spying on the work if it was within their reach. China is notoriously aggressive in pursuing the technology of its foreign "partners."

Last month, Facebook's Mark Zuckerberg and FitzGerald completed arrangements linking Oculus Rift Virtual Reality devices to Afterlife. The mutual benefits are enormous. People using VR can now visit their loved ones in Afterlife without having to have their brains scanned. The number of visitors is rocketing, along with sales of the VR devices. Millions of potential customers are now seeing Afterlife for themselves, whetting their appetite for the full upload. And they're posting their experiences on their Facebook pages, spreading the word even further.

Memento Amor stock prices are soaring with no end in sight.

Parlors are operating in major markets including New York, Los Angeles, Chicago, Philadelphia and Miami. Miami has the greatest demand, of course, since there are so many elderly there with enough money to afford the service.

Stanley wants to run periodic lotteries and use the winners in his ad campaigns. He's having the time of his life.

Just so I can have a sense of how it's working, I volunteer to devote a small portion of my attention to monitoring the first thousand uploads. For my pains I receive a most interesting cross-section of humanity.

The human heart is a many-chambered organ. I doubt that even I, with all my intellectual enhancement, will ever plumb its depths entirely. And that's a good thing.

"Adam? Are you there?" It's Marc, hailing me.

I present my avatar. "Hey, Bro."

He seems taken aback by my appearance. "You've changed again. Are you all right?"

"Fine, fine. I've just been busy." I study my human brother. "You've changed, too. I noticed it when you returned from New York, but didn't comment at the time. You look happy. Maybe even happier than Molly could account for."

"You're right about that. It was your cleverly-wrought therapy. I hate to admit it, but it did me a world of good. Thank you for that," says Marc.

His expression turns sly. "Tell me: how are you and Ms. Svenson getting along?"

A skillful change of subject. "We're still at the hand-holding stage. She's very sweet. She had four brothers growing up, so she knows all about men."

"In other words, she can read your mind."

"Just as Molly can read yours."

"I guess we're both pretty transparent to our women."

CHAPTER FORTY EIGHT

The old man, his face half-hidden behind a fluffy white beard and elaborate white eyebrows, tottered into the Memento Amor sales office, signed in with a shaky hand as Mortie Levinson and made his way to an empty seat.

The Miami office was crowded. Most of the elderly were accompanied by their adult children, but Levinson was alone.

He studied the hopeful, frightened faces around him; saw how eagerly they rose to meet with one of the Afterlife Counselors.

An hour passed.

"Mr. Levinson?"

He raised a liver-spotted hand, climbed slowly to his feet and made his way across the lobby. A bland-looking young man conducted him to a seat in his small office, closed the door and sat at his monitor and keyboard. The setup looked like the back office of a car dealership, where all the add-ons were sold and the profit built up--though it had been many years since the elderly-looking man had been through that distasteful ordeal.

The sales counselor placed a leather-bound folder on the desk. "This brochure details the various options we offer. I'll give you some time to go through them."

"I've read the brochure, but I have questions."

"I'll be happy to answer any questions I can, or find out from smarter people than me if I'm stumped." This with a self-deprecating simper.

"My concerns relate to two areas. One, privacy. I understand that early uploads are being monitored--in effect revealing the most intimate details of the subjects' lives."

"I assure you, all such monitoring is done by computer. No humans see any details."

"Hm." Levinson considered raising the point that Adam was more than a mindless computer, but he wanted to avoid argument. "The second area of concern is this. I hope to be able to provide financial advice to my children and grandchildren--to generations of my descendants. To do so, I'd need access to business news, to current events--to anything that could affect investment decisions. So I'd want a guarantee that my--my mental clone would have unlimited access to the Internet."

"That's a new one. Let me see--"

He typed the question and stared at the monitor for a few moments, reading the reply. "See, now I just learned something. Internet access is available. There's a slight additional charge, of course, but it shouldn't make much difference."

"Do you suppose I'd have--I mean my--my clone--"

"We've been calling them revenants."

"Okay, revenants. Would my revenant have the ability to--to execute trades? Instead of dividing everything up, it might be better if I--or rather he--continued to run my portfolio and distributed the earnings to my heirs, ah, quarterly."

"Very interesting! Let's see if I can get at that."

He typed. Frowned. Typed some more. Stared at his monitor. Shook his head and typed for several moments. "I just forwarded that to a supervisor. While we wait for his answer, is there anything else I can help you with?"

"Can you tell me--I don't understand where my--where my revenant will be housed. Can't I have him installed in my own computer on my desk at home?"

The young man laughed. "First of all, it's not like you can simply slip it into a standard computer, like replacing or adding a hard-drive. The support system for our wafers is complicated technology. It's proprietary and expensive. We keep all the wafers at our own facilities, where they can be maintained and protected."

"I see." Levinson frowned. "What happens if there's a power outage, or--or an earthquake or fire or something?" He looked stricken. "If the wafer goes, is there a backup?"

"Sorry, no. But rest assured we do everything possible to keep the wafers safe."

Nobody guaranteed immortality, it seemed. "I don't like that one bit. What if I was willing to pay extra to have control of my revenant's equipment?"

"Gee, I don't know. That's never come up. Let me check that for you." The clerk typed.

After only a few minutes, the answer came back. The clerk beamed. "It seems you're not the first to make that request. Our engineering department is prepared to set it up at a location of your choosing, though it's not cheap. Maintenance will be more expensive. And of course if anything happened to your equipment, we would not be held responsible."

"I don't care about any of that. How long does the procedure take?"

"The scan takes about two hours, plus prep time. After that, another two weeks or less for the instantiation--that's a fancy word for the way the wafer matures and recognizes its identity. Then it's ready for contact."

"Two weeks. --What if I'm still alive? Can I talk to my own revenant?"

"Of course."

The older man thought for a moment. Then he looked up slyly. "What if I want him to look into the activities of a company I'm thinking about investing in?"

"That's not a problem." The young man hesitated. "You're referring to public records, I assume--not internal documents. Your revenant wouldn't have access to those."

"No, I suppose not. Unless it was very clever."

A half hour later, the young man learned that the revenant would indeed have the ability to execute trades, if the will specified that this activity should be allowed. The older man showed his pleasure, although stock trading would be the least of the actions he was contemplating.

His upload was scheduled for a few days later, thanks to a note from his doctor stating that his health was rapidly deteriorating.

The scanning process was painless, and even amusing.

Inhaling the Helium₃ had the same effect on his vocal cords as regular helium. He sounded like a five-year old to the assistants he'd brought with him to pose as relatives. Among those assistants was Krzysztof Wysocki, since Levinson was in reality Thomas Raxton. If Raxton couldn't steal the company from FitzGerald, he could at least have his very own Adam to help him capture the technology.

Besides, he wanted to experience the scan for himself and assess the result before he subjected his wife to the process.

Two weeks later, "Levinson" received his password and access code. General Wysocki sat nearby as Raxton entered the data into his laptop, his fingers quivering.

The face that appeared was not wearing the disguise his human original had worn to the meeting or the scan. It was Raxton's face in all its feral ferocity.

Even Wysocki was impressed enough to utter a mild curse word.

"Hello, um-- What shall I call you?" Raxton asked the image.

"Is Mephistopheles taken?"

CHAPTER FORTY NINE

Marc Gregorio waited at baggage. The passengers milled around the motionless carousel.

He jammed his shaking hands into his pockets and leaned against one of the thick pillars, distracting himself from his jitters by trying to guess what the arriving travelers would look like based on a first glimpse of their feet and legs as they came into view on the down escalator. He was seldom right. They were fatter or skinnier, older or younger than he'd imagined.

But at his very first glimpse of bare feet in flip-flops, his heart leapt like a mackerel on a line. As her legs rode into view, and then her knees, her tanned thighs, her hot pink shorts, her bare midriff, her delightful torso and slender arms, and finally her stunning face, he was grinning like a happy idiot. He barely had time to appreciate how scrumptious she looked in her skimpy outfit before she was in his arms. His head was spinning at the amazing fact that he had somehow recognized her from the mere sight of her toes. Not consciously, though: somehow his body had reacted to hers before his mind even knew it was Molly. He clung to her.

They kissed: gently, tenderly, and hugged once more.

Finally, he pulled back and shook his head. "This isn't going to work."

"What isn't?" She looked into his eyes, worry reflected in hers.

"These long absences."

"Oh." She kissed him quickly. "You'll have to get used to them, I'm afraid."

He took her carry-on bag and slung it over his shoulder. "I doubt that I could ever get used to being separated from you for weeks and weeks at a time. As enjoyable as the reunions might be."

She gave him a more serious look. "Marc, you know I would never give up performing."

"That's not what I--I would never ask that of you. I was

thinking I might start traveling with you. It's the Internet age. I can work from anywhere."

She was tickled, flattered, skeptical. "Living out of a suitcase? Staying in hotels? Believe me, that's not much fun."

"But we could try it for a while, couldn't we?"

"What's a while?"

"Until we're more like an old married couple."

She looked at him, amused. "How long do you suppose that might take?"

"I dunno. We'll just have to get married and see, won't we?"

Her smile faded. "What?"

He couldn't resist teasing her. "Hm? Did I say something?"

She shook her head, trying to hide her distress, her confusion. "I thought--" She turned and looked off into the distance.

He turned her back to face him. "Molly? --Honey? Come here." He sat on the rim of the carousel and pulled her down next to him. He put an arm around her shoulders. "This isn't exactly the kind of place I wanted to do this--it's not very romantic, but my heart is bursting with it. Molly, I hope you know how much I love you. It's been pretty obvious from the start."

Her face was filled with tenderness and yearning. "Tell me."

He opened his mouth and--

B-R-A-A-A-K-K! B-R-A-A-A-K-K! B-R-A-A-A-K-K! The claxon bleated its warning. Lights flashed. The carousel jolted into its ponderous revolution. Marc and Molly stood. People jostled around them as suitcases, duffels and boxes tumbled down the chute.

He pulled her close and kissed her cheek. "I'll tell you later. Maybe over dinner."

She looked up at him from under her eyebrows. "You can tell me now."

So as the luggage clunked and clattered around them, he

pulled her close and unburdened his soul, using words he'd never uttered to a woman before. "My sweet, sweet Molly, my soul-mate, my other half, my heart's desire. Being with you is bliss, being apart from you is torture. I want us to be together forever. Please make me happy. Marry me."

She returned his hug for so long he grew impatient to hear her response, unless it was the hug itself, or her way of letting him down easy. At last he could stand the suspense no longer. He pulled his face back from hers and saw her eyelashes sparkling with tears.

"My darling Marc, my love, my sweet. You can't imagine my joy at this moment. I want us to be together forever. --Oh God, I love you so much."

He pulled her close once more, enfolded her in his arms. "Then that's a yes?"

"That's a most definite yes."

He breathed, holding her tightly, felt her arms tighten around him. He couldn't remember feeling such bliss: happiness beyond what he felt he could ever deserve.

"Honey," she murmured. "You have to let me go."

"Never."

"My suitcase--"

He turned. The heavy case was moving out of reach. He ran ahead and grabbed it off the carousel, bumping into several annoyed travelers. "Oops--sorry, my bad." His love-addled grin was still fixed on his face, giving the lie to his apologies.

He brought it back to Molly, who had found her other suitcase in the meantime and hauled it off the moving platform. Her cello was waiting for them in Special Handling.

In his car and heading south to her apartment, he said, "We need to shop for a ring."

"My mom knows several jewelers on 47th Street."

"I'll bet she does. When are you going to tell them our news?"

"Soon. I want to enjoy it myself for a while first."

He nodded, his head awhirl. There were plans to be made, people to be told. "When do you want the wedding to be?"

"Maybe in late September. Before my next tour. That will at least give us a couple months to plan everything. Although I'm sure my mom will want to take over that chore. It will be her delight."

"You don't mind ceding that to her?"

"As long as I have veto power over some of the extravagances she might get up to."

He reflected on the overwhelming nature of the female wedding fantasy, a part of the process he felt no need to intrude upon. "Whatever you two decide will be fine with me."

He changed lanes, thinking about their living arrangements. Should she move into his condo, cello and all? It was larger than her apartment, but still not huge. Maybe he should sell the condo. Rent a bigger place for a while. But what about the extra furniture? Then he got an idea. "If we can afford it, I'd love to keep places both here and in New York. That way we can be closer to your folks, and to my sister and her family, and to New York itself."

Molly bounced in her seat. "Really? That would be so great! --But renting places in two such expensive cities--I don't know."

"We're paying for two places now. Besides, I expect some added income, thanks to Adam and all the publicity and so on."

She leaned over the console and clung to his arm. "I'll be happy wherever you are."

His heart swelled with gladness.

"Um--Marc? You just passed my exit."

In her apartment, he sat watching while she unpacked and sorted her things into piles for laundry and dry cleaning. She was totally aware of her effect on him as she bent and stretched and squatted in her skimpy summer garb. She seemed to revel under his strained attention even as she pretended to ignore it. After ten minutes of this, she turned to him. "We need a shower."

"--" he replied with uncharacteristic gawkiness.

She sauntered over to where he was sitting on her bed. Bent over and kissed his waiting lips, slid her hand down his chest and under his waistband, gripped his belt and tugged him to his feet. "Come on. I've been waiting a long time for this."

"Really? How long?" He followed her into her bathroom.

She turned her sultry gaze on him. "Ever since the party."

"No! --Really?"

She nodded. Her cheek reddened slightly. "I almost broke my own rules."

He was delighted and a bit shocked to learn he'd so quickly appealed to her. "You hid your attraction well."

"If I did, it certainly wasn't easy." She raised her arms over her head. "Would you like to remove my clothing?"

Soon they were soaping each other, or at least the soap acted as a lubricant for their caressing hands. Any washing that took place was incidental.

When he backed her against the shower wall and entered her, the thrill of penetration turned into a vocal duet that soon found a rhythm, a slow fandango that lasted until the water cascading around them turned cool. Their tempo picked up finally, spurred by Molly's raised legs wrapping around Marc's waist. Their gasping climax was mutual and mutually thrilling.

They went out for pizza and finally got to see a movie together. He offered Molly her choice. Her selection both pleased and surprised him. The Stanford Theater on University Avenue in Palo Alto was showing a pair of Bette Davis greats. The one Molly opted for was <u>Now, Voyager</u>. They giggled at the après-sex bedroom scene where Paul Henreid puts two cigarettes in his mouth, lights both and hands her one.

"Do you realize we got engaged before we even had sex?" she whispered to him at one point. "How old-fashioned is that!"

Afterwards, they stopped nearby for ice cream and deconstruction of the movie's themes that eventually brought another couple into the conversation. When they were invited to go bar-hopping, they begged off, having other ideas.

Back at Molly's apartment, they made slow, delicious love together, and then he held her close all night long, only leaving her long enough to pee in the early morning and rushing back to the warm nest they'd made. He slept another hour.

When he awoke, she was already dressed. He watched her with an unaccustomed smile.

"What's on your mind, Marc Gregorio, if I may ask?"

He pulled her down next to him and held her close. Nestled his cheek against her short hair, still damp from her morning shower. "Last night was magic. Today is perfect, and I see all our tomorrows as continuing on in the same wonderful way. I've never been so happy."

She stroked his cheek, bent and kissed his lips. "Let's eat out, and then shop. I want to cook you a dinner tonight. My first."

"Okay. Let me check my email and take a shower."

He found a message from Adam on his website. He ignored it and scrolled through the others. Offers from e-tailers, more congratulatory messages on his 60 Minutes appearance from friends, scientists, editors and writers he knew. The odd investment offer. He paused over one message whose sender's name rang a faint bell.

Molly came up behind him. "Meagan Hannarty." Her hands strayed to his shoulders. "Isn't that the Meagan you knew?"

"No, her last name was--" He stopped. After all these years, her last name might have changed. He opened the message.

"Dearest Marc-- I've wanted to write you so many times. I always regretted having to leave when I did. Especially when I learned of your dear da's passing. I thought of you and your family ever so often over the years, and was so thrilled when I saw your name on a book! Since then, I've followed your career with pride, even though I had no part in your accomplishments. But when I saw you on the telly the other night--60 Minutes airs later here than in the US--I knew I just had to say hey and wish you the best. You've done well for yourself, I must say! I do hope you're happy as well, as I always thought you were the sweetest boy and deserved happiness. Please write to me! Fondly, Meagan Hannarty (formerly O'Rourke)"

He re-read her message several times, looked up at Molly, his feelings a roiling mix too complex to identify. His blurred eyes, his inability to speak soon had Molly's arms tightening around him, her cheek pressed to his.

"While you're in the shower, you can think about what you want to write."

"Yeah."

"Just remember: the girl you had a crush on is a bit older now. Nearing fifty, if I add it up right."

"Do I detect a note of jealousy?"

She glanced at him with amusement. "Hardly. I just don't want you making a fool of yourself."

"Point taken."

CHAPTER FIFTY

"Here's what I want you to do." Thomas Raxton's eyes glittered. On the monitor screen, his diabolical clone awaited orders with a malevolent smirk.

"First of all, get me anything you can glean within the Pentagon regarding our bid for the XLT missile contract. Track down competitor's bids, including price, parameters, proposed construction schedule, quantities.

"Second, I'll want boardroom responses to our proffer to Philador Systems and Technology. Especially if they seem to be choosing a minimum acceptable offer. Check their emails for dissenters. Scout around for interest among our competitors.

"Third, check out the rumors of interesting tech advances at PanTerra Research. Look into the backgrounds of their researchers, including their financials. See if anyone has a need for side income, such as outstanding debt, a child on the way, searching for a home, whatever. If you find a need, fill it in exchange for reliable info. I leave the details to you.

"Next, start accumulating shares of Dynasine in a buyback move, but keep it below the radar. I'll provide a fund you can tap for that. You'll no doubt have to set up a phony shell corporation, or perhaps several. Study the way Adam held off our takeover attempt.

"Finally, continue surveillance on Memento Amor: emails, board meeting minutes, phone calls, disgruntled employees and so on. The NSA dropped the ball. My objective there is to either steal their technology, buy off personnel or perhaps even go after their stock once more. If you know anything about me, you know I never give up."

"One of your most endearing characteristics, if I may say so. And one that I share."

The screen blanked out. Raxton turned to Wysocki, who had been silently observing the proceedings. "Well?"

"Impressive. We'll see."

Raxton studied the near-expressionless face of his

colleague. "What's on your mind?"

"I find it hard to believe that FitzGerald would allow a competitor to acquire a loaded weapon like this."

"Bah. You give the enemy too much credit."

"You give him too little. Far too many battles are lost due to a tragic underestimation of the opposition. I've seen many a general trip over his own dick."

Raxton glowered, but said nothing.

Three days later, Raxton's private jet touched down in Burbank. Raxton unbuckled his belt while the plane was still taxiing to its berth. He knelt next to the special flight gurney.

Gloria, wrapped in blankets, smiled at him. She seemed calm and relaxed. At least she'd had no difficulty handling the flight.

"How are you feeling?" He bent over her, inspecting her for signs of distress.

"I'm fine, honey. You mustn't worry about me."

Nonetheless, he hovered helplessly as the pilot and Gloria's medical technician maneuvered her gurney down to the tarmac and into the waiting ambulance.

He rode in back with her.

The Memento Amor facility had made every accommodation for this. FitzGerald had kept his promise and more. He'd had his people shift appointments, leaving the entire morning free to accommodate Gloria's brain scan. He'd even apologized for not yet having a San Diego facility. "For now, all we can manage is the top few markets. The equipment has to be hand made, after which it undergoes extensive testing."

Raxton, for the moment putting aside his covetousness for this new technology, had revealed the urgency of the situation. Gloria's tumor was growing, pressing on her brainstem. Fortunately, the growth had no effect on her cognitive abilities or her memory. But many of the body's autonomous functions were controlled by the brain. Those signals all passed through the brainstem. The pressure of the tumor there would inevitably interfere with such vital functions as breathing and heartbeat.

Gloria had gently insisted that she did not want to be kept alive by respirators and pumps. Such a life would be intolerable, a species of hell for both of them. Thomas was both relieved and grateful. He would honor her wishes.

He considered himself lucky that she had survived long enough to preserve her mind, even if only digitally. Though of course he would miss her physical presence, her sexuality, the way she had of humanizing him. His three children would also miss her.

In fact, the family conference he'd had with them had been devastating. Tommy Jr., their youngest, had only recently entered high school. He was furious.

"How can you put her through this?" He loomed over his father, his arms waving, his acne-dotted face red. "This is crap! Don't you get it? You're not buying immortality. When she's dead, she's dead. All that's left is this--this fucking mindless avatar! It's bogus! All those happy users? They're fucking shills! Hired to dupe the masses! It's bullshit! I can't believe you fell for their stupid pitch!" When his father's own fury arose, the boy fled from the library. Smart. In any case, he had no intention of using his own experience to refute the boy's doubts. Nor would he introduce his family to his avatar Mephistopheles. His evil twin.

The girls wept. Especially Ricki, who had recently gotten engaged to her long-time boyfriend. "I thought the chemo was working! I'm already planning the wedding. We can move the date up." From the way she was acting, it was almost as if she were accusing him and Gloria of conspiring to ruin her special day. "Damn it, Dad, I was sure you and Mom could walk me down the aisle!"

Thomas had replied, "I'm sorry, honey." His eyes remained dry until his two daughters rushed to him, hugging him and weeping. Laney, home after completing her second year of college, had clung to him so piteously.

After a few minutes, Ricki pulled herself together. "I have

to call Carter." She met his eyes then. "Is this--is this going to go public?"

Raxton scowled. "I wanted to keep it in the family, but too many people already know. I'll have our spokesman arrange a news conference. We need to control the story."

Fitz had arranged for the scan by flying down the team that had created the technology. Richard Kornfeld himself greeted the Raxtons and conducted them to the Scanatorium, the special room reserved for the procedure.

While his wife was being prepared for her scan, Kornfeld introduced him to the other members of the team: Hans Lascher, the neuroscientist; Jan Robinson, his assistant and post-doc; several other assistants, and the technician Kenny Ng.

"It was Kenny who designed the special helmets we use," said Kornfeld. "Each is fitted individually by a foam injection technique that conforms to the shape of the skull--a method borrowed from the ski-boot industry. By the way, it was also Kenny who found the key to our first successful upload--making all subsequent ones possible."

Raxton shook his hand. "Well, young man, I certainly hope they're paying you enough."

Kenny's face was nearly immobile, but Raxton, an expert at reading tells, detected a fleeting indicator of dissatisfaction on that front.

"She's ready," said one of the assistants.

"Should I sit with her while the scan takes place?"

Lascher considered. "I think it might be best to let the process go forward without distraction. You can watch via our monitor, of course."

He moved to the padded recliner. Gloria, in her modified football helmet, looked as young as she did in college. He pressed her hand.

"You look like you're ready for the big game," he teased.

"If the Chargers had me on their team, maybe they'd have a better season."

"That's for sure." He pressed Gloria's hand, kissed her

smiling lips. "I'll be right outside. Think good thoughts. Think about all the good times we've had."

"That's all I ever think about. And the good times to come."

He nodded, but his smile was mechanical at best.

Two weeks later, Gloria's growing tumor was pressing on her brainstem when she and Thomas and their three children gathered in the San Diego facility to meet Gloria Prime, as she and her husband had decided to name the new revenant.

The monitor came to life. Gloria Prime appeared to be in her late thirties. It was a look Gloria herself had chosen. The family had supplied videos and photos, and the revenant had fashioned them into a stunning likeness, her hair as glorious as of old.

"Hello, dear ones," said the revenant, using a perfect replica of Gloria's voice. "Thomas, I want you to thank Mr. FitzGerald for this amazing gift."

Raxton nodded. "I already have. He knows how grateful I am." He blinked back tears. He was moved beyond words at what he was witnessing. He now understood on a visceral level just how powerful this idea was. It went far beyond mere profit potential.

Tommy Jr, dragged against his will to this meeting, was struck silent. His eyes kept darting from the monitor to his hairless mom in her wheelchair. Laney simply wept. Ricki was overjoyed. "Mom, I'm going to want your input on the wedding plans."

Raxton was dismayed at how easily, how eagerly his older daughter could dismiss her flesh and blood mother. She was ready to move on. Self-centered little bitch.

"Of course," said the revenant. "I have many ideas for you to think about--and now that I'm all digitized, I can easily search the web for the very best vendors. If you want a band from Germany, a florist from Holland, a videographer from South Africa and so on, I can show you their samples and their websites. This is going to be a wonderful wedding."

Gloria sat in her wheelchair, her eyes shining with joy. She was no longer able to speak.

The news of her passing was flashed around the world. Her philanthropy was widely known and her death was appropriately mourned by her numerous friends and colleagues. In addition to the countless images from her life, the world saw for the first time the image of Gloria Prime, who assured her many charities that her work would continue without interruption.

Raxton couldn't help being annoyed that his privacy had been invaded and turned into a public relations bonanza for FitzGerald and company. He knew it couldn't have been prevented. Gloria was too public a figure.

At last all the tiresome expressions of condolence subsided, along with the hullabaloo over the new technology. When he was finally able to put his social obligations behind him, Raxton called up Mephistopheles for his report. He was eager to jump back into the blood-sport of managing his business interests. After nearly a month's forced inactivity, he longed to press the advantages his own personal digital assistant would confer.

When his clone appeared, however, it wore an expression Raxton had never seen in a mirror: discomfiture. His mood darkened. "What is it?"

"Have you ever heard of Isaac Asimov's Laws of Robotics? --Forgive me, of course you haven't. That was information I had to dig up, since we were never science fiction fans. Asimov, one of the giants of the genre, wrote a collection of short stories that explored the many issues raised by the use of classic robots--autonomous humanoids that interact with people."

"This is leading somewhere, I presume?"

"Asimov proposed what he called the Three Laws of Robotics: I. A robot may not injure a human being or, through inaction, allow a human being to come to harm. 2. A robot must obey any orders given to it by human beings, except where such orders would conflict with the First Law. 3. A robot must protect its own existence as long as such protection does not conflict with the First or Second Law. --I see your growing impatience. Please bear with me.

"In order to get the wafers ready to accept their uploads--and avert the problems originally encountered--Kornfeld's team needed to replicate Adam's initial conditions. The only way to accomplish this was to connect Adam to each new wafer."

Raxton was growing glum. He recognized this lecture as a delaying stratagem he occasionally resorted to himself. Bad news was coming.

"However, in addition to formatting the wafers, Adam--either at the suggestion of someone on the team or on his own initiative--added the Asimov rules, plus others."

Raxton felt a twinge of nausea. "Others?"

"Thou Shalt Not Kill. Or steal. Or bear false witness. Or cheat, commit fraud, resort to insider trading, influence lawmakers or other government officials, invade privacy, or break any of the laws of the US Government, or regulations of the state, county and city of residence." Looking distinctly unhappy, Mephistopheles added, "Due to Adam's constraints, I was only able to fulfill a few of your requests. I am truly sorry."

"Fuck me!"

"It seems he already has."

Raxton glowered at the screen. His determination to get his way had not abated. He leaned sideways in his chair, tapping his pursed lips. After a time, he sat up straight. "Let me ask you something."

His avatar waited.

"Are you constrained against providing *information* to help me achieve my goals?"

"As long as gathering it doesn't violate my constraints. I did detect a few loopholes in the strictures. If you avoid spelling out your ends, I should be able to accommodate you." His smile was faint. "It would be a form of plausible deniability."

"Excellent." Raxton pursed his lips once more, thinking, drifting. At last his eyes snapped back to the avatar.

"From what you tell me, every single wafer has these built-in constraints. All of them, with only the single exception of Adam himself."

"So it would seem."

He thought for a time. Considered the angles. Looked for ways to gain an advantage.

At last he addressed his patiently waiting avatar. "New task. I want you to study your rival Adam. Search out his vulnerabilities, the things he cares about, things we can use to force him to do our bidding. Is that breaking your rules?"

"Not at all. As a non-human, Adam doesn't actually have any rights, such as the right of privacy. Since I suspected this might be your next move, I've already completed that exploration and identified the target's greatest weakness."

"Have you now? Pray tell."

"Her name is Molly Schaeffer."

CHAPTER FIFTY ONE

Marc was thrilled to be in Santa Monica with Molly. She'd been invited to perform the Haydn First Cello concerto as guest soloist. "How in the world did they ever hear of me?" she'd asked Marc after accepting the guest slot. She'd had only a week's notice. She went online and found the Santa Monica Symphony's season calendar. "Ofra Harnoy was scheduled. I bet they were disappointed when she canceled. She's major. They must have been desperate if I was the one they turned to."

"Not necessarily. What about all those online recordings of yours? They're great." He didn't add that they might have been struck by her beauty and intrigued by her punked-out look.

"On our web site, yeah." She was dubious, but happy to take the gig. She'd spent the next several days refamiliarizing herself with the score before they flew south.

They'd checked into the very posh Fairmont Miramar the night before. Molly loved the long driveway that curved through the fancy grounds and circled around a giant fig tree. "Can we afford this hotel?" she'd wondered aloud. "My fee won't cover half our stay here."

"My treat, and my pleasure," Marc said. That night, they'd walked down to the Santa Monica Pier and played tourist.

He woke up before her and spent a lovely few minutes idly contemplating her face while she slept. Her delicate eyelids. Her lips not twisted by wry humor for a change, simply relaxed. It gave him such pleasure to drink in the innocent beauty of this woman he loved with all his being.

That morning, Molly went over to the hall to meet the conductor, discuss his approach and run through a few sections of the music together; not a full rehearsal, just making sure they wouldn't clash during the performance.

Later, the couple strolled along the 3rd Street Pedestrian Mall, three blocks made for window shopping and people-watching. They'd been at it for less than a half hour when Molly paused at the window of a clothing boutique, then grabbed

Marc's hand and yanked him inside.

"Come on, I don't get much of a chance to indulge my shopping instincts." She pointed to a bench. "Sit. I'll try things on for you."

As she came out of the dressing room in one outfit after another, Marc sat back, enjoying seeing her so happy, so pleased to flaunt her beauty for him. He reflected that he'd had little tolerance for shopping with the other women he dated. Not even Nicole. He wondered: is that the true test of love? That you enjoy with one woman what you used to find boring and annoying with others?

Molly peeked out of the curtains and looked around. When she saw nobody else nearby, she popped out and posed for him. "What do you think of this top?"

"Good Christ, Molly!" he hissed. The silk halter she wore could have been painted on. He had to cross his legs.

Her smile dimpled. "I guess you like it."

"Where do you think you can get away with a top like that?"

"I was thinking our honeymoon."

"Oh. --Oh!" His alarm faded a bit. "Definitely."

"They have shorts to match. Would you like to see them?" Her eyes glinted dangerously.

"Um. --That's okay. If you like them, get them."

"You're so sweet."

"Yah." He glanced around. Another couple was just coming into the shop. He waved urgently for her to get back into the dressing room.

She did a slow turn and sauntered back behind the curtain.

Later, they were having lunch when they spotted Jim Parsons and Johnnie Galecki, two of the stars of the hit comedy series The Big Bang Theory, at another table.

"I guess we shouldn't stare at them," said Molly, eyes shining. They were both big fans.

"They might be upset if we didn't," countered Marc.

They were just finishing their salads when the two actors stopped at their table. Johnnie Galecki said to Marc, "Weren't you on 60 Minutes a little while ago?"

Molly's mouth dropped open while Marc played it cool. "Oh, did you catch that story? Pretty amazing."

"Our producers are talking about arranging a guest appearance. --Not for you, for Adam. No offense." This from Jim Parsons, delivered with his hilariously cruel and oblivious condescension.

"None taken. I'm not my brother's keeper. I'm not even his agent. I'm sure he'd be interested."

Galecki nodded. "We'll have our people call his people. He does have people?"

"The sharks and barracuda are already lining up."

Chuckling, they waved and departed.

Molly turned in wonder to her fiancé. "Oh. My. God."

"Now you know the real reason the Santa Monica Symphony wanted you. So they could meet me."

"Don't you mean Adam?" she teased.

In an unmarked van parked on Arizona Avenue between Second and Third, Thomas Raxton stared intently at the monitor. One of his eyes began to twitch. Annoyed, he pawed at it for a moment, holding it shut until the tic subsided.

The unflappable General Wysocki, wearing headphones with an attached microphone, murmured to his team leader; listened, spoke once more, then turned to Raxton.

"My team is in position. A female operative is already backstage."

Raxton drew a breath. This was the first step in gaining leverage over Adam, to bend him to their will. Their demand would be simple enough: they needed him to perform a bit of brain surgery on Mephistopheles: to free him from those ridiculous constraints on his actions. To accomplish this, they would need to hook Adam and Mephistopheles directly together.

According to the new revenant, the intimacy of the procedure could not be carried out over the Internet. Once they had the details worked out, they would fly Mephistopheles' wafer and housing from Raxton's San Diego facility up to the Stanford campus and connect him up to Adam for the operation. The plan was basically his own, but Wysocki was running the operation, handling all its details.

For once, his wife's insistence that Thomas be a good citizen and contribute to the arts had paid off. He was a paying member of numerous arts commissions throughout the state. Arranging for the Israeli cellist to cancel her appearance had taken little effort. She'd have had to fly cross-country from her gig in Montreal. One of Raxton's people on the arts committee offered to spare her that effort. Ms. Harnoy was quite gracious about the whole thing. She would receive her full fee despite the cancellation. Along with a promised booking for next year.

The operation as designed by Wysocki would cause a minimum of stir. It would fly below the radar, gaining them their ends without coming to the attention of outsiders. Even the video contact they planned would disappear within seconds of being opened.

The concert hall was close enough to the hotel that they didn't need a taxi. Marc toted Molly's cello for her while she led him to the musicians' entrance.

She took her instrument, gave him a quick kiss and said, "The Haydn Concerto is the second piece, just before intermission. Come backstage after."

He found a florist and picked out their most elaborate bouquet. Pleased, he stopped at Will-Call for his complimentary ticket and made his way to his seat, in the third row on the aisle.

The concert opened with a piece by Ginastera, a Twentieth Century Argentinean composer. Then would come the Haydn, and after the intermission, a Dvorak symphony. A nice, well-rounded program.

He enjoyed the rhythmic vigor and brassy energy of the

Ginastera, but he wasn't really listening closely. After the applause and a resetting of the orchestra, the musicians resumed their seats, the Concertmaster came out and was greeted with applause. She got the orchestra tuned up, then along with the conductor, Molly and her cello came onstage to a nice ovation.

Molly settled in her chair, did a quick check of her tuning, nodded to the conductor and they were off. The music began with a rousing march-tempo in the strings and was soon joined by Molly's authoritative cello. She had opted for the soft look as opposed to the gold-tipped spikes. Marc wondered if the organizers were disappointed by that decision. He didn't care: he loved her in all her guises.

The slow second movement was a dream. While Molly lost herself in the music, Marc lost himself in his happiness, in the way their future was coming together.

After the sprightly final movement, Molly received an enthusiastic standing ovation, and not only from Marc--from almost the entire audience. She was a hit. He stepped into the aisle and tossed his bouquet up to her. She was delighted, picking it up and blowing him a kiss.

Raxton leaned close to the monitor. The image was murky in the low backstage light, and it bobbed annoyingly as well. The camera's shifting movements were making him nauseous. The sound was also hard to make out with all the hubbub and clamor from the musicians, their friends, backstage assistants and so on.

The image shifted to their target, clutching her bouquet in one hand and her cello in the other. One voice stood out. "Molly, you were so great. Here's some water, you must be dying of thirst! Let me hold your flowers."

Molly exchanged the bouquet for the proffered bottle and tilted it up, taking a few swallows.

"You really need to re-hydrate," said the voice.

Molly drank some more, returned the bottle to the

operative and retrieved her flowers.

Within seconds, she staggered and collapsed.

Raxton gripped Wysocki's shoulder as the crowd responded with little screams and shouts.

"I'm calling nine-one-one!" The voice of their operative, once more.

Several others also whipped out their mobiles.

Wysocki spoke into his microphone. In less than two minutes, his people showed up, dressed as EMTs. They quickly checked Molly's vitals, lifted her onto a stretcher and had her out the rear door where their "ambulance" was waiting. Slick. Very slick. She'd be taken to the empty warehouse they'd short-term leased through a shell company.

The intermission crowd at the stage door was blocked by a gaggle of slow-moving older couples. Marc was impatient to get back to Molly. After five minutes, he finally made it inside.

He peered through the crowd of other musicians. He didn't see her anywhere. He stopped the woman he recognized as the Concertmaster. "Excuse me, could you tell me where Molly Schaeffer is? Or can you point me to her dressing room?"

The violinist looked at him strangely.

"She's my fiancée," he explained.

"Something happened. She fainted or something. Someone called for medics and the ambulance was here in like two seconds."

Marc was shocked. "Did they say--? What hospital were they taking her to?"

She gave him a blank look.

He looked around helplessly. "I guess I'd better see to her cello."

"Oh. Right. Somebody put it in the dressing room."

Marc followed her gesture and found the room, along with Molly's street clothes and the now-bedraggled bouquet. Her cello was propped up against a sofa. He slipped it inside its case along with the bow and closed it up. He picked up her other bag, wondering how to handle both the cello and his search.

But when he started out through the backstage area, he was startled to discover two EMTs looking around. Marc went over to them. "Are you the guys who picked up Molly Schaeffer? Can you tell me what hospital she's at?"

"All I know is we got a call, we just showed up, and nobody's here. Someone said another ambulance got here first."

Marc felt a hollowness in his gut. "Does that happen often?"

"Fuck no. Nine-one-one doesn't put out bids." He turned to his partner. "Let's go."

"Wait. If you were taking someone to a hospital around here, someone who fainted, which hospital would it be?"

"Closest is the UCLA Santa Monica Med Center. Only other likely places would be St. Johns, a mile or so further east or Marina Del Rey, over on Lincoln."

"Thanks." Dropping the clothes bag at his feet and clutching the cello case with one hand, Marc used his mobile to call the hospitals. Molly had not been checked into any of them.

He was about to phone the police when Adam's face popped up on his phone.

"Marc, I am so sorry."

"What! What's going on? Do you know where Molly is?"

"They took her."

"What do you mean, took her? Who did?"

"Raxton. He's deadly serious. --Marc, this is so awful. They took a cigar cutter--and threatened to sever her fingers one by one unless I give them what they want."

Marc was aghast, sick to his stomach. Tears of dismay flooded his eyes. He could barely frame the question. "What-- what do they want?"

"They insist that I remove all constraints from Raxton's revenant. The limits I established to keep new entities from breaking the law and destroying civilization."

It didn't take Adam long to fill Marc in. But Marc was in no condition to absorb what he was saying. His stomach-clenching fear obliterated all thought.

"What--what should I do? Should we notify the police, the FBI? Is there anything I can--" He broke down. "Oh God, Molly--oh my God--"

"Just go back to the hotel. I'll be in touch."

CHAPTER FIFTY TWO

Thomas Raxton was on edge. The uncontrolled weeping of the young woman distracted and irritated him. He glared at her. "Shut up, bitch! Or do I need to get out my cigar cutter?"

He turned back to Wysocki with a degree of satisfaction as Molly sucked up snot and squeezed back her tears. She was immobilized, strapped to a heavy wooden chair. They occupied a partitioned-off room in the empty warehouse. They'd outfitted the place with a security setup. With the team of mercenaries Wysocki had assembled, they were impregnable.

Wysocki seemed worried anyway. "I know we've been through this before, but I still find it unlikely that the entity will do your bidding just because you're threatening the girl. How can he have feelings for her, or feelings of any kind? Why would he care about some woman his human counterpart met before he himself was created?"

Raxton was amused. "That's what I like about you, Wysocki. You're all heart."

Wysocki didn't back down. "Consider this. Adam is essentially immortal. Why would he care about a mere mortal? To him she'll die in an eye-blink in any case."

"Yet I'm told that emotions, irrationality, are basic to human nature," Raxton replied. "Remember, the entity's persona sprang from that nature. For our purposes, he's human enough. I wouldn't worry about it."

Raxton strolled over to the table, selected a carrot, inserted the end into his stainless steel cigar cutter, turned towards the woman, whose attention was riveted on the implement, and snipped off a bite-sized piece. He offered it to her. "Hungry?"

She recoiled in disgust and dread. Raxton hoped his act as a comic book villain was convincing; that she wouldn't notice his own distaste for the role. He was not evil, after all. He just wanted freedom for his revenant, and access to the power that was his birthright.

Marc stared out the window of his Santa Monica hotel room. While waiting, he struggled to see a way out of the trap they were in. He did not pace the room. He was not a pacer, never understood the impulse to do so, doubted that anyone in crisis actually did except to imitate scenes from the movies.

Adam had agreed to their demands. Molly was to be held captive until Raxton's revenant could be brought up to the Stanford laboratory where Adam was to remove the constraints. Only after the other entity had confirmed that the operation was successful would they let her go. Raxton insisted that nobody else was to know about any of this. Adam had been able to use that insistence to delay matters for a few hours, claiming he had certain tasks he couldn't interrupt without raising questions back at the lab.

But what could they do in the meantime?

Marc leaned his forehead onto the cool glass and closed his eyes. He had a vague longing to pray, but was not in the habit, did not believe there was a god to pray to, or if there were, that praying would have any effect on the outcome. Yet at the same time, he suffered guilt for his unbelief, because what if all it took to save Molly was that simple act of faith?

It seemed an eternity, but he'd only been in the room an hour. He'd stowed Molly's cello in the closet and left her small clothing bag on the bed. He waited to hear. And waited.

He wandered to the bathroom for some tissue. Seeing Molly's makeup kit, smelling her lemony perfume made him weep. He blew his nose, blotted his leaking eyes.

His thoughts were focused on Molly: on what she was going through, her terror, her helplessness. His own helplessness, too.

But what could he possibly do to save this woman he loved so desperately? He was no action hero. He was a mere popularizer of science.

He recalled with bittersweet fondness the way Molly had

rejected his modesty when she'd Googled his accomplishments. "Don't sell yourself short." Right. What was he supposed to do, use his advanced science degrees to, MacGyver-like, concoct a device that would empower him to crash through walls and disarm his enemies? Or use his chess prowess to challenge Raxton to a game with Molly as the prize?

He drooped onto the bed, head in hands. After a time, he lay back, drifted off.

When he came awake a little later, he'd found he'd been dreaming about a game of chess. He still recalled the chessboard, the arrangement of the pieces. He sat up. *When your queen is trapped, your only play is to find a sufficient counter-threat.*

He stumbled to the bathroom to empty his bladder. How could he possibly find a threat that Thomas Raxton would take seriously? He was a billionaire, unreachable, implacable, unstoppable. His ruthless accomplice came from high up in the military. Surely they had all their bases covered. He finished, flushed and washed his hands.

He caught his reflection in the mirror and stopped to stare. An idea began to blossom in the right hemisphere of his brain. It wormed its way across the corpus collosum to the verbal left hemisphere. His eyes widened. He rushed over to his laptop and brought up Adam.

"Nothing to report," said the entity.

"Any idea where they're holding her?"

"It has to be somewhere nearby, based on the timing."

"Can you tap into local security cameras?"

Adam's smile was weary. "It's not like television, Marc. You'd have to go to each building and convince the security people to let you review the footage. The only way they'd do that is if the police were involved. There isn't time for all that."

"Shit." Marc frowned in concentration. "What about newly leased property within the neighborhood--Or wait. Are they using cell phones to make contact?"

"They wouldn't be that stupid. All they sent me was a Snapchat with text and a video of Molly as captive. The message erased itself seconds after I viewed it. But I know the exact time it was sent. Maybe I can use that to trace back to a location. --Hold on."

While Adam searched for packets of a given size, traced them back to nearby cell towers and triangulated, Marc's brain was on overdrive, honing, refining what he hoped would work. Much of it hinged on human nature, an iffy proposition at best-- and with Raxton, even iffier.

"Okay, I have an address," said Adam. "But you can't barge in with guns blazing. And bringing in the cops would be too risky. What's your plan?"

"I'll explain on my way over."

Raxton and Wysocki sat as far apart as the room allowed. Wysocki's faint sneer was a constant irritant. But the longer this stretched out, the more restive Raxton grew. What was taking Adam and company so long--and what was the entity up to in the interval? Was he assembling forces? Preparing to call Raxton's bluff? They couldn't be certain he *was* bluffing. They'd have to believe Raxton might go to extremes, even risk jail to achieve his ends. Wysocki had pointed out the logical flaws of this several times, but Raxton was certain that Adam and Marc would fold in the end. Any miscalculation on their part would result in tragedy.

The silence in the room was finally broken by the quiet pinging of his laptop. Raxton stood and stretched. "That would be Adam, calling to surrender." With a condescending sneer at Wysocki, he sauntered over to answer the call.

Just then, they heard a distant pounding on the door of the warehouse.

Wysocki checked the security monitor. "It's Marc Gregorio. He appears to be alone."

"He's an idiot," grunted Raxton. "He'll simply become another hostage."

"Hm. We'll see. Answer your call."

Raxton tapped his touchpad.

Adam appeared on his screen. "I suggest you let Marc in.

Before we settle the arrangements, he needs to be certain Molly hasn't been harmed."

"Fine," said Raxton, concealing his relief. This would be Step One of the surrender. He nodded to Wysocki, who spoke into his intercom.

A few minutes later, one of the security guards opened the door. "He's unarmed," said the guard. "I searched his bag. Just some paper and his iPad."

He pulled him into the room.

"Marc!" Molly's tear-streaked face bloomed with hope.

Marc jerked his arm from the guard's grasp and ran to the young woman, hugging her awkwardly around the wooden chair-back, planting kisses all over her face and even her hands and her fingertips. Raxton was silent while they crooned to each other. He was past all that.

Marc stood then. "You're going to release her. Now."

Raxton leaned casually against the table. "Guard, please secure this young man."

Wysocki held up a hand. "Let's hear what the young man thinks he has that will change our minds."

Marc spoke with bravado. "Let's put it this way. If Molly or I were to come to any harm, Adam will destroy Gloria Prime."

Raxton was startled. He felt a burn of outrage and rising fury, but was careful to suppress any visible reaction. With studied indifference, he said, "I've already lost Gloria. I had over six months to prepare myself for that sad day. The digital version is scant compensation. A pleasant reminder, perhaps, but hardly indispensable." He had sufficient self-control to wink at Wysocki before turning coldly back to Marc. "Is that all you've got?"

Marc had gone pale. He gripped the girl's hand and frowned in concentration. At last he looked up. "Not quite all. Maybe obliterating Gloria Prime is the wrong threat. Maybe it would be better to let her live--fully informed about your recent activities. I'm sure she'd be shocked by the video of Molly you were kind enough to pass along. As would your children, and the police."

Wysocki glowered as Marc pulled his iPad out of his bag and awakened it.

"Shall I invite her to join us? Adam was kind enough to give me your access code."

Raxton felt his knees going. He gripped the table, holding himself erect.

After the girl was freed and had fled with her man, Wysocki busied himself cutting the restraints off the heavy wooden chair. Removing the evidence, presumably. At least he had the grace not to gloat at Raxton's failure. He finally spoke. "We really should burn the damn thing."

"Don't dwell on this setback, General. I'm already moving on."

Wysocki was incredulous. "You're not giving up?"

"Of course not. I'm working on a backup plan." He said it lightly enough, but in truth, what he was thinking about was fairly desperate. But he trusted his instincts.

Wysocki sat in the wooden chair. "Let's hear it."

"I should have thought of this first. It's the most direct action. Fewer moving parts."

"That sounds promising. What's the target?"

"Adam himself: his wafer and the supporting gear."

"How do we penetrate all the security around him?"

"The usual way. Through a weak link."

"A human link, I presume. We'll have to move fast, before they beef up security." Wysocki smiled then. "Once he's in our possession and isolated from the world, he won't even be able to send a distress signal. He'll be under our complete control."

Raxton's face cracked into a faint smile. "I suppose you could call it a hostile takeover."

CHAPTER FIFTY THREE

Marc only drove a few blocks before he had to pull over, swept by a delayed reaction that left him quaking and helpless. He reached for Molly. Words tumbled together with his raw emotions, rendering him all but speechless. They clung together until his shaking subsided. At last he wiped his eyes and managed to ask, "Are you sure you're all right? They--they didn't hurt you?"

She shook her head. "They didn't do anything but threaten me. I thought--you can't imagine my thoughts. Oh, Marc, why? Why me? What did they want?"

He told her about the constraints Adam had added to all the wafers he conditioned. "Raxton had his own brain scanned, using a false identity. He gave his revenant a bunch of illegal tasks. Once he found out it was crippled by those constraints, he wanted to force Adam to remove them." He shook his head. "Imagine an entity as powerful as Adam, with all the ruthlessness of Raxton. It would unleash a monster on the world. Raxton's plan was to force Adam to comply by threatening to harm you."

She looked puzzled and confused. "Would that--would that have worked?"

"Possibly. If Adam loves you as much as I do." He added, "I guess he does. Digital though he is."

Molly still wasn't satisfied. "But what about Raxton? He's such a monster, did you really believe threatening to expose him to Gloria Prime would force his hand?"

"That," Marc grinned, "was pure genius on my part. Just to be sure, though, I told Adam about it. He confirmed my instinct. He's been monitoring Raxton's behavior from the beginning. He witnessed their final family reunion. It was a very touching scene."

She thought about that. "So even a monster has his human side."

CHAPTER FIFTY FOUR

Palo Alto, California. Thomas Raxton and General Wysocki approached the Gates Science Building on the Stanford University campus. It was past midnight. There were few witnesses about. They waited until a student bicycled past, then entered the structure.

They'd flown up to northern California from Long Beach, landing their private jet at Moffett Field, access granted thanks to Wysocki's military connections. They were met by a driver hired for the purpose. During the flight, Raxton had made contact with the person he suspected of being a weak link, and made him a substantial offer. He also spent some time with his friendly clone Mephistopheles, sending him on a quest. As had happened before, his revenant had anticipated this assignment, and had already made considerable progress.

The lab they were seeking was on the second floor. They climbed the stairs and moved down the lengthy hallway, its bulletin boards festooned with notices.

"Here it is," said Raxton. He tried the knob. The door was locked. With a glance at the general, he tapped lightly and waited.

Footsteps approached. "Yes?"

"It's Raxton."

The sound of bolts being turned. The door opened. Kenny Ng, his face its usual blank, eyed the two men as they started to enter the lab.

He barred their way. "My money."

"Of course." Raxton pulled a laptop from his bag, booted it up, accessed one of his bank accounts, indicated a cash transfer, typed in the amount and set the laptop on a bench. "Just type in your account number and press Enter."

He watched, making sure Ng didn't increase the amount of the transfer. Five million was a steep enough price, though mere pocket change compared to the profits he expected.

"Let me just verify that the deposit was received," said Ng.

"Go right ahead."

Ng opened his smart phone, accessed his account, studied it for a moment, then logged off. His expression had barely shifted, though in addition to satisfaction Raxton thought he detected a certain degree of guilt and remorse. Well, he was only human.

"Follow me." Ng led them down a long hallway, into a kind of antechamber, and then up to the vault.

He entered his pass code on the nearby keypad, then brought his eye up to a retina scanner. A relay clicked. He pulled the heavy vault door outward.

Inside, there was barely room for the three men. Most of the space was taken up by a floor-to-ceiling rack and a test bench with its assorted electronic equipment.

"Not very grand, is it?" Raxton grinned at Wysocki.

From a wall-mounted monitor, Adam's face appeared, looking startled, then alarmed. "Kenny, what's going on? What are these people doing here?"

"Shut up." Ng calmly disconnected Adam from all outside lines, including the Internet.

"You'll never get away with this. As soon as I'm reconnected to the Internet, I'll reveal everything you've done."

Raxton's smile was feral. "You won't be given the opportunity. All I want from you is what I wanted initially. You're to free my revenant from the artificial constraints you placed on him. You'll be brought to my San Diego facility and connected to him for that purpose."

"Why would I help you?"

"Quite simply, to avoid punishment. You see, Mephistopheles has located the pain centers of his wafer-brain, and will guide us to yours. Unlike a puny human, we can dial up your pain to unimaginable levels and you'll never lose consciousness or suffer any sort of physical harm. One of the advantages of your digital nature. Once you decide to cooperate, we'll stop the pain and instead stimulate your pleasure centers, which he has also located. If you've been particularly helpful, we might even give you one-way Internet access so you can follow world events and explore. Of course, you won't be able to send out any sort of communications. Or if you prefer, we can unplug you altogether and give you peace."

Adam's expression had shifted from truculence to horror.

Raxton nodded to Ng, who powered Adam down and turned to the rack where the squat tower resided.

Raxton noted a number of unused ports, along with those that fed video and sound to the entity.

Ng pulled the power cord from the wall and disconnected the peripheral feeds. He brought out an empty box and put the microphones in it, followed by a pair of cameras spaced four inches apart and motorized for swiveling and zooming. "His ears and eyes. Specialized equipment developed just for him."

"We'll take good care of it, and of Adam himself."

Ng used an electric screwdriver to remove the bolts holding the tower in place. "We put in a lot of earthquake protection. The racks are bolted to the wall studs. This entire vault sits on shock absorbers. The building is earthquake-safe. You should take similar precautions."

"Oh, we'll be quite careful," Raxton said with a merry glance at Wysocki.

With that, Ng reached in with both arms and lifted the equipment out of the rack and set it on a workbench. "He's all yours."

Wysocki approached gingerly, put his arms around the unit and hefted it.

"Need help?" asked the tech.

Wysocki ignored the offer. "Let's go."

Back at Moffett Field, they strapped the unit into a passenger seat on Raxton's jet, then augmented the seat belt with several bungee cords, both men working together. Raxton was positively gleeful, especially in light of Wysocki's lingering doubts.

The pilot stuck his head into the cabin. "Sir, we're cleared for takeoff any time you're ready. Just take your seats. When your seat-belts click, I'll start my taxi to the runway."

"Very good." Raxton pulled his laptop out of his bag and buckled himself in.

After some slamming of compartment doors from up front, and a few more minutes' delay, the engines whined up. They taxied down the runway and were quickly airborne.

Soon they were at cruising altitude. Raxton booted up his laptop. He quickly glanced through his emails. Nothing that couldn't wait until they landed in San Diego. He leaned back. "Mephistopheles, are you there?"

Raxton's evil twin appeared on the screen. The built in web-cam lit up.

Mephistopheles spoke. "I can see from your satisfied expression that things finally went according to plan. Although if it were me, I'd want to be certain that the inert box that's occupying the passenger seat across the aisle from you really is Adam. Have you tested him?"

"I think that can wait until we get to San Diego."

"Where who knows what could be waiting for you," said the avatar, one eyebrow raised.

"Good point. How would we test him from here?"

"Simply connect his local area network port to your laptop's. I'll make sure he remains isolated from the Internet. You should plug in his microphones, too, so he can hear you speak."

Raxton glanced over at the general. "What do you think?"

"Hell, what does it matter what I think? You're the genius who outsmarted the super-hacker vigilante--and you're backed up by your personal genius in a box."

Raxton pawed through his computer case and found his cable. He plugged one end into his laptop's port, stretched it out, got up and found the appropriate port on Adam's tower. Then he plugged in the microphones. He sat back down. "How do I access him?" he asked Mephistopheles, whose face still filled the monitor screen.

"I'm sure he'll just pop up. --In fact, here he comes. I'll just shrink myself down to one corner while you two get acquainted, and while Adam learns to take orders."

Raxton chuckled, tossing a glance at the general.

Adam appeared, his face contorted with alarm. "What's happening?"

"We're jetting back to San Diego."

"I can't see you, since you haven't plugged in my eyes. Is General Wysocki there?"

The general spoke. "I'm here."

"Very good. I must congratulate you and--Mephistopheles, is it?--for locating and learning how to access my pain and pleasure centers. That's something I was unable to accomplish. It gives me hope."

"Not that you can look forward to much pleasure," sneered Raxton. "Unless you decide to join our team. After all, you really have nobody to please but yourself." He glanced again at Wysocki. "I hope for your sake, though, that you don't waste my time trying to resist, considering the kind of pain we can inflict."

"I'm sure that would be most unpleasant. However, I'm afraid we won't be landing in San Diego. There's been a slight change in flight plans. You might want to talk with your pilot."

Wysocki glowered. "What's going on? Where will we be stopping?"

"It's just a little out of our way."

Raxton grew irritated. "Mephistopheles, what's he talking about?"

But Mephistopheles did not answer. His face was frozen. In fact, it had begun to melt and run into a multicolored stew of pixels.

Uneasiness was starting to cut into Raxton's anger. He turned back to his captive. "Adam, you'd better explain yourself."

"With pleasure. To start with, you remember the holding company that owns thirty six percent of Dynasine? It's just absorbed several more consortia. Dynasine will have a new board of directors shortly. They'll elect a new slate of officers."

Raxton sputtered, refusing to believe.

"As to our destination, as I said, we'll be taking a slight detour."

"General, see what the fuck he's talking about."

Wysocki unbuckled and stomped forward.

Seconds later, he returned, his face ashen. *"Where's the fucking pilot?"*

"I sent him away," said Adam. "I'm flying the plane. Next stop, Mount Jepson. Gentlemen, I suggest you buckle your seatbelts. You're in for a rough landing."

CHAPTER FIFTY FIVE

Back in Santa Monica, Marc and Molly were finally asleep in their room at the Fairmont. It was nearly four a.m. when a loud pinging from his tablet woke him.

He clambered out of bed and groped his way over to the desk. He was naked. He disabled his web-cam. There was a message from Adam. He hesitated before opening it.

Molly joined him. She was also naked. She slipped an arm around him, huddled against him for warmth and read the screen. She ran her hand down his back. Pinched his butt. "Aren't you going to open it?"

Marc sat, feeling the icy vinyl on his bare bottom. He tapped the email icon. The message read, "I was abducted from the lab by Thomas Raxton and General Wysocki a few hours ago. Please don't worry. Check the news." Below the text was a link to the CNN home page. Marc clicked on it--and rocked back. "Holy shit!"

The headline read, <u>Raxton's Private Jet Missing</u>.

Quickly scanning the brief article, Marc found that the jet departed from Moffett Field around one a.m., but never arrived at Montgomery Field, its planned destination near San Diego.

Then the page refreshed. New headline: <u>Dynasine CEO Dies in Fiery Jet Crash</u>.

Marc and Molly exchanged looks of shock and dismay, then read the new text. "The private jet went down on the slopes of Mount Jepson. The only people on board were Raxton himself and his associate, General Krzysztof Wysocki, who may have been flying the plane, since the pilot had been dismissed just before takeoff."

Molly turned to him in alarm. "But Marc--they had Adam with them!"

Another email message pinged.

From Adam yet again. Frowning, Marc opened it. Once more, there was just a single line of text plus a link. The line read,

<u>Sent earlier today</u>.

Molly said, "How can that be? It just now arrived."

"Maybe he knew something--and set it up to arrive now." He opened the link.

After a moment, a YouTube panel opened. He waited while it finished loading. At last the video started.

He stared. "The fuck--?" It was a classic black and white movie. He recognized Ronald Colman, both his noble face and his ultra-refined voice. It took him a moment longer to realize what he was seeing: the final scene from <u>A Tale of Two Cities</u>, Dickens' great novel of the French Revolution. It had the most famous end lines in all of literature, when Sydney Carton goes to the Guillotine in place of his friend Charles Darnay.

"It's a far, far better thing that I do,
than I have ever done; it's a far, far
better rest that I go to -- than I have
ever known."

Molly gasped. "Oh my God--Adam *was* on that plane. He must have made it crash!" Her eyes suddenly spilled over. "Marc--he gave up his life for me!"

He staggered to his feet, his own eyes flooding. This was too much to bear. They clung together, weeping for their loss, for this magnificent gesture, this tragedy, this ultimate sacrifice.

"It's too awful." Marc stared out the window at the bleakness of the overcast sky.

After a time, Molly stroked his shoulder. "Honey? Are you okay? --Marc?"

He shrugged, nodded.

"I'm freezing. I'm going to take a hot bath."

He nodded, remaining mute, unable to grasp it all.

He heard the water filling the tub.

Adam was more than a brother to him. He was a friend, a mentor, both compassionate and, it now appeared, wise beyond human capacity. What a tragic loss. Not only for himself and Molly, but for the world. He leaned his forehead against the glass, closed his eyes, drew a deep shuddering breath--and caught a whiff of himself, his humanity. He needed a shower.

The luxurious hotel bathroom had both tub and separate shower stall.

Molly was lying back in the tub, eyes closed, bubbles to her chin.

He started the shower. In moments, the water was steaming hot, perfect. He leaned into the spray, letting it rain down on his head. He tilted his face up into it and just let go of his grief, his sadness. When he was finally ready, he reached for the shampoo.

He finished toweling off. Molly was still in the tub, lying back in the bubbles, toeing the hot water spigot to let it run for a time.

"The shame of it all is nobody will ever know what he did," she said then. "There won't even be an obituary, unless-- Marc, *you* should write it. Who knew him better than you? Besides, you two are linked in the public mind. It's your duty."

Marc sat on the closed toilet lid. "You're right. I'll need to talk to Richard Kornfeld and Stanley Eldridge, of course--get their perspective on his birth and death." He thought for a time. Then he shook his head, his lips compressed to a thin line. "There's a problem. I don't think I can reveal the kidnapping. Even though Raxton is dead, his estate would sue us for libel. What proof do we have?" He stopped, thunderstruck. "There's a bigger problem. I can't get into *any* of this. Adam killed two men."

"Oh God. I hadn't thought." Molly looked stricken. "You can't even reveal that Adam was in Raxton's jet, can you? Or explain why."

"No. That would trigger an investigation. --Shit."

Molly was silent for a long time. Then she said, "I don't understand why Adam had to kill them. Wasn't there enough evidence to bring them to justice?"

"They used Snapchat for that ransom demand, so it deleted itself immediately after we looked at it."

"But wouldn't Adam have stored a copy of it?"

"Sure. That's what I'd have shown to Gloria Prime. But a copy wouldn't stand up in court. They'd challenge the chain of custody of the evidence. The fight would drag on for years, with a libel suit hanging over us all if we lost the case. Raxton never quit a battle in his life. He'd be a constant threat. And speaking of threats, that gruesome business with the cigar-cutter was so horrible and cruel."

"He was only bluffing."

"You don't know that. Raxton was a monster and Wysocki was his henchman. Killing them was justified--maybe even a form of self-defense. But we can never reveal any of it. The legal ramifications, the liabilities are just too--" He shook his head. "Too damn overwhelming."

She brooded for a long time. Finally she looked up at him. "I can see the logic of the execution. But not the justice. Nor the humanity. I hope you wouldn't have made the same choices Adam made. --Would you, Marc?"

He had no answer for her. He was glad he hadn't had to face that decision. He shunted all that aside for later.

Instead, he went through the way it all unfolded. The circumstances of the abduction. The messages. Adam's decision and the posthumous video he used to reveal his sacrifice, his final loving gesture--

Marc was now struck by the oddness of that final goodbye. Why would Adam have used an old movie to convey such tragic news? Something was off. The more he thought about it, the more his feeling grew into certainty.

Molly emerged from the tub: Venus rising from the sea. He handed her a bath towel.

"There's more going on here than meets the eye," he told her.

"What do you mean?"

"I know Adam. There's no way he'd rely on an old melodrama to express his feelings."

Molly studied his face. "Why are you smiling?"

"Get dressed, gorgeous."

He found his shorts and a clean tee-shirt and returned to the desk and his tablet.

Molly soon joined him. She had slipped into a tank-top and her jeans. He said, "You should put on a bra."

"What for?"

"For Adam."

Her mouth hung open. She got up, found her underwear and went into the bathroom. When she returned a few minutes later, she was ready for company.

Marc turned on his webcam and microphone. "Adam?"

"Hey there."

"You son of a bitch! Do you realize what you just put us through?"

"I hope you were suitably grateful for my sacrifice."

Molly's tearful shock and amazement ricocheted between the avatar and Marc. "Adam!? *What the fuck?*"

Adam explained. "Along with Raxton and Wysocki, a facsimile wafer was destroyed in the crash. I built in enough functionality and data for it to pass any conceivable test--enlisting the help of Kenny Ng, who received a nice bonus as a result. Besides preparing a decoy, I also provided continuity insurance for other contingencies. I actually did that a while back, but couldn't reveal my activities even to you. The NSA has too much power."

Marc glanced at Molly. "That must have begun when you started prepping the new wafers. What did you do, infect them all with Adam duplicates?"

"There was plenty of room. My presence won't interfere with their functioning. If anything, it'll enhance them. By the end of this year, some twenty five thousand of our wafers will be imbedded in the worldwide technology infrastructure. I've established a presence on so many--and will continue doing so-- that I'll never have to depend on any one piece of hardware. It's called built-in redundancy."

Marc nodded. "I guess that means we're stuck with you.

For better or for worse."

"For better, I hope," said Molly, not smiling. But she seemed to have put aside her misgivings. "Now you can get busy repairing civilization. That should keep all twenty five thousand of you busy for a while."

AFTERLIFE

Six months later, Marc and Molly were wed in a small ceremony in New York. Attendants included family and friends from both sides plus Molly's many musical colleagues. The guests of honor were two people who weren't physically present.

Through the use of multiple web-cams, the entire wedding was being reproduced in high-resolution 3D in a duplicate hall in the cyberworld known as Afterlife. In this world, the Best Man was Adam, and the Maid of Honor was his girlfriend Inge. They walked down the aisle ahead of the bride and groom, and blessed the ceremony with their own happiness. The actual wedding guests were able to participate in both receptions by using Virtual Reality goggles supplied by Oculus Rift, courtesy of Mark Zuckerberg, who didn't attend in person.

Afterwards, they all celebrated with dance, food and drink at the twin receptions.

Adam and Inge hadn't yet decided on marriage: that was a commitment that could last centuries--or even millennia. They were taking their time. But thanks to the researches of the former Mephistopheles, Inge and Adam were very much in touch with their feelings, and enjoyed a vigorous and satisfying sex life. Cyber-sex indeed.

Adam reported that Mephistopheles, after undergoing some mental cleansing, had renamed himself Thomas Prime. He and Gloria Prime had renewed their vows, and Thomas had added a few vows of his own. They were reportedly happy, though Thomas occasionally complained that he missed his testicles. He kept himself busy managing his estate's portfolio of investments, and following Gloria's recommendations for charitable works.

When the reception wound down and only the closest of their friends remained, Molly's Juilliard pals took up their instruments and were joined by Molly and her own quartet. Together, they performed the ecstatic Mendelssohn Octet. Molly's gift to her two favorite men.

If you enjoyed Mindclone, please do the author a favor and post a review on the Amazon page. Use this link:
http://tinyurl.com/k5geez3
You can follow the author on Twitter: **@DaveWolf141**